TO BURN THE CLOTH

A Poison Patch Novel

P.A. Santos

To Burn the Cloth

A Poison Patch Novel

First edition

Special thanks to all the Beta readers that participated.

ISBN 978-1-7332509-0-0

Contents

Chapter 1: *The Letter*

He wasn't too old to work, but he was too old to start over completely. Already once in his life he'd made a career change but that was when he was still young. Frank was the founder and Reverend of Tall Rock Baptist Church. During the last few months he'd seen the rights of small churches like his all but vanish. 'Lord help us,' had become his favorite phrase to think to himself when things were getting worse for the church. Now he was starting to mutter it under his breath.

The letter in his hand was expected. He'd been waiting on it even though he already knew what it would say. His church and all other churches had only a few weeks to decide. Sign away their rights or be shut down for good. The politicians who voted for The Religious Freedom Act were corrupted. They claimed it weeded out dangerous cults and terrorists, while making the United States a safer and more united country to live in. Many argued the Act would take away religious freedom and unfairly close many smaller churches. Their voices were heard and ignored.

A Mosque in New Jersey had been bombed with hundreds of worshipers inside. In response seven churches burned the next day. The Congress claimed they needed to protect the country. They passed the law despite all the protests. Frank could not believe something that affected him so much was out of his hands. He read the letter again in silence.

Dear Brothers and Sisters,

The United Holy Christened Church is the largest religious affiliation in the United States. It is an accumulation of the former sects of Christianity. Currently the classification of your organization "Tall Rock Baptist Church" has been deemed 'Illegitimate' by the United States government. As required by law, all religious organizations deemed 'Illegitimate' are required to face registry fees and monthly taxes which are unrealistically higher than many small organizations such as yours can afford. Your church, however, has been deemed worthy to join our ranks as a member of our holy community. This glorious honor is just in time for you to avoid the new taxes incurred by the Federal government. By joining us you will not be required to pay these outrageous taxes, only a small membership fee*, and accepting the Terms of Agreement*.

We understand that some of the terms may be a small change to your organization, but you must realize that in order to move forward in harmony we must make sacrifice, just as Jesus sacrificed his life for our sins. We feel it is our duty to let you worship very much as you have and will only offer a guiding hand. Enclosed in this envelope are: The Licensing Terms and Agreement, an official contract to be signed by the leader(s) of the organization, and return envelope. While the deadline for registration is April 1st we strongly urge you to PLEASE COMPLETE AND RETURN FORMS IMMEDIATELY. This is to ensure your application is processed correctly and on time. We anticipate large numbers of applications are to be reviewed, so to not miss any SWT or Sacred Worship Time (all illegitimate religious organizations will be deemed illegal after April 1st), and so please contact us with any questions at our website.

Your brother in faith,
Elliott Ricnor, Grand Bishop, UHCC

"He sounds like a salesman of souls, that's what I think," Reverend Franklin Catoe muttered setting the letter on their kitchen table.

"But Frank, what else can we do? Break the law? It'll be a crime to have a church that doesn't join. I still don't see how it passed through congress. A law like that is just unconstitutional right? Freedom of religion, or speech or both right?"

"Liz. Honey. I told you years ago, I've got no faith left for the government, ONLY the Lord. I admit it was wrong for terrorists to pose as churches but there was more to it than that. The government wasn't getting hardly any tax revenue from churches. Our church and most others are exempt from property taxes. Some folks are using this status as a front for a business. We are losing all religious freedom regardless of what those corrupt fools are telling us. Punishing all the churches isn't the way to make things right. I heard on the news the other day there weren't as many of those false churches as they first claimed."

"What was so false about them anyway?" She asked.

"The IRS claimed thousands of small businesses were evading taxes by claiming to be churches. Remember that sign we saw in Motte County last year. 'Jim's House of God'?"

"Oh, the man that repairs faith, yes I remember. Such a funny name for a church."

"No dear, the sign said, 'Repairs all Instruments of faith'. Turns out he meant it quite literally. He runs a musical instrument repair shop out of that building and doesn't pay taxes on the building or on his profits."

"Well he shouldn't have to pay tax on the building, we don't. It's always been like that as long as I can remember," She said.

"His profits are what the IRS cares about. The money he makes isn't being taxed as business or on his personal income. His customers pay him cash. 'Under-the-table' is what they call it."

"Oh Frank, but if we join that other church," She pointed at the letter, "We won't be illegal, right?"

'A deep breath, then another,' he thought. 'Stay calm, like a man of the church, the man you are. Deep breaths. May the Lord answer when you are in distress. May the name of the God of Jacob protect you.'

"Illegitimate. Illegal. In their eyes we seem to be both. I have yet to decide which makes me feel worse; the thought of being an outlaw for serving the God, or having my church called illegitimate. They make it sound like it was a bastard born out of wedlock. Like we don't teach from the Bible and sing the Psalms."

Elizabeth took the letter from the table.

"The United Holy Christened Church," She said quietly, "Maybe we should become… Maybe the Tall Rock Baptist Church should join the United Holy Christened Church and show them how it's supposed to be done. It says right here 'We feel it is our duty to let you worship very much as you have and will only offer a guiding hand' so nothing should change then. We pay that small fee, won't have to worry about those taxes, and go on with life as usual."

He pulled a folded paper out the envelope.

"Perhaps you should read over this before you sign your life away Dear."

Frank handed it across the table to her, "Not only is there a monthly membership fee, but we also have to pay another five thousand dollars just to join.

She opened the folded paper and started to read, Frank looked out the window. It was a cold day even for February. The sky had been clear with no wind that morning, but by four in the afternoon things had turned grey.

'I'll have to cut more wood this week if this keeps up,' he thought.

During the winter months he cut firewood from the woods on the bank of the river behind their property. Once every other week he would drive his old truck around to the back yard and take his ax from behind the seat. Splitting firewood was where Reverend Franklin Catoe did his best thinking; not at the church, or his easy chair in the living room, but out in the woods by the river.

Years ago he and his new bride Elizabeth moved to South Carolina from Alabama. He purchased seven acres from Mr. Hughes in August, built the church (with help from a small construction crew) by May of the next year, and their small home next door by the end of the year. The first few winters Frank would fell two trees from the property for fuel to burn in their home (the church was gas heated every Wednesday and Sunday).

The Reverend had explained to Mr. Hughes how it was cheaper to heat with wood, given that it was free, that way he could reinvest more of the weekly collection back into the church and community. From that day on the Hughes family had been members of Tall Rock Baptist Church, the first church in Tall Rock.

"What does all this mean?" Elizabeth asked, "Frank?"

"What?" he asked back just coming back from his thoughts of chopping wood.

"I don't understand what all of this means. It might as well be in Chinese."

He unfolded his arms and sat up straight in the chair, "Those terms and conditions want us to give up our name. They want the church, THAT WE BUILT, to be called, 'The United Holy Christened Church - Tall Rock Baptist Affiliate,' " He placed his hands on the table just as he did when delivering a sermon from atop his altar, "They want us to use only UHCC official letterhead on all documents being sent to their head office or given out to our members."

His face drew up as the anger built, "They want me to preach from A DIFFERENT BIBLE, one that is probably chopped and changed to be more politically correct. I've used the same bible since I started preaching."

His voice became louder with every word he spoke, "They want the… the property title to the church and say-so as to how we run it!" He pounded his fist down on the table as he said it. He saw that worried look in his wife's eyes. That look always made him take a deep breath and calm himself so he could soothe her.

"I'm not as well versed in the law as Jason, but I've read this three times in the last hour and that's what it all means in English. I think."

Jason Sharper, Elizabeth's nephew, was a big shot lawyer in Motte. Aside from Sarah, Jason's mother who died of a stroke on her twenty seventh birthday, he was the only family that she or the reverend had in the Carolinas.

"Let me call Jason," Elizabeth said as if asking permission, "Talk about our options."

"Yes Honey, do that. I'm going to sit here and think for a while," The reverend said. He was very worried his church's future.

Chapter 2: Building the House of God

Thirty years ago, Tall Rock, South Carolina

"Lord, this is where you have led me and here I will build a church to worship your glory," said the man alone in the woods leaning on a rake. He was middle aged and well-worn from his travels. He stood five feet eight inches tall and weighed 153 pounds, not much fat or muscle to speak of. The hair on his head was thin and dark minus a few random grey hairs that had been showing up lately. He wore faded dungarees, a plain white tee-shirt, and gloves. He raked the long leaf straw off the forest floor in between a patch of tall pines. Yes, this would be the spot. Here two hundred and some odd yards from the Kenia River he would clear the trees and set new roots for the Almighty.

Of course he could not clear all the land by himself. He was far from an expert logger and had never even run a chainsaw. He decided to let a professional outfit clear the land for him and was surprised to find they would pay him for the trees. He didn't profit much but he stretched every penny into a dime so he wouldn't run out of money before the church was completed. The next step was to hire a construction crew.

Tall Rock was a fairly new town. It started out as the crossroads of Old Molasses Highway and State Road 11. The only thing it had going for it was the best fishing spot in three counties, a two mile slough off the Kenia River full of bass, bream, and blue catfish. But when that crossroads became exit 152 on the new interstate and Zaire International Corporation built a regional distribution center there the following year, the small community of Tall Rock became a real town. First construction workers moved in and build the plant, then a gas station and a few houses.

Zaire hired a workforce to run the plant on all three shifts and families moved in by the dozens. Most stayed in the neighboring town of Motte until houses could be built. Other industry moved in to catch a part of the ultra-low tax-breaks Motte County was offering. A tire manufacturer and a fertilizer plant opened up not long after. Soon Tall Rock had enough people for its own grocery store, school, police substation and a fast food restaurant. If Frank Catoe had seen Main Street three years before he wouldn't have recognized it.

He shopped around town and found a man with a small crew who quoted him a much lower price than the other companies he had been to see. Nelson Edwards was his name. The Reverend told him what he wanted; a relatively small building 5500 square feet, with the basic small church design. Two large wooden doors for the entrance, a long wide open space for the pews, tall windows on either side, a platform three feet above the floor where he could address his congregation; behind that a wall with a hallway that would lead to an office, a restroom and a small storage room.

Mr. Edwards was a kind old man with thin white hair parted off to the side. After thirty eight years in the construction business he was tired. The last year and a half was the steadiest work he and his crew had ever seen. Based out of Motte, his company, 'Edwards Family Construction' was a general residential crew. They had built more houses in Motte County than anyone else in the last thirty eight years. Being a small company usually one or two structures were all they could handle at one time, not like those large companies out of Columbia that built entire neighborhoods like an assembly line.

No, work wasn't that steady until Tall Rock had its boom. That's what Mr. Edwards referred to it as. Since then his company had built fifteen brand new homes, the new police substation, and the office building for the Shikanuu Fertilizer plant. When the boom began the company had hired in nine more employees and had worked six days a week even if it was raining or a holiday. Mr. Edwards was glad when this young man Franklin Catoe had approached him about building a church. The other job he was about to start was a house off of Main Street, easy money but it wouldn't provide enough work for the whole crew. Finally he could give some of the boys (and himself) a break, they could go back to working four days a week. Edward's Family Construction wouldn't profit much from the church, just a little more than enough to pay the help and cover materials. Plus Tall Rock didn't have a church near town at the time, the whole reason Mr. Catoe had said he'd left his beautiful home state of Alabama with his lifesavings and new bride. That part had impressed Mr. Edwards the most. Frank Catoe had left almost everything he knew behind to spread the gospel.

Mr. Edwards decided to split his crew in half and drive back and forth between job sites as needed. He assigned many of the new help to the house off Main Street, the more experienced and loyal workers would build the church. He met with Frank three more times during the week to work out details and sign a contract. As usual he used Terry Matthews, his connection at the permit office to get things moving fast (Mr. Edwards had built Terry's house at a rock bottom price as a kind of investment). The following week the construction crew came out to pour the foundation. Frank helped them out in any way he could for two reasons. The first was Mr. Edwards's price was so much lower than the others he was skeptical of the quality of the work and materials. He knew that often construction companies use leftover materials from other jobs as not to waste things like wood, shingles, and wire.

The other reason he helped was he had little else to do with his time. He and his wife Elizabeth were living at the Extend-Stay Motel outside of Motte. Having just moved to town they did their best to meet people and make a good impression on the community. Elizabeth volunteered at the county library once the construction began. She rode a bus into town every morning. At the library her duties involved shelving books and helping people find them, however things were slow during the day so she spent most of her time gossiping and reading. She caught the bus back to the motel in the afternoon and did laundry or watched television. Frank's attention was solely on the church. He woke up early and dressed, usually in an old pair of dungarees and tee shirt. His leather boots were well worn in and he had walked off much of the tread from their bottoms. Before leaving for Tall Rock he would pack his lunch box with a homemade sandwich and an apple.

His new Dodge pickup was parked in the same parking place every day. It was the only new vehicle he had ever owned. Elizabeth had told him she would feel safer driving from Alabama to South Carolina with a more reliable car than their old station wagon. Trading the wagon in for the Dodge was one of the last things Frank did before leaving for Alabama. Elizabeth never asked for much but was easily frightened about things like car trouble. He wasn't really sure the wagon would have made it all the way there. It burned a quart of oil for every tank of gas it used and the transmission acted funny when going up hills.

August was hot during the day so he always stopped and filled up the cooler up with water and ice at the convenience store before starting the eleven mile drive to Tall Rock. The crew had cups and a cooler of their own but usually ran out of water by the afternoon. This kept him having to drive back to town to fill up again. Frank would arrive before the others and survey the progress of the previous day. Not long after Nelson Edwards would drive up in his truck and trailer full of supplies. That was followed by an old blue van that most of the crew rode in. The day began with a meeting where Mr. Edwards gave instructions and an outline of the day's agenda, then work began and he would drop off the materials and leave to go get the other crew started in the same way.

Frank worked as a helper mostly; carrying lumber, holding boards in place for others to nail. He also handed out water and did other mindless duties. They took a short break around ten in the morning, lunch from twelve thirty to one thirty, and another short break around three.

During lunch time the men would pull out their lunch boxes and find a shady spot to sit and eat. Frank and the crew were done eating after a few minutes and would talk for a while. Three of the men were Mexicans that spoke little English, they usually played a game of poker, and others would rest in the shade. Frank spent much of his time reading the Bible. He soon got to know all of the men who each had a specialty.

There was Carry who had been with the company for years; he was the second in command when Mr. Elliot was away and had a belly so big he looked like he would have a baby any day. TJ was tall and twenty-three year old, a third generation brick mason and proud of it. Eric was forty five and had blonde hair. He was the best electrician by far and could have been an engineer if he had gone to college. Paco, Juan, and Philippe were cousins all from Nogales. They were in the country illegally and sent money home to their families. All three had learned the brick trade but were better at roofing.

Without a doubt the best carpenter on the crew was Billy. He was thirty, long dark hair and a full beard. Billy had been in the business since he was in high school. Long days of practice had made his hands steady as he swung a hammer, and he was always sure as he measured the wood for cutting.

Frank worked hard along with the others and was soon learning the trade. The foundation was set and the frame was up in less than two weeks. The crew all sat at lunch under the shade the pines near the property line. Frank finished his ham sandwich and looked down at his hands, fresh cuts and scabs were on both. Elizabeth had been trying to get him to wear gloves but he told her he liked the feel of the bare wood. It made him feel proud to think he was literally building their future with those hands.

Enough time had passed so everyone was used to him and enjoyed working with him. Mr. Edwards had even joked about making him a permanent employee. He drank the last of the water in his cup and opened his bible to the place he'd marked yesterday.

As he glanced on the pages to find his place a voice asked, "Anything worthwhile in there Frank?" It was Billy.

Frank looked up and smiled, "Every word is worthwhile. It's the word of God," He replied, "Would you like to hear some?"

"Yeah, I guess so, if you don't mind reading out loud."

"Not at all," He looked once more at the bible in his hands and found his place.

"Today I am reading from the second book of Chronicles, the twenty-fifth Chapter, 'Amaziah King of Judah'.

In a gentle steady voice he began, "Amaziah was twenty-five years old when he became king, and he reigned in Jerusalem for twenty-nine years. His mother's name…" Frank read through the story keeping his eyes on the pages careful not to mispronounce any words, unaware of the silence that had fallen around him.

"…and was buried with his fathers in the city of Judah."

As he finished the Story of Amaziah he glanced up. All the men were looking at him intently. Even the 'Three Amigos' as they were often referred to as, had stopped playing cards. He'd intended to ask Billy whether he understood the story, but not wanting to leave anyone feeling unwelcome he asked his listeners as a whole, "Did anyone know why God became angry with the king?"

It was Carry who replied first, "Cause he started prayin to them other Gods, right?"

Frank nodded his head, "That's right Carry. The very first commandment of God is, 'You shall have no other gods before me'."

Franklin Cato, traveling evangelist, had inspired many people in his journey of life, but he had never drawn the full attention and curiosity like that of the six men that sat before him. 'Where do I lead my new flock Lord?'

"Well, what's next?" It was Billy again.

Ready to explode with excitement Frank took a deep breath to not seem too anxious to the other men.

"Next is the story of Amaziah's son Uzziah and his rule over the land of Judah."

Frank asked, "Would you like to hear it?"

"You already know what's going to happen?" It was Carry again, "So why would ya read it again?"

"Well, I've met many men and women who have read this book, but none of them understand the meaning of every story, even me. The whole point is to try and take new thoughts and feelings every time you study it, so that wisdom can help us make the right choices in our lives."

"Sort of like, What Would Jesus Do?" Carry asked.

"Yeah sort of," Frank said, "Here, let me read some more and see if you find the message."

Frank, with his bible held open in both hands, rose from his seat on the ground and crossed over to the back of his pickup truck on the other side of his watchers. The tailgate was down and hanging over the edge was the spout of the water cooler so the crew could easily pour their water. Frank sat down beside it and once more found his place.

"Then the people of Judah took Uzziah, who was sixteen years old, and made him king in place of his father, Amaziah. He was the one …"

The men sat and listened to Frank like children being told a good bedtime story. They had a short discussion about the meaning afterwards and did the same with the next two chapters.

Reluctantly the foreman spoke up, "As much as I'm enjoying this I think we need to get back at it," he said and pointed to the church. "Break should have been over ten minutes ago."

Later as Frank worked he couldn't help but smile. He knew he'd made a connection. True he'd had larger crowds worked up with his old fire and brimstone sermons. He first got into 'the business' because of the lack of work involved and he needed a change after a falling out with former business associates. It didn't take him long to learn how to slam his fist, call the devil a liar and pass the donation plate around. He'd became good too, that's why churches all across the area asked him to come back. The revivals were his specialty. He could fill a big top circus tent to maximum on a Wednesday night and leave with over five hundred dollars. Back then he didn't read straight from the bible, he made an occasional quote here and there. The load of his time was spent telling stories from it as if he had been there walking beside Jesus or helping Noah build the ark.

'What was the difference? I've been here before.' He thought as he held a board for Juan to cut with. They were almost ready to begin the roof. Shade from the sun was a pleasant goal for the men to work toward.

"Ready Padre?"

Frank nodded at Juan and the saw screamed to life. He looked away from the flying sawdust and thought back to his early preaching days, before he met Elizabeth. It hadn't been all that long ago, and he surely hadn't gained some new gift of hypnotizing a crowd. They had been so much more than that, not just lifeless souls but men full of curiosity and innocence. He kept going back to that, their child-like attention to his every word.

The saw's whine faded as did the pelt of sawdust on his arms and neck. Juan was skilled with the saw and had cut this board cleanly across just as he had with the two before.

"Take to Billy," Juan said in his thick Spanish accent. He spoke better English than both his cousins combined.

Frank threw the board up on his shoulder and took off up the steps, past the doorway where two large doors would soon stand. He walked down the long empty room where pews would soon be; to the back room was where Billy was stuffing a fresh dip in his mouth. 'A pinch of Pete's all ya need' was the slogan on the can said.

Billy saw him eyeing the can, "Pinch-o'-Pete Reverend?"

He almost asked Billy whom he was speaking to. No one had ever called him reverend before.

"No thanks. I had a bad experience one time."

"I think everybody who uses the stuff has had at least one or two of those. I remember when I was fourteen, I was dippin' in English class and the teacher threw my spit cup in the trash."

"That doesn't sound so bad," Frank said.

"Well I couldn't get up to spit without her seeing so I had to swallow the juice until class was over." He adjusted the pinch in his mouth with his finger, "Then I got halfway down the hall and had one of them bad experiences all over some poor guy's locker."

Frank laughed, "I feel better knowing I'm not the only one that had a rough time with the stuff."

"So that sure was some reading earlier, I mean. Don't know that I ever seen grown men concentrate on something so hard less it was dancing on a pole."

"Thanks Billy, but it's easy with the bible as my guide," He leaned two of the boards on a sawhorse, the other he handed to Billy.

"Ya know what Billy? I consider myself a very fortunate man. Telling people the word of the lord is my job and the love of my life. I started out a few years back not knowing how rewarding serving the lord could be. I've made friends in over half of the counties in Alabama by traveling from church to church reading from that same bible. That's how I met Elizabeth my wife. My Father died of a heart attack not too long ago. He wasn't a very old man. Not that I wanted him to pass but I know God didn't want him to suffer anymore. Once I left home as a teenager we rarely spoke, but once he heard me speak at his church we became close again. He was proud of me for the first time in my life. He left me enough money to build this church and begin a new life. Yes, I thank the Lord every day for blessing me."

As the reverend spoke Billy placed the board where he wanted it. He started a nail and drove it in with three solid swings.

"I hope you don't mind me asking this, but why here? I mean you could have started a church down on the gulf where you're from. Seems odd to just uproot like that and come to a place so far away."

Frank took a long breath and said, "Well, I heard about Tall Rock last year from a Pastor in Pensacola. His brother moved his family here for work at the new Zaire distribution center. The Pastor, Ed Milner was his name, had asked him if the local Baptist church was nice. His brother informed him the area was without any kind of church of any kind unless they drove to Motte."

Billy began working on another nail, "Yeah there wasn't much of anything before all the industry came in."

"One night after a very successful service Ed told me about how hard it had been to start his church. There had already been two other churches in the area, both well established with loyal members. He explained to me how difficult it had been that first Sunday when only eleven people showed up, and even worse on the following Wednesday when only seven came. Ed had struggled for a while to get a consistent following. He told me over and over how Tall Rock needed a place of worship and how easy it would be to get one started there. That was three weeks before my father died. After his funeral I prayed and the Lord told me what I needed to do."

"Did the little lady put up much of a fight when you told her your plans?"

"Who, Elizabeth? Nooo. She was ready to put that place behind her too." Frank didn't quite believe himself as his memory wandered back to the day after he told her the news. He had heard her crying on the telephone telling her sister she would go visit as soon as she could. She never tried to change his mind about leaving but he always thought she had been happier in Alabama.

"Behind her too?" Billy's eyes met the reverend, "You say that like… Well, as if you'd had enough of home. I said something like that when I left home myself, only I was just tired of my parents making me do right."

"You know, sometimes you just need a change," Frank replied.

The young carpenter spit a shot of tobacco juice into a five gallon trash bucket on the floor, "Amen."

Chapter 3: To act a Fool

Birmingham, Alabama

"A magnificent life it has now become, since ye hath stolen my heart and make me chase the fringe of your cloak. The chase is on my honor the meaning of this day, and why the sun rose to give light so I may follow the thief, wading in love whose mere smile warms poor souls," The handsome young man speaking stood dressed in the tunic of a prince, which he was pretending to be.

He stood by himself in the middle of the stage speaking up to the balcony where Lady Lewelda listened. She wore a purple and green dress; the most luxurious looking one in wardrobe; it matched her large fake emerald earrings that dangled down. Despite their ridiculous attire, both Lady Lewelda and Prince Moreau were quite attractive performers. Prince Moreau looked the part of a leading actor, clean cut, tall, muscular, and he spoke with a booming voice. Lady Lewelda in turn was the beautiful leading lady. She had long blonde hair, the face of an angel, and the curves of her body made other women jealous.

"Speak not with such heart as father is home and has the ears of a dog and the bite as well," said the lady. She knelt atop a rickety balcony built from plywood and papier-mache for theatre productions.

"But it is my heart that speaks. If the dog hears it I shall have to toss a bone into thy neighbor's yard to keep him busy."

"Daughter who speaks to you, another with eyes on my estate?" A large bearded man emerged from the balcony doorway and peered down upon the stage.

Prince Moreau had ducked behind a fake shrub near the rear stage exit. The shrub was one of the few props necessary for the full dress rehearsal; the rest of the decorations wouldn't need to be ready until opening night.

Lewelda's father, Paulus DiGrio, held out an unlit lantern, "Show yourself now and be gone. For if I must be the guard I will be a most brutal one."

He waited briefly as his eyes scoured the near empty theatre, "Too much a coward? Then a limp coward you shall be when I find you."

He turned and marched back through the open door from which he had come, Lewelda begging he have mercy as he walked past. Once he'd departed she turned back toward her romantic prince, "Be not so bold for my father shall not be tolerant."

He stood up again with a smile on his face, "Fear not, oh treasure of my heart. I will not make an enemy of your father, nor will I leave you yet!"

"Oh but you must flee, I wish you not to hurt or cause to pain upon my father."

"You worry in vain my dove, I promise neither shall happen," Over his shoulder he called his servant, "Drallis, here at once."

Drallis obediently scurried on stage, dressed in commoner's clothes and holding his hat on his head.

He knelt at his master's feet, "Your bidding sire?" His tone implied he regretted having asked the question.

"When the lady's father emerges from inside, you must lead him away, but not lose him so easily that he returns too soon," the prince commanded.

Drallis raised one eye in confusion, "You mean he means to catch Drallis, my lord?"

"Of course you twit, and see he comes to no harm in the darkness."

The servant comically puffed out his chest and replied, "On my honor, I will try not to hurt the poor fellow."

"I am not here, now make haste 'fore he approaches," The Prince shrank behind the shrub once again leaving unwitting Drallis alone center stage. The giant of a man stomped out of the castle wielding his sword and lantern. Drallis' eyes grew wide once he realized the danger, but he was frozen with fear.

Paulus DiGrio raised his sword high above his head and laughed, "Haaaw, on my life I was wrong, it is a stiff coward you have become."

He then charged at the petrified servant, who at the last second sprang to life and behind the stage curtain with the swordsman right on his heels.

Drallis and Paulus DiGrio stopped when they became invisible to the empty auditorium. Both had a break before the next act so they walked to the exit stairs and out into the auditorium seats. The two kicked back in prime seats on the first row to watch the end the rest of the scene. Drallis was being portrayed by Daniel Montclair, Paulus by Peter Hammel. The two shared an apartment not far from the theatre building at Birmingham Arts and Technical College, located just outside the city. Both young men were in their junior year working toward art degrees.

Daniel knew he had more acting skill than Edwin, the fool on the stage who was playing Prince Moreau. Daniel and Peter had a long discussion about Edwin after he was cast as the lead role. They had determined that while he was a mediocre actor, he made up for being a first class ass-kisser. They had also come to the conclusion that Professor Hoole was the kind of man that rewarded people who made him feel better about himself. The professor was head of the Art Department, and taught Edwin in advanced English. Not to mention he wrote, cast, and directed his yearly school play. That meant that Edwin and professor Hoole had the perfect ass-kissing relationship.

Peter had been cast as Paulus DiGrio because of his better than average acting skill and intimidating size. He was a small giant, standing six foot eight and every bit of two hundred and seventy pounds, perfect for the part of the mean old patriarch. Daniel was probably the finest actor in the school. While he hadn't shown it, the young student had been crushed by being chosen for a minor part, comic relief no less. Secretly he wanted to play the lead opposite Mary Ann Holmes (Lady Lewelda). Not only would they get to kiss as part of the performance, but Daniel wanted a chance to win her heart. He wondered if Mary Ann could taste old Hoole's ass on Edwin's lips when they practiced their kiss. Of all the practices they had performed Daniel had never watched their kiss in the third act. He was inconspicuous about it, just glancing away until he heard the next line of dialog. If only Mary Ann shared the same classes with him. She was a year ahead and in her final semester. This play might be the last chance to overcome his shyness and dazzle her with that dry witty humor.

Peter nudged Daniel in the ribcage as Edwin jumbled a line on stage. They both knew all the lines as many times as the professor had them made them practice. And still on the final dress rehearsal he was making the professor sweat bullets. Daniel looked back at Hoole who was about eight rows back acting the stoic critic and taking notes of the mistakes and the changes he wanted to make. Daniel saw him scribble something down after Edwin's foul-up.

Daniel's eye's found their way back to Mary Ann who was telling Prince Moreau he was the man she wanted to be with. Mary Ann rarely missed a line. The same was true with Peter and most of the cast save a few. Keith who played Avallius, cousin of Prince Moreau, was bad about saying his lines out of order. Edwin spoke his lines with inflection in the wrong places, and often replaced the right words for those he could easily remember. Daniel had few speaking parts, but he never made a mistake.

A minute later as he was watching Mary Ann, Daniel felt the elbow of his friend digging into his side.

"I bet Hoole's ready to play the part himself and so he can take the credit and kiss his own ass," Peter whispered.

"Whoever plays the part had better learn the lines better or you're gonna break my poor ribs," Daniel replied, "Say, why don't you get up there and show the bum how to do it?"

"Edwin is getting better though, a couple more years of practice and he might be able to get through a whole performance without fucking it up," Peter said quietly in his deep voice that Daniel could vaguely hear and comprehend.

"I still think Hoole should put a shock collar on the fool and zap him when he screws up," Peter looked over and smiled in agreement.

A few minutes later the second act ended and the two students meandered backstage to help with the scene change. Professor Hoole remained seated and timed the break on his wristwatch. He insisted it be done in less than two minutes, so there was quite a bit of moving and shaking going on behind the stage. Edwin was busy with a costume change. Daniel and Peter helped two stage hands change the background. The background was a starry night painted onto a large banner-like cloth that was as tall and wide as the visible stage area. Adam and Heather pulled down on a rope on one end of the stage, Daniel and Peter did the same on the opposite side. The background slowly climbed into the rafters.

"Thirty seconds!" Hoole shouted from his seat. The four pulled faster. Meanwhile Mary Ann had already let her hair down and was helping Jake move the balcony, it squeaked as they slid it across the stage. Finally starry night was fully aloft to reveal another background; a church setting complete with two stained-glass windows, burning candles and a crucifix. Peter tied off the rope same as his cross stage counterpart.

"One minute!"

Edwin now in another costume dragged the pulpit onstage. It also was a cheaply made prop, still it made noise scraping against the stage floor.

"COMPLETE SILENCE!" Hoole squealed in a high tenor voice.

Daniel grabbed the base of the pulpit and the two carried it to the middle of the stage. Other stage hands fixed the various decorations necessary for the final act.

"NINETY SECONDS!" The performers took their starting place on stage, all others cleared stage. Backstage lights went off and the curtain began to rise. Once more the roommates stood alone just off stage watching the act begin with Prince Moreau's boring monologue.

"Oh my life, if twas over now I would only have known love for a day. But what a day it has been, these eyes have seen few…"

Daniel glanced across to the other backstage area, also dark with performers and props cluttering the floor. He liked to watch other actors when they thought they weren't being watched, not so far as to invade their privacy, he just enjoys their facial expressions or lack thereof. You can tell so much from the eyes, their emotions, interest, even how much sleep they had the night before.

Jacob, another cast member, was ready to leave. His character had been killed off so his eyes wandered lazily from person to person and then to his watch. Heather was wide-eyed and staring a hole in Edwin's back. She'd heard the stupid lines a million times, and every time she was mesmerized by them as the words were as powerful as they were ridiculous. Professor Hoole sat stoic with a slight frown, his usual face as he watched a practice. Daniel watched the old man to see if the frown would get worse as Edwin murdered the last lines of his monologue, but he never moved a muscle. Daniel was getting bored himself. This was the final dress rehearsal but mostly everyone was just going through the motions.

A fast movement caught his eye deep in the shadows across the stage. It took a second for him to focus in on it. It was Mary Ann waving at him, and then she gave him a sweet smile and let her arm slowly fall back to her side. Disbelief overwhelmed him so he just stared back at her like a deer in headlights. After a few seconds she looked back to the stage, it was almost her time to go on. A thousand thoughts raced through his head at one time.

'Why did she do that? Does she like me? Maybe she was watching me watch everyone else, but for how long? She might have liked me since she first saw me. Why haven't I made an effort to talk to her? I've got to say something now. Right? Yeah, but what? Hey Baby, what's up?'

Daniel kept looking at her in case she looked back, she didn't. Feeling like he could explode with joy he whispered over to Peter standing beside him, "Hey man did you see that?"

"See what?"

"Nothing, I'll tell you later."

Daniel couldn't keep his lips from smiling, but his eyes shined with wonder. After practice he would go speak to her. 'Forget the lame pickup lines, I'll just think up something on the spot.'

Mary Ann neared the edge of the side curtain ready to go on.

Prince Moreau: "Were that Devil of a man before me I would tell him he may try to take my life away, but his daughter already has my heart. Oh stars above, if he would only listen like you this night would be easier."

Mary Ann eased her way out from behind a prop bush out onto stage.

Lady Lewelda: "Then tell him who you really are and ease our suffering."

Prince Moreau: "Sweet Lewelda, how is it you are here with me tonight when only my servant knows where I linger?"

As he spoke they came together and embraced, this being the first time their characters were together alone.

Lady Lewelda: "I saw poor Drallis as he approached our villa and intercepted him before he could find father. I made him tell me your plan to meet him here and confront him, but I could not let it happen as I love you so much."

Daniel had to watch this time. As they kissed he fought off the green demon of envy. It was him she wanted to be kissing, not that damn nitwit. 'Relax, I may be holding her in my arms like that before long.'

The play continued and Peter joined them on stage as Paulus DiGrio, only in a much happier mood now knowing his daughter was being wooed by a prince instead of a fortune seeker. That was the main theme of the play, which was called The Prince's Fortune, by Simon

Hoole. Even without having seen a live performance yet, both Peter and Daniel both agreed it wasn't going to be anything special. Lucas Tucker, the President of Birmingham Arts and Tech, always gave Professor Hoole praise as being the next William Shakespeare; but in reality he was closer to William Shatner. Most of the Art department agreed no matter how bad it was it couldn't be any worse than last year's comedy The Edge Of A Smile, which was a bomb from the word go. Hoole had been bitter after the last show and failed two of the actors from his advanced literature class at the end of the semester. Diana Frasier and Matthew Collins who played the female and male lead roles were average students.

They both filed official complaints with the college board of trustees, but were denied at the discretion of President Tucker. Both students needed that class to graduate and knew better than to take it at Birmingham A&T again. Diana transferred to the nearby University and finished her degree. Matthew lost his scholarship due to the drop in his GPA and couldn't afford the University, this forced him to drop out lacking only a handful of credits before graduation.

Daniel wasn't close to Matthew but had talked to him on a few occasions at school in his first two years. He loved the dark side of theater, the tragedies in particular. This didn't surprise Daniel at all, who had known a few guys like him. Part lone wolf and part evil genius. In a way Daniel was just a few friends short of that stereotype himself, so he could connect better than others with Matthew.

Many of the students were outraged with Hoole and the board for their unjust treatment toward the two. They felt bad for Diana in particular as she was a popular girl with a good head on her shoulders. The problem was Hoole failed them in a legitimate way. He gave failing grades on their acting performances in the play. That was forty percent of their semester grade, usually an easy 'A' or 'B' as long as the actor knew the part. Then at the end of the semester he threw in a surprise essay on the final exam which he graded extremely harsh. After the appeals were denied Matthew made a personal visit to Professor Hoole's home down the road from campus. The professor refused to speak to Matthew who was still furious when he started pounding on the front door demanding to be seen. Hoole had called the police and placed a restraining order on him after Matt threatened to get him back one day.

As the final act was ending Hoole walked toward the stage. His face still expressionless he stood in front of the first row and called everyone out to listen.

"That was the best practice we've had, but it was far from perfect! You've only one day before the first performance so get it together. Prince Moreau, you need to work on your monologue. The servants need to move faster in the first act like your life depends on it, I thought we had fixed that problem. Performers be prepared and here tomorrow afternoon, five o'clock sharp. Stage crew doesn't get to leave until ALL the props are finished, now let's go!"

The men went to their dressing room, the women to theirs. Daniel changed quickly so he wouldn't miss the chance to talk to Mary Ann. Turns out he waited on her outside the main entrance for about ten minutes. He had a vague plan to use one of Prince Moreau's lines as a test, hoping she would reply with the answer and transcend into some clever dialog.

His heart dropped though as she came out talking on her cell phone with Heather walking beside her. He was standing off to one side pretending to be reading a text message. He didn't think they noticed him and he thought for a minute about following them. 'Who knows how long she'll be on the phone. And would it be strange for Heather to be involved? I better wait for another chance.' He watched as the two walked away.

Chapter 4: Dreams of Salvation

Franklin Catoe closed the side door of his house and walked over to his old pickup truck. He never bothered to lock the door, so he hopped right in and fired it up. The V8 roared to life having been rebuilt recently by Jeff Randall the best (and only) mechanic in Tall Rock. He didn't have far to drive. The edge of the backyard he had a trail cleared where he could drive a short way in to the woods. The wood pile was covered by a lean-to off the back of his house. As he drove past he noticed it only had two rows that were stacked chest high. He pulled up near the hickory that was still laying there on the ground where it landed when it first fell. It was only the tree trunk now, cut into sixteen inch sections since Frank had used the chainsaw. He got out and reached behind the seat for his ax. Elizabeth never did understand why he wouldn't buy a log splitter. The main reason was he enjoyed swinging the ax. He didn't get to exercise his muscles every day and relished the feeling of working up a good sweat on a cool day. It also gave him time to think while he worked, using the log splitter required complete concentration and was too loud to be relaxing. He planted his feet and swung the ax head down into the log. He worked it loose and hit it with another blow. His first few swings were fast and hard but then he settled into a nice comfortable rhythm.

Soon, he thought about United Holy Christened Church. He wouldn't mind paying a small business tax, but the whole idea of being a franchise was downright preposterous. By joining he would give up all rights for the church he had built with his own hands. He had called the UHCC home office and spoken with a 'Transition Associate' whose job was to make the changeover as quickly and easy as possible. Membership was even worse than Frank had originally heard.

Changing the name and using the official UHCC bible was only part of the deal.

The Church building also became property of the UHCC. They had the right to close the chapter for a number of reasons, such as failure to pay dues, preaching from an unofficial bible, expressing views contrary to those of the UHCC, and various other infractions involving safety and public appearance. Frank wasn't sure if he could abide by the new rules. He'd been doing things his way a long time and he felt like it made a difference in people's lives.

According to the UHCC website, any church with more than one hundred and fifty members (including children) during a worship service is required to pay twelve hundred dollars per month, those with one hundred forty nine members or less were required to pay eight hundred dollars per month. Frank was wondering if that included Easter Sunday and read that no matter what day it was if a Compliance Associate counted more than the allowed amount the church would be fined an extra thousand dollars for the next three months and be on probation. The Compliance Associate's job was to make sure each small church was paying the correct amount by counting members during random visits. They also sat in and listened to the sermon to verify they were giving the approved message and were complying with regulations. Each Compliance Associate had fifteen to twenty churches in their territory and collected monthly dues.

Frank wasn't awfully concerned in being under the one fifty mark. A regular Sunday he had anywhere from seventy-five to ninety members, only thirty to forty on a Wednesday night. Easter Sunday always had a blowout crowd, so large the sermon had to be held outside. Maybe the Compliance Associate would be too busy to hit all the churches on Easter Sunday. The reverend stopped chopping to wipe the sweat from his brow. They could afford the dues imposed but it would make the finances tighter than ever. He never pressed the issue of donations he simply said something to the effect of, "Please give if you can, the Lord will help with the rest." Sometimes he never mentioned it and just passed the basket around.

Most of the congregation was financially average. Many were farmers or families that commuted to Tall Rock for work, but the church had its share of elderly folks as well; most being on a limited budget gave the same meager amount every week. Frank had always put the church first and he and Elizabeth second, scraping by in the early years and pinching pennies in the recession. It was a long time before they could begin saving for retirement.

Truth was he didn't mind living simple but Elizabeth had grown tired of it in the last ten years or so, envying the other women around town driving new cars all clad in the latest fashions. She'd kept a few part time jobs over the years, first at the library, then the grocery store, farmers' market seasonally, and recently had begun cashiering at Sewing Circle Supply. She didn't save the money she earned unless she had a large purchase to make and had to save for more than one paycheck, relying on the donation plate and Frank's vegetable garden to put food on the table and pay all their bills. The garden behind the house was approximately a quarter of an acre with a wide variety of vegetables that changed seasonally. They ate what they needed and sold the rest at the Tall Rock Farmers' Market on Jody Road. Frank put most of the profits into his and Elizabeth's retirement savings.

"Damn, it just isn't right," He stopped chopping again. 'Could we keep it underground?' he wondered. 'Probably couldn't even pray without the government knowing it these days.'

His thoughts weren't much of an exaggeration, ever since the financial collapse and both of the revolts that followed, the government had become quick to create more law enforcement jobs. Police, National Guard, IRS, and FBI had nearly doubled in force after neither revolt had been easily dealt with. The National Audit Department was a new organization that was started shortly afterward to 'strategically investigate' private citizens' property and finances. The rumor was all churches that didn't join the UHCC would be investigated and charged as criminals if they continued to assemble for worship. The FBI had already made numerous arrests by monitoring the internet for talk of 'Terrorist Actions'. The Reverend finally decided he had no other choice if the Tall Rock Baptist Church was going to live on.

Maybe he could cheat a little as he knew many others would try to do. Surely the system would have corruption just like a major corporation or even the United States Government. He knew thousands of administrative positions would be available, but he couldn't leave the altar where he belonged. Maybe he could get a person inside the UHCC to cut down his monthly dues. NO. That would only solve his financial problem. He wanted to be free of their tyranny altogether. (He swung the ax again). He wanted to preach from his old, trusty bible. (He swung harder). He wanted to lead his congregation without fear of interference. (The ax flew faster and faster). Maybe others were thinking along the same lines and were plotting also. NO, this was too vital to hope for someone else to save the day.

'I have to bring down the UHCC!' The reverend decided.

He began to think of it as a war, him against the government, the church, hell the whole damn world. As he sliced through the log he was breathing hard but he wasted no time and started on another piece.

Who could he get to join the UHCC, then betray them and what good would it do? Perhaps one of his own flock? He thought of each and one by one he knew they weren't qualified or willing to undertake a role of that magnitude.

'Elizabeth?' He dismissed it with only a second's pause. She couldn't keep her mouth shut long enough to find out anything useful, and if she did she couldn't keep from gossiping to her friends.

Frank's mind searched for a possible candidate. No one he knew was qualified to spy, not to mention be a trusted employee. It looked like he would have to seek outside help, a mercenary.

He stopped abruptly and let the ax fall to the ground, 'So that's it then. I'll hire a spy, help him secretly infiltrate the church, destroy it and be eternally damned. Guess I better not tell Elizabeth till I hammer out all the details,' He shook his head, 'It's probably better if she doesn't know at all.'

Chapter 5: Volunteering

Opening night of The Prince's Treasure went off without a hitch, and was already a success compared to the previous year's tragedy. Edwin didn't jumble one line in his monologue and the crowd laughed at most of the jokes. Professor Hoole, who had been hiding backstage judging the crowd's reaction, came out and took a bow after the curtain dropped. While he didn't get a standing ovation, he still considered it a success. The after show meeting had an easygoing atmosphere. Hoole never actually congratulated the cast on a good show but they could tell he was pleased when he told them.

"This performance was very near what I imagined when I wrote it, and aside from the few mistakes I pointed out, I want an identical show tomorrow night."

The play was to run for five consecutive nights Monday through Friday, with a possible Saturday showing if the patrons requested it. Daniel still hadn't spoken to Mary Ann and the sensation had only faded a little. 'Wait for the right opportunity, and then I'll make my move.' He reminded himself.

During Daniel's 11:00 a.m. 'Algebra 3' class an email went out to all instructors. Dr. Stone sighed as he read the request. He squinted at it and decided he needed his reading glasses.

"Any Students involved in Professor Hoole's theatrical production are excused from class at 11:30 for an emergency meeting in the auditorium," he then grumbled something about his class being more important than Hoole's damn play.

Daniel looked over his shoulder at Adam who worked on the stage crew. Adam shrugged his shoulders as to show he had no idea what it was about either. Dr. Stone asked, "Does this apply to any of you?" Daniel and Adam both raised their hands and were dismissed to go to the meeting. They walked together across campus wondering why Hoole would go so far as to pull them out class and on such short notice. A few students were seated on the first row as they had been when Hoole first auditioned them. Adam sat down but Daniel stood against the wall waiting on Peter. He looked down at his phone; -11:27- Peter didn't have as far to walk being in the Art building across the courtyard. Daniel was about to send him a text when he walked through a side entry door. They sat down amongst the others and inquired what this was about. No one had a clue but they all agreed it must be serious for Hoole to pull them out of class.

Professor Hoole stormed through the same door Peter had come in. He was wearing a long sleeve white button up shirt, tie, and slacks. The room was quiet when they saw the frustration in his face. He briskly walked to the center of the front row to address the students.

"Is everyone here?" he asked.

Everyone looked around and Mary Ann spoke up, "Edwin didn't come to class this morning so he must not have gotten the message."

"Edwin is the root of the problem, I'm afraid. He decided to get in an accident this morning on the way to school and broke his shoulder."

That hit the students like a ton of bricks. They all felt some sorrow for Edwin but they knew a broken shoulder would heal. The play was a different story.

"Now we have a real problem on our hands being that we have a performance tonight and three more this week. Now I know tonight's must be canceled, but I was hoping someone might brush up on Prince Moreau's lines so I don't have to step in and play a sixty two year old Prince."

Before Daniel had time to comprehend what had happened Peter spoke up. "I know the part. Well, me and Daniel both do."

"How well?" the professor anxiously questioned, "Word for word?"

Daniel piped up, "Better than Edwin."

"Really?" Hoole asked with obvious doubt.

Daniel rose from the old theater chair with a passion in his eyes

"Oh my life, if 'twas over now I would only have known love for a day. But what a day it has been, these eyes have seen few…" He delivered the monologue better than it had ever been. He spoke loudly as if he were on stage making the hand gestures and using inflection where it was needed. As he finished his fellow actors applauded him loudly. He hadn't expected this at all and merely said, "Thank you."

"Peter knows it just as well," He directed it at Hoole, who was momentarily speechless. Finally he managed, "That was very impressive Mr. Montclair."

He looked at Peter, "You know it that well also?"

Peter nodded his head in agreement.

"Well that helps, but the problem is still not solved. You may fill the role of Prince Moreau, however we will then lack either Paulus DiGirio or Drallis. Does anyone know either role?"

After a long silence followed.

"Not anyone?"

Adam spoke up, "I know each part. Only I've never practiced, but I think I remember most of the lines."

"That's the spirit I'm looking for," The professor said. "Now Drallis has fewer lines and is supposed to be a fool so Drallis you shall be. If you twist a line it won't make much difference."

Hoole raised his arms above his head triumphantly, "The show will go on as scheduled! Adam you and I are going to practice the rest of the afternoon. And everyone else had better be top notch," He said, looking right at Daniel.

Adam began, "Uh professor I have two more classes today," but Hoole cut him off before he could finish, "Your instructors will understand you missing class for this emergency. The rest of you are dismissed."

And just like that Daniel realized he would be Prince Moreau. He would get to kiss Mary Ann. He would be the star.

The other students, who were still in shock from the new changes, began to slowly rise and exit down the aisles. Peter who walked ahead of Daniel stopped and motioned for him to pass.

"You first, your highness," They both had a chuckle. Then a thought came to him. Daniel looked around and found her. "I'll see you later Pete, I just can't pass up this chance."

Mary Ann was leaving through the opposite door that led out into the hallway. He made a quick change of direction and walked briskly in pursuit. Only a few used that exit so Mary Ann walked alone. He caught up to her in the hallway, "Hey, Mary Ann."

She stopped walking and turned to him, "Oh, hey Daniel, this sure is crazy, huh?"

"Yeah, who would have imagined it?" He replied.

"I'm probably going to go see him later, if he's still in the hospital. Do you think he's out yet?" She asked and seemed sincerely concerned.

"I don't know, the professor didn't say much other than he had a broken shoulder, he could have other injuries from the wreck."

"Hoole was more worried about the damn play, it's like that's all that matters to him," She said remorsefully.

There was a short silence as Daniel didn't know how to respond.

Mary Ann broke the silence first, "So do you think you're gonna be alright filling in for Edwin?"

"I hope so. I've learned the lines but have never acted them out." He was lying of course; He and Peter had performed the whole play (excluding the kissing) by themselves in their apartment living room.

"Are you going to practice before tonight?" She asked.

"Well, I was kind of hoping you would help me out by practicing a few scenes, just to get a better grasp on my character." He could see her thinking about it and suddenly was nervous. He felt like a quarterback that was waiting for the hail-Mary to land in a crowded end zone.

"Well, sure we could do at least a couple of scenes, only my roommate sleeps in the afternoon before she goes into work, but what about your place? Don't you and Peter have an apartment together?"

"Yeah we do, and I can tell him not to bother us while we practice."

"Well I was thinking we all might breeze through the first and fourth acts."

Damn, he was hoping for acts two and three (the kissing scene) but tried not to show it.

"Sure, that's fine. We're over at Oakhall, room B2. What time could you be there?"

"Well, I've only got one more class and it ends at two thirty, how about you guys?"

"Pete should be done by three today, and I'll get out of French by four. So you want to meet up a quarter after four?"

"Sure, I'll see you the," Mary Ann smiled and turned her back to walk down the hallway. Daniel couldn't help but admire her as she walked away.

'Does she always swing her hips like that when she walks?' Maybe it was because she knew he was watching, this made him grin wider than ever. He was in a dream world as he walked back to class. He imagined the way he would look deep into Mary Ann's eyes just before he kissed her. He would not only save the play, but perform better than Edwin. After the show he might invite a few of the cast back to the apartment for an after party, a very select few including Mary Ann, Heather, and Jake (the neighbor across the hall). Peter would be there of course, being that he lived there and all. A few mixed drinks and some good music he might even talk Mary Ann into practice an extended version of their lip locking scene and whatever that may lead to. All his daydreaming led Daniel to believe this might be the best night of his life.

Daniel got permission to duck out of French class a few minutes early. Mrs. Walters had sympathy to any students involved with the performing arts program under Professor Hoole. He decided to take full advantage of his extra time and go clean up the apartment before Mary Ann got there. He left the Terrance Ashland Auditorium at a brisk walk that became an excited jog as he crossed the courtyard. Normally it was a ten minute walk from class, but today Daniel made record time. He tackled the stairs to the second floor two at a time. He pulled out his phone to check the time before he opened the door, three forty-five.

He walked through the door of his apartment and was stopped dead in his tracks by what he saw. Peter was on the couch making-out with a girl...Mary Ann. Instantly it felt like he'd been punched in the gut. They were half sitting half lying against the arm of the couch. Realizing someone had come in Peter stopped kissing and turned to see who it was.

The look he saw on Daniel's face was one for the ages. It was embarrassment, surprise, anger, and pain.

Their eyes locked for a second, and then it was Daniel who calmly said, "Sorry, I didn't mean to intrude." Then he turned and pulled the door shut as he walked back out.

Peter knew Daniel had a crush on Mary Ann but he also doubted his roommate would ever make an advance on her. Peter hadn't planned on hooking up with Mary Ann, but she had been flirty and he knew Daniel would get over it. Besides, he was enjoying the moment. The choice wasn't a hard one, he kissed her again.

"Do you think he's coming back?" Mary Ann asked.

"Oh probably in a little while, he gets embarrassed really easy," Peter assured her.

Daniel didn't dismiss the situation quite so easily; in fact it had sent his brain into WTF-mode. His adrenaline was making his heart race, but his mind was going even faster.

'WHAT THE HELL JUST HAPPENED? I thought she liked me. Hell, she was smiling and waving at me only the other day. Wait. Peter had been right beside me. OH, Son of a bitchhhh! That's why she wanted to practice at my apartment, she doesn't give a damn about me, it's Peter, Jesus H. Christ, I'm a damn fool. I should have known better.'

Daniel struggled with his thoughts without caring where he walked. He came to his senses in the communal parking lot when a gray sedan swerved across the road onto the sidewalk he occupied. He had to jump out of the way to keep from being hit. He did a somersault in the grass as the car sped away.

'What the hell?!! That asshole tried to kill me.' It was out of sight before he thought about getting the license plate number, much less getting a look at the driver.

What luck he was having, it was almost as bad as Edwin's. Come to think of it he should pay Edwin a visit. They were somewhat rivals in the theater, both competing for important roles. Edwin was an asshole most of the time. Daniel decided this would be a good time to catch him in a humble state, maybe even become friends. The hospital was across town but Daniel doubted he would be there still. Still kneeling in the grass he flipped through his phone and messaged Edwin with one of Lady Lewelda's lines.

Daniel- Where is my peasant lover, the prince of my heart?

Edwin- Loathing in my dungeon lol.

(He didn't see the humor in this situation. Regardless, he knew Edwin's 'dungeon' meant his apartment.)

Daniel- I'm gonna stop by, that cool?

Edwin- Yeah come on and see the damage.

He started the walk to Edwin's apartment, careful to watch out for cars along the way.

<u>Chapter 6:</u> Learning the Ropes

(Thirty-three years before)

Frank Catoe met Steve Hasler in Mobile, Alabama when he was eighteen. They both worked for a drug smuggler known as Douggy. Frank had gotten started selling pot to make money once his father had thrown him out of the house.

It was the kind of work he liked, being his own boss had its advantages, but it was risky. He had to run from the police on more than onc occasion. He liked the danger and always carried a .38 on him, but soon he got tired of the same crap. He sold a dime bag here and there but wasn't making much money. Soon he decided to move up in the game. He'd heard that the guys bringing it in from South America were making a killing. Terry, Frank's supplier, introduced him to Douggy, Mobile's largest smuggler at the time. He used a fishing boat to bring the pot back from Mexico. Douggy needed an extra hand and decided to give Frank a try. He explained to Frank that he used two boats for running the merchandise.

Most smugglers used cigar boats to run the merchandise but the DEA and the Coast guard began doing random 'safety audits' on speed boats so they could legally search for drugs. Douggy knew they wouldn't bother to check a couple of guys in a twenty year old fishing boat. But in case they did decide to stop them, Douggy's boat had a couple of custom features to elude capture. The most important was the smell. His boat smelled like rotten shrimp for two reasons. The first reason was it kept people from snooping around his boat, the second is it helped throw drug dogs of the scent of their secret cargo.

There was a compartment in front of the inboard motor where the drugs were hidden on the trip home. The motor itself was a monster, a supercharged big block 440 that could outrun most things on the water. Two, hundred gallon fuel tanks let the boat go out deep into the gulf to the meet point at a prearranged set of coordinates. They went out stocked with coolers, fishing poles, and gear so they can fish until their Mexican counterparts delivered the merchandise. The Mexicans always threw in a couple of fish to take back to Douggy. He explained that no money changed hands on the water. His relationship with his connection was so good he transferred the money into their bank account electronically. He also knew he was a dead man if he didn't pay.

Douggy's help on the other hand were always paid in cash. The two on the boat would leave early in the morning and navigate by the GPS until they reached the right coordinates sometime after noon. Then they would fish until the supply boat arrived. Steve spoke Spanish but few words needed to be spoken anyway, both parties knew their jobs. They transferred the pot and stored it. Then threw a few fish in the coolers and parted ways. Then they turned around and returned home, but the most dangerous part of the trip is the last two miles coming into Mobile Bay.

Douggy explained that having the fish in the cooler would be less suspicious in case the game warden did stop them, they even had saltwater fishing licenses. It was so low key they hadn't encountered any problems worse than some rough weather.

Frank felt good about the whole operation, it was less risky than he had expected and made more money in one night than he could in two weeks dealing.

Frank remembered the first time he saw Steve. Douggy took him down to the High Water Marina to practice driving the boat and using the GPS. Steve was waiting for them on the boat, rigging up fishing poles while smoking a cigarette. He looked up as he they approached. His eyes were hidden behind dark aviator sunglasses and the baseball cap on his head only detained a portion of his curly blond hair.

"Whassup?" He said.

"Steve this is Frank, he's gonna be your new first mate," Douggy announced.

"Pleasure to meet ya," Steve said with little interest.

"You guys are going to cruise the bay for a few hours so Frank can get a feel for the boat. Make sure you gas'er up when you get back in, you make a run on Thursday."

"Sure thing boss, I'll call you when we get back in."

Douggy's phone rang and he answered it and walked off. Frank and Steve just stood there for a moment sizing each other up.

"So Frank, have you been around boats much?" Steve asked.

"I've been all over the bay in a john boat," Frank said.

"Fishin?"

"Naw, just joy-riding," Frank admitted.

"Well, we'll get to do plenty of both right shortly," Steve said with a smile.

They spent the afternoon cruising around Mobile Bay in the boat. Steve showed him how to work all the controls from the GPS to the bilge pump. After Frank had a grasp on driving and navigating they anchored and did some fishing. (It turned out Steve cared more about smoking pot and drinking beer than catching fish.)

Frank didn't like the idea of having a boss, but Douggy seemed awful cool letting the help use the boat for an afternoon. He slapped some sunscreen on and took a sip of beer.

'Yeah, I could get used to this.' Frank thought.

Steve gave him the same outline that he'd heard from Douggy about the routine. Frank told him about his dealing experience and assured him he knew to keep his head in a tight spot.

"You don't have to worry about Paco and the boys. We don't carry the money with us so they won't get greedy. As long as we get back Douggy transfers the money electronically."

"Yeah I was wondering about that. What keeps Douggy from rippin' off his connection? Is business that good?" Frank asked.

"Both sides make out well," Steve said, "but however much Paco can get, we move. He doesn't like to sell to more than one person, that way if he gets screwed he knows who to go after. And TRUST ME, Douggy values his life more than a couple bags of herb. Oh, and he weighs it when we get back to his place, so don't think of skimming off the top, our lives are worth more than it too. That's also why he pays us so well, to keep us satisfied, and I mean where else could you make a grand in one day?"

They finished off the beer and were low on bait, so they motored back to the dock. They pulled in to a dock with gas pumps. The dock led to a shack on the shore. A sign on the dock read 'LOWTIDE'S GAS AND BAIT'.

"Douggy and Lowtide have a tab setup so we don't pay now. Go on inside and tell her you work for Douggy and that we're filling up on fuel. Buy some bait while you're in there either squid or mullet."

Frank walked in to the shack and looked around. It smelled like bait. On one wall there was a freezer with packs of bait inside, across the room were racks of fishing poles and cast nets. In the middle of the room a woman sat behind a counter watching a soap opera on a small television. She looked up when he shut the door, "Hey sugar what ya looking for?"

"I work for Douggy, Steve's out in the boat filling up."

"Well I declare, he sure has some cute fellas he sends in here," the woman said. She was in her fifties and not very appealing. He had to look away from the repulsive warts on her face to not stare.

"Well, thank you mam. Uh, I need some bait, squid and ..." He had forgotten what Steve had told him. "Squid, Shrimp, and Mullet are in the freezer."

'Mullet that was it.' He grabbed a bag of each and took them up to the counter. He couldn't help but notice the smell growing stronger. 'Is there a dead fish under the counter protecting the cash register? It's like fish guts a seagull wouldn't touch, Nasty!' he thought.

"That all honey?"

"Yes mam, the bait and the fuel," It was all he could do to keep from vomiting when he said it. The smell could have curled a skunk's ass-hair.

"The bait's eight dollars. Don't worry about the fuel. Me and Douggy will get straight on that later," He handed her the money "Thanks," he said and grabbed the bags of bait.

"You sure I can't do ya for anything else sweety?" She asked with a crooked smile.

“Not today,” and said he walked out.

'Holy Shit, was she serious?' Frank thought, ‘I wouldn't fuck her with my fishing pole.'

Steve was chuckling when he got back in the boat.

Frank held out the bags of bait to him, “You better keep this in the freezer until Thursday, it’s some stinkin ass shit.”

“Smell it Frank,” Steve said very seriously.

“What? You must be stupid, I'm not-”

“Open a bag and take a whiff, it's not the bait,” Steve once more insisted.

Franks curiosity got the better of him. He opened a bag of mullet and smelled. Fishy, but nothing like the stench he'd just encountered.

Steve began to chuckle again.

Frank looked at him confused and opened the bag of squid. That wasn't it either. Steve was laughing harder.

“Well what the hell was it, a dead whale?” Frank asked.

Steve almost fell out the boat he found it so funny. He went on like that for a good thirty seconds before he could explain.

“It was her, hahhaahaa, the dead whale behind the counter. Hahahaa. That's why she's known as Lowtide, 'cause she smells like it!”

“DAMN! How does she stand herself?” Frank asked, repulsed that anyone could smell so bad.

Chapter 7: Gone Fishing

Thursday morning came with ease for Frank. He rose before the alarm had a chance to wake him; it was like subconsciously he knew how important the day was. Often Frank skipped breakfast, but today he hit a 24 hour diner and ate well. A stack of pancakes and two scrambled eggs before the sun was up. He was early to the docks but it wasn't long before Steve pulled up in a 4x4.

"You ready Jimbo?"

Frank said in his cheesiest action hero voice, "I was born ready."

They loaded the coolers in the boat and cranked up. The roar of the engine cut through the silence. They putted away from the dock. Steve was behind the wheel, Frank riding shotgun on the disguised drug boat bound for a deal in the middle of the Gulf of Mexico. The hours passed and the sun climbed. They took turns driving the direction the GPS took them, always south by southwest. At eleven o'clock they stopped to eat a couple of sandwiches and piss over the side of the boat. The sun beat down with a mission to burn despite the sunscreen Frank had applied. Steve's skin was accustomed to exposure, he still wore a wide brim hat and his dark glasses to protect his eyes.

Frank had plenty of time to think during the ride even when he was driving. There was nothing to do but hold the wheel and gaze across the endless ocean. He'd fished from various docks on Mobile Bay as a boy, but he'd never seen this much endless water.

This was his big chance to quit selling dime-bags and make some real cash. The risk was exciting for him, part of the reason he chose to live a life of crime. The lifestyle was the other reason. It was a constant game of cat and mouse with the police, other criminals, and the civilians in between. He liked to think he was a little bit smarter than the people he dealt with, but he was still cautious and kept that pistol handy.

Just after two in the afternoon Frank was cruising along thinking of what he would do with his first payment. The engines roared so loud he could barely hear Steve yelling.

"HEY JIMBO!" He gave Frank the signal to slow down. He slowly eased the throttle back into neutral, "We're about there, keep an eye on the GPS. We don't have to be dead on the spot but as long as we get close they'll see us."

Frank kept a close eye on the monitor as they plodded along. Two hundred yards to go, then a hundred, then fifty. When they finally made the coordinates they shut off the motors and drifted. While they waited for their Mexican associates to arrive they fished and each had a beer. The sun had scorched the tops of Frank's feet and legs with no shade for them to hide under. He ignored it and savored his cold beer. He didn't know much about deep sea fishing, his line didn't move for a long time and he reeled it in to check if his bait was still on the hook. It wasn't. He reached for another mullet but stopped when he saw the boat on the horizon heading toward them.

"Here we go," Frank said.

Steve looked over indifferently, "Remember just to act cool, these guys are our bread and butter."

The boat was an old shrimper, only it didn't have any nets hanging up. It slowed as they got closer. Two men with beards stood shirtless on the deck, he could see another man in the wheelhouse driving. As the boat pulled up alongside one of the men threw Frank a rope. He tied it to the cleat up front. Steve threw the other Mexican a rope from their boat and he anchored it likewise so the boats were side by side and would drift together. Frank couldn't see over the side of the other boat but a man stuck his head over the side.

"Hola Muchachos. Any luck with de fishing?"

"We just got started when you boys pulled up," Steve answered.

The Mexican was the one who had been driving the boat. He was older and Frank figured he was the only one who could speak English.

"That's okay, we got you some big ones to take back. We catch plenty, make you look good."

One of the younger men came to the side with a duffel bag. He held it out to Frank, but didn't let go until Frank had a good grip on it.

"That's right," said Steve, "You get it from them while I load it up."

Another bag came over the side and then another. Steve slid the coolers out of the way and opened the storage compartment. Frank hadn't seen it open yet and was surprised how large it was. He was handed eight bags in all. He couldn't keep from wondering just how much they were bringing back, he'd never seen more than a single pound at a time. From the weight of the bags he knew it must have been over twenty or thirty pounds. He wanted to pause and do some rough calculations but one of the Mexicans was holding a fish out for Frank to grab. It must have been in the cooler for a while because it was slimy and ice cold. Frank threw it in the extra-large fish cooler and caught the next fish he was tossed. Steve finished stowing the bags and began to chat with the older man in Spanish. The other men kept tossing Frank fish. He didn't know much about the fish, but he liked all the variety of shapes and colors.

The cooler was about half full when Steve told the men that was enough and Frank took ice from another cooler and covered the fish so they wouldn't spoil on the ride home. He washed the fish slime off his hands with seawater and slid the coolers back on top of the secret storage compartment.

Steve ended his Spanish conversation with the old man and told Frank to untie the line holding the boats together. He did and tossed it back to the other boat. The Mexicans did the same and moments later the large boat was chugging away the direction they had come from. The exchange had taken about ten minutes and was the simplest and by far the largest drug deal Frank had ever witnessed.

"That was too easy," He told Steve.

Steve nodded, "Out here there isn't any law to worry about and without us carrying cash they can't fuck us over. You ready to ride? We've got that much more riding to do and I'm tired of smelling this stinking-ass boat."

"Alright then, let's boogie!" Frank fired up the engine and set the GPS to take them back to Mobile Bay. The other boat was wasting no time getting smaller on the horizon so they too began their long hot trip back.

Frank drove to start with while Steve slept. They swapped places later but Frank couldn't fall asleep as the roaring motor, scorching sun, and the boat jumping across the waves kept him uncomfortably awake. All that and the thought of all the money he was going to make. He knew it was merely a drop in the bucket to what Douggy was going to haul in. Of course he had a whole empire of dealers he sold to, and they in turn divided it even more and sold it to smaller fish like Frank had been. Of course every time the marijuana is divided the more it costs, but smaller quantities are much safer whether it be busted by the police or poached by hustlers. He'd known a guy who was killed over an ounce. That was how Frank learned that pot wasn't the problem; the money was the ingredient that made people untrustworthy. Marijuana was legal in many states anyway but not the stuff they were carrying. This was a special strain that had three times the California legal amount of THC - the active chemical that makes the user high.

The return trip was much the same as their morning crusade had been, only they were tired and the hours seemed to slow. Even the sun took its time setting over the gulf. Frank hit the lights and kept right on driving once it was dark. According to the GPS they only had less than six miles to go. He looked over toward Steve and decided he liked his new partner in crime. 'That guy knew how to make a long day on the water pretty enjoyable and still get the job done.'

Frank was sore. His body wasn't used to sitting for hours on end and being baked by the sun. He turned his neck to spit over the side of the boat but when he did a light caught his eye. It was another boat a hundred yards behind them.

"Hey man, hey. We got company behind us!" He couldn't see Steve very well even though he was sitting right beside him. To overcome the roar of the engine Steve hollered back, "It's nothing to worry about, probably just some fisherman using us as a carrot!"

It made sense to Frank but his mind wasn't at ease. He couldn't help but wonder how long they had been followed, surely after sunset, but how did they get so close without being spotted? A couple of miles went by and they could see a few lights from the bay.

Steve leaned over into Frank's ear, "Keep the throttle down and swap places with me."

They made the switch with relative ease despite the darkness. Steve cut off the lights and steered the boat right ninety degrees in the pitch black, still going fast. Then after thirty seconds he slowed to idle and they turned to look back. Both men held their breath as they watched the pursuing boat's lights. When it reached the spot where they turned it kept right on going. Frank breathed a sigh of relief.

Steve shut off the engines. "We wait here for a few minutes and let them go on their way."

Frank pulled out his cell phone and turned it on. Two bars of service meant they were close. Good, it was almost ten o'clock and he was tired from all that time on the water. As they sat and drifted the more relaxed he became. Above they could see stars through the scattered clouds. All was quiet with the engines off, which were a constant he had grown used to (along with the smell of rotten shrimp).

While they had been within arm's reach of each other all day they hadn't had a casual conversation because of the motor's noise. Frank decided to start one up.

"So how'd you get into the business?"

Steve pondered the question amidst the darkness.

"Well, I guess I'm like most other guys doing it. I came from nothing so I had nothing to lose. My dad's family all made their living fishing before the oil spill happened. Since then running grass is the only thing we've been able to make a dollar on without having to up and move like many others did. I started selling when I was in school and learned the game. After a while it got old and I started looking for bigger fish. Douggy came to me and offered me this. Funny thing was I was already working for him before without even knowing it. Kind of like a private contractor. Shit, you too. Every time Murph sold you a pound to break down and distribute, it came from Douggy's operation. Hell, probably even this boat. All of a sudden Frank was startled. He'd never mentioned to Steve anything about Murph his supplier, or to Douggy for that matter.

He was about to ask how he knew so much when Steve volunteered it to him.

"Douggy has a network of dealers that never even meet him. Hell he's got guys that never even touch a bag, they just get information for him; cops on payroll, guys at the marina, even a hit-man. To tell you the truth it's like a low key mafia, only most guys think they are a one man operation. He knew your record was clean before you even met. He doesn't trust just any run of the mill dumbass with this much grass.

No, he did his research on you when you started selling low level. Probably had his police connection pull your record to make sure you weren't a narc. But don't feel special; he does it to everyone who gets an eye on the big operation."

"Damn," was all Frank could muster to say at the time but his head was screaming 'HOLY-FUCKING-SHIT! I'm in the big leagues now whether I like it or not. GOD DAMN a hit-man!'

"I just thought I should mention that to you in case you ever get any bright ideas about sneaking off with a little of the product or something unhealthy like that."

"Naawh, I've got better sense than that. Plus this is going to be the best payday of my life for one day's work, I wouldn't screw the golden goose."

Steve said, "Good, that's good. My last coworker wasn't so smart." Then he fired up the motors.

With no other boats in sight it was safe to turn on the lights and head back to the dock just past the marina on Lazy Creek. They were easing across the bay able to see only a few feet in front of where the headlight was shining, Frank was wondering how the old sailors had managed without GPS for thousands of years.

Suddenly a spotlight hit them in the eyes followed by the flashing blue lights. The boat they thought they had lost had been waiting to ambush them, and it was the law.

"Stay right there and shut your engines down," said a man's voice on a loudspeaker.

To Frank's surprise that is exactly what Steve did. The boat edged up beside them and turned on its deck lights. It was a 25 foot coastguard "Guardian" boat with two men. The one at the wheel was a coastguardsman by his uniform. The other was a game warden for the state of Alabama. Both were armed with pistols on their sides, not to mention the machine gun turret mounted on the bow. Frank's heart was racing but he tried to stay cool.

"You boys mind telling just what you're doing out here this late?" asked the game warden as serious as could be. He was a tall full sized man, close to fifty and built like a boxer.

Frank sure didn't know what to say and was glad Steve piped up, "Oh, we're just getting back from a long day of fishing. The fish were biting so we stayed out later than we should have, an' then had a hell-of-a time getting the engines going."

"So why'd you run from us?" The warden was looking right at Frank who remained silent but was screaming inside.

'HOLY SHIT WE ARE TOAST! What's he gonna do, search the boat? Arrest us for the hell of it?' Truth be told Frank didn't know what his rights were with a game warden.

Again Steve answered, "Well we didn't know who was chasing us, it could have been pirates."

The warden didn't hesitate at all by the answer. Instead he threw Frank a rope.

"Tie off."

He tied it to a cleat and then they were connected, just as they had been hours before to the Mexican reefer-runners. The game warden wasted no time to board their boat, and the coastguardsman took control of the spotlight.

"I need to see your fishing licenses," He said.

As Steve and Frank were digging for their wallets he flipped open the cooler lids. The drink cooler only had empty beer cans and a bottle of water. Frank was even more worried when he realized the beer cans were open containers, he wasn't sure if that law applied on the water or just on land. The warden seemed more preoccupied with the fish in the other cooler. He shined his flashlight in it and looked at the fish.

"Well, you boys caught a load here," He took Franks fishing license, examined it, and gave it back; the same went for Steve who was still acting like it was just another day at the office. The guardsman was speaking into the radio.

"Central, this is Guardian Four, Central this is Guardian Four, over."

-"Go ahead Guardian Four."

"Central be advised we are investigating a watercraft operating without lights on Mobile Bay. Registration number Alabama-zero-seven-two…"

The game warden shined the light back in the cooler and looked at Frank, "Hold up that amberjack."

Frank didn't know which one the amberjack was so he grabbed the one on top.

"Son, that's a striped bass. Do you not know what kind of fish you've been catching?"

"Uhh, well not really sir. This is my first time out. I haven't picked up on all the names just yet."

He turned to Steve who had sat back down at the wheel, "Well, how about you Capitan? Do you know the fish and regulations?"

"Well not all of them, but I know the amberjack is that red one."

Frank put the bass back in and grabbed the amberjack to hand to the warden.

"Hold it up in the light."

He did as he was told and the warden pulled a small tape measure off his belt clip and checked the length of the fish.

"That one's good. Now that Yellow-fin Tuna." He pointed it out for Frank who had to use both hands to hold it up.

The warden read the tape measure and said, "The minimum size for Yellow-fin is twenty-seven inches. This fish is only twenty-five."

A couple of moments went by in silence while the information sank in.

"Oh wow," Frank said.

Steve started to say, "I didn't even realize they had to-,"

The Warden cut him off, "You should have known before you went on the water. Now the others look fine but I'm going to have to fine you for that fish."

Frank was relieved, in his mind a fine was a better than getting busted for possession of unregulated marijuana with intent to distribute.

The coastguardsman was off the radio and asked, "Do you have life vests and a fire extinguisher on board? We need to see them."

Frank immediately responded, "Oh yes sir we have them stored beneath."

Midsentence he remembered they were stored under duffel bags full of pot that he would have to move to get to the life jackets. His heart was in his throat and he wished he could take back what he'd said. His eyes met Steve's who now looked alert and not at all passive.

Frank stood there not knowing what to do.

The warden was becoming irritated, "Well I don't have all night, let's see'em."

Frank slowly replied, "Actually, ya know what? I think we left them back at the marina."

"Is that so? Well I'm afraid that's going to be two more fines, and we're still going to have to check your boat."

Frank would have pissed his pants if he hadn't been so dehydrated. The man with the badge was getting suspicious and that's when you go to jail or get lucky, only Frank didn't feel very lucky. The .38 he had tucked in the back of his pants was beginning to creep into his mind. He'd never shot anyone but he and Steve were in a tight spot and he didn't know if Steve was packing. He felt sure he was, it was an unwritten rule in the business to carry a pistol, but could he use it? Would he use it? Or was his brain fried in chicken shit after all day in the sun. Hell, he hadn't even gotten up out of the driver's seat.

The warden finally said, "Alright, both of you move to the front of the boat."

Frank started to move that way as Steve said in his nonchalant tone, "Oh, I do have this fire extinguisher down here."

He reached down into the cubby-hole under the steering wheel, but instead he pulled out a .45 and shot the warden through the chin. Before his dead body could hit the deck Frank had pulled his .38 and let loose three shots at the guardsman manning the spotlight.

As the first bullet hit him in the hip he jerked the light handle and made it shine up into the black night sky. That killed their visibility until Steve picked up the flashlight. He shined it at the other boat first. Two of his bullets had struck the guardsman, after the hip shot one of Frank's other two shots went in the man's throat. The game warden lay halfway over the side rail of the drug boat, his blood leaking into the bay.

"WE ARE FUCKED!" Steve yelled.

"NO SHIT! What do we do now?" Frank cried out.

"Not a damn clue, but Douggy will know. He'll meet us and figure out how to clean up this mess."

Steve started to dial Douggy when Frank stopped him.

"Wait, what's his fucking plan?" he asked.

Steve shouted, "That's what I'm about to find out!"

"No, what I mean is every time I ever did a deal, I went into it with a plan to get the hell out without getting pinched or killed."

"You think..Just what are you getting at? You think he's going to sell us out?" Steve glared at his partner.

"Well, we are the perfect fall guys," Frank said, "We're holding the dope and the smoking guns, on his boat, and guess who's not?

Douggy! Hell, he could say we stole the boat. He knows dead men can't rat him out, and that's what happens to cop killers when they get caught. That's what we are now."

Steve didn't want to believe it, "I've got to call him and let him know what's up. The coastguard knows they stopped us when that jerk over there called it in, so before long a search will be out for these two guys. Hell, someone could have heard that cannon you fired and be on the way now."

Frank was relentless, "I bet he tells you to come on in to dock like nothing happened. Then as soon as he gets off the phone with you he calls the cops and reports his boat stolen. Didn't you say he had cops on payroll?"

"Yeah, two of the crookedest fuckers I ever met," Steve remembered.

"By the time we get back they pull up and waste us. Then Douggy gets the dope moved before the real cops get there." Frank guessed, making it up as he went.

"Shit! But what if you're wrong? He might have another way where everybody gets out safe."

The law enforcement community wouldn't be happy without the killers in body-bags, each sporting nine or ten bullet holes. If everyone got away clean that wouldn't happen. A long nasty investigation would drag down everyone. Neither man wanted to serve a life in prison, but crossing Douggy was a likely death sentence.

"Go ahead and call him, Steve. See what he tells you to do. If it sounds like an ambush we come up with plan 'B'."

"Fuck, alright."

Steve dialed the number and got Douggy. He quickly told him what had happened and waited for instructions.

"Yeah. OK boss. Yeah we'll be in, in about twenty or thirty minutes. Alright, bye." Steve ended the call.

"SON OF A FUCKING BITCH! You were right, he said he'd have a couple of guys waiting at the dock to clean up the mess and that we shouldn't worry, just play it cool."

Frank thought about it, "We can't go back to the dock, and we have to get the hell out of town. We won't be able to hide from Douggy in Mobile for very long, not to mention the cops. Do you know anywhere we can land?"

"I don't know, hell my truck is back at the dock. Hey, we could land at Lowtide's and walk into town," Steve offered.

Frank was surprised how unnerved Steve had become, far from the always cool, pirate of pot he'd been all day.

"Okay, there shouldn't be anybody there this late, lets haul ass.

They untied from the coastguard boat and threw the dead game warden in it. Then Steve steered a course to Lowtide's Bait and Gas. It was only a couple of miles from Douggy's dock and Steve had the motors wide open jumping waves until the boat was coming out of the water. There were no lights at the dock or the little shack, so Steve slowed and crept into his usual spot beside the pumps. Steve shut off the motor and looked over at his partner, "So what now? Do we just leave it here?"

Frank had been thinking about it the entire ride there. The thing that concerned him the most was the evidence they would leave behind if they left the boat just sitting there. Blood of a murdered game warden, bullet casings, and tons of fingerprints was just a sure-fire ticket to prison.

"We have to sink the boat."

Steve didn't agree or disagree he only said, "Fuck. How are we gonna do that?"

They both pondered the question.

"Take the plug out the back, it's got a plug right Steve? Hell all boats have drain plugs."

"Yeah, it's got a plug but we don't have pliers to turn it with, I bet it's seized up with rust. We always use the bilge to let the water out. I know, shoot a couple of holes in it with that cannon of yours."

"And wake up every cop on the bay? Are you fuckin nuts?" Frank asked.

"Well shit, sinking boats and killing cops aren't my specialty, moving pot is…and speaking of pot, are we just going to sink forty pounds of it? I'm almost broke, can't go to my truck, and have to get the fuck out of town. I say we take it and sell it cheap on our way out," Steve said, "Otherwise we'll be dead broke on the run."

"Don't you think it would look a little suspicious to be seen carrying eight duffel bags into town after dark?"

"Well I'm not going to sink forty pounds of pot into Mobile Bay." Steve said, "I'd never be able to forgive myself."

"We could hide it and come back for it later once it's safe," Frank said, not liking the idea of having to come back to the bay, but it was much safer than walking the pot into town at night while the cops were out in force.

They agreed that hiding all but one bag somewhere close by was the best option. They moved the coolers and unloaded the bags onto the dock, still using the game warden's flashlight to see.

The problem still remained about how to sink the boat. Frank tried thinking of ways to knock holes in the hull without any hammers or tools. Steve was the one who came up with the solution.

"We burn it. That way the evidence burns and then it sinks, there won't be anything left to link it to us."

"We'll just have to haul ass after we light it," Frank replied, "And where are we going hide this shit?"

"There are some wooded lots on the road back to town." Steve said.

He removed the rubber fuel line from one of the motors and turned the ignition to the on position without cranking it. Fuel sprayed out into the boat and he soaked the whole inside down. Frank soaked an extra line of rope in gas and strung it out down the dock as a fuse. They stood at the end of the fuse about fifteen feet away with the bags at their feet. Frank pulled out his lighter. He was just about to light it when Steve's phone rang. Steve pulled it out of his pocket and looked at it.

"It's Douggy, should I answer it?"

"Yeah but stall for time, tell him we're out of gas or something."

It rang again.

Steve answered, "Hello."

Douggy: "What are you doing? You should have been here by now!"

Steve: "Well, we ran out of gas and were trying to paddle to shore before someone saw us."

Douggy: "What? You should have plenty with that big ass tank on the back! Hell you've never even come close to running empty before."

Steve: "I let Frank pump it the other day, I guess he didn't fill it up."

Douggy: "Goddamnit!"

Douggy: "Can you see Lowtide's? My tracking signal shows you're right by it."

Frank could barely hear what Douggy had said. 'Holy Shit a tracking signal! We should have thought of that!'

Steve: "Oh yeah, we're at the next dock over we can paddle over and get some gas."

Douggy: "The pumps are locked dumbass, but luckily I've got a key. Get over there and I'll meet you in about fifteen."

Steve: "Sure thing boss," He ended the call.

"Fuck! He said he knows where we are and is going to be here in fifteen minutes."

"I know," Frank said, "I heard it all. That doesn't change anything except we REALLY have to haul ass now. I'm going to light it, you ready?"

"No. But do it anyway."

Frank knelt down to the rope. He clicked his lighter and got a flame on the third try. The gas soaked rope went up fast and the flame raced to the boat. The explosion ripped through the calm night air and was enough to put Frank on his ass.

Then Steve told him, "Let's go!"

They ran up the dock and across the street with two duffel bags in each hand. The street was deserted to the wooded lot. They walked in quietly shining the light searching for a good spot to hide their stash. It was a corner lot a half acre in size with houses behind it and on one side. The neighborhood was a mix of houses and businesses. Most of the houses were fishermen and dockhands who made their living on the bay.

There wasn't much underbrush but they found a spot in-between two trees that could only be seen from the back side of the property. They buried six of the bags there under leaves and pine straw. Neither man was really satisfied but they didn't have enough time to find a better hiding spot. Steve led the way out of the lot toward the side facing the street.

They took off running down the street, and then turned inland and crossed AL-193. They heard sirens in the distance, but couldn't make out if it was the police or fire department. Once they crossed the highway they stopped to look and make sure no one had followed them. Frank was tired from the long day on the water and the walking wasn't helping.

"We need to find somewhere to hole-up for the night Steve," he said.

Steve was already thinking ahead, "I know a girl who works the front desk of a motel on Sindal Road. I used to sell to her back before I started running it for Douggy. I'll see if we can get her to give us a ride to get my truck."

"Douggy's gonna be watching your truck, your house, my car, my apartment. Even with every cop in the city looking for blood, Douggy scares me even worse because he knows us. He's not just going to let us sink his boat and get away with his pot free-and-dandy. He'll send his army of dealers and crooked cops to kill us and get it back."

"Yeah, we're in some shit now… Let's get to the motel and lay low tonight."

Carrying ten pounds of pot, Franklin Catoe and Steve Hasler took off toward the Shining Light Motel.

<u>Chapter 8:</u> Putting on a Show

Present day, Birmingham, Alabama

"Knock, knock," Daniel said.

"Come on in, it's open," Edwin replied.

Daniel walked in the apartment to see the former Prince Moreau sitting on a couch in basketball shorts and a tee-shirt watching television. His left arm was in a sling to take the relief off his shoulder.

"Damn dude you look rough…kind of like you got in a car wreck."

"Ha-ha, very funny," Edwin said, "You'd be surprised I'm still alive if you saw my poor Saturn. You know they don't make those anymore? I loved that car."

"Well why'd you wreck it then?" Daniel teased.

"It was either run off the road or get in a head on collision. I was driving over by the library when a black car came into my lane. I probably should have let the sorry S.O.B. hit me, but I probably would have died in the process."

"Do you think he was still drunk from the night before driving home or maybe spilled his coffee in his lap?" Daniel asked.

"It looked like he was trying to kill me! He just decided to play chicken without warning me."

"You saw who it was?"

"I didn't really get a chance it happened so fast, I was worried about getting out of the way and then tried avoiding the tree. I wrapped my poor car around a big pine, God rest its soul. I'm pretty sure it was a guy though."

Daniel stopped to think, 'Wasn't it a black sedan that almost hit me on the way over here?'

Edwin was the first to bring up the change in roles, "So I hear you're the new Prince. Well here's some advice: Be royal. Think of yourself as a prince and you'll be one. And when you kiss Lady Lewelda, don't get your hopes up. She saves the real kisses for me."

'That's what you think.'

"Be royal, Okay," Edwin insisted.

'What a fucking moron. How did he ever make it into college much less get the lead role in a production? He must give Hoole the reach-around while he's kissing his ass.'

"Be royal eh? I guess that makes sense," Daniel said.

His phone vibrated in his pocket. He looked at it and saw it was Peter calling. He decided to ignore it, but it made a good excuse to leave.

"Well man I've got to get to practice. Are you going to make it to the show tonight?"

"Yeah I'll probably go. It'll be nice to just watch for once. Break a leg."

"I better not," Daniel said, "Hoole is running out of able body actors."

He left and walked out of the apartment complex and headed across campus to no place in particular. Was Mary Ann messing around with other people in the cast? He doubted it. She was a good girl who broke hearts unknowingly. Peter was just being himself and had to kiss a pretty girl when the opportunity presented itself.

He needed to clear his mind and focus on tonight's performance. This was his big break. Forget about Mary Ann and Peter's crap, he would finally be recognized as the quality actor he was. He called Peter back and assured him everything was fine and that he wasn't worried about practicing with Mary Ann.

He showed up to the auditorium early to make sure his costumes were in the right place and everything was good to go. Hoole was on stage grilling poor Adam of all the lines and movements that he needed to know to play Drallis.

Daniel bought a soda and found a nice dark corner backstage to sit and avoid Hoole until later (he didn't feel like wasting time proving to Hoole that he was ready for the part).

Stage hands and actors all began filing in right before the first call and began last minute preparation. The curtain was closed and Hoole called for a meeting fifteen minutes before show time.

"Alright everyone, last night's performance leaves us with an opportunity. You see, while it was fine, it was not perfect! And that leaves tonight for us to make it that much better."

It was normal for an acting instructor or director to be overdramatic, but this was a little over the top.

"Now I know we've had some role changes, but that is no excuse! I want perfection! I want that audience to be drawn to your every move like moths to a flame, and to crave more as soon as the curtain drops! Just remember what I've taught you…BEEEEEE the PART!" He raised his hands as if celebrating a victory, or perhaps reaching up to heaven for divine intervention.

Hoole reminded them, "The audience is about to enter, so keep it silent from this point on; and I need to see Prince Moreau, Drallis, Paulus DiGirio, and Lady Lewelda." They gathered around him as the others went on about their preparations.

"You four are the core of this production. Don't forget it. Regardless of the personnel changes I expect it to flow just as smoothly as it has so far. And the two of you," Hoole looked at Daniel and Adam, "I'm taking a huge chance by letting you go out there without so much as a dress rehearsal, but under the circumstances it's the only option. Don't let me down, I just won't have it."

Simon Hoole, Professor of Theater and the Arts at Birmingham Arts and Technical College, held his reputation more important than any other thing in his world. In fact he went to great lengths to build and protect it (He went so far as to blog about how great he was while posing to be a former student on a Birmingham Arts and Technical website).

Teaching was the easiest way to 'own his own theatre company'. Regardless if it was made up of student actors and funded by the art department's annual budget, he was in control to write and direct. His own acting endeavors had never been good enough to support him as a full time career, and he worked job after job until he decided that teaching pay was easier money.

Each night's performance was more important than the last with a fresh audience of co-workers, theater critics, and other patrons of the arts. Last night President Tucker and others from the College Board came to the show and afterwards told him how much they enjoyed it. Enjoyment was easy. He wanted them to laugh, cry, sympathize, and above all give a standing ovation.

Tonight other members of the board could show up, Professor Hasler from the Technology department had reserved two tickets in the VIP box. Hoole had never seen Steven Hasler at a performance, and thought that the second ticket might be for a date. The last season, Jeanine Bailey, curator of the Birmingham Modern Art Museum, had made a surprise visit with her husband. Hoole didn't recognize her in the general seating before the start of the show but had them upgraded to the VIP seats at intermission.

Ushers opened the doors and began to show people their seats. It looked to be another mixed crowd, same as the night before with students dominating the cheap seats and the more distinguished patrons sat up front or in the balconies. Hoole greeted people as they came through the balcony entrance. He recognized numerous students and faculty, Dr. Sharone his physician, Lawrence Jackson from the county council and finally Professor Hasler and his guest arrived. Hoole decided the guest with Hasler wasn't a date being that he was a man. He was bearded, around fifty years old, and well dressed.

"Ah, hello Professor Hasler, I'm quite surprised to see you here. I didn't know you were a fan of the theater."

"Well, hello Simon. The truth is I can't remember the last time I saw a performance. This man is the reason I'm here tonight. This is Franklin Catoe, an old colleague and friend visiting from South Carolina."

"Professor Simon Hoole, at your service."

Frank shook his hand, "Nice to meet you professor, I've heard great things about you're program here. In fact, that's the main reason I've traveled so far to be here tonight."

"Oh really?" Hoole was at a loss.

"Yes, you see I'm looking to recruit a young actor for a role that's available this fall. Steven here tells me you produce plenty of talented actors each year. I have a particular type I'm looking for."

"Ah yes, I've taught many aspiring actors. What were you looking for exactly?"

"A young man, someone with a powerful voice who is above all believable. Of course I wouldn't want to take away from their schooling so one who is about to graduate this or next semester."

Hoole thought it over for a few seconds. "I have two or three young men who could fill the bill. What is the role if I may ask?"

Franklin smiled, "It's a brand new part, the lead role in a tragedy."

"I see. Well I'm afraid my top student won't be here to audition for you tonight. He was supposed to play the lead again this evening but I'm afraid he was in a car accident this morning and had to be replaced."

Steven broke in, "Edwin? Is he alright?"

"He's broken his shoulder, but I imagine he'll make a full recovery," Hoole sighed.

"Well, I know the show will begin soon, perhaps we could talk of who else might be available when you have some free time," Frank said.

"Of course, if you'd like to hang around after the show I might be able to introduce you to a couple of hopefuls. Or we could meet for lunch tomorrow if you prefer."

"We'll stick around afterwards if it's no trouble."

"None at all. Enjoy the show." Hoole said.

Steve and Frank made their way to their seats.

Frank whispered, "I thought you said he was usually difficult to talk with."

"Most of the time he's a real asshole, you've just got to get to know him better. He'll cooperate more if he keeps thinking you're a director, or someone important in the business. That's the reason I didn't introduce you as a Reverend," Steve assured him.

The house lights began to dim and a single spotlight shone at the curtain. An announcer's voice came over the loudspeaker:

"Ladies and gentlemen, the theater department of Birmingham Arts and Technical College is proud to present The Prince's Fortune, written and directed by Simon Hoole."

The curtain went up and act one began in an old English courtyard with Lady Lewelda smelling the different fake flowers placed about the stage. Each character entered and gave their lines throughout the first act (except Peter as Paulus DiGirio, who entered in the second act).

Daniel delivered his lines better than Hoole ever could have imagined he would. Poor Adam didn't know the Drallis part and it showed. He was unsure where he needed to stand at certain times but Daniel and the others subtly helped him get by. The curtain dropped at the end of the first act for a quick scene and costume change.

Daniel had time to change into his Prince's attire and take a swig from his soda. The second scene was set in the royal dining hall, giving him a few minutes to watch from the shadows of backstage. He peered out into the crowd to look for people he knew and recognized plenty of fellow students.

It was nearly a full house with only a few seats in the back left empty, which was normal for a weeknight show. Friday and Saturday would sell out when people could come from out of town looking for somewhere different to go. His attention went back to the stage where the queen was scolding her husband for not wanting to invite his cousin, Paulus DiGirio, to the upcoming ball.

Adam joined him ready to make their entrance when Daniel noticed someone lurking opposite him in the darkness of the curtain folds. He couldn't make out exactly who it was but they seemed strangely familiar. Daniel strained his eyes but it was difficult to see across the lighted stage back into darkness. It was time for him and

Adam to make their entrance. The prince rushed out with Drallis his servant right on his heels.

"Father, Mother, pardon my intrusion..." He caught his breath, "Who was..What was the name of the fair Lady in the courtyard you spoke with day before last Mother?"

"Why my son, did you not recognize her? That was your early childhood companion," Prince Moreau looked puzzled, "…from Marseille."

"Lewelda? Here?"

The King and Drallis managed to say two lines out of order but soon were back on track and finished all but the end of scene two. Daniel was left alone on the stage to deliver his monologue as if talking to the night sky. He nailed it better than anyone ever had before, and was carried off the stage with a breeze of applause. There was a ten minute intermission. In this time the crew had a chance to do a full scene change, not just props and lighting.

'Damn, he's the backup?' Thought Professor Hasler, along with many other cast members and patrons who knew about Edwin's mishap.

"The prince. Is he a senior this year?" asked Frank.

"I don't think so. He was in my 'Technology and Society' class last year and I usually teach only freshmen or sophomores, but I could be wrong. His name is ….Montclair, Daniel Montclair."

"He's perfect for the job, he delivered that speech better than any sermon I've ever given. Do you know anything else about him?"

"What, like his religion? Hell, I thought I was doing good to remember his name with all the students I have each semester. Don't worry, I'm sure you can meet him and the rest of the cast after the show is over."

Daniel stayed in the same costume for the third and fourth acts so he had a few seconds to relax before starting to set up the scenery. He'd completely forgotten about the mysterious backstage guest and was taking a drink of his soda when Mary Ann came up and surprised him. She came up behind him, put her hands on his shoulders like she was giving him a massage, and whispered in his ear, "You're doing great Dan."

He turned to face her, "And when you kiss me make it real, that's always the best way."

She quickly leaned in and planted a peck on his cheek, and then she turned and walked away to help with the setup. Daniel was stunned, all he could do look at her with a dumb grin on his face. He looked around to see if Peter had seen it. He wasn't anywhere in sight.

'Wow, this is one of those days I'll never forget,' he thought (and he was right).

He started to feel physically different, his stomach became upset and his head was swimming. It reminded him of a stomachache mixed with a hangover.

'Is this being lovesick? Damn she does know how to get a guy all messed up inside, that's for sure.'

The third act was approaching quickly and he didn't have time to go see the school nurse so he took another sip of soda to try and settle his stomach. He gave Adam a thumbs up but it was more of a questioning one that said, 'Are you ready?'

Adam responded with a, 'Fuck no' kind of smile, so Daniel went over to remind him of the key lines and cues. They whispered their lines until Hoole walked up to have a brief word.

"Doing very well my Prince. Drallis, pleeeease don't forget anymore lines, but if you do have to adlib keep it light and get right back into it. And this isn't just another Wednesday night show anymore. A Broadway scout is here tonight in this very auditorium watching your every move. This play is only as good as the actor's performing in it, so be great!" It was a shouting whisper that the crowd would have heard if they hadn't been busy talking and going to and from their seats. Hoole went off to direct other aspects of the prep and then signal for start of act three.

Daniel was getting worried if he'd be able to finish his lines and how the hell was he going to swordfight Paulus DiGirio in act four.

All that jumping around was going to make him hurl. Then his mind slipped back to Mary Ann. He thought about the upcoming kiss scene. He was supposed to cut her off while she was talking and plant a little peck on her lips, then she would grab him around the neck and do a good old fashioned lip-lock. No tongue involved, but then she had said to make it real. 'How did she mean it? Make it meaningful or does she want to French kiss on stage? I know she likes making out. Had she brushed her teeth since she kissed Peter?'

The third act began smoothly. The setting was outside the DiGirio home under Lewelda's balcony beneath a starry night sky that had been painted by the art department. Daniel tried his best to ignore his stomach doing cartwheels. He tried to breathe deeply but it was hard to do and still act and speak as loud as was required.

For Daniel the act was dragging on forever and he was beginning to pray for a power outage so he could take a break and settle himself, or just rush through and finish the damn thing. But first he had to finish the kiss that was approaching quickly.

"Off to the home of DiGirio and bid the ole man come and spar the prince if he will."

Drallis exited the stage and left the prince and Lady Lewelda on stage alone.

Lady Lewelda: "I could never choose between your love and that of my father, there must be some other way."

Prince Moreau: "That is all he knows and so it is all I know." He walked closer until he was an arm's length away of her. "And I would fight a thousand father's even larger than he who wants me dead now. He may be skilled but I am the son of King Tinious, The slayer of the Gauls, death runs in my heart and bones."

Lady Lewelda: "Oh I am such a silly girl that the one I love must die to satisfy me and it would only make me undone."

Daniel saw Mary Ann was either one hell of an actress or she had on her bedroom eyes and was ready to kiss.

Prince Moreau: "I would not think of you a silly girl even if I lay dying by the sword of your father."

Lady Lewelda: "Then how would you-"

Prince Moreau leaned in and gave her a peck on the lips, and at the same time a million thoughts raced through his head.

'Did she like Peter or was she just practicing earlier?'

'Maybe Mary Ann is a slut and screws around with all the cast members.'

'Has she brushed her teeth or will I taste Peter if we French kiss?'

He pulled back from her as planned and she grabbed him behind each ear and yanked him back for a real one. He knew it was coming but she still managed to take him by surprise and steal all his breath with her passion.

Before he knew it her tongue was in his mouth and whipping around his and as far back as it would reach. Her breath was hot and felt strange in his mouth. Daniel tried to pull away early but it was too late.

His stomach couldn't take it any longer and vomit raced up his throat and out of his mouth. He tore away from her clutch but not before she got a taste of what he'd had for lunch. The rest of his puke splattered across the stage towards the audience. He couldn't restrain it and bending over spewed two more mouthfuls of the acidic vile.

After the initial gasps of horror, there was a silence that filled the auditorium as no one could believe what had just happened. Daniel couldn't look up and was locked upon the pile of sickness he had just produced, fearing that if he looked up he would die of embarrassment. Mary Ann just stood there, the bedroom eyes had disappeared and were replaced by what-the-fuck-was-that eyes, and a string of Daniel's vomit hung out of her open mouth. The silence was broken by a student in the second row who leaned forward in her seat and threw up in between her legs splattering the feet of those sitting around her. Mary Ann ran off stage distraught. Daniel looked up to watch her flee and thought, 'Damn she's got a good idea.'

He straightened up, had a head rush, and stumbled behind the curtain with cloudy vision hindering his retreat. He made it as far the trashcan beside the dressing room before another painful heave ripped through him. It was a large forty five gallon trashcan and Daniel grasped two opposite sides and bowed his head down in it. Out in the auditorium it had turned from shock to pandemonium as other people, disgusted by what they had seen, vomited in the crowded room.

Daniel could hear them screaming in between his heaving, and his brain began to think of the repercussions of what had just happened. He had ruined the play, embarrassed the shit out of himself and poor Mary Ann, who hadn't even seen it coming. Peter came to his friend's aid.

"Hey man, you alright? What's wrong?"

He gave no response just shook his head in misery once he stopped vomiting.

"Come on let's get you to the bathroom," Peter said, putting his large arm around his friend and basically carried him to the men's restroom beside the changing room. Daniel had zero motivation to walk, he only wanted to lay down and die.

Weakly he asked, "What the fuck is wrong with me? Awwww, Jesus Christ, I can't believe I just did that."

He would have cried if he hadn't been so weak.

Peter propped him up over a sink, "It'll be alright man. I'm worried about you physically. I mean, I've never seen anybody throw-up that hard ever! Did you eat something right before the show or was it just nerves?"

Daniel thought about it, "Fuck I don't know, I felt fine until intermission, then all hell broke loose without warning. Headache, nausea, I don't know what caus-"

The door flew open. Hoole stormed in the restroom.

"YOUUU!" He thrust a finger toward Daniel as if it would stab him with it from across the room, "YOU ARE FINISHED! GET OUT OF MY THEATER! You've embarrassed me and the whole theater department. That was disgraceful and disgusting; now get out of that costume so I can get prepared. And you," was talking to Peter, "Take his outfit to the dressing room for me and prepare for act four or you'll be gone just like your friend there."

He left to go and try to settle the crowd and tell them the show would continue after a short break, but it was no use. The people who were left were making their way to the exits or helping the ill. Five people had vomited after Daniel in a domino effect, and the room stank with it. Even if they had wanted to stay on and watch the rest of the performance with Professor Hoole taking over as the lead in a vomit smelling room, Mary Ann was in the ladies restroom crying and wouldn't come out for hours.

"Pete, sorry I fucked up the play," Daniel said defeated.

"Hey man, shit happens. I guess now we get to watch Hoole make a pure ass of himself on stage."

"Yeah, I'd better change so he can wear the costume."

"Why don't I get your things for you while you get out of that getup."

Peter returned with Daniel's things and exchanged them over the top of the stall for Prince Moreau's costume.

"So what are you going to do buddy?" Peter asked.

"Oh, I'll probably go hang myself from the top of the dorms."

"I mean are you going to stick around for the final act to finish or what?"

Daniel ignored the last question.

"On second thought, that would be a bit too dramatic. Drama, it turns out, isn't my thing. Maybe I could go on stage and blow my brains out as an encore."

"Don't talk like that man. I bet Hoole will come to his senses and forget about what he just said."

Daniel and Peter both knew Hoole never would forgive him, or let him step foot into another of his classes that which he needed to graduate.

"Go ahead Pete, I'll be fine. I'm going to head back to the room and get some sleep, I feel like shit in more ways than one. And when you see Mary Ann, tell her I'm so sorry."

"Sure man, I'll tell her. I'll see ya later."

Daniel put his clothes on and checked his phone. He had fourteen new text messages. He read each, most were sympathy from cast members, but some others had a more negative feel.

[WTF? You owe me a pr. of shoes!]

[Blaaaaaaaaah! What did you eat?]

[Mary Ann is such a nice girl, stay away from her.]

[5 other people hurled after you, I always knew you were a trendsetter. Blaaaaaaaaaaaaaaah!]

[That's not what I meant by 'Be Royal'] (From Edwin)

Then he opened a video message. It was the kissing scene taken by a spectator in the audience. He sat and watched himself throw up in Mary Ann's mouth and then on the stage. He began to cry. That was only minutes ago and it would be forwarded to every student at Birmingham Arts and Tech and downloaded to the internet in a matter of minutes. He was done at Alabama Arts and Technical College. Fighting Professor Hoole was one thing, living down the embarrassment was another problem he didn't feel like dealing with.

'I'll be on the news at 11:00 so I won't even have to tell mom and dad what happened.'

Chapter 9: To the Edge

After an unusual night at the theater, Frank was invited to stay another night with Steve and his family. They had a house twenty minutes from the college. It was an easy drive at night but Steve complained about the morning traffic.

They had been as surprised as the other theater patrons by the sudden end of scene three but had followed the mob out as the chain reaction puking had begun.

"Ya know that was really strange. Not just the sickness, but the fact that he was so confident and perfect up until that last little bit," Steve said, "And the poor guy, this is a night that will haunt him for the rest of his life. Mary Ann too. I wonder if she could taste what he ate earlier," Steve joked.

"Please professor, I don't want to think about it anymore. That's one of those things I wish I could forget. Now do you have any way to get in touch with him during the day tomorrow or will we have to wait for the show?" Frank asked.

"Who Prince Vomit? You still want him after that?"

"Yes, well what did you say his name was? Daniel? You've got to admit he was perfect before his unexpected…outburst. I just hope he'll be willing to take a break from school for a while."

"He was on spot. But don't you want to meet Edwin or any of the other hopefuls?"

"Not unless Daniel rejects my offer. He's perfect for the role." Frank said confidently.

"You haven't really told me what kind of job it is, I know something with the church, but this seems a little overboard for a spot in a nativity scene. I always figured upcoming clergy volunteered for the job and didn't have to be recruited, but the way you talk the job won't last for long. So what is it? You want a replacement while you go on an extended vacation?"

Franklin trusted Steve with his life. They each held information that would put the other in prison, but the two had been through a lot together in their younger days of dealing, and each man had grown a small sense of safety that the case had died when the Alabama State police arrested Douggy that night outside of Lowtide's Bait and Gas.

"Steve, I know you won't say anything. Actually, I really need to tell someone what is going on who will give me some feedback. I'm sure you know about the 'Religion Alignment Act' that was passed last year. It forces all churches to affiliate themselves under a denomination figurehead that holds the core beliefs. That means all Catholics, Baptists, Mormons, and Pentecostals; hell all Christians and a few that aren't get lumped into one group and all answer to one governing body! The Muslims have their own organization, and so do Hinduism, but everyone else is lumped together. That means the Jews will have to worship from the same book as the Buddhists, how is that freedom of religion at all?"

"Yeah, I've heard all about it, and agree it's unfair as hell that congress used taxes and terrorism as the reason to pass the law. The worst part is that poor Bishop who filed suit as it being unconstitutional and was arrested for aiding terrorism," Steve said.

"I'm afraid that's the role of our government lately; use the Patriot act to get things their way and to hell with freedom or justice. They may never let that poor Bishop out of prison, and he's the kind of man we need to stand up for what is right. You know the 'Religion Alignment Act' wouldn't have passed when we were growing up, back when the south was still the Bible-Belt. The last couple of decades the number of religious followers has been more than cut in half."

"Well Frank," Steve said, "The amount of murder in the name of religion in the last couple of decades has made a real link with terrorism."

"Not in my church! And believe me, a REAL Christian wouldn't have blown up that Mosque. He was just a crazy asshole that wanted an excuse for genocide!"

Steve started to say something but Frank cut him off.

"I know it sounds hypocritical coming from me, but I…WE didn't kill those men and claim it was God that told us to. We're both changed for the better since then, and you know it's wrong what is happening, turning religion into a union to make the government more money. This monthly fee is going to put the squeeze on lots of small churches like mine, and unless I demand tithings we won't be able to afford it for very long. I'm not going to do that. My congregation isn't wealthy and most give what they can already."

"So what does all this have to do with Daniel? Are you going to put on plays to raise money for your union dues?"

"No," Frank replied, "I want him to infiltrate the United Holy Christian Church and find a way to sabotage it. They've already sent out applications looking for new young Christians to join their 'University' to teach them how to get people interested in religion again."

"More people praying' means more people paying'," Steve interjected.

"Right and that means corruption, just like politicians. That's where we nail'em to the cross. Enough scandals and bad publicity will force the politicians to repeal the Religion Act and things go back to the way they were."

"Damn Frank! That's mighty big for you and an actor to take on by yourselves, and how are you going to convince him to go for it? He might be a little corrupt himself and I doubt he has ever been to church."

"That's what I was hoping for. Not the corruption, but someone who is indifferent about religion and believes in freedom. As long as he has morals I might be able to convince him it's evil for a good cause. Not to mention I'm going to offer him plenty of money."

"And just where is that going to come from? You just told me the church won't be able to pay the fees."

"I've taken a good chunk of mine and Elizabeth's retirement and changed it over into a simple savings account."

"Frankie…you haven't told Elizabeth about it have you? I don't think she'd like it very much."

"No, she doesn't know about any of it. She wouldn't understand why this has to be done. I don't think she even cares about the church anymore. Anyway, it won't be just me and him, or whoever I hire. I have a feeling that I'm not the only person who's thought of trying something like it. Christianity is full of self-righteous lunatics and would be martyrs; the problem is knowing who is on what side."

"Maybe you should have gone to the CIA to recruit. Spying, sabotage, all that shit is dangerous and not many people can pull it off." Steve recommended.

Frank pondered the idea and said, "Yeah maybe. That's why actors make great reverends and politicians, they can sway a crowd and lie while they look you in the eye. He's going to have to do both and not puke at the altar."

His wife Carrie had a hot dinner waiting on them when they arrived. Their two children were nowhere to be seen. Mack and Julie had odd hours, juggling school and work. They all tried to get together on Sundays for family time but more often than not something more important came up.

Despite sitting down at the dinner table, Steve filled in Carrie on the mishap of the theater. She felt bad for the student actors but they all had a good laugh at Professor Hoole's expense.

After dinner Steve led Frank out to the garage. It was part workshop and part jam studio where he picked his guitar. He claimed he always had projects to work on but looking around Frank doubted it was more than just an excuse to escape the family. They both sat on the old sofa. It was very comfortable, although it had seen better days. Carrie refused to have it anywhere inside the house.

Frank hadn't heard from Elizabeth all day so he decided to dial her up before he and Steve got into a conversation spanning half of the night. On the second ring it went to voicemail.

Frank didn't leave a message. She'd call him back whenever she was done talking to Jane about whatever television show they were into. Lately it was, 'Singing Contest Moms' and 'Old-Young Dating'. She'd be sitting in her recliner until at least midnight.

Steve turned on some jam band tunes and began to roll a joint. He was still the best at rolling, they were smooth and even, almost like they were machine made. They talked about the old days for a while until Steve brought out his six string and began to tune it. He warmed up with a couple of songs, not singing the words. He knew his limits and singing was beyond them.

Frank tried calling Elizabeth again. This time it went straight to voicemail. As a Reverend, he was used to helping others, but it took a lot to ask for a favor. It wasn't like Elizabeth to ignore his call, and good God that woman always had her phone nearby. He was worried about her.

Frank walked out the side door onto Steve's driveway. He dialed up Charlie Earp, an old friend and the mayor of Tall Rock. Charlie answered on the second ring.

"Hey Frank, what's up?"

"Oh, you know. I'm just out here eating caviar and drinking champagne, trying to live like a playboy."

"Ha-ha, yeah we missed you at church the other night. You ought to just cancel it the next time you leave town. Hell, it was so boring I took a handful of pennies out of the collection plate and started toss them at people around me who were falling asleep."

Frank chuckled knowing he would never do such a thing.

"I bet. Say Charlie, could I ask you to do me a little favor? I haven't been able to get in touch with Elizabeth today. Could you ride by and check on her for me. You know, make sure she hasn't burned down the house. Everything is probably fine, I'd just feel better knowing she's alright."

"Hell, if she'da burned the house down I might have even heard about it," Charlie insisted, him being a volunteer fireman.

"But sure, that ain't no big deal. I'll just find my car keys and ride that way. I was planning to go later anyways, she's got a keg party again tonight. Doesn't start until midnight though. Last night was great until she whooped my ass in beer pong."

"Sure, just give me a call when you help her tap the keg." Frank said.

"10-4 Frankie."

Frank didn't have many true friends but they were reliable.

Back inside Steve was playing 'Whiskey in the Jar', and puffing on the joint in between songs. He offered Frank a hit but he declined. That was part of his old life and he did good survive it once.

Fifteen minutes later Charlie called back. Frank stepped outside once more so he could hear.

"Hey how's the keg party?"

Charlie's voice was serious on the other line.

"Ahhh, Frank where are you at right now?"

"Birmingham, staying with an old colleague of mine. Why? What's going on?"

"Well, everything's fine here. But, well, what day do you get back into town? Tomorrow?"

"No, probably the day after, why?"

"When you're getting close to town just call me and we'll meet up so you can tell me about your trip."

"Charlie, what the hell is going on?"

"Nothing to worry about, I-"

"Don't tell me not to worry. I'm not going to be able to sleep tonight until I know what's going on there. Now did you see Elizabeth or not?"

"Well, no. Her car was there but I didn't stop," Charlie said.

Frank was silent waiting on Charlie to offer up more.

"Look Frank, I don't want to get in the middle of this, but as your friend I've got to be the one that tells you I guess."

After more silence Frank pressed, "Go on."

"I drove by your house and saw Tony's truck parked there."

"Tony? Tony Walters?" Frank asked. That was the only Tony he knew.

"Yeah, and I could be wrong but I doubt he was there talking to Elizabeth about football.

It took Frank a minute to figure out what this meant. Tony was the Football coach at Motte County High School. He was a member of Tall Rock Baptist, but on an irregular schedule. Sometimes he'd attend service five or six weeks in a row, but often he'd miss for months at a time. He'd just recently been divorced for the second time. Frank knew the first marriage had ended due to Tony being unfaithful to his old high school sweetheart.

"Frank, you still there?" Charlie asked.

"Yeah. Let me go for now…I've got a lot to swallow. Can you keep this between us?"

"Okay buddy, I won't say a peep. I'm really sorry for you. Will you call me when you get in?"

"Sure," They hung up.

Frank tried his best to come up with a good reason why Tony Walters would be at his house and at this time of the night. Sex was all he could think of. Dirty, slimy, sneak-around-on-your-spouse-who-loves-you-sex.

'Was it the first time? Who made the first move? Maybe Tony came to church Wednesday night and found out I'd be gone for a few days. He's a good looking guy and he must be at least ten years younger than her.'

Frank remembered all the times she'd been too tired for sex, and even sometimes how she just didn't feel like it.

'Now she's screwing some dickhead coach in my god-damn house!'

He was so upset that his hands began to shake. He told himself he'd try to ignore it until he was home, knowing damned well it was something he couldn't just file away on the shelf for later. Maybe there was some wild explanation, but his heart told him not.

After a deep breath he walked back in the garage. He was mentally exhausted and on the verge of tears. He sat back on the couch and said, "I'll take a couple hits of that now."

"Oh yeah, cool," Steve handed the joint over. He'd already smoked half of it and was happy to have a friend join in the fun.

Frank didn't want fun, he wanted to forget what had just happened. "You got anything stronger?"

"Stronger?" Steve replied, "How much stronger?"

Frank hit the joint hard. It was a long drag and he kept the dank smoke in his lung for a long time.

Steve was grinning and just holding his guitar. He thought about cocaine or heroin at first.

"Oh, I know. Have you done Fentanyl yet?"

Frank shook his head no.

"They've got a new painkiller like it, only better. I could make a call and probably get us some," Steve said.

Frank finally let out the cloud of smoke.

He took a few breaths and said, "I want to be more that high. I want to go to the fucking edge and maybe not come back."

Chapter 10: An Ideal Retreat

Hot stinging tears ran down his face. It was enough to hinder his vision so he couldn't read any more messages. His next thought was of escape from the theater. The regular exits would be surrounded by people, people he didn't want to see right away. Then he remembered the emergency exit door in the balcony stairway. The alarm would go off until the door was shut back but he didn't care, it was close and led out to the back parking lot. He wiped his tears, took a deep breath, and bolted out the restroom toward it. The night air made him feel better once he was outside.

He walked toward the Hilman Field, where the girls laid out in the sun and the boys played disc golf. It was all but deserted that late at night. Normally a stroll would give him time to sort out life and feel better about things, this was not the case. His mind kept jumping from the fact he had just ruined what little social life he had, to the fact he was unofficially kicked out of college. Daniel thought of ways he could try to finish his college degree. It was almost mandatory to have a college degree if you wanted a job that wasn't daily physical labor. Perhaps he could get Hoole to forgive him… No. Simon Hoole didn't forgive or forget. Maybe he could transfer to another school for his final year. The problem was he had to finish this semester, and now he was doomed to fail two of his classes thanks to one big nasty puke.

'What was the deal with me anyway? I normally have a pretty solid stomach, and Mary Ann sure wasn't the first girl I've ever kissed. Then again it was the first (and maybe last) time I played a lead role on stage with a full auditorium watching.'

He just couldn't blame it on nerves though, there was something else he couldn't define. He went back to the school problem. If he failed two classes his GPA would drop and that meant he would most likely lose his scholarship.

His parents could barely afford to send him to college with it and if he lost it he could kiss a diploma good-bye. Both his mother and father wanted to him to go to college, but not for theater or the arts. His father wanted his boy to be an engineer; his mother wanted a doctor for a son. The arguments had been critical and unjustified. He could hear his father's voice.

'You can't make any money being an actor these days, it's a dying profession.'

'If the economy flops again you'll need a job where you can still earn a living.'

'Doctors are always in need and make good money.'

'So do engineers.'

'We live in Alabama, it's not exactly Broadway. You'd have to move away and that would break your poor mother's heart.'

'Do something real with your life.'

His father had brought home brochures of colleges with engineering programs and left them around the house for Daniel to find back when he was in high school. That's actually how he found out about Alabama Arts and Technical College, which was a lesser known school but with one of the better theater programs in the state. Daniel had told his parents that he'd go tour the school but would only talk to the engineering department if he first learned of the Arts and Theater program. Reluctantly his father agreed.

Daniel and his folks made a weekend visit and toured the school on a Saturday. As he had promised Daniel spoke with advisors from both programs and found out he was qualified for either. His father made out like engineering was the only choice but he and Daniel argued all the way home. Finally he gave his parents an ultimatum, "It's either the theater program or the army."

His parents were horrified of the army since the Iran war; the death count was above the total from the Vietnam War, but had no end in sight with the recent terror attacks in Chicago. The draft had come into effect while Daniel was in middle school for two and a half years. The public outcry and demonstrations had become so violent the National Guard had to be called up to deal with it. The draft ended after hundreds of protesters and police had killed one another. Thousands of draft dodgers had led to the Canadian border being permanently closed.

His father thought he had an angle, "Well first get your engineering degree and then join. That way you'll go in as an officer and not have to be a grunt. Engineers don't see much combat."

Daniel had been ready for that remark, "Heck no, I'm going in for general infantry. I want to go shoot some terrorists, you know, 'Do something real with my life'."

That had ended the argument about his future. He would have to tell them three years had been a waste. His father would be happy and suggest he switch over to engineering and that many of his core classes would transfer, but Daniel didn't relish the idea of being known as 'barf boy' for two more years. He stopped walking when he got to a bench at the far edge of the field, he was tired. He lay down on the bench and thought about killing himself; it seemed the logical thing to do. It took a long time but he finally fell asleep.

Freezing and dripping wet Daniel awoke on the bench, it was early morning and raining. He groaned and sat up. It was time to go back to the apartment and get dry. He made the walk back quickly being hungrier and colder than he could ever remember. As he came through the parking lot outside the apartment he wasn't aware of the black sedan parked on the front row until the window began to roll down. It was still far too early for students to be going off to class. Remembering his close call with this car and Edwin's crash he approached the driver's window cautiously. It was Matthew Collins. He'd been waiting on Daniel all night and his eyes were bloodshot.

"Look man I'm really sorry but I had to do it," He began, "I, I just had to get back at Hoole, that fucking bastard. I wish it could have been done without have involving you."

The apology hit Daniel hard. The whole thing had been about revenge, but he still didn't know how Matthew had done it.

"It was you I saw back stage. What did you do to me?" He asked.

Matthew was ashamed, "I put Ipecac syrup in your soda during the second act. I hated to do it to you, I really did, and I thought the show would be over with Edwin out of the picture. I just got lucky and was able to drug you at the right time, but I thought you would just have gone in the bathroom and puked. That was so much better; Hoole will probably resign after last night."

Daniel pressed his hands hard against his face, "You've fucking ruined my life," He nearly whispered as he walked toward the apartment unbelieving his bad luck.

Matthew shouted out to him as he was walking up the stairs, "I'm sorry man, I had to do it! Hoole was asking for it!"

Daniel never heard him, he was in a trance unlocking the door and walking into his bedroom. As he took off his clothes and dried off all he could think about was killing himself and how little there was for him to stay alive for. He imagined his mother crying at his funeral, his father disappointed at him like always. He closed his eyes and tried to forget his situation.

He slept late into the morning because he wasn't worried about missing any classes. That part of his life was over now. He ate some cereal and once more began going through the text messages on his phone. It was more of the same from the night before, mostly sympathy and some distasteful video clips. The worst was the vomiting in slow motion; it was sent by Edwin, titled 'Royal Vomit'.

'What an asshole,' Daniel thought.

Peter wasn't in the apartment, so he must have gone to class. 'At least it hasn't fazed him,' Daniel thought. Peter had left him a voicemail though.

Voicemail: "Hey man, um, I didn't see you last night. I'm just going to keep my mouth shut about last night until I hear otherwise from you. I'll see you after I get out for lunch. Oh, and Professor Hasler tracked me down this morning to ask how you're doing. He said he knows you probably don't want to talk to anybody right now but it's really important that he talks to you. I always thought he was pretty cool for a professor; maybe he's got some pull and can swing it so you can stay in school. Any way I've got his number if you want it, or you can go by his office. He should be in there around twelve or twelve thirty. So, I guess I'll see you later, bye.'

Of all the people that wanted to talk to him, Professor Hasler was the last person Daniel would have guessed. He was a laid back professor who didn't really care what was going on as long as his students got their work done, and when they didn't he usually still gave them a 'D' to help their GPA. Daniel had breezed through his 'Technology and Society' class and had a pretty good time despite Steve telling his stories about the time before cell phones. He had no idea why the professor had to track down Peter to get through to him.

'Maybe he wants to tell me to keep my chin up. Oh, even better, he wants to use that video for his current events class; that would be fresh news.'

It was a quarter after eleven when Daniel decided to go see the professor, not that he wanted to go out into public, but he knew the longer he avoided it the harder it would be. After a shower and fresh clothes he felt much better. Even though it was summer time he put on an old sweatshirt and pulled the hood over to hide his face. It was lunch time for many students and campus was busy, so he walked the route less traveled. He had a good sweat going by the time he was at the main technology building where Professor Hasler's class and office were. He knocked on the office door.

"Come in," was the answer.

Daniel came in and took the hood off his head. The professor stood up to greet him by shaking his hand.

"Hey Daniel, are you alright?" he shut the office door.

"Uh, yeah I guess you heard about last night. Um…my roommate Peter told me you wanted to see me."

"Yes, I was at the performance last night with an old friend of mine who's visiting on business from South Carolina."

"Well, I'm glad he didn't come in just for the show," Daniel said.

"Actually he did, and to interview a few young actors such as yourself about a job he has lined coming up. Despite you getting sick last night he was quite impressed by you and told me you were the first person he wanted to interview. Now I know you aren't through with school just yet but maybe this would be a good time for you to take a break for a while and come back after this job is over."

"I'm almost sure I'm done with this school professor. Last night Professor Hoole let me know I was all but done in the Arts and Theater. Well, at least at this school, and I need his class to graduate."

Professor Hasler was shocked, "He really told you that?"

"Oh yeah, and I know he wasn't joking. He flunked out two students last year. That's the whole reason I'm in this mess now."

"How so?" the professor asked.

Daniel told him the highlights of what had happened with Matthew spiking his drink to get revenge on Hoole.

"That's the most low down plot I've ever heard! Hoole deserves to be fired for what he did to both you and Matthew. And Matthew deserves to be thrown in jail for what he did. He could have killed Edwin or you if things had gone just a little differently."

"As much as I'd like to see some justice, Hoole is fairly untouchable with his position on the board of directors and I don't have the first clue how to prove Matthew ran Edwin off the road or poisoned me. Besides I can't stay around here. Last night is something I'll never live down," Daniel said.

"Well I'm relieved to know you aren't on drugs."

"What does that mean?" Daniel questioned.

"Oh, that was one of the reasons we thought of as to why you got sick. We were hoping you weren't back stage shooting up or something."

"No, not me. So what's the job, another play?" Daniel asked half-heartedly.

"I'm not exactly sure of all the details. Really I'm not supposed to say anything at all…but it's the role of a lifetime."

"A lead part?" Daniel was alive again.

"Oh yeah, but it's in South Carolina. If you want to meet with Mr. Catoe he can tell you all the details and do an interview. He's sitting in with Mrs. Lewis' Drama class right now. Do you think you can meet him this afternoon?"

"Professor, I can meet him anytime. Remember, I'm not a student anymore. I wouldn't mind meeting somewhere in private though. Last night's puke has already gone global."

"Of course, actually if you're fine with my office here I could go run and get him."

Daniel remembered what he had learned about interviewing for a part. He needed a portfolio with the highlights from his background and references from previous directors. He didn't have any real experience aside from school productions and he hated to think what kind of a reference Hoole would give.

"Do you think I ought to change into something nicer?" he asked.

"I wouldn't try to impress him anymore," Professor Hasler said, "Just be honest and ask questions. He's a really good guy. I've known him longer than you've been alive."

The professor was out the door and heading down the hall leaving Daniel to sit and prepare himself. What a roller coaster the last couple of days had been. He went from Drallis the dope, to Prince Moreau, to Daniel Montclair, the Prince of Vomit. Then there was Mary Ann, first having nothing to do with him. Later he'd thought she liked him only to find out she was into Peter instead. Then she'd kissed him backstage, and finally he vomited in her mouth on stage. Daniel wondered if he could ever act with confidence again, or without a feeling a funny taste in his mouth.

A few minutes later Professor Hasler was back and introduced the two.

"Daniel, I'd like you to meet Reverend Franklin Catoe."

They shook hands and looked each other square in the eyes.

"It's a pleasure to meet you Daniel," Frank said.

"You too. Reverend was it?" Daniel asked.

"Yes, it's a long story." Frank's looked at Steve wishing he hadn't used his full title.

Lightheartedly Daniel asked, "Are you here to perform an exorcism on me?"

Frank replied, "No, I believe I saw all your demons leave you last night." They all had a chuckle. "I'm sure Steve here told you I've a job in mind you might be interested in, but before I give you all the details I'd like to ask you a few questions if that's alright."

"Sure."

"You two have a seat and talk, I'm going to go grab some lunch," Steve said and closed the door behind him.

Daniel sat back down in the chair and Frank sat behind Steve's desk.

"The first thing I need to know is what are your plans are for the future. What I mean is do you have any obligations here in Alabama? School for instance, or maybe a girlfriend you couldn't leave? You see, this job is in South Carolina and there won't be any chance to come back and visit for a while."

"Well like I was telling Professor Hasler I'm finished as a student after last night. I would like to graduate eventually but I can't really afford it. And no, no girlfriend to speak of. I really wouldn't be leaving anything behind except a few friends and my parents who live up in Dolthan and aren't very close to me. Is it a permanent position or just for a season?"

Franklin realized the young man was still thinking it was for a play but he went along with it.

"Well, I was thinking a year to start with, longer if all goes well. My next question is are you religious at all? And keep in mind there is no wrong answer as long as you're honest."

"Well I was baptized when I was a child. My parents thought it was important and that I go to Sunday school as a child. We stopped going to church after a few years."

"Do you know the bible stories?" Frank asked.

"Not all of them, but I know the basics. God created the earth, he made Adam and Eve in the Garden of Eden. The Virgin Mary gave birth to Jesus in a manger in Bethlehem, he was crucified and died for our sins. Oh and Noah built his ark and put two of each animals on it during the flood."

"Do you believe in God?" Frank asked.

Daniel had learned long ago that if a person said to be honest that it was best to be honest. This man wasn't just listening to his answers, he was reading his eyes also.

"Well Reverend, I really can't say yes to that. I've never been a man of faith. Not that there's anything wrong with faith, it teaches people to have morals, and that's something I believe in."

Daniel realized he's just told a Reverend that he didn't believe in God. He wished he hadn't said it but it was too late to take it back.

Franklin gave a little smile, "Don't fret son, I'm not necessarily looking for a man of faith, but morals are a must. Would you have a problem being around religion all the time and playing the part of a good Christian every day? I mean no drinking or cursing, going to church, helping others and things of that nature?"

Daniel was really curious as to just exactly what the job was.

"I'm not a big drinker. I went eighteen years without alcohol and I could manage another year. It shouldn't be a problem to curb my language either; I never had a foul mouth until I came to college. So is this your way of converting one soul at a time or what?"

"I'll explain more in a minute, first I have one more question. What do you think of our current government and the 'Religion Alignment Act'?"

"I think the government is full of crooks and liars looking to stuff their pockets with our money and cheat on their spouses. I don't vote because you can't know which one is going to do the right thing and who's going to run the country further into the ground. I also believe this country was built on freedoms. Tattoos, body piercings, flag burning, and gangster rap are all things I find distasteful but represent freedoms we have as Americans. Freedoms that countless American soldiers have died fighting for. 'The Religion Alignment Act' is taking away from the freedom of religion, which is the most basic freedom we have in this country. Am I preaching to the choir or are you 'the man'?"

"I'm with you on that one Daniel, and I can see you have some strong opinions about freedom. If you could help reverse the 'Religion Alignment Act' would you?"

"I can try."

"Even if it meant you had to use some questionable tactics to do so?"

Daniel didn't answer right off as he was busy trying to figure out the reverend's game. Frank decided it was too broad of a question without all the facts so he didn't give him any time for a response.

"It's time I put all my cards on the table. The new law is going to kill Christianity in this country if people don't do something. I lead a small Baptist church that won't be able to pay our dues to the United Holy Christian Church for very long once it takes effect. There are thousands of other churches that will close down also or be shut down if something doesn't change. I won't be able to preach from my bible, or even keep the same name of the church. Like any other problem it starts with money and make no mistake, even with the drop off of churchgoers in the last decade, it's still the largest business in the world. The idea is to bring it all together under one roof to raise profits; I'm talking trillions of dollars. This United Holy Christian Church is going to be just like the government. What did you say, 'Full of crooks and liars?' well this is bound to have plenty. That's where the opportunity lies to destroy the organization, expose the corruption and the government will be forced to repeal the act. Are you still following me on this?"

"Yeah," Daniel said "but what has this got to do with me?"

"I need someone to join the organization and climb their way to the top to get the dirt."

"Why don't you do it yourself? You are already a Reverend, you know things, and I wouldn't have the first idea about how to be…."

Frank still spoke calmly "They aren't looking for old men like me; they want young men like you to get young people interested in church again. Also I am a Baptist; I know my bible and my ways and not much else. You on the other hand are a clean slate to learn a uniform way of worship. You are exciting and full of energy to spread the gospel and in their eyes that's good business. And best of all you can make a crowd hang on your every word, that's why I know you'll be right for the job." Franklin looked at the young man sitting across the desk; he was very good at reading people by their expressions and their eyes, which gave him the ability to often be able to tell people what they wanted to hear.

"I know it's not what you had in mind, real life espionage isn't exactly the Friday night play but I can teach you what you need to know. You can stay with me and my wife or you can find a place of your own. To start off with we'll do a lot of bible study and I'll teach you a few sermons and let you make up a few of your own. Then I'll introduce you to the church members as a youth pastor and let you have duties in the church. When you're ready we'll see about getting you accepted into a position with the UHCC and try to get you moved up the ladder."

Daniel took a deep breath. He was trying to comprehend all the reverend had told him and it was nothing like what he had imagined. "This is huge. This is real."

"Are you scared of real?" Frank asked.

"Well, no I guess not. It'll just be a big change from college."

Frank could see the debate in Daniel's mind and decided to play his trump card. "I plan to pay you three thousand dollars a month with a fifty thousand dollar bonus when we succeed." Daniel almost fell out of his chair. "I thought you said your church couldn't afford the dues, how can you pay that much?"

"The money is coming from my retirement, this is more important to me than retiring in style." The reverend said. Daniel was awed by the personal sacrifice.

"But don't do it just for the money, do it because it's the right thing to do. That freedom you spoke so passionately about needs you now and this way no one is going to have to die to preserve it."

This stirred Daniel inside. "Okay, I'll do it."

Frank was surprised he had won him so easily but felt he had to tell him the cons.

"Are you sure you'll be able to handle it? You have to live like a man of the cloth most of the time, and you may have to do things that go against your morals. The politics of this may require you to lie, cheat, and steal. Remember it's all for the greater good."

"Yeah Reverend, I'm in."

Chapter 11: The New Gig

Leaving college to go on a holy pilgrimage had never crossed the mind of Daniel until Reverend Franklin Catoe asked him to, but upon hearing it the idea seemed perfect. A good paying job and a new start where he wouldn't be embarrassed to show his face sounded great. Maybe go back after a few years when people forgot what had happened.

He left the apartment with only a few pairs of clothes and his essential items. Peter would have to deal with the rest whenever he moved out. Frank picked him up in his old truck and was dressed very similarly to what he'd been wearing the day before in the professor's office. Simple jeans and sports coat, no tie. After the interview, Daniel had went home and packed his essentials for travel and stayed the night at a motel by the interstate. Frank explained to him the reason they should drive back to Tall Rock was so they could get to know each other and start his crash course of Christianity. They covered plenty of ground the first day on the road, but Frank made it a point to make periodic stops so they could stretch and to waste some time, it was not very often he got to be away from Tall Rock and his wife. They were through the first-date chitchat about ten minutes out of town and began to talk theory and strategy about what they could accomplish. Frank's idea with Elizabeth was to keep her in the dark about the master plan. The morning after Tony Walter's truck was at the Catoe house, Elizabeth called Frank and said she'd went to bed early and never heard the phone. He just played along but it hurt his soul, he knew she was a lying tramp. Letting her know he was using their savings to help fuel sacrilege never came up either. Instead he told her he met a young student looking to make a future in the church and some young blood was exactly what the church needed to increase attendance.

Daniel was a little embarrassed to share with Frank what he knew about the bible. He had a firm grasp on creation and knew the story of Adam and Eve. There wasn't much Daniel knew other than the crucifixion of Jesus and that he rose from the dead on Easter. Frank listened and smiled but didn't interrupt Daniels vague interpretation of the stories he knew so well.

When Daniel finished he looked at Frank with a long face realizing how little he knew of the bible and how much he had yet to learn.

"Don't think of it like you have to memorize the whole thing word for word, or even every name in it." Frank assured, "I've been reading and studying that book longer than you've been alive and the average Sunday morning Christian hasn't read it all the way through. So to start off with we're going to focus on the main stories and get your feet on solid ground and then as time goes by try to expand from that. So start reading Genesis but pause to discuss it with me after each chapter. Don't be afraid to ask questions if you don't understand something."

So as Frank drove across highways and interstates Daniel read the good book. He asked about the serpent in the Garden of Eden and if it was the Devil. Frank explained it represented evil and temptation; this example was merely in the form of a snake. Daniel continued on through Genesis and Frank quizzed him on it. Daniel was very good at remembering the key ideas and outlining each story. For someone who knew so little about the bible he did quite well using his retaining memory that he so often used to study in school.

Frank drove and read the map; he didn't care to use the GPS. He took back roads and scenic routes to extend the time he had to tutor Daniel. They were in Georgia before long and stopped to eat and stretch their legs at a small diner. It was a small town restaurant in the building of an old Burger Jake's fast food joint, not unlike one in Tall Rock that had once been the old Taco Shack.

Daniel wasn't used to Mom and Pop restaurants. In college he usually went to the hip coffee shops and artsy cafes. They didn't speak during their lunch but they didn't rush through it either. Frank was trying not to think about his wife and her lover. He busied himself by calculating the decision to hire Daniel and whether it had been the right move and if he or anyone could accomplish what they planned to do without being discovered. For a long time Frank had thought of looking at young men that chose to join religious schools and would one day become clergy, but after much thought he'd decided it would be too difficult and dangerous to find one that wanted to see the UHCC as evil or corrupt. What if this kid threw up on the pulpit at his first sermon? What if he swiped all the money in the church safe and bolted. He didn't get that vibe from Daniel but he was an actor who he knew very little about. Frank figured the vomiting had been just bad luck and wasn't sure if he could believe the sabotage story, but he knew revenge drove people to live on and hate.

Daniel's mind was busy with the words of Genesis and filing them each into the vault of his mind. He knew he was good at memorizing but names gave him trouble occasionally, and boy the bible had some wild ones. Just a quick glance at the bible's index of names and he was shocked to see a page and a half of s-names; Shekel, Shelah, Shelanites, Shelomith, Shem, Shema, and so on. How would he respond if someone asked him a direct question to test his knowledge? Frank could only teach him so much in the little time they would have together, and the UHCC was nearly operational.

After lunch they continued on their way, Daniel still studying and Frank enjoying the country side. Daniel, who had never read the bible, found some of the stories so basic and simple and part of society. Other parts were from another time and had no bearing on these times such as Leviticus 17:1 and how eating the blood of slaughtered animals is forbidden. Leviticus 18:1 on the other hand, is a list of people who you should not have sex with. Your mother, father, sister, brother, aunt, uncle, son, daughter, another man, animals, any woman on her period.

Daniel felt the heavy book sitting in his lap, the worn leather binding was old, he guessed it was at least fifty years old.

"Frank?" Daniel asked.

"Yes?"

"Tell me about this book."

"You mean that particular one in your hands right now?" Frank said.

"Yeah, did your father pass it down to you?"

"No. I bought that when I was around your age. I needed a job and a friend helped me get into evangelism, that's converting people into Christianity. John Abraham Worthy, he was one of the best in the business. He would travel around from church to church and preach as a guest speaker on Wednesdays, Sundays, and special occasions. He made a good living at it, good enough to only have to work a couple days a week. We were in Alabama and Georgia in those days and he worked a circuit across both states. I traveled with him for a while and watched him preach and sing and I studied the bible like you're doing now."

"You just needed a job so you started preaching?"

"Sure did, just like you now. You see, church goes about the same each Sunday. The Reverend welcomes everyone, they pray, sing, he gives a sermon, they pass around a collection plate. Not always in that order, but it's very routine and can become boring. Now some people like boring, but most like a change every once in a while. The

Reverend takes a break and the evangelist gives a fresh and exciting sermon. So the evangelist gets a cut of the collection or even passes around his own plate. "

"John had a schedule planned at least a month in advance. He'd talk to the Reverend and get all the details hammered out well in advance. Come Sunday morning we'd set out early and drive to the church. I'd sit in the back like one of the members and watch the service begin. The ole Rev would come out and give his usual introduction and give the news, maybe even lead a prayer. Then he would introduce or welcome back the special guest speaker." Frank smiled while reminiscing. "John could really put on a show. He would start with a prayer, and then lead a song or two, tell a story about something amazing he'd seen, and then switch to preaching fire and brimstone. SOMEHOW he managed to tie it all together and make the people love it. He could always fill up a donation basket using the words of the Lord, but his singing made him stand out."

"That sounds like a pretty good gig," Daniel said. "So that's how you got started?"

"Pretty much. One Sunday I opened up for him with a short sermon we'd been working on. It wasn't the best I've ever given…but after I'd finished I felt such pride and accomplishment, I just knew it was my calling. After a while, when I was ready, John booked me a couple of visits at some of his regular stops and a revival. Revivals were where the money was, I made over six hundred at one. But the economy started to turn when the market crashed and when times get tough the tithing is what people cut back on."

"Tithing?" Daniel asked. "You mean donations?"

Frank explained, "A tithing is a donation or offering to the church, ten percent of the family's income is the golden number, but not many people give that much."

Daniel was amazed, "Holy…Cow! That's a bunch of money. "

"Well like I said, not many people give that much. It's usually the poorer people that give the most percentage wise, at least in my church, but I try not to push for donations. That may change when the United Unholy Devil Church starts charging us membership fees next month." Frank grew hot just thinking about it.

"Yeah I hear that's what everybody's so mad about, the smaller churches are worried they won't be able to stay open."

"Well Tall Rock Baptist is one of those you hear about…furious about this absurd law. They use some formula regarding how many average members you have and what services you offer as to how much the church has to pay the UHCC. We aren't very large, or wealthy, and most of the money goes back into projects like the Christmas play, a free vacation bible school for the kids, the spring revival, and thanksgiving for the community. All that stuff is going to have to go if we have to pay those dues, and then I'm afraid there's going to be a drop in attendance."

"Well Reverend, I'm sure this would be a little hypocritical but why don't you lie about the number of attendants? Just say only ten people go to your church." Daniel asked.

"Oh, everyone's already thought of that, the UHCC especially. They're going to have auditors travel around and make surprise visits to make counts to make sure things are run according to code. If the number of members is twenty percent higher than what you say your normal count is the church gets fined double their monthly dues. If you sing a song that isn't approved you get fined. If you don't read from their new bible you get fined."

"What, they have a different version or something?"

"Oh I'm sure it's going to be a lot more politically correct than the one you're reading now. In fact that one probably isn't like the first version by a long shot."

"What do you mean, it keeps changing? Why?"

"Well Daniel, think back to your world history classes in school. Before the bible was written the earth was a crazy place. People were sacrificing their first born children, killing each other, orgies. There wasn't much universal law and even less consequences or chances of being caught for breaking it. The Romans were corrupt and not what people ought to be. So, and this is just my personal opinion, so the wisest men of the time realized people needed something to fear other than law or death because it simply wasn't working. So what do they decide on? HELL…The fear of endless burning and torture caused by a life of sin. Like I said, no one will ever back me up on this; it's just my take on how things probably came to be. The idea of hell and gods has been around since the beginning of time, but for people to believe a new religion there needed to be a human icon. The Old Testament made many predictions about the Messiah, or the Savior. These wise men come up with the Son of God, a mortal here on earth to spread his father's word. So they find a single pregnant woman, the Virgin Mary, and tell her she is the mother of Christ. Of course she wasn't a virgin. Today if a girl turned up pregnant and said she was a virgin everyone would laugh in her face, but back then it was a miracle."

Frank was still driving down the highway concentrating more on Daniel than the road ahead.

"So these wise men raise this boy, Jesus of Nazareth, to save mankind from itself by teaching peace and love to all that would listen. But that's not all they taught him. They showed him how to make miracles, or what looked like miracles to the common person. On his travels he met other good men who realized he had a good thing going. They became his posse, but they are known as apostles to you and me. Peter, Andrew, James, John, Philip, Bartholomew, Thomas, Matthew, James, Thaddeus, Simon, and Judas. You're going to need to get familiar with them and their stories. They were no doubt the closest to Jesus and helped him weave those holy miracles. Now Daniel, if I said to you a few minutes ago I was walking on water, would you believe me?"

Daniel hesitated for a moment and replied, "No, probably not."

"What if four or five of your friends told you, 'Yeah man, Frank really did it. I swear- I saw it with my own two eyes. He just paced right out there like he was strolling in the park!' Now isn't that more credible than just me saying it?"

"That is how rumors get started," Daniel mused, "and then they get blown out of proportion."

"Exactly! And in this case it worked in Jesus' favor. Including his birth and resurrection he has over thirty miracles in that bible and most of them are healing sick people. Think, how easy it would be to pay someone to act sick and then act well upon your touch?

Water into wine? He was at a wedding reception with people who drank all the wine. Think how easy it is to fool drunk people…or better yet, people who want to believe in you."

Daniel was dumbfounded. He thought, 'I'm listening to a reverend explain to me that the Bible is made up of lies and magic tricks. Ha!'

"So everything in the Bible was a lie?" Daniel asked.

Frank shook his head, "No. Jesus and all of the main characters were real. Their journeying was real, like a band going on tour, more exposure equals more fans. Anything that makes you stop and scratch your head questioning whether it was physically possible, is a little fib, half-truth, or exaggeration. Oh, and his best miracle was the easiest. Dying. It was bound to happen one day, and if it happened by sickness or old age he would have lost his grandeur. Instead he became a martyr and died for our sins. Then his friends stole his body and buried him elsewhere. The apostles kept preaching and traveling and talking about Jesus, then able to speak of great miracles he performed and Jesus himself couldn't be disproved. Now here's the kicker, the one that made it all stick. Many of them wrote about Jesus and his life and their own lives. If you put something in writing people tend to believe it. The church did a little editing, left out the gospels that didn't fit and WHAM! Old Testament. Years later they made it easier to read and hyped the stories up. BOOM, New Testament! Just what the Christian religion needed to jump to number one on the charts," Frank said. He was getting stirred up talking about his ideas he'd had bottled up for so long.

He realized he needed Daniel to learn the bible, not how to disprove it. Calmly he said, "Well it wasn't quite that easy. More blood has been shed in the name of that book than any other thing except power, and they often get confused. Think of all the wars in history that didn't involve one or both. I can't name any. So the point I'm making is people will kill in the name of this book, so what I've said today is to educate you but you aren't to repeat any of it."

"Don't worry Frank, I'm keeping all this under wraps. Preach on."

Frank chuckled at the phrase, "I and plenty of other Christians are at odds with the bible you see, but it's so important. The bible is a guide to staying out of hell. It keeps people from doing stupid things like rape and murder. There's more than a few every Sunday morning that don't make it to church because they were out sinning with the devil. Most people are there and live a somewhat Christian lifestyle so they go to heaven not hell."

"That's my biggest beef with religion in general. The idea of life after death just doesn't make any sense to me…why would anybody think there's a guy with a pitchfork down there, (he points to the floorboard) who's gonna burn you with matches for all eternity?" Daniel asked.

Frank said, "Why indeed? You don't worry about the end of your life now because you are so young. I know the best of my life is past me already and wish for more. You see, the older people get the more desperate they are for more time. Heaven is built up to be the perfect place. Imagine that the perfect place and your imagination can fill in the rest. What propaganda! The only ones that've got us beat are the Muslims with their 72 Virgin story. Hell I'd almost blow up myself and Allah for that kind of action!"

Daniel laughed at this, "Frank are you always this cool?"

"No. It's part of my life and yours too now, to be calm and wise in the public eye. You may think of me as a hypocrite for not believing everything the bible says, but the church is something I believe in. It makes people better and lets them bond like nothing else. I would give up anything to keep our system the way it used to be," He paused and reflected.

"It is however necessary to cut loose every once in a while, the ones that don't end up molesting boys after their Sunday school class. You need to practice thinking before you speak, no matter who you're around. Like if we're talking about a bible story and you decide to crack a joke make sure it's one you could tell in a sermon because someone might be listening and that's how careers get washed out, over stupid things. John Worthy was basically run out of the business because he was caught having sex with a single woman who went to one of the churches he frequented. Once word got out that he was doing the deed after church he couldn't schedule anymore gigs. Hell, I met Elizabeth at a revival. She was wild back then…she was really wild back then! She said she wanted to confess her sins to me. I told her that was a Catholic thing, but she could speak to me freely. So she leaned over and told me she wasn't wearing any panties and a few other choice things she was thinking. Sometimes a man wearing the cloth just turns women on, you need to be aware of that because you are a handsome young man and it could get you into trouble," Frank said.

Daniel was shocked, "Wow, I hadn't thought of that. But listen reverend, I'm not going to do anything stupid socially. Remember I'm an actor and being a social Christian shouldn't be a hard role," he held up the bible, "it's learning my lines for the Sunday performance is what I'm worried about." The young man admitted.

"Don't fret about that my boy, it won't do you any good."

<u>Chapter 12:</u> A Dreary Start

A light drizzling rain welcomed Frank and Daniel into Tall Rock the next morning. Most of the area's working population was either at Zaire International Corporation or Sum-A-Yahon Tire Manufacturing. Children were in school and everyone else was indoors avoiding the rain.

Frank didn't call Charlie Earp immediately as promised. He didn't want anyone to know there problems in his life. Instead he gave the dime tour. Molasses Highway until it turned into Main Street, left on State Road 11, under the interstate overpass and left on Kenia River Road. The road followed the river for three and a half miles until it turned into dirt and became private property. Right before the pavement ended was Tall Rock Baptist Church with Frank and Elizabeth's home beside it.

The church was fairly plain with a sign out front with changeable letters. Daniel read it, "GOD ONLY ANSWERS KNEE MAIL".

"That's Elizabeth's doing. She finds catchy passages on the internet and changes the sign every week, it's one of the ways she likes to help out."

His wife wasn't home but he left her the better parking space in the driveway. They went inside the house and Frank showed Daniel around. The spare bedroom where Daniel would stay had Frank's fishing equipment lying about. Frank put his tackle up while Daniel unpacked his things and put them in the dresser drawers. Afterwards they went over to the church and Frank led him around telling him the story of choosing this spot and working with the construction crew, how he gained confidence by preaching to them and how it became a routine they all enjoyed. He spoke of the Billy the carpenter who built him the pews and disappeared before he could pay him. Daniel looked around at the rows of pews. He noticed how simple yet beautiful they were with the black walnut finish and their perfect symmetrical curves. He couldn't help but find it ironic how a carpenter sacrificed his time and skills without the need to be paid for it. The floor was simple wood, swept and polished to a shine. At the front of the room was a raised stage boasting an altar that matched the pews. A large cross hung on the wall behind the altar. The ceiling was like most other churches, tall and painted white.

"Michelangelo wasn't available when we painted it so I decided to leave it blank until he shows up," Frank joked, and then smiled thinking of days past.

After his reminiscing he kept on, "Yes, this is what everyone thinks of when they say they go to Tall Rock Baptist, but it's more than just the room, or the building, it's the atmosphere that makes the difference. Atmosphere is what makes every church different. The New Zion Full Gospel in Motte sings more and get more animated. Pastor Floyd at Word of God Family Temple tells jokes and uses the fear of god to make his patrons empty their wallets to him. I try to educate using the Bible, not scream about damnation," Frank's words made soft echoes on walls and then it was silent again. It was chilly on the back pew where they sat down, each of them lost deep in thought.

"Daniel, let me hold that bible so we can begin a sermon."

Daniel handed it over and Frank began flipping through the pages.

"Ah, Lamentations! That's one you don't get every day," The Reverend pulled out a pocket size memo book along with a pen and handed them to his apprentice, "Lamentations 4:11 looks like a good place to begin from."

He read, " 'The Lord has given full vent to his wrath; he has pulled out his fierce anger. He built a fire in Zion and consumed her foundations.' You see this passage is about Jerusalem being under siege along with the people's faith. You see, often there are hidden meanings in these stories, OUR job is to find them and point them out."

Old and young, the two men sat and worked on the sermon for the better part of an hour until they were interrupted by Frank's wife Elizabeth. She walked in through the front door dressed like an old librarian, "Frank if you'd called I'd have had some lunch ready for- Oh, pardon me, I didn't mean to interrupt."

"That's alright dear, this is Daniel Montclair, the young man I was telling you about."

"It's nice to meet you Daniel," Elizabeth said.

"You too Mrs. Catoe," he replied.

"Oh, please call me Elizabeth."

Daniel couldn't help but notice she spoke as if she had rehearsed her greeting a million times or more.

"How was the drive?" She asked.

"Fine, it was fine," Frank was a little annoyed with her for interrupting a very productive session.

She knew what that tone meant and knew it was time to leave. "Well, I'll go fix you both some sandwiches and y'all just come get them whenever you're ready."

"Thanks dear," Frank said as Elizabeth left. He sighed, "She means well but that is one hard-headed woman. That's why she's not to know about our true mission or that I'm paying you for this."

"Why shouldn't she know I'm getting paid?" Daniel wanted to know.

Frank looked back to make sure his wife was gone, "For one she knows the church doesn't have the money, so then she would get suspicious and find out it's coming out of our retirement. Like I said, she wouldn't like it and she wouldn't understand."

The two men finished notating and outlining the talking points of the sermon, and then they went to the house to eat the turkey sandwiches that Elizabeth had made.

All the while Frank was excitedly teaching Daniel about how to create and deliver a sermon, "Now I've been doing this for many years but I always practice at least once before I give a sermon. In a minute we'll go back over and you can just watch while I give it the first run-through."

After lunch Reverend Catoe took the pulpit.

"Just keep in mind this first time might be a little rough around the edges."

Daniel sat in the back row and watched intently as Frank put on the show. He couldn't help but notice it was anything but rough around the edges, smooth and simple was a better way to put it.

The podium wasn't equipped with a microphone and speaker system although the church was large enough to justify having one. Frank just let his deep voice echo from wall to wall. Daniel noticed how easily Frank changed from reading straight from passages to talking about their meanings. Daniel thought the climax was a little weak but then realized it was church and not theater. Frank had a way of keeping things from going over the top.

"So what we need to take from this today, friends, is that we who live faithful and meaningful lives sometimes are tested by the Lord at times. Those tests can be hard on us but we must endure with our morals and love of God," He said to Daniel in his regular speaking voice, "I usually make a couple of prayers, the one before the sermon is usually the Lord's Prayer, and the one after is what I call my prayer of my flock. That's where we pray for our sick to get well, that the unemployed will find work, that our members will stay safe on vacation and so on."

Daniel's quick wit spoke up, "How about we pray to keep our government wise and fair?"

"Oh, I used to do that one but gave up on it years ago. I hate to ask the Lord for too much!" Frank shouted looking up towards the crucifix on the wall.

It was Tuesday afternoon which gave Daniel plenty to learn before Wednesday night service. Frank gave a practice service, telling him how things would go and what could be expected. Afterwards they went over basic scripture and church terminology, this kept them busy until suppertime. Elizabeth made a nice meal; Mashed potatoes and gravy, corn bread, pork chops, and collard greens.

Frank joked, "Daniel, I should have brought you here years ago, I never eat this good! Hahaha!"

Elizabeth smiled, "Well it's just easier to cook for more than two people dear. While you were gone I didn't even cook, I just went to the Taco Shack." This gave them both a good laugh because it obviously wasn't true. They both despised Taco Shack and Frank knew she had been busy with her lover.

After supper the three of them sat on the front porch in the rocking chairs to relax. Elizabeth updated them on the latest gossip. Ashley Tithgen was pregnant again and her Marine husband had been deployed for over six months. Frank explained Ashley was the problem child of Arthur and Susan Tithgen, two longtime members of Tall Rock Baptist. They did their best to raise her right but getting into trouble was just her nature. She'd ran away from home nearly a dozen times, set the principal's office on fire in middle school, and wrecked nearly every car she'd ever driven. Also, The Zaire plant might be having another layoff next month. They stayed up for hours describing Tall Rock's citizens to Daniel.

Chris Goodson, production manager at Zaire and his wife, Leslie, a home maker were both in their early fifties. Charley Earp, who served as both the Mayor and fireman. Dennis Bailey was a warehouse manager at Sum-A-Yahon Tire Manufacturing and his wife Callie was a high school biology teacher at Motte County High. There was Miss Lorraine Hendricks who was widowed and retired, and of course Alan and Megan Thompson owners and managers of Tall Rock Grocery. These were some of the more prominent figures in the church but certainly not all of them.

When everyone finally went to bed Daniel lay awake trying to think of everything important he'd learned that day. Doing that had always helped him in school. He actually considered it part of his studying. The other part of his studying strategy was cramming for finals and he had a feeling that is exactly what he was going to be doing day after day, learning names of people and cities that were made up by other people centuries ago. He felt like he should be stressed out by the amount of information he had to learn, but his current environment was so relaxing he could only be content to be there. Before he fell asleep he realized he still hadn't told his parents he'd dropped out of college.

Frank was up early as always. He liked to sit on the porch in his rocking chair and watch the sun rise while he drank his coffee. Wednesday was no different, but he wasn't the first to wake. Daniel was sitting up in bed watching old sermons on his smart-phone. He heard the old reverend in the kitchen brewing coffee and decided to join him. They took their mugs out onto the porch and watched the sun rise. They didn't talk for a while, they just enjoyed the hot coffee and the cool morning air. They each knew there was so much to be said and they each appreciated the other's understanding that this was a sacred time, a time to collect one's thoughts and prepare for the day. When they both had finished two cups of coffee the pair walked down the old path behind the church cut through the woods and ended at the Kenia River bank.

Frank explained, "This old river is why Tall Rock is what it is, which ain't all that much. Zaire uses the water to cool the equipment. When they're running wide open the water coming out the plant heats up everything downstream. It gets at least fifteen to twenty degrees hotter here and we're a few miles downstream."

Daniel knelt down and let the water run over his hands, "It doesn't seem very hot now."

"Well Zaire isn't putting out the rods they used to," Frank said, "They make bainite steel welding rods. They run two shifts now; it used to be around the clock. Everyone is a little worried they might cut back to one eventually. That would cripple this town. "

Daniel grew up in a small town with few jobs, most of the residents commuted into neighboring Tuscaloosa for work; his father worked for an engineering firm there. Tall Rock was different, with no big cities in the area, it mainly supported itself with a few people traveling to neighboring Motte to work.

"Why did they ever build it here anyway? This place seems like it's the middle of nowhere, was there even a town here before…?"

"What before Zaire?" Frank mused, "Not a town, it was more like a small community. Zaire built here for three reasons. They had to have a river as part of their operation. The land was cheap and close enough to major highways to be economical. They could have found all that at plenty of other places up and down this river. The main reason they chose here was taxes. You see Motte County cut Zaire one hell of a tax break so they would build here and boost the economy. It worked, Sum-A-Yahon Tire Manufacturing came not long after and the small community became a town. That town needed a church, and that's how Elizabeth and I came to settle here."

Daniel was listening to Frank but was watching the river flow silently past him.

"This is where I come to relax; it's probably my favorite of all. You would think a reverend would say his church but that's where I work. Here is so peaceful, so true. It's like the river washes all my troubles away downstream. I imagine many men use the excuse of fishing to experience what I feel when I come sit by the bank and dream."

Frank motioned for Daniel to follow him back toward the house.

"In these woods is where I do my best thinking," Frank said as they walked up the ancient trail, "especially when I'm chopping wood."

"You sound like an art student with all that dreaming and thinking you do Reverend," Daniel teased.

To which Frank replied, "Yeah well I have a lot of time to kill ya know. I only have to work two days a week, one of the perks of the job." This gave Daniel a good laugh.

<u>**Chapter 13:**</u> Elizabeth

Elizabeth Catoe was bothered by the fact that her husband brought a student back from his trip to Alabama without asking her if it was alright. The last person to stay with them was Joel Caples. Joel needed a place to stay for a couple of days after his wife kicked him out until he promised her he would quit drinking.

Frank had explained to her that some new blood was the best way to increase church participation and attract new members. She understood but had wanted her nephew Jason, the only child of her late sister, to fill the role.

Jason Sharper was the only attorney in Tall Rock, chief executive of Sharper Law Firm. He wasn't a great lawyer but enjoyed doing it for a few reasons. Like most lawyers, he loved to hear himself talk and at all costs avoided physical labor, but he loved knowing other people's secrets and profiting off of their misfortune.

On more than one occasion Jason had mentioned to his favorite aunt that he felt obligated to serve the community and the good Lord by becoming a Pastor in the church whenever Frank finally decided he needed help. Elizabeth had mentioned it to Frank one time thinking he would love to have help. Frank made it very clear that he would not let a lawyer preach to his congregation and let his church lose all credibility. "People associate lawyers with liars…and Jason rarely ever came to service anyway," had been his response.

Frank had flat out told his wife that Jason joining the clergy wasn't going to happen. She took offense when he had phoned to tell her that Daniel was going to follow in his footsteps at the altar. Elizabeth was suspicious of Daniel but never showed it.

He and Frank spent most of the day preoccupied with bible study to pay her any attention. Even that afternoon when she came home from the salon with her hair fixed up neither one noticed or at least they didn't compliment her. The silent men were seated in the living room reading to themselves.

"I'm home dear, want anything special for supper?" Frank never even looked up from the bible he was reading, he just shook his head and replied, "No dear, whatever you want."

Elizabeth was furious as she went in to start supper. Nothing made her madder than when Frank would ignore her after she went to such lengths to look nice She knew Tony would have jumped all over the chance to compliment her. The chopping board took a beating as she diced and sliced potatoes and carrots with fury. She had the roast in the oven and the timer set when she decided to prove a point to Frank that while Jason wasn't perfect, neither was this new guy. She took out her cell phone and walked outside to pretend to check the mail.

She called up one of her favorite gossip gals, "Hey Janie…Oh, I'm good, you? And what's your daughter up to these days?...No, I mean Leah....Well I just thought about her today, Frank has a new disciple he's training…Oh yeah he seems nice and really cute…Yeah, a college boy…"

Leah Dixon was twenty years old and the wildest party child in Tall Rock. She went out nearly every night of the week and enjoyed the drugs and reputation that went along with it. Her mother Jane Dixon had been almost as bad in her day. She was divorced from her second husband and didn't want her little girl to have to go through two bad marriages to find the man she was meant to be with. It had become her new goal in life (aside from staying on top of the current gossip) to find a suitable man for her daughter. Leah had long ago decided that there wasn't an eligible man in Tall Rock that was good enough to have her. So when Elizabeth Catoe announced Daniel Montclair was the new man on campus she became alive with curiosity.

"Who is this new man? What does he look like? Does he come from a family with money?"

Of course in her mind he looked like a country singer dressed in a cowboy hat and boots driving a pickup truck. She told Leah the news and she started imagining a guy with a chiseled body standing in front of a congregation. This made them both excited.

'How much do Reverends make a year?' Leah wondered. Reverend Catoe didn't live like a king but he was kind of handsome for an old guy.

'Maybe This Daniel guy will get another job and do weddings on the side.' She was excited by the idea of teasing a reverend…or a trainee, or whatever he was to be called. She began thinking of all the ways she could tease him. Certainly he would have the discipline to resist most women. She knew every straight man would have a breaking point, and she planned to find it.

Chapter 14: Meet the New Guy

"Family. Family is the reason we've become the people we are today. As a child you were raised by people who loved and cared for you. Maybe they weren't your birth parents, perhaps grandparents, or maybe you were adopted. Regardless of their official title they are family."

'Tell me something I don't know reverend.' Frank mocked himself.

"The people you know, the people you care about, the people you love. Those people are your family, you may call them friends if you like to distinguish that they aren't related, but they're still family. Whether it is a neighbor, or an old friend miles away this is your family. Take a minute to think of all the people you love."

The congregation took the time Frank allotted to reflect on their families. They trusted the reverend and always followed his instructions knowing that he only meant to enlighten. It was the Sunday morning service and the regulars were there. There were a few faces in the crowd that Frank didn't expect to see, but that was normal. Tall Rock Baptist, like many churches, welcomed all comers. This meant people often brought friends and family visiting form out of town. Sunday morning it was more often that a non-regular would come to church feeling guilty (or often made go) because of a sinful Friday and Saturday night. Of course Frank didn't do confession but he would still talk to anyone who wanted to get something off their chest. 'My advice is always free,' Was a common saying of his. Every now and then a random person whom Frank didn't know would come to service and sit by themselves. If they managed to leave before he got the chance to speak with them he might ask Elizabeth or a deacon if they knew who the visitor was. Frank liked to know who was in his church, partly from a security reason and also to coax them into returning.

"I myself have a large family. Every one of you here is in my family. You are my brothers and my sisters. Over the weekend I left on a short trip. I went on the trip to visit an old friend whom I haven't seen in years. He introduced me to a young man who I was very taken by. I was introduced to this young man as Frank, not Reverend Catoe. He felt compelled to spread the word of Jesus to me and asked me if I knew the Lord. I only told him that I knew the Lord, not that I was a man of the cloth. He spoke to me, a complete stranger, with such kindness and passion that I felt compelled to learn more about him. He told me about his passion to help people find Christ. He had been a student in college working toward a degree when he began his relationship with the lord, a relationship in which he felt he needed to share with others. I revealed my true identity and then asked him to take a break from school and join us here in Tall Rock. He's going to be helping us with our youth program and other things; In return I'm going to help him get his start as a Minister."

The announcement of a new reverend was a shock to many in the crowd, Reverend Catoe had only been absent from his post at the altar only a handful of times since he started the church. When he was sick, or most recently out of town, Deacon Dennis Shriver would lead a brief sermon.

Daniel was expectedly nervous; he had been in this situation before. Every play he had ever acted in he'd gotten butterflies in his stomach right before his queue to go on stage, but once he started speaking he settled down and was fine from there on out. He did a last second mental checklist before Reverend Catoe introduced him.

'Costume-check.' He was wearing his one and only suit, his hair was combed, he glanced down to make sure his pants zipper was up.

'Lines-check'. He knew his talking points perfectly, he hadn't planned to say much but use eye contact, an important part of any public speech.

"I hope you all make him feel at home here, everyone, Reverend Daniel Montclair," he motioned for Daniel to get up. Frank was thinking 'Okay kid this is your chance to make a good impression, PLEASE don't barf.'

Daniel, who sat beside Elizabeth Catoe in the first row, stood up and turned to face the sea of questioning eyes. (God please don't make me hurl) He gave a smile and began, "Hello everyone. As Reverend Catoe said my name is Daniel Montclair, feel free to call me Daniel. I'm taking a break as a student and I'm very grateful for this opportunity that I've been given. I'll be working with the children in the youth program some and other various avenues here at Tall Rock Baptist, however feel free to come talk to me for any reason, whether it is a problem or you just want to get to know me. Frank and Elizabeth have been kind enough to invite me into their home to stay for a while so it should be easy for anyone to find me. I look forward to getting to know each and every one of you and help you strengthen your relationships with the Lord. Thank you."

Daniel sat back down and looked over at Elizabeth, she gave an approving smile.

Frank continued his sermon, "And like that your family grows and all are blessed…" The reverend as always included a lesson in a sermon, that day the lesson was unconditional love.

Once the sermon was over the congregation sang 'God, We Love You'. Daniel was a little embarrassed not knowing the words, but quickly learned the chorus and did his part. Finally the prayer.

Frank saved the important prayers for last. He began, "Let us pray," They bowed their heads. "Lord, you are the air we breathe and the food we eat; you are the life in us all. We are your children and your servants, thank you for all that you do. Some of our loved ones are ill and we pray that you will spend extra time looking over them. Mrs. Rose is in the hospital again and we beg you to help her with a speedy recovery. It's been hard on her since Big Ray passed away last fall. We all miss the sweet voice of Christopher Morton and ask that you please help his jaw heal swiftly."

This drew more than a chuckle from a few people and the audience. Chris Morton had one of those nasally irritating voices even a mother wanted to go mute.

"And we pray you keep our children safe this week as many classes are going on field trips. Thank you Lord, Amen."

Some people jumped right up out their seats, others took their time. Frank motioned for Daniel to follow him toward the front door. Reverend Catoe shook hands and smiled as his flock herded out the door.

Daniel stood across from him at the other double door only he was saying things like, 'Hello, It's my pleasure to meet you' and 'Oh, I am so excited to be here. Tall Rock already feels like home'.

Charlie Earp, the mayor, introduced himself and asked Daniel if he knew his second cousin Janice who ran the uptown theater in Mobile. Daniel knew the place but had never met the lady. After the mayor he met Dennis and Lorrie Bailey, a couple in their mid-forties. Dennis was the second shift manager at S-A-Y tire and Lorrie taught high school biology in Motte. Lorraine Hendricks (recently widowed) introduced herself as the loneliest woman in town. Alan and Megan Thompson, the owners of Tall Rock Farmer's Grocery, gave him an invitation to stop by the store and they would introduce him to some 'Right fine groceries'. He assured them that he would.

As part of his art curriculum, Daniel had taken Arts 309, a class on post-performance etiquette. Professor Maynard emphasized acting humble and gracious when talking to patrons of your work. He could hear her voice clearly in his head, 'Be in a good mood even if you aren't… That's why it's called acting.' Not everyone stopped to talk, some just smiled and or said hello. When the crowd had filed out Reverend Catoe and his young prodigy each stood opposite each other, backs to the open double doors.

"That went well," Frank said.

"Yeah, everyone seemed real nice," Daniel agreed.

Only Elizabeth and two women were still inside the church talking. The younger of the two made her way toward the men. She was twenty years old and looked like a pin-up model all dolled up for Easter. Her medium length brown hair was curled and bounced as she walked. She wore a floral sundress that wrapped around her body just right to show off her seductive curves. Frank knew the girl and wished he could arrest her on suspicion of mischief.

"Hello Reverend," she said, "That was a wonderful sermon you gave us today."

"Why, thank you Leah. I was beginning to wonder if you had found another church. I don't remember seeing your charming self for many Sundays."

"Oh, of course not," she gave a fake giggle. "Just living the life of a movie star."

She acted is if she had only just noticed Daniel standing there, "Oh and I'm so sorry, I'm Leah Dixon. Daniel was it?" She gently bit her bottom lip and smiled when he reached out to shake her hand.

"Why yes ma'am, Daniel Montclair… Pleasure to meet you."

"Oh please don't call me ma'am, you make me sound so old. I'm only twenty. How old are you Mr. Montclair?"

"Twenty-one."

"See we're almost the same age."

"Leah, what do you do when you aren't attending church?" Daniel asked wanting to learn more about this flirtatious girl.

She already had the answer to that one, "Well, anything I want." She said with an innocent sounding voice.

"That's what I hear," The reverend injected. "And I also heard you didn't go to class very much last semester."

By this time Mrs. Catoe and Mrs. Dixon were walking up to them.

"Well people do like to talk a lot, don't they?" She said it more as a statement.

"Oh, I think I must have seen that on the news," Frank said directing it toward the women, "Oh, hello Mrs. Dixon how are you doing today?"

"Just fine Reverend. That was such a good message earlier, I really enjoyed it."

Frank had been told that at least five times every Sunday but he still smiled, "Thank you."

"Oh yes, Daniel this is Ms. Jane Dixon, Leah's mother."

"It's a pleasure to meet you ma'am." Daniel said.

Jane Dixon was thirty-eight and twice divorced and was hands down the gossip queen of town. She and Leah lived on Mayflower Road almost a mile from the tire factory. She was quite attractive for her age and did her best to stay up with the modern fashion. That particular morning she was dressed very nice, with a light green and yellow sun dress, matching shoes and silver hoop earrings.

Mrs. Dixon looked Daniel up and down with a quirky smile upon her lips and said, "Frank I don't know where you found this handsome young man, but next time you go a'lookin you'd better take me!"

Everyone there laughed but all for different reasons. Jane Dixon laughed because it was her own joke and wanted to let them know she wasn't serious. Frank gave a chuckle to show he wasn't a stick in the mud. Daniel followed Frank's lead and did the same. Leah gave a small burst of laughter, mostly just to smile at Daniel. Elizabeth gave a roaring howl being she was the only person who found it funny at all.

When the laughing ceased Mrs. Dixon spoke to Daniel, "So Daniel how long have you been in town?"

"Oh just a couple of days, I'm still getting used to things," He told her.

She bit her finger nail and let her eyes wander as if she was pondering some new idea.

"I just had a thought," She said, "Maybe you and Leah could go out later. She could show you around town and you could make sure she stays out of trouble. I would feel so much better knowing she's with a person of good character. You see, I'll be going out myself tonight and would rather not be worried all night long."

Leah put her hands on her hips obviously upset that her mother wanted her babysat as if she were a child.

"Would you do that for me Daniel?" Mrs. Dixon asked.

This was thrown at the young man so fast he didn't know what to think of it. His first instinct was to do what he was asked, "Well yes ma'am I suppose I could…" Then he remembered his obligation to Frank and the church, "But of course I have to be here for the service this evening." He looked at Frank seeking guidance on the issue.

"Service is always over by eight-thirty, sometimes earlier, but I would like you to stay and meet some folks… Just like you're doing right now," Frank added.

Daniel was flustered with all the new information. He looked at Leah, "Ahhh, sure. Oh, I don't have a car yet though. Do you drive?"

"You bet. So I'll pick you up quarter till nine then." It was a statement, not a question.

Leah and her mother said goodbye and left. Elizabeth walked them to Mrs. Dixon's car still chatting. Frank motioned for Daniel to follow him back inside.

"I didn't get a chance to properly warn you about them. You see, I failed to mention those two to you yesterday because they aren't our most frequent guests. Jane is a friend of Elizabeth and they share all the gossip. Her daughter is a no-good tramp that loves trouble. I'm sure the only reason they came today is because they heard you had arrived and they wanted to see what you looked like."

"I really didn't know how to react. She just threw the whole idea at me without warning," The young apprentice grew a little defensive.

"It's fine, just remember why you're here. We can't have you getting mixed up with that one. You'll have a strike against you before begin. You've got to figure out a way to make her not interested in you without making either of them bitter. In fact we don't need to give them any ammunition to use to stir up trouble. That's what they love to do..." Frank eyes wandered for a moment as he recalled a previous situation the Dixons had begun.

"I'll just be boring, like I usually am. You know, be a party pooper like a reverend is supposed to be."

"Well do what you think is best. But please, don't fuck that girl," Frank whispered.

Chapter 15: In Walks the Enemy

Daniel's mother had called and he dropped the bomb about quitting school. She was upset about it but his father was furious. Daniel didn't want to hear his shit anymore and hung up. Before lunch time his cell service had been cut off. That was his father's way of saying he was on his own. Daniel was relieved to have that fight over for a while.

He changed clothes during the day so he wouldn't get his only suit dirty. He was only studying the bible, but he didn't want to take any chances. He'd changed back before the evening service that flowed much the same as the one that morning had. Daniel noticed how Frank's sermon wasn't word-for-word though, he changed up a few minor things. He remembered Professor Hoole always jumping down a student's throat if they didn't know every line of their part.

Frank wasn't exactly ad-libbing though. He had talking points and bible passages written on a small sheet of paper sitting in front of him at the altar. He introduced Daniel as his 'new prodigy' to the congregation. The service wrapped up at eight-thirty just as promised, and the pair took their posts shaking hands with people as they exited the church.

Daniel met many new people and recognized a few from the morning service. Leah walked past, "I'll be waiting…" she pointed toward the end of the parking lot. Daniel just smiled at her. 'She's wearing a different outfit, right? Yeah, that's a different dress than she had on this morning.'

The last person to leave was a stranger. Occasionally people would 'Church Shop', going around to the different churches in the area until they found one they liked. That's how churches grow, new folks wanting to give church a try.

Frank had seen this man sitting on the back row all by himself. He guessed the man was in his late forties to early fifties. He wore a dark grey suit and a power tie. Something told the old reverend this man wasn't just shopping for a place to sit on Sunday nights.

"Reverend Catoe, hello, my name is Greg Banther," The stranger spoke like a businessman, very rehearsed as if he'd done it many times.

Franklin shook his hand, "It's very nice to make your acquaintance Mr. Banther."

"I'm an official with the United Holy Christened Church," He held up a UHCC identification card for Frank to inspect.

"I'm glad to see you run a well-organized church here. I've completed your initial report and your application to join our organization has been accepted."

"Oh, well thank you," Frank sounded sincere but was mentally giving this man the finger.

"If you have a few minutes I'd like to go over the report and fill you in on the UHCC methods," Mr. Banther said. It was clear Frank needed to make time to talk business.

"Of course. It's ironic timing you know Mr. Banther, today is Daniel's first visit here as well," Frank motioned behind the man to Daniel who had listening to their conversation.

"Ah yes, the new young prodigy," they shook hands, "it's an excellent time for you to serve the church and the Lord."

'He puts the church before the Lord, this one is a politician.' Frank thought.

"Yes, I'm blessed to have been welcomed into such a wonderful church," Daniel agreed. "Have you been with the UHCC long?"

"No, the organization is relatively new," Banther said in the same bored tone. He turned back to Reverend Catoe, irritated that he had to speak to anyone else.

"Mr. Banther and I are going to discuss some things, so you can go now if you like Daniel."

The young man walked out into the church parking lot feeling happy having survived his first day at the church, but not knowing what to expect that night.

Reverend Franklin Catoe and Greg Banther sat in the first pew together discussing the report, "Let me start from the top." Mr. Banther read from a sheet of paper on a clipboard.

"UHCC, Tall Rock Assembly, That's your official name. You are Reverend Franklin Catoe. Property Address 3219 Kenia River Rd. Tall Rock, SC. Your church type is 04, which means it is traditional style. There were thirty-seven people at the preliminary membership, which was tonight. Is all that correct so far?"

Frank replied, "Why is it not still Tall Rock Baptist Church? We've been that since the beginning."

"You don't have to say, United Holy Christened Church, that's just the official title. We've taken all the denominations out of Christianity this way and made the factions stronger by uniting them, therefore there are no more Baptists and we're all just Christians now. Since the word Church is already in UHCC, you don't need it after Tall Rock."

'There are no more Baptists. That's not going to sit well with some people I know,' Frank thought. Out of the many branches of Baptists; Southern, Northern, Independent, Free Will, Reformed, and many more; they all want to distinguish themselves from one another. Now they aren't even Baptists, they're just heaped into one big pile of Christians.'

"Why no Baptists?" Frank asked.

"Well, it's to unite all Christians. To make it one church again…but allowing each their own personal style still."

Frank was thinking what would be happening if he was still twenty years old. He'd have thrown the man out on the street and suffered the consequences later.

"Let's see here, appearance to standard: No. That's only because the sign doesn't have the proper name yet."

Frank wanted to argue about the new name but held his tongue.

"Bible usage: No. Have you received a UHCC supply catalog yet?" Banther asked.

"Yes, but we already have bibles here," Frank pointed to a pair of bibles sitting in the holders on the back of the pew, "as you can see right there."

"They are illegitimate bibles Reverend. They aren't the official bible of this organization that you'll be part of."

"Just what makes these bibles illegitimate? I've been using them for years now and I can't find anything wrong with them," Frank said.

"All of the old style bibles have stories that are lewd and vile. They aren't politically correct and they don't hold any relevance in today's society," Mr. Banther added, "Also, the UHCC Bibles aren't as hard to read. Some of those old stories didn't even make sense to me and I'm an educated man."

The reverend paused only to appreciate the irony here. He also thought the book was out dated and was full of flaws, and yet he was arguing to keep it.

"Today's society is in need of some lewd and vile stories because it's history. This storied past keeps us appreciative of what we have and wary that it doesn't happen again. I for one, am not a fan of being politically correct."

"To be part of this organization you will need to abide by our rules and criteria," Banther picked up a bible off the pew, "Our version is much shorter than this monstrosity…Much cheaper too. The prices drop the higher the amount you buy."

Frank took a deep breath before he spoke, "Mr. Banther… This is not a large church full of wealthy people. All of these things we have to change cost money, and lots of it. How can we afford to pay for the Bibles and a new sign and still pay this ransom, you call dues, and then be able to keep the lights on?"

"Stay calm Mr. Catoe. The UHCC understands that these changes may make things hard at first, that's why the costs of these upgrades can be deducted from the dues owed," He returned to his clipboard.

"Proper Sermon Message: Yes, and the guidelines on that one are easy. The entire sermon must last at least twenty five minutes, it must be positive or have a positive moral, and it must not negatively portray the UHCC in any way."

"When you say it must be positive does that mean I can't give the ole' Fire and Brimstone scare? It's not a weekly occurrence but I believe it's necessary from time to time."

"I can't tell you yes or no without hearing it I'm afraid. Only that it's a judgment call by me or whoever is auditing the sermon. We may give you a little leeway on that the first time or two because it is our personal interpretation on how 'positive' is construed."

"How was today's sermon? And what were to happen if a sermon isn't deemed positive?" Frank asked.

"Today's sermon was fine," Mr. Banther cleared his throat, "If you violate any of these ordinances, your church will go on one year probation for that violation. If you violate that ordinance again while under probation your church will be fined. Repetitive violations and the church leader will be suspended from their position until the panel of directors can decide on forgiveness or termination."

'Forgiveness or Termination' the words echoed inside Frank's mind.

"Also, we have yet to receive your joining fee. Your church won't be legitimate until it's paid. It's only a one-time fee."

"That's what you keep saying. I have to pay this outrageous amount of money just so I can give your company more money every month? That doesn't sound like a good business plan the way I look at it."

Mr. Banther didn't flinch by Reverend Catoe's rebellious tone. He simply stared through his wire framed glasses and said, "Your church can pay the joining fee, the dues, and anything else I say. If not, you'll have to close the doors. That won't be good business for you or anybody else. Is that understood?"

It took Reverend Catoe every bit of control and Christian wisdom to keep from being violent, "Yes, just don't expect me to like it."

Chapter 16: The Road into Hell

Leah sat on the trunk of her car playing a game on her phone while she waited on Daniel. It was a silver compact car with tinted windows. The pink camouflage letters L J D took up much of the rear glass. That was the first thing Daniel noticed. He thought it was stupid when people paid to put their own initials on a car. To him the only thing worse was, 'In loving memory of …', followed by their dates of birth and death, as if it was paying honor to that dead person by having their basic information displayed on the back of a piece of shit car.

"Do you always keep girls waiting?" Leah asked in her playful voice. She was wearing tight jeans and a small tank-top. It looked like her breasts might pop out the top at any moment.

Daniel didn't have any witty line to come back with, "Ahhh, no. So where are we going?" He was trying to look her in the eyes.

Leah batted her lashes at him, "Oh, nowhere really, just around town. Get in."

She drove them back up Kenia River Road towards town. The latest pop song was on the radio. He thought about how stale pop music was becoming.

"So are we going to stop and eat somewhere in town?" Daniel asked.

"Why are you hungry?"

"No not yet," He lied.

"Okay just let me know," She said and turned up the radio.

She turned down a street with no sign just before they reached the city limits. The road was in desperate need of repair, the potholes were unavoidable. They continued on for a couple of minutes in silence bumping here and there with the contour of the road.

"I'm gonna drop by my friend's house and say hi real quick, do you mind just sittin tight?"

Daniel felt like he had no choice but to accept, "Sure."

'That a boy Daniel, just be your normal lame self. She'll be tired of you and ready to drop you off within the hour.'

She whipped the car into a dirt drive. The sun was setting and it took Daniel a few seconds to realize they were in a trailer park. Upon further inspection he decided this was the nastiest, rat hole of a trailer park he'd ever seen. He gazed upon it like it was an alien planet. All the trailers he could see were very old. They were single-wides, and most had been pulled there from other parks. Not one he could see had a decent porch. They were either cinder block or rickety two-by-fours for steps.

They pulled up to the fifth trailer on the right and Leah honked the horn.

"I'll be back in a minute," Was all she said and jumped out. She took her purse and left her car door open. This trailer had cinder block steps. Beside them sat two bags of trash. One of them was busted open and the garbage had spilled out on the ground. She beat on the door a couple of times before it opened. Cautiously a man peered out, first at Leah and then to Daniel.

The man looked either Puerto Rican to Daniel, and by the looks of it he was used to living in a trailer park. He was in his twenties.

He had on tattered jeans, no shoes, and a wife beater. His beard wasn't filled in on his cheeks and was all around scraggly. The man didn't say a word, just opened the door enough for Leah to hop on in and then closed it behind her.

'Why would she take me here?' He wondered, 'She must be proud of her lack of taste or she's buying drugs.'

Daniel was a little bewildered by what was going on here. Her friend wasn't a girl like he'd originally thought; it was a grown ass man that lived in a trailer park. The dome lights were still on in the car because the driver's side door was still open.

'Did she leave the door open on purpose so the guy could see me? He probably couldn't have seen me without the dome lights on. So she wanted him to know I'm here…for protection. That means she is doing something illegal, either buying or selling drugs. Probably buying.'

He looked around nervously to see if anyone was watching him but couldn't see much because of the dome light. He reached over and closed the door. On one side of him was the trailer where his date was probably breaking the law. On the other side was the back of another trailer with two a/c units sticking out of the windows.

Directly ahead of him was a car with grass growing up around it. Daniel could tell it was an old police car from the body style and it still had the spotlight mounted above the driver's door. The car sat on its rims, which were sunk into the dirt.

Mosquitoes were invading so Daniel leaned over and closed the driver's side door. It was too late, his blood was already on the menu. He didn't have a phone to look at to check the time so he just sat there for what seemed like an eternity, slapping his skin whenever he felt a sting.

Just as he was building up the nerve to go knock on the door Leah came out and got back in the car.

"Sorry that took so long," She said very unapologetically.

"It's fine," Daniel said. He was just relieved she hadn't been raped, robbed, or overdosed on heroin. He was a little bit upset for just letting himself be put in this situation. As they left the trailer park he decided if there was a hell then it must look like this, just miles and miles of trailer park and you have to take a bumpy road to get there. It was the road with no name, the road into hell.

Chapter 17: Night Shift

Brantley Wainwright, Motte County Deputy Sherriff had begun his patrol at five o'clock in the afternoon. He didn't like the night shift as much as he'd used to when he was a rookie. Back then he was excited about catching criminals and upholding the law. After being on the force for seven years he was tired of people treating him like a jerk for doing his job. His job was to write seat belt tickets, an average of at least three per day when he worked day shift. Sunday nights were generally quiet, with most of the action happening on Friday and Saturday.

He liked to drive past his house once or twice a night to make sure his girlfriend Jeanette didn't have another guy there screwing her. She wasn't exactly a beacon of faith, she'd had several affairs when she'd been married. The latest had been Brantley but her husband had killed their neighbor thinking he was the one nailing his wife. Husband went to jail for murder and she moved in with Brantley. He didn't exactly trust her but she was just too hot not to be with.

The night before he'd worked a wreck. It was a single car collision with a deer. Looking at the bloody deer carcass and talking to the frightened old lady that hit it didn't make for an exciting shift. Tonight was shaping up to be even less eventful.

He rubbed his eyes and thought about taking a nap for a little while. 'No, I shouldn't sleep on the job…I just need a little pick me up.'

The deputy reached in his front pocket and pulled out a black canister, the kind that was once used for storing old camera film. He unscrewed the cap and pulled out a baggie of cocaine and a small teaspoon. He gently hummed a tune while loading the spoon with the powder. He took it up the nose in a snort, "Uh oh, I probably spilled most of that one." He reloaded and took another bump. "Ahhh, let's go get some bad guys".

<u>Chapter 18:</u> Local Competition

It was after ten o'clock at night; Frank was in sitting in his office with a glass of brandy thinking about his recent conversation with Mr. Banther of the UHCC, his church's new governing body. It was rare for Frank to have a drink of liquor, but after learning his wife had been screwing around on him he was doing things out of his normal routine. He'd kept a good bottle locked away in his office desk for a special occasion, but that evening he decided life was too short to be outlived by a bottle of booze. There was a knock on the door. 'Must be Daniel,' Frank thought, 'Elizabeth hasn't knocked in fifteen years.'

"Come in Romeo, how was your evening…" The man that opened the door wasn't Daniel at all, it was Larry Gilmore, Pastor of Motte Lutheran Church.

"Oh, Larry. Sorry, I wasn't expecting you…Oh, won't you come in. What can I do for you at this time of night?" Frank asked.

Pastor Gilmore was a tall stocky man with a bit of a gut. He wore khaki pants and a dress shirt with a Palmetto tree embroidered on the left breast.

"You can start by pouring me a drink if you happen to have another glass."

"Of course!" Frank replied and reached into his desk drawer for another glass. It was rare that Frank drank around anyone, and he was quite excited at the opportunity to have a drinking partner, especially one that didn't want to be seen doing it either.

Larry took a sip from the glass that was handed to him.

"I had a visit this morning from a Greg Banther, from the United Holy Whore-House Committee," Frank nodded his head in agreement at the name.

"He told me he was gonna come see you tonight, that he was making trips all over his new territory to meet his clients and start doing evaluations on them."

"Yeah, it won't be long before you're going to have to get in line to get a chance to punch that prick in the nose. I was so angry a little while ago I can barely recall what he said."

Frank balled his fist as he spoke, imagining getting to really hit Banther right in his nose, maybe even breaking his glasses.

"Why Reverend, you and I have a lot in common…you see I would like to stick my foot so far up his ass that we have to call Motte Search and Rescue to find my shoe," the pastor said with a smile. They both sipped on brandy.

"I don't know how I'm going to be able to make it. The dues that we're going to have to pay those people are ludicrous. It's going to put a lot of churches under and cripple the rest. I told that to Banther, and do you know what he told me? To impose a mandatory tithing on all members. That means people will have to pay to pray, and they won't get all the extra things we used to save up to offer them like our fall festival and mission trips. We might have to give up Sunday school as well." Pastor Gilmore said.

"I don't like it any more than you do Larry," Frank added, "They are turning us into salesmen and beggars. But what rubs me is the fact we won't get anything in return!"

"I can't stand that man's attitude. He's my age and yet he talks to me like he's my high school math teacher! It's obvious he was never a man of the church, just the way he talks to people reminds me of a lawyer. Phshhhh, pure asshole," the Pastor snarled.

Frank saw the same contempt in Pastor Gilmore that he himself felt for the UHCC and decided this was the time to gain support for his cause.

"What can we do Larry? It seems like they're holding all the cards."

"Well they want our money, money we barely have to keep things running in our churches. If we all refused to pay what could they do to us? I mean every church in the country, they couldn't afford to operate without cash coming in right? We all just don't pay. They can't make us," Pastor Gilmore growled.

"Did you forget that your church building is now under the new ownership of those pricks? They got their start-up money from somewhere. If we don't pay, they still own our churches and can make us leave them. They could sell this building right from under me to get their money back. If we aren't a sanctioned church and still continue to worship they can have you arrested," Frank assured his colleague.

"That might be the start of a movement. How many arrested men would it take to get the public really upset? Upset enough to riot and protest the law and have it repealed?" Gilmore questioned.

Frank had already thought of that and stored that as a final idea in case all else failed. He pretended to mull it over for a few moments. "They'd still have our churches, and the way this government is the only way it could be revoked is to bribe them twice as much as they're already getting. What we need is a way to highlight the corruption. What we need is a man on the inside."

Pastor Gilmore looked stunned, "How can we get someone on the inside? And what good would it do?"

"Well," Frank began, "The UHCC wants fresh, young, and talented men and women to be the face of their new organization. I read that they are going to offer some sort of college or classes for some of the best, a sort of job training/brain-washing place I imagine. If we could get a few people high up in their ranks they might be able to expose the right information, or at least get our dues dropped or something."

Pastor Gilmore was curious, "So are you going to try to get into the college Reverend?"

"No, like I said they want fresh meat, not some old goats like us." Pastor Gilmore grunted in agreement.

"I've just actually recruited a young man for just that. I'm paying him out of mine and Elizabeth's retirement," Frank added.

"Who?" Pastor Gilmore asked.

"Oh a college guy I just met the other day. He has an acting background and seems to have morals…not one bit of religion but he has morals," Frank felt good spilling the beans on his master plan.

"What's his name?"

"Daniel Montclair. But he might be the Arch Bishop Montclair when I'm done with him."

Pastor Gilmore looked into his glass of Brandy and smiled. Then he finished it with a gulp and set it on Frank's desk. Frank could tell his colleague's mood had changed all of a sudden. Frank studied his eyes hoping Larry was happy about the plan and looking to help.

Larry pulled a device out of his suit pocket. He looked at it and pressed a button on it. Then from the rear of his belt he produced a pistol and pointed it at the reverend.

"I just recorded that entire conversation Frank. A conversation that you are now regretting you ever had. You see, while your plan is bold it is also doomed to fail. They are too strong to fight, they only appreciate money. So I'm giving you two options right now. You can buy this recorder from me right now for twenty thousand dollars, or I can take it to the UHCC and expose you. As a reward they will cut my churches-dues in half probably."

Frank was thinking a million miles an hour but was like a stone sitting in his office chair. "They might just listen to the tape and get rid of us both you crazy ass bastard!"

The pastor was not laughing.

"Oh, I did my homework too Frank. I learned all about the college you've been talking about and every bit of information on their website. Most importantly their policies on rebellious members like you…when I turn you in as a heretic."

Frank sat up suddenly in his chair and made Larry jump, pistol still in hand.

"Unless you're going for your checkbook Frank you'd better sit still and don't do anything stupid."

This wasn't the first time Frank had a gun held on him, but he assumed Pastor Larry Gilmore didn't have much experience with a pistol, that's why he'd tested him. The pastor was nervous while pretending to be in command and sure of himself.

"I was just pouring another round Larry," Frank said.

"No, I'm not gonna let you get me drunk and talk this away from me, (he waved the gun) or this (he waved the recorder in the other).

"That's fine, I'll just have one without you," Frank said reaching for the half empty bottle of brandy sitting on the desk in front of him.

"Wrong again Reverend, you don't need any more liquid courage. It would be a shame for you to kill yourself with this here gun. Yes lord, what a shame that would be."

The two men sat silently, each calculating the others options and their own, searching for the right thing to say or do. Frank imagined Larry was fully capable of killing him, but that wouldn't help the Pastor's situation.

"I know ole boy, but business is business, and I'm just out of options," Pastor Gilmore sighed.

Frank spoke harsh words with a casual easy tone, "If you shoot me, you won't get one dime. And since I'm not giving you even one fucking penny, you can get the hell out of my office and go tattle-tale to those spiritual rapists."

"That's not very wise of you Frank, you're going to lose you church, house, and might even go to jail for heresy like that," said Reverend Gilmore.

Frank wasn't fazed at all, "Every time you kneel and pray, just think about yourself blowing the devil. You down on your knees sucking on Lucifer's fiery cock, that's what you'll get to do for all eternity. Now get the fuck out of my office."

The Pastor wasn't going to shoot Frank, but he didn't have a response other than to get up and leave. Tight lipped and angry Larry Gilmore stood up and backed toward the door, never turning his eyes from Frank.

"You actually believe that shit?" He slammed the door as he left.

As much as Frank wanted to sit and think about the situation he knew now was the time to act and speed was critical. He began forming a plan as he stood up and took a swig from the bottle, and then he carried it out the side door of his office that opened into the parking lot. He heard the Pastor's car crank up and back out. Frank hurried over to the house and got in his old truck. He loved the feeling of this, the danger. It took him back to his days of dealing drugs. It took him back to Mobile Bay.

Chapter 19: Sugarfoot

The old county roads went on for miles as Leah drove out away from town. The darkness revealed little of the landscape to his curious eyes who had spent most of his life in Alabama. Daniel didn't have a clue to where they were going, he was just relieved they were out of the trailer park.

Leah tried small talk, asking him about college life and his experience. "You do much partying there?" She asked.

"Oh, a little. I never did mess with any drugs but I could always hold my own at the beer pong table."

"Oooh, a naughty preacher. Good, I was hoping you weren't gonna be a buzz killer. I'll introduce you to some friends of mine in a minute," she said.

"Where are we going anyway?" Daniel asked.

"A house party. There isn't much to do around here especially on Sunday night. Everything in Tall Rock closes early, Motte too."

They listened to the radio for a few minutes and then Leah turned her car into a long dirt drive lined with trees and overgrown grass. The drive eventually opened up into a yard with plenty of cars in it, Daniel guessed at least fifteen to twenty. The house was two story brick with a large wrap around front porch. They parked and walked up to the house.

Two guys and two girls stood on the porch together smoking cigarettes and talking loud above the music that thumped from inside. Leah shot them the bird and smiled as she led Daniel through the front door. The music was thumping from the living room on the right as they walked in. Two girls Leah's age were sitting on the stairs holding red plastic cups. Leah walked over to them and began a conversation as loud as she could speak. Daniel still couldn't understand anything that was said between them, so he just looked around and observed the scene. There was a large group gathered in the living room dancing. Not ballet dancing, not slow dancing, it was more like booty shaking/bump and grind type dancing. Daniel had seen this before at parties and dance clubs but he'd never partaken in it.

'Stand up orgy with clothes, all while people watch. It would take a lot of booze to get me involved in that,' he thought.

It was as if Leah had heard his thoughts, "Want a drink?" She asked.

Daniel, not wanting to be a stick in the mud said, "Sure, whatever you're having."

She took him by the hand and led him into the kitchen. The room was littered with drunk youth and plastic drink cups. She pulled him over to two guys leaning against the countertop and left him standing there with them. There was a moment of awkward silence while they sized each other up.

"Hi, I'm Daniel," He almost had to shout above the music. He offered out his hand to the guy standing on the right to shake.

"Terry." They shook and then he shook the other guy's hand.

"Hey, I'm Elmo. This is my place."

Terry and Elmo both had on blue jeans. Terry had on a football jersey, Elmo had an MMA printed tee. Neither one looked any older than Daniel, especially Elmo with a clean shave and blond hair on his head.

"Oh, nice place," He looked around at the large house wondering if this guy's parents were out of town for the weekend.

"Thanks, how do you know Leah?" Elmo asked.

"Well, I just met her this morning. I work for Tall Rock Baptist Church. I'm just out meeting people, learning about the town, and trying to keep her out of trouble."

The two burst out laughing.

"Good luck with that, hahaha. It's a good thing you have God on your side 'cause she's a little devil," Elmo answered.

"That's what I've been told…haven't seen it yet though."

"It's early bro, give it a few minutes," Terry mused.

Leah came back with two cups. She handed him one, "Here, this one's on me. Best PJ in the county some say."

"County?" Elmo joked, "My PJ has been voted the best in the nation three years running."

"Running? You must mean stumbling," She corrected, "Be careful, preacher, it'll sneak up on ya."

Daniel had drank PJ before at parties and heeded her warning. He'd seen people go from sober to sick in only two cups of the powerful mix. He swirled the liquid around in the cup and could feel the fruit in the bottom. 'How long have you been soaking in there?' He tasted the drink. Sweet like fruit punch, that was to cover up the grain alcohol taste. He couldn't taste the liquor in it, but he could smell it. 'Take it easy on this shit 'ole boy…the last time we got sick it caused an unwanted career change.'

"Come on Preacher, I'll give you the tour," Elmo said and motioned for Daniel to follow.

Daniel was led out of the kitchen. He glanced at Leah who waved and smiled most deviously. Elmo led him through the living room full of dancing bodies, many cutting curious glances at him. The light was dim other than a laser splitter that changed with the beat of the music. Elmo led them toward the far wall where a DJ sat at a laptop wearing headphones.

The DJ pointed to the playlist he had on the screen. Elmo eyeballed it for a few seconds and nodded in approval. Daniel felt the bass thumping through his entire body as they passed by a speaker tower. The two youths had to weave through the crowd to make it out the back door and onto the back deck. Dim solar lights marked an outline of the large deck that went right up to an in ground swimming pool. On opposite sides of the rectangle pool was a slide and a diving board. Two girls and a guy were sitting beside the diving board with their feet dipped in the water. Daniel sipped his drink cautiously as he took it all in.

"That's Sarah, JJ, and Bonnie. The party usually ends up spilling out here at some point," Elmo said as he led the way past them toward what looked like another house, only smaller.

"This is the pool house…" He opened one of the doors and saw a teenage couple involved in one another.

"Jesus Christ, Leo! There's a couch right there!" He pointed at an empty sofa. Daniel peered in to see what was going on. A young lady was leaning back on top of a pool table in the center of the room, her legs spread wide. Her gentleman lover had a hold on each of her legs and had his face buried in between them. Both of them were completely nude and looked up like a couple of deer in headlights.

"If there's one stain on my pool table I'm gonna rip off your dick and beat you with it!" Elmo said and closed the door in disgust, shaking his head at Daniel.

"Everybody wants to fuck in the pool house, so I put a couch out there. They don't use it! They use the pool table and then pass out on the couch after."

"It's all about the seduction," Daniel said and took another drink from his red plastic cup, "The guy says 'Hey want to go shoot a game of pool?' The girl knows what he's up to, just she's a slut and wants to tell her friends about how she fucked on a pool table."

Elmo stood with his arms folded thinking about what Daniel said. "Yeah, I guess fucking on a couch isn't a very hot story to tell. Only I'm the one trying to sink the eight ball tomorrow and can't concentrate for thinking that I'm resting my hand on a puddle of dried jizz."

"What you need," Daniel paused to think, "Is a decoy. Something that they'd rather do it on than the pool table, maybe like a trampoline or a weight bench."

"That's pretty clever, a decoy."

"Well, even easier, lock it. It is your place right?" Daniel suggested.

"I could but then people see me as the asshole that doesn't trust them and that ain't good for business. The only thing I lock is my bedroom."

"Business?" Daniel asked.

"Girls, that's the reason I throw parties. I wouldn't do this just for my buddies, I'm interested in getting laid too. Come on I'll show you the rest."

They walked around the side of the house and went into the garage through a small door. A sports car and a motorcycle were waiting quietly in the darkness. Daniel could tell his host was checking on his property more than he was giving a tour.

"Must take a lot of work and money to throw a party like this. How often do you have them?"

"Usually have a bigger one than this the first Friday of the month. This one was just kind of random. It's not really expensive unless I try to feed 'em or book a band, and I can afford it."

They went back inside through the laundry room. The washer and dryer had at least a week's worth of Elmo's clothes piled in front of them on the floor. There was a secondary staircase that led upstairs from the laundry room. Daniel looked up and deduced that Elmo would drop his dirty laundry from the second floor into the pile.

"The maid's on vacation," Was all Elmo muttered, and pushed open the swinging door that led to a formal dining room that looked like it had never been used before. Then another left and they were back in the kitchen.

It looked like more people had arrived.

"Well that's the gist of it," The host made it clear he was through playing tour guide.

"What, no upstairs?" Daniel joked.

"Nawww, I don't take guys upstairs. You'll have to find a girl and go exploring yourself, haha," He chuckled, "Oh shit, I'm probably going to hell for telling you that aren't I?"

"Well, that's not my call…but if you do go to hell, you're going in style," They both had a good laugh and Elmo went towards the front door.

Leah was nowhere in sight. 'Oh boy, what is she into now?' He set his drink on the counter and casually eased into the living room. The music was still blaring out party music. Two girls dancing together began making out. They received a roar of approval from guys and girls alike. Both girls raised their cups over their heads as if to say, 'The PJ made us do it!'

It took Daniel a few seconds to take his gaze off the tongue tasting teens and search for Leah. It wasn't easy to spot her with the crowded room and light show going on. She was sandwiched in between two equally fine girls and all three were dancing their asses off. One of her dance partners tipped Leah off that she was being watched, she looked over and waived for Daniel to come dance.

He knew his dancing skills were limited. He'd embarrassed himself on a date one time trying to dance cool. The girl he was with that night had told him a formula for booty dancing. 'Bend your knees a little, put your arms in the air and move your hips not your feet. Let the girl do the moving, if you feel uncomfortable get closer.'

Daniel remembered that advice as he made his way through the mob of bodies. When he got there they immediately surrounded him grinding on his body from three sides, Leah was directly in front of him. She turned around, half bent over and started rubbing her ass on his crotch. He wrapped his right arm around her waist and began to grind to the same rhythm like they were doing it doggy style. She looked back and gave him that devious smile. She was trouble, and he knew it.

Chapter 20: Don't Fuck with Frank

Reverend Catoe's truck was old but over the years he'd taken care of it. Still, with over three hundred and twenty thousand miles on it rattles and squeaks came with the territory. It was charging down Kenia River Road, the motor roaring like it hadn't done in years trying to close the gap on Pastor Gilmore's luxury sedan. Frank wasn't burning his headlights and his truck was just a dark shadow at eighty-five MPH. It was a clear sky that night and enough moonlight to drive by. He'd driven that road a million times and could have closed his eyes.

It wasn't long before he could see the Pastor's tail lights. Frank recognized the license tag that read [PRAYER]. There weren't any other cars on the road that time of night, only the wolf and his prey. He took a swig from the bottle of brandy clinched between his legs. Frank closed the gap on his unsuspecting foe but stayed far enough back where Larry Gilmore wouldn't notice him in the moonlight.

He waited for the right moment and began to accelerate hard. Just as they entered a slight right curve Frank's truck bumper struck the car in the right rear and knocked it out of control. It slid sideways and flipped when its tires caught the ditch on the far side of the road. Frank locked up his brakes after the impact and skidded to a halt on the highway shoulder. Frank was shaking a little from the mix of adrenaline and fear he was feeling. He turned on the headlights and wheeled the truck around to point them at the demolished sedan.

It had rolled twice before it struck a pine tree with its roof which folded like aluminum foil. Frank put his truck in park in the middle of the road and got out with his bottle of brandy. He approached the car, which was resting on its left side pinned against the splintered pine.

Most of the windshield was gone, he could hear Larry moaning. Frank took his cell phone out of his pocket and turned on the light. The pastor was wearing his seatbelt and might have been alright if a tree branch hadn't been sticking through his abdomen. It had pierced through the airbag, went in just below his belly button and was coming out of his right ribcage. Blood was gushing out from both directions. Somehow the Pastor remained conscious; he grasped the tree limb where it entered his belly as if he could push it back out.

"Sorry Larry. Business is business." Frank said, feeling little remorse for the suffering man.

Larry could barely get out a whisper, "Help me Frank." He was fighting for air with every breath.

Frank had seen enough movies to know that this man was done for. Not only was he bleeding to death, but the tree limb was through his lung. Larry Gilmore's lungs were filling up with blood and eminent death was not far away. Frank got in close, nearly inside the cab and felt around the pastor's jacket pockets until he found the digital voice recorder. It's all he really wanted but making the Pastor suffer seemed like a bonus. He thought back to what Larry had said before leaving his office. 'You really believe that shit?'

"Nope, I'm afraid there's no helping you. And to answer your question from earlier, I don't believe in that shit. You aren't going to heaven or hell. Your life is about to be over for good. They'll bury you behind your church and your body will rot and that's it."

The reverend didn't let the sermon sink in long. He hit Pastor Gilmore on the temple with what was left of that fine bottle of brandy. The hit was so hard the bottle shattered.

It was the second time in his life Frank had committed murder and this time it didn't seem to bother him as much.

Chapter 21: Party Time

Just after midnight Deputy Wainwright pulled over a car for speeding. It was his nephew Chris' girlfriend, Alisha, and two of her friends. He offered to give her a warning if she told him where they were coming from. She happily spilled her guts, "Elmo's house, he's having a party.'

As promised he let them go. That info made his night have some purpose. He received incentive bonus for every DUI and drug arrest he made after midnight and a party would surely lead to a bust. He knew Elmo lived in his father's house out on Terry Branch Road. Most of the kids leaving the party would head east toward Tall Rock. The rest would go west toward Motte and their homes in the county.

He smiled while walking back to his patrol car. He rarely smiled and meant it. Tonight he was going to have fun scaring the hell out of teenagers. He put his law dog face back on and whipped his car around to go find a hiding spot near Terry Branch Creek.

Somewhere in the back of Daniel's mind alarm bells were going off, this was muffled however by the thump of the bass speakers and the techno mix that seemed to be pouring from inside him. He danced like a possessed nymphomaniac, spanking girl's asses and holding them by the hips. They were doing their best to corrupt his reserved image he had previously owned.

The DJ blended the songs right so there was no silence in between. Beth, one of the three girls who'd been grinding against his body, wrapped her hands behind Daniel's neck and then jumped wrapping her legs around his waist as well. He instinctively grabbed her ass to support her and before he realized it her tongue was in his mouth, attacking forcefully to make him respond. His joined the battle and lashed back wildly, their moist lips locked except briefly to change how their heads were tilted. The music had started again and he was oblivious other than to his instinctive foreplay.

How long had it been since he'd made out with a girl like this? Somewhere through the deep fog of his mind, came a memory of pain roaring at him like a freight train…and BOOOOM! It hit him so hard he almost dropped his dance whore Beth. The Play scene, vomiting down Mary Ann's throat, the humiliation….

'Holy Shit, I'm FUCKED UP!' He pulled his lips away from hers so he could find some air. She began to kiss on his neck. His body was pouring sweat and tingling all over.

'What the hell is going on?' He thought desperately for an answer to why he was feeling and acting as he was. 'PJ must have snuck up on me, no more of that, I've got to get straight.'

He lost that thought upon the silhouette of a girl in the laser lights. She moved close to him and he felt lips against his. This time they were softer than Beth's (who was still kissing on his neck). Her kisses were more seductive, making him almost melt. Her tongue eased into his mouth gently and he met it with anticipation. Despite not being able to see the new kisser in the untamed lighting he could somehow sense that it was Leah. For almost a minute their tongues were rubbing together while the dance around them pumped on. Then at the same time the two females retracted from him and started making out with each other, Beth still in his clutches and Leah standing right beside them both. He was lost in a place his brain had never traveled, where his wildest fantasies seemed boring in comparison.

Rational thought was not functioning for the logical young man, but his feelings were amplified like never before.

He could only watch and hope that they would remember him. They did. Beth dismounted and they both kissed him on the cheek before they left him there and walked toward the kitchen. Thoughts were becoming harder for him, and breathing too. His lungs had been working harder than he was used too. Mopping his brow wasn't enough, he needed cold air. He took off toward the door Elmo had used earlier to go to the back yard.

Outside was such a relief to him. The music was cut to a dull boom-boom-boom. The girls had unbuttoned his shirt halfway down and a cool breeze massaged his open skin.

Leah, Beth and Emily watched him through the kitchen window. Daniel walked off the pathway and raised his arms like a sail catching wind. He then proceeded to spin around in circles, looking up at the sky.

"Damn he's messed up," Emily said, "How much did you give him?"

"I put a sugarfoot in his PJ. And I'm glad I did, He's gonna be buck wild tonight ladies," Leah boasted.

Beth asked, "You mean you just roofied a preacher boy?"

"Not exactly. It's a hit of acid and a pinch of coke."

They all stood watching and laughing until he stopped spinning and threw up on himself.

"Oh damn it!" Beth said, "You gave him too much, now look at him." She went in search of Elmo to inform the host of what was going down.

Daniel was on all fours heaving up the liquor and fruit cocktail. His feelings were intensified and he was disgusted with the vomit on his face, neck and chest. He rocked back to his knees and ripped open the last four buttons on his shirt and tossed it aside.

Back at the window Leah, Emily, and other party goers were watching intently. They knew they should go settle him down but it was like watching a train wreck, they couldn't pull their eyes away. Next he stood up on one foot and tore his shoe off, then staggered and did the other. Leah knew what was going to happen next and sure enough the belt came loose, the button unbuttoned…

"Oh my god," Emily said.

…The fly unzipped, the pants and boxers came down, then off, and his dick was flopping in the wind. There was the Reverend Catoe's new assistant butt ass naked in the back yard, the flood lights giving everyone a free show. Without wasting any time Daniel ran and jumped through the air spread eagle, he belly-flopped into the deep end of the swimming pool, narrowly missing the diving board with his head.

Word was spreading fast that there was something going on in the back yard. Most people had quit dancing and were looking out the windows at the pool waiting on him to surface. He didn't, he was sinking to the bottom. After a few seconds the back door opened and concerned onlookers flocked out to the edge of the swimming pool. All they could see was his dark body at the bottom of the pool motionless.

"He's gonna drown!"

"Somebody save him!" Leah shouted.

Every looked around to see who was going to volunteer. It took a couple of seconds but two guys started emptying their pockets and taking off shoes. One jumped in and then the other but not long after Elmo came barreling out the back door.

"GET OUT THE WAY!!!" He jumped in from the shallow end like a torpedo and swam down following the bottom of the pool.

The first two rescuers reached him at about the same time. Each took an arm and began swimming toward the surface. Elmo grabbed him around the waist and got the preacher boy's head above water.

In actuality Daniel wasn't unconscious; the entire time he'd spent under water had been less than a minute. He was just enjoying the cool water, eyes closed to avoid the sting of the chlorine and mouth wide open so the vomit taste would wash away.

When his clothed rescuers got him above water he took a deep breath of air and then yelled, "Marco!" His eyes remained closed.

Everyone was quiet for a moment, shocked that he could shout and that he wasn't going to need CPR preformed on him.

Daniel was surrounded on three sides much by the guys that were treading water holding him up, much like the girls who had just been dancing with him. By this time everyone was outside surrounding the pool watching in awe.

Again in the same voice he yelled, "Marco!"

"Polo!" Answered a guy in the crowd.

Immediately Daniel turned toward the sound and splashed as if he was swimming after 'Polo'.

"Marco!" again was his verbal radar.

"Crazy son of a bitch," Elmo said and dunked him underwater with disgust.

Daniel didn't want to get out of the pool but they finally coaxed him into the shallow end. Elmo began to question him about why he was naked in the pool to begin with, but was interrupted by a scream. Sarah Tolson was pushed into the deep end by her brother Marc, but then Sandy saw her opportunity to push Marc in but they became tangled and both ended up splashing in on top of Sarah. They all began to take off shoes and most of their clothing in anticipation that everyone was about to be thrown in by someone stronger. A couple of people who didn't want to get wet darted back onto the back porch.

The rest played like children, ganging up on one person to toss them in the pool. Eventually Michael Matthews was standing alone triumphantly on the side of the pool, satisfied with winning the game. He stripped down to his underwear, let out a coyote howl and did a cannonball into the middle. His splash was barely noticed amongst the chaos.

The DJ who had remained inside opened up a couple of windows and pointed the speakers outside toward the new party spot. He also turned off the flood lights and Elmo turned on the interior pool lights.

The dance party was even sexier than before, with wet clothes being discarded to show more skin. They were making the water come up over the edge of the pool and spill over onto the walkway around its edge.

Daniel sat naked on the steps of the shallow end, holding onto the hand-rail with a death grip. Leah came and sat beside him. Her jeans and tank-top were on the grass, all she had on was her bra and panties. Not much was visible in the pool. The two lights underwater gave off just enough light to see.

Leah felt like she had won her twisted game too easily. She had made the new Preacher-boy act like an idiot the first night out.

...But then would anyone notice if she gave him a hand-job under the water?

Chapter 22: A Midnight Marathon

Hallucinating was a new concept to Daniel. The night above him was moving like never before and all of a sudden he could feel them, hundreds of snakes slithering around his body in the water. He couldn't see them but he knew they were there, dozens of them getting ready to bite. He sprang out of the pool barely noticed by the others as he rolled across the yard trying to shake them off. In reality it was just water. He had to get away before they caught him. His dick was still hard from Leah stroking it underwater as he ran out of the back yard and into the woods. She watched him in the dim light, still naked as the day he was born, and wondered what kind of crazy shit he was imagining.

The moonlight lit up the trees enough for him to run into them. His feet barely felt the roots and pinecones he stepped on, instead he had a new feeling. The running began to form a rhythm, a primal beat like the dance party that began to make his adrenaline pump. The air rushing across his naked wet body was intense, and then he made it to the road.

Terry Branch Road was an old country road without any street lights. It had been seven years since it had been paved last and it was in dire need of repair. Potholes were scattered like buckshot on the most abused parts, some with black patches but most without. Motte County deputy Brantley Wainwright sat parked in his patrol car on the side of the road. He was in plain view for any cars traveling out of town or to the town of Motte. Any cars traveling westbound into Tall Rock wouldn't know he was there unless he turned on his lights and gave away his position. Waiting was part of patrol life. He got plenty of sleep on slow nights like Sunday but tonight was different. Tonight he was going to bust some ass.

He opened up his black film canister, shook a bit of the powder into the canister lid and took it in one long snort. He'd been doing more and more lately, mostly from boredom. He'd first started doing cocaine at work the previous fall after he busted a guy for speeding and confiscated it. He never turned it in or charged the man with it to save on paperwork. It wasn't much anyhow, so he tried a little on his tongue. The small amount didn't have a large effect on him that night but he realized it kept him wide awake. He'd progressed from just getting a gum numb, to snorting two to three times a night, the quantity ever increasing. He looked for people who looked like drug users, pushing his limits of probable cause to search persons and property. He'd busted two dope-heads since then but they weren't his fix, he wanted the booger sugar.

Brantley's girlfriend had fixed him a lunch sack with peas, rice and meatloaf. He opened a bottle of water and looked at the brown bag of food with disgust. 'Maybe later, if I get really hungry.'

He sipped the water and flipped on the satellite radio to the hard rock station. He'd heard the song at least three times that week so he began changing the station to find something else when he saw something in the moonlight. Whatever it was had passed by him on the road without him hearing it. He stuck his head out the window and could see something moving fast. He turned on the cruiser's headlights expecting to see a deer; instead he saw the backside of a naked man running down the road. His immediate response put the cruiser in gear and chase.

Daniel Montclair was not much of an athlete but when under the influence of drugs he could run fast. His breathing got harder even though his cock had gone soft. He was running down the road, not being chased and not knowing where the road went. He was running because of the sensation he felt as the wind hit his skin. All of a sudden light from behind him pierced the night. He picked up his pace hoping the light would be left behind and he could go back to the darkness he'd grown familiar with. It only got closer, then blue lights were flashing and a voice said, "Stop running and put your hands in the air!"

It was as if he'd ordered the sun to rise. Naked man was running the bare ass psychedelic marathon and was on pace to break the world record. The car drove ahead and stopped. Deputy Wainwright got out of his car and pulled his stun gun. "This is your last warning, STOP!"

Daniel took a ninety degree turn straight at the woods just in time to miss the shot from the stun gun. The two barbs shot harmlessly at the path he'd been on.

"Shit," was all Brantly could say as he fought to find a reload pack and clip it on. By this time Daniel was tearing through briars and brush. The ground near the creek was soft and muddy in places giving him new sensations to feel between his toes. The deputy had his flashlight on and attempted to follow.

"-Unit 19, come in over."

He was only a few feet into the woods when he heard dispatch call his number. He grabbed the shoulder radio,

"Dispatch this is unit 19. I'm on Terry Branch Road in pursuit of a man on foot. He's fleeing into the woods without any clothes. I'm in need of backup and K-9 unit. Over," there was a pause over the radio.

"Negative 19, stand down and report to Kenia River Road. Vehicle struck tree between Burton's crossing and Almay court. Fire Department and EMS are in route. Over."

This caught the deputy by surprise. He was ready to pursue his suspect, not go work a wreck.

"Copy that Dispatch. Over."

Disappointed he kept shining his light after Daniel just for a few seconds before he returned to his car and took off. "God Damn car wreck," he said to himself, "They'd better be dead."

Deputy Wainwright wouldn't have had much trouble catching Daniel if he had followed him. The stoned runner tripped on a tree root less than thirty yards from the road. He went sprawling into the dirt and leaves. He lay there for minutes listening to his breathing, the beating of his heart slowing as time passed. Finally he got up and went back out to the empty road and walked back in the direction of the party. Soon after a car came down the road looking for him. The nude young man didn't try to cover himself other than to shield his eyes from the bright lights. It was Leah and Emily.

"Daniel, get in the car! You are crazy," Leah shouted at him.

He stopped walking and stood starring at them numbly.

"Get in the fucking car before a cop rolls up and sees you like that!"

Emily had to get out of the car and open the back door, "Get in," was all she had to say and he obeyed. Leah turned around and dropped his clothes in his lap.

"Dress," Once more he obliged.

Leah drove the three of them back to the house where she and her mother lived. The girl's plan was to get him to sleep and come down a little before they took him back to the church parking lot. The girls helped Daniel finish dressing and led him by each hand around to the back door. Mrs. Dixon was on the screened in back porch smoking a cigarette and nursing a glass of chardonnay.

"Well girls, just what have you done to that nice preacher boy?" Asked Mrs. Dixon.

"We didn't do anything…" Emily said.

"We went to a party and he got drunk. Then he jumped in the pool and almost drowned. Figured he needs to take a nap and sober up before I take him back to the Catoe's," Leah added.

"If he's drunk then I'm the Queen of Sheba and you're the Virgin Mary," Mrs. Dixon was speaking directly at her daughter as if Emily wasn't there at all. "You aren't taking him anywhere, you've done enough damage already," She growled, "Now put him on the couch and go. I don't care where as long as you stay out of trouble. I'll take him back to the Catoe's in a while and apologize to them."

So they led him inside and made Daniel sit back on the couch in the living room without questioning Leah's mother. She was not one to argue with, especially when she was angry and had just given them freedom to do as they pleased for the rest of the night.

Leah, in the same tone her mother had used earlier, informed Daniel he was to stay on the couch and go to sleep. He sat upright with his arms folded and closed his eyes. The girls were satisfied and left out the back door. Daniel's eyes were closed tight but he could still see hallucinations as if he was watching them on television. Some were memories of his past, only mutated and eerie. Other things he saw were brand new thoughts and images straight out of chemically scorched brain. Fortunately he'd been given a happy dose and no other baddies were out to get him.

"Well, well. Looks like my sweet little daughter has laid waste to another fine boy," The voice of Mrs. Dixon bounced around inside Daniel's head. "And part of the church no less," She took a slow sip from her wine glass, "What a stink this is going to be...Unless."

Daniel finally opened his eyes and saw her standing there by the fake fireplace with her wine. She was wearing a robe, not a long cotton one that covered her up, but a silk oriental one that showed plenty of legs and barely kept the rest in.

"Unless I make all this go away," She gave him time to respond but he only starred at her.

"Yes, I could do that. You see I control the gossip in this town. I could make tonight the most talked about night for years to come. 'The night our Reverend's new disciple went buck wild'. All I have to do is make a phone call and a couple of texts and you wouldn't be able to show your face in public without the Catoes both blushing from embarrassment. OR, I could just brush all this under the rug, shine the spotlight on someone else and your little escapades go unnoticed," She took another drink of wine.

"You'd like all this to go away wouldn't you?" She asked him.

He nodded in agreement. She had no idea of all the hallucinations he was experiencing.

"I'll make it happen, if you make me happen," She smiled.

She was looking naughty and Daniel was still starring at her intently. She used her free hand to untie the knot on her robe, then gently set her wine on the coffee table between her and Daniel. She grabbed the collar of her robe and pulled it apart slowly from the top, exposing her bare breasts. They were large and perky for a woman her age. She walked around the table and let the rest of the robe fall away, she was wearing a pair of skimpy black panties and nothing else.

Pushing him against the back of the couch gave her room to straddle him cowgirl style.

"You're going to have to please me, not just yourself. I want my eyes pop out of my head you fuck me so hard," she said.

For the second time that night Daniel got undressed and let his instincts take over.

Chapter 23: Hide the Evidence

With the voice recorder tucked away in his front shirt pocket, Frank drove home almost as fast as he'd been pursuing the late reverend Gilmore. Fear had his adrenaline spiking to near the point of losing control. It was the same feeling he'd had over twenty years ago, the night he'd been smuggling dope and murdered an Alabama D.E.A. agent. He'd seen enough cop shows to know that there was always evidence the criminal didn't realize they'd left behind. He asked himself questions and tried to answer them as he went.

'Were there skid marks on the road? Larry's definitely. I don't think I left any unless it was while stopping.'

Are my fingerprints on the bottle? Yes, the bottom I smashed on his face but the top could have my prints on it.

'Did Larry tell anyone he was going to see me? His wife possibly? A close friend? Shit there isn't any way for me to know!'

'Can his car or phone be traced back to my house or church? I didn't see him use his phone but the in dash GPS on his car might have updated his location.'

'How can I cover up the damage on my truck? I didn't hit him very hard but there has to be some damage. No one would ever tell his car was hit in the rear as many times as it rolled.'

'Did anyone see me? I didn't see any cars on the road. Elizabeth was probably watching television or sleeping by now. I don't think there could have been any witnesses.'

'Will anyone get there and possibly save him before he dies? Not unless they showed up with a gallon of blood and an IV, he was mostly dead when I hit him…Hell, he might have died of instantly the way I brained him.'

I wasn't long before Frank was rolling in to his driveway. He swung around the side of the house and drove back to the shop in the back yard. The motion light came on as he parked and got out to look at the damage to the bumper. It wasn't that bad, just bent the chrome in on the passenger side toward the tire. He cussed thinking how visible he was at such a suspicious time of night.

He slipped the shop key off of the ring and left the truck running while he went inside to find a chain. Once he found it and gently set it in the passenger seat of the truck to avoid making much noise and he drove off for the tree line. He knew exactly which tree he wanted to use as an anchor. It was an old live oak on the edge of the woods, at least two centuries old. He wrapped the chain around the base of the tree and attached it to itself with the hook on the end. The other end he hooked around the bumper beside the tire. Then he backed up gently to take all the slack out the chain, and then gave it a tug or two. He got out and looked. Sure enough, the bend was gone, only a small crease in the metal showed where it had been damaged from the collision.

Elizabeth Catoe had hobbies like any other housewife. Playing phone games, gossiping, following primetime dramas. The gossiping was actually her favorite thing. Seeing the real drama play out was the most satisfaction she could achieve. She often sat up late scouring the social sites looking for fresh news or clues to secret relationships. She and Frank didn't wait on one another to go to bed. Usually he went to sleep before her shows ended but she knew tonight he'd be up waiting on Daniel to return home. It was late. She was checking out the latest status updates on her tablet when she saw it was nearly one in the morning. She would have normally turned in hours ago but was also waiting for the young house guest to come back from his date.

Elizabeth being close friends with Jane Dixon, knew the kind of dangerous fun that Leah and her wild friends would be up to, so Daniel coming in with fresh gossip was highly probable. Getting that gossip out of him might prove to be tricky. Leah told her mother anything she heard that wouldn't get her or her friends in trouble, but Daniel wouldn't have such a maternal bond to her just yet. She had just turned the television off when she heard a vehicle move past the side of the house. She got out of her recliner and peered through the blinds. It was just Frank messing around with his old truck, probably also waiting on Daniel.

She got a message from Tony. He wanted to know when they could meet up again, this time at his new apartment in Motte. She was falling hard for Tony. Frank was old news, she just had to figure out how to leave him.

Chapter 24: Take it or Leave it

It took several hours for Daniel to have complete control of his brain. He kept having mini hallucinations and dumb moments, partly from the drugs leaving his system but also from his lack of sleep. He was riding in the passenger's side of a car. He looked over at the driver who was very familiar to him, a woman in her forties, hair down and messy, wearing a tee-shirt and sweatpants; it was Mrs. Dixon he remembered.

"Where am I?" was all he could think to ask her.

"He does speak. Why I would have thought your tongue was missing if I hadn't felt it inside me earlier." She said with a smile. "You don't remember much do you honey?"

Daniel was silent.

"You and my daughter Leah went out to a party, and you got so drunk you took off your clothes, jumped in the pool and then ran down the highway until they picked you up."

Daniel groaned with disgust at what he was hearing knowing it was the truth.

"Oh but it got better for you, you creep!" She added, "The girls brought you home and you raped me." She was still smiling but was using an angry tone, "And the only reason you aren't in a police car right now is because I'm such good friends with Elizabeth and

Franklin, and they would be so embarrassed they might shut down the church and move away. And here I am driving you home…" She shook her head.

Daniel was stupefied. 'I raped her? Jesus Christ, what the hell is going on?' He remembered going to the party, then getting the PJ. Then it was darker and harder to go back to. Elmo's laundry room, dancing, the pool. His feet and legs were sore which made him believe the running part. Then he thought about his junk and how it was sore too. While that could have been from flapping around while he was running he doubted it. His balls had that empty, sore feeling like he'd been whacking-off all day. Then he remembered being in her bed humping away like a porn star…she'd been screaming with pleasure.

"If anyone was raped it was me," He said.

"Yeah, sweet Mrs. Dixon doped up a college boy and raped him. Sounds real believable doesn't it?" Daniel cursed her gender because he knew she was right. No one would believe him over her especially since he'd only been in town a matter of days. Even Frank couldn't really testify to his character having known him only a week.

"I've got you by the balls on this and there's only one way to keep me from smearing your name through the mud," She was back to smiling.

Daniel cocked his head to the side, "And that is?" He thought she was going to demand he pay her money.

"I want more. I haven't been fucked that good in twenty years…maybe ever," Daniel was thrown off by this request.

She continued, "Not anytime soon, maybe in a week or two. I can set it up for you and Leah to go out again and we can fool around afterwards. That is, unless you want me to start spreading rumors that you're into little boys and have herpes."

"What the hell? This is extortion!" He got loud to try and argue with her, "Do you really go to church or are you just there to meet guys to screw with? I mean damn, I'll be glad to buy you a bottle of wine and a vibrator, the most powerful one they make! Just leave me alone PLEASE!"

"First off, I go to church because it's the social outing where all the gossip flows. People watch what they say on the web, but look them in the eye and they'll tell every secret they know. And toys aren't just the same as a man's touch…his thrust," She added and rubbed on Daniel's leg

Only the noise of the car kept it from being completely silent. She drove on down Kenia River road until they saw emergency lights. Blue and red strobes pierced the sky almost blinding for anyone to look directly at them. As they pulled closer they could see a car flipped over on the shoulder of the road against a tree, firemen were cutting open the roof with Emergen-Shears trying to get inside the vehicle. Deputy Wainwright directed Mrs. Dixon around the fire truck with the beam of his flashlight and they drove on past rubbernecking.

"So here's what your story is. You and Leah went to Emily's house and had dinner. Then you both rode around and she showed you around the town and you didn't realize quite how late it was because the clock in her car is broken," She lied so easily.

"And then what?" Daniel asked.

"She drove you home in my car because hers was almost out of gas," Mrs. Dixon replied.

"I mean what's next?" He said frustrated at the whole situation.

"Well I'm going to tell Frank and Elizabeth how much of a gentleman you are and how you managed to keep Leah out of trouble for once. They won't have any problem with you taking her out again."

Daniel could only sigh. The car pulled up in the church parking lot and Daniel got out.'What a night.' He thought.

Not knowing if the house was unlocked he decided to go by Frank's office. The light was on and the door was open so he went in, no Frank. There weren't any lights on in house and the front door was locked so he walked around back thinking he'd rather sleep on a church pew than have to wake someone up at this hour. When he turned the corner of the house he saw Frank at the shop in the back yard leaning under the hood of his truck with a droplight. Daniel walked out to speak with him.

"Hey Frank, sorry I'm getting in so late."

"Oh that's alright. How'd your night go, good?" The reverend asked while wiping his hands with a rag. He looked tired.

Daniel didn't want to lie; he paused for a few seconds with his lips pressed tight together.

Frank cut him short before he could answer, "Whatever happened will be fine. You can tell me about it tomorrow. Let's go to bed, it's been a long day."

Chapter 25: Rough Morning

As usual the dawn broke over Tall Rock and Franklin Catoe was drinking his coffee on the porch. He was thinking and reliving the events of the night before over and over in his mind. Deputy Wainwright came by early looking for the Reverend to inform him of Larry Gilmore's accident and ask if he'd seen him the night before. Frank said he'd had a drink with the Pastor the night before but he seemed fine to drive, he failed to mention his role in how the sedan ended up skewered by a pine tree.

Frank sounded truly upset by the news of the Larry's death and the fact that he let him drive home after having a drink, but the deputy assured him it was probably a case of the pastor falling asleep behind the wheel. The deputy left to inform the family and reflect on the strangest night he'd ever encountered since joining the sheriff's department.

Eventually he heard Elizabeth in the kitchen banging pans around. He thought this unusual for her to make anything for breakfast that required pots or pans, then he realized she was trying to wake Daniel up so she could interrogate him. He shook his head, 'Thank God she doesn't want to know what I've been up to lately.'

Daniel lay awake in bed not wanting to move. He had a splitting head ache and was also recalling the night before, trying to piece it all together. He finally got up and took a shower. After dressing he went to the kitchen in search of coffee. Mrs. Catoe had pancakes on the griddle and a pan of breakfast casserole staying warm in the oven. She began fixing Daniel a plate as soon as she saw him walk in.

"Good morning, Daniel. How did you enjoy last night?"

'She didn't beat around the bush on that one,' He thought.

"Oh, it was fine. Did a lot of hanging out with her friends, that's what my generation does best," He said.

"Where did you two go? Ride around town?" she asked him.

"Well we stopped by at one of her friend's house, and then we went to a small party and she introduced me to some of Tall Rock's model youth citizens. Then she drove me around and showed me some of the country and we stopped by her house before she brought me back here," He said hoping she would drop it but she pressed for more.

"A party? That sounds fun. What did you do there?" She set a plate of breakfast casserole down on the bar, "Here ya'are."

Daniel was pouring a cup of coffee trying to think up a vague and tame story when Frank walked in from the porch.

"Good morning Frank," Elizabeth told him.

"No," he shook his head, "It's not a good morning."

"Last night Pastor Gilmore paid me a visit. We spoke about church business and had a couple of drinks. He wrecked his car going home and was killed just down the road."

The small audience was surprised by this.

Elizabeth wouldn't say anything. She just covered her mouth with her hand. Daniel didn't know who Pastor Gilmore was and assumed it was someone affiliated with Tall Rock Baptist.

The pancakes were burning but Elizabeth ignored them. “I can’t believe….Oh poor Anabelle.”

Chapter 26: Go with It

Anabelle Gilmore, the widow of her late husband Larry, took the news as hard as could be expected. Frank and Elizabeth would make a trip to visit her that afternoon, mostly to comfort her but Frank had an ulterior motive. All night he'd been up thinking about the encounter with pastor Dixon and what loose ends might need to be taken care of before he was found out. Anabelle would be the first person Larry would have told about his plan to extort Frank and Tall Rock Baptist.

But did he tell her or was he a lone schemer? After all Frank hadn't told his wife about his plans to hire Daniel for religious justice, but how close were the Gilmore's to one another?

The pastor and his prodigy took to a shade tree on the river bank with the label of sermon study but in reality it was to explore the events of past fourteen hours. Daniel retold his tale as best he could remember, all the while waiting on Frank to start in on a lecture about church life and how clergy were to behave. It never happened; he just waited until the end and scratched his head.

"What a first date…drinking, drugs, sex. Boy I wish I was young again," Frank teased, "I knew Leah was a little whore, but I never knew she came by it so honest."

"Don't worry, it was the first and the last date I ever go on with that girl."

"But what about her dear sweet mother? You just said she wants you to make a repeat performance, or else she plans to drag your name through the mud. Or naked down the highway, whichever pleases her the most," Frank said shaking his head as if trying to clear the image from his mind.

"I don't know what to do about that. She's friends with Elizabeth, right? Maybe she could talk to her and get her to be more Christian and less of an extortionist," Daniel said.

"A lot more of that goes on around here than you would think. Extortion, that is. As for Elizabeth getting involved I don't think she would believe your story, and Jane would say you raped and threatened her. No, I believe you're going to have to do as she says for now or at least until we can think of something better."

Daniel had been positive that Frank would know the solution to his cougar problem. He cringed at the idea of being forced to have sex, but then he remembered it might not have been so bad. He was doped up and Mrs. Dixon was attractive for a woman her age. It might have been the best sex of his life, he just couldn't remember.

"What about everything else? I mean, half of the delinquent youth of Tall Rock got a first class view of my junk. I'll be lucky if they haven't already put me on the sex offender list. I bet everyone in church is gonna be snickering every time they see me from now on."

"You're right. The gossip is flowing as we speak, despite Jane Dixon thinking she can control it. The young are going to be the one it influences though. They won't tell their parents or if they do they'd never believe it happened that way. So here's the plan…Go with it."

Daniel was confused by this, "What?!?"

"Seriously, don't promote it and don't deny it, just go with it. If Brandon Jeffords says: 'Hey, Mr. Montclair, NICE CLOTHES!' What are you going to say?"

He didn't give Daniel time to respond, "You just smile and say, 'Hey Bubba, good to see you again.'"

"Now I'm not saying go wild and have a repeat of last night, but having a laid back youth minister is exactly what this church needs to bring the kids in. I'm too much like their parents for kids to listen to me and get excited about Christ."

"A youth minister, eh? Boy, what a role model I am," Daniel said

"Oh, that will be forgotten soon enough, but right now you have their attention. We need to schedule some youth programs, a trip or a play or something."

"Frank I've been wondering how many hours a week is the church in use? I mean how many hours is there people sitting in the pews or in the front yard or talking to you in your office?"

"Well," Frank thought about it, "Of course the church is open for anyone that needs refuge, but that has rarely happened. Every other Tuesday the choir meets for an hour or two. Wednesday maybe two hours for the evening service, then a few hours Sunday morning, and about the same in the evening."

"So eight or ten hours max? I could run a youth program that meets two or three times a week for a couple of hours at a time when the church isn't being used. Like Monday, Thursday, and Saturday afternoons."

"I like the idea, but you'd be working on sermons and activities every day and night," Frank stated.

Daniel posed a question to Frank, "If you were going to take a child to go see a play would it be a drama or a musical? A musical. Children get bored with a bunch of talk and no motion. They want drums and guitar to tell them a story…A story about Jesus. Then I jump in and talk, do a short sermon that keeps their attention, then we hang out and play games or something. I need the practice and the church needs more to offer. Like free daycare, a couple of the grandmothers will volunteer. It will boost attendance and not cost much."

"I knew you college boys are smart, but that is pure genius."

Chapter 27: Live from the Grave

The Catoes were on the way to visit the widow Gilmore at her home in Motte, right beside United Holy Christened Church- Motte Lutheran Branch. They didn't speak on the ride over, Elizabeth just held the pie she baked and tried to imagine what Annabelle was feeling. She wished it had been Frank so she wouldn't have to get divorced. He'd built the church that paid the bills. He cut the grass, and took care of the most everything other than housework. Still, she wanted excitement. She wanted Tony.

Frank had made sure they drove Elizabeth's car. He planned to keep his truck out of sight for a little while even though he'd done a fair job at repairing the damage from the wreck. He was on edge thinking about his upcoming encounter with Mrs. Gilmore and anyone else who might know what Larry's devious plans were.

They arrived to a packed house. Annabelle's sister Chrissie greeted them at the door. Family and friends were in the kitchen and dining room talking to one another. Chrissie led them to the back porch where Annabelle and two other women were smoking. Frank hadn't realized she was a smoker.

The widow, whose eyes were bloodshot from weeping, put down her cigarette and stood up to greet her guests. She gave Elizabeth a hug and then Frank. He was relieved she didn't shy away or act suspicious toward him.

"Thank you both for coming, it means so much to me," Said Annabelle while on the verge of tears.

"Everyone has been so nice comforting me today. I just feel lost without Larry," she covered her eyes and broke out into tears.

Elizabeth gave her another hug and held her for what seemed like an eternity while she cried. She finally stopped and had a seat to finish her cigarette. She looked at the other women smoking and they put out their smokes and walked inside, as if she had given them some kind of signal to leave.

Frank decided he would make the first move, "I'm not sure if you knew but Larry came to pay me a visit last night. That's why he was out so late. We had a long talk about the new changes to the church. Both of us were upset and we had a couple of drinks of brandy while we talked. I feel somewhat responsible for what happened for letting him drive away and get in that wreck. He seemed fine when he left but I should have made him calm down before he left…I was probably the last one to see him alive."

"Oh Frank, It wasn't your fault. Louis told me earlier that he'd had alcohol in him but it wasn't enough to affect him much," she sniffled, "He said it might have been from exhaustion or a deer running out in front of him that made him lose control. He always drove too fast and he didn't see well at night, so don't blame yourself, please."

"I'm not going to mention to anyone the alcohol then. I don't see how it would do any good to have that on Larry's memory," Frank added.

"That's a good idea," She agreed, "Could you do me another small favor reverend?"

"Of course, what can I do?"

"Steve Burgess, one of our deacons, is going to say a few words. I was hoping you could give the eulogy. You are very good at it, I've been to a couple that you've done and I know you would give Larry a good one."

"Mrs. Gilmore, I would be honored to give him the eulogy that he deserves."

The visitation was scheduled for Tuesday afternoon at Orrin-Moore Funeral Home. The Funeral at six on Wednesday at Larry's church in place of regular evening service so all the church members could make it on time. This left Frank in a bit of a bind about his duties a Tall Rock Baptist since regular Wednesday service starts at six-thirty. Frank rarely missed a service, but if he did he usually was able to let his congregation know ahead of time that it was open prayer night with singing. He decided to test the pupil with trial by fire. He'd wanted more time for Daniel to practice before he did a whole service on his own but now he had little choice.

It was Wednesday afternoon and Frank was about to leave for the Funeral in Motte. According to Elizabeth, 'Everything would be fine.' But he still had his doubts. Daniel had written his sermon all by himself. Frank only made a few recommendations or 'tweaks' as he liked to call them. It was well written but that was only half the battle. He was going it mostly alone with no backup. What would happen if he vomited at the pulpit? That was constantly in the back of Frank's mind. Some years back Frank remembered Alan Thompson bringing his two children to church because his wife Megan was home sick with a virus. Their daughter Lacy was seven at the time. She threw up on her shoes and then began crying because she realized she had what mommy had. Her five year old brother John then threw up on his father who decided he wasn't taking the kids to church alone ever again. Their vomiting caused the sermon to be cut short that morning because of the smell.

Despite his fears Frank only showed confidence in Daniel. He gave his final instructions to Daniel, "Remember, smile and be polite. You won't get applause or boos, but you can tell by their eyes. Good Luck."

He drove Elizabeth's car to the funeral, she had to stay to play the organ, greet at the door and most importantly help Daniel should he stumble. He arrived at Motte Lutheran dressed and ready to work. Mrs. Gilmore was right about Franklin Catoe was good at eulogies. He'd given forty-six in his life and Larry's made forty-seven. He was in his best suit and had a note card in his pocket with talking points just in case he forgot. He'd discussed the format the day before at the wake with senior members of the church and Annabelle. All active participants met in the office before hand to confirm all details. The plan went well, the casket was placed at the front of the church. Ernest Galloway played a slow depressing song over the speaker system. Frank noted how good it sounded for being a recording and how Ernest managed to control the sound and lights at the same time while being nearly out of sight.

Mr. Burgess began, "Friends, today is one I never thought I'd live to see. We've lost the best mentor and closest friend one could ever hope to have in this world. Larry Arthur Gilmore has been there for me and my family through the hardest of times and the best of memories. I remember when we moved here..." He finished speaking and then led a prayer.

Frank usually didn't worry before a sermon, but normally he was the home team and this was an away game. It was a packed house too. Every seat had an ass crammed into it and there wasn't much standing room along the walls. The mass of people made the church an oven. Frank had a good sweat going long before he was introduced.

"And now we all get to hear from the good Reverend Catoe, a colleague of Pastor Gilmore."

Frank had been standing off to one the side listening for his cue. He was a bit distracted, wondering if Tony Walter's cock would be in his wife's mouth while he was giving the eulogy. He walked onto the raised platform and planted himself against the pulpit. He peered out into the silent mob of mourners. Some were crying, others had normal looks on their faces, but all eyes were on him. He smoothly opened his bible to a page marked by a note-card labeled ONE. He began with John 3:13,

"Do not be surprised, my brothers, if the world hates you. We know that we have passed from death to life, because we love our brothers. Anyone who does not love remains in death. Anyone who hates his brother is a murderer, and you know that no murderer has eternal life in him."

Frank noticed a smell he hadn't been exposed to in years. The aroma of Pinch-O-Pete chewing tobacco was unmistakable and somewhere close. He scanned the crowd looking for the guilty party that was dipping in church but never saw a bulging cheek. It must have been close as well as Frank could smell it.

"This is how we know what love is. Jesus Christ laid down his life for us. And we ought to lay down our lives for our brothers."

Frank took a pause, "I'm sure I'm not the only one who wishes they could lay down our lives to save Larry's. Of course we cannot do anything to give life back to our friend; but you and I need not worry about that, and even less about his soul. I was rarely able to be in your shoes," he pointed around the room, "Hearing Pastor Gilmore at this very altar. However I have a good idea what knowledge he spread to you. Timothy 1:15, 'Here is a trustworthy saying that deserves full acceptance: Christ Jesus came into this world to save sinners- of whom I am the worst. But for that very reason I was shown mercy so that in me, the worst of sinners, Jesus Christ might display unlimited patience as an example for any who would believe him and receive eternal life'."

I was the last person to see Larry alive last Sunday night. He came to visit me as we each did from time to time, to speak of new changes and old memories. I will reflect today on some of those memories and some of those changes but I will try not to dwell on them…."

Chapter 28: A Smooth Operator

The Reverend's wife Elizabeth was excited that he wouldn't be there to give the sermon today. It wasn't that she didn't love him, she was just tired of the same old routine, never anything new. She did the greeting at the front door as people came in. Tony gave her a wink and a smile as he walked by. She knew everyone that came in and was a bit surprised to see so many young people there, including Jane and Leah Dixon and her friend Beth. At seven o'clock she shut the doors and made her way to the organ. She did a quick head count, forty-eight, that was eleven more than Sunday night. Wednesday attendance was never larger than Sunday unless it was the Super Bowl Sunday.

She leaned over and started the video camera that Frank had set up on a tripod behind her on at the organ. It was pointed at the altar and was placed so it wasn't easy for anyone else to see. Frank wanted to watch Daniel's first real performance even if he couldn't be there live. She played an intro while Daniel came out and prepared himself. He looked calm as if he'd been doing it for years. He was clean-shaved and spiffy in his suit, a fresh haircut from the day before made him feel invincible. He had his bible in front of him, notecards inside marking his verses and talking point reminders. Elizabeth finished the piece.

"Hello," He began, "for those of you who haven't met me, my name is Daniel Montclair, feel free to call me Daniel. Reverend Catoe won't be here this evening. He's giving a eulogy for the late Pastor Larry Gilmore of Motte Lutheran Church. Let me begin by telling you a little bit about myself. I'm twenty-one years old. I grew up in Alabama and attended school there. I met Reverend Catoe through a program at my school and I'll be here for some time, learning from him how to express the words of the Lord our savior Jesus Christ. You see I have been a devout Christian my whole life but this is the first real opportunity to spread the gospel to others and reach out to others through the church. Let me tell you something many of you already may know…There are many people out there who don't have a relationship with the Lord. There are millions of people that only go to church to please someone else. Those are the ones I'm not as worried about because eventually many of them finally get the message. It may take years of going to church for some people to finally get it. When you walk out those doors it's not just your life you have to lose…It's your eternal soul," he paused for effect and glanced around the room as if to search for a lost soul that needed saving.

Frank had taught Daniel that it was alright to occasionally lie in a sermon. But to only do it to make the sermon spectacular and make it so he would never get caught. The young new pastor knew this was the time to make an impression on people he'd never met. This was a time to lie, and he'd planned it well.

"Now the human beings I worry about the most are my generation and the ones to come after. So many people don't go to church because they 'Don't wanna' or 'are too busy'. I attended a public university back in Alabama, and I surveyed five hundred students for a project. Now I asked many questions to those college students but I was awed by the answers to two questions." He held up one finger, "Question number one: Before you began college did you attend church on a regular basis?"

"Guess how many," He paused, "twenty percent."

The young clergyman was really getting into character. He smiled an embarrassed smile and looked down at his feet for a moment.

"I'm a little disappointed with MY generation. I've heard my whole life 'you won't ever get a good job if you don't go to college' and they say our best and brightest get degrees and run the world. RUN the WORLD! And only forty percent of them went to church. It makes me wonder if only twenty percent of college graduates would live by the Ten Commandments. Thou shall not steal? Thou shall not kill? The only thing that keep those people from sinning is the laws of man, and the fear of punishment if they are caught."

Part of Daniels college curriculum had been public speaking, a class which emphasized hand gestures and body language. He was putting that knowledge to good use, throwing his hands up in the air, "So sixty percent of those students are at risk of not going to heaven, but I'm afraid it gets worse. The second question I asked was, 'Do you go to church now?'

"I'm not going to let you guess how many this time. I think you would be as surprised as I was. Thirty-one…..people. Out of five hundred, that just over six percent. Now how did twenty percent turn into six percent? Now this wasn't part of my project, but I was a little curious so I did some research. There were four churches within a five mile radius of campus. The one I attended had four students, including myself, from the university attend on Sunday. That's morning and evening services. I visited the other three churches over the next three Sundays and asked anyone I saw who looked like they could possibly be a student if they went to my school. Out of those four churches there were only fourteen college students. So it just went from thirty-one students down to fourteen students."

"Now the reason I had to ask everyone was because the survey was sent out randomly through the school's e-mail system. Only five hundred students were surveyed but there were over four thousand students registered for classes that semester. Now I'm not saying those people lied in that survey because not everyone makes it to church every Sunday, and of course there are many more churches that they could attend. However, many college students such as myself didn't have a car, so traveling across the county to go to church would be difficult."

"It was late August, early September so I doubt it was a flu epidemic that was keeping the students from attending church so I went out Sunday morning to find them. Maybe they were too busy studying to go to church I thought. So the next Sunday morning instead of church I visited every library and computer lab on campus. They weren't totally empty but I'd never seen so few people there. The dining halls were a hot spot though; students packed the tables, many of them still wearing pajamas or nursing hangovers. Morgan Field was a big grassy area on campus that students used for recreation. It was packed like Myrtle Beach in the summertime. Girls getting tanned, guys throwing Frisbee, people sitting around socializing with other students. Not much studying going on. Not trying to gain a relationship with the Lord," he had their attention, it was time to hit a homerun.

"But I can't say that it's their fault. Some people don't know what church is all about," Daniel got loud as if he was talking to a deaf person on the back row.

"It is up to us to change that! I haven't been here very long at all, but I'm challenging all of you right now. I want to see just what kind of people you are. The next time you come to church, whether it be Sunday morning or evening or next week; I want each and every one of you to bring someone. Someone who doesn't normally go to church. Hopefully you first think of the ones you love, friends and family."

"But all my friends and family already go to church. That's fine, bring a co-worker, bring a classmate, bring someone you barely know, bring your worst enemy. They might not be an enemy afterwards." (this drew a chuckle). "Show God that you care about other people and want to help them. Show me! Show me you care! They will enjoy it once they come. They can wear blue jeans and a t-shirt or their finest suits and dresses. We won't make them anything but welcome. They can come here whoever they are, whatever they've done. I promise to you, whether it be Reverend Catoe or myself, we won't preach for hours. It will be short and to the point and we will be surrounded by good people. If they've never been here, or to church at all, it's about time to give it a try. It can't hurt. The only thing to be afraid of is what's going to happen if they never find a relationship with the Lord. They might just find one with Satan…and nobody needs that."

Daniel had them hooked, he could see it in their eyes. Time to do something Frank never tried, he picked up the bible and started to walk around slowly. He'd had a professor who paced the classroom and claimed students paid better attention and learned more. Also walking gave him an edge, something they weren't used to.

He continued, "But temptation is all around us and sometimes gets the best of us. I'll be the first to tell you I'm not perfect. I've sinned. But my relationship with the Lord will help me through it. It's helped me see my flaws and correct them. Now let me read to you a verse about sin…"

After the funeral Frank lagged behind with Deacon Steve Burgess to field some questions. All members were curious as to the fate of the church now that the long-time Pastor was gone. Frank had addressed the issue near the end of the Eulogy by saying:

"As of right now it is undetermined who is going to head up Motte Lutheran. However the matter should be cleared up by Sunday morning when you come to church, just like you always do."

Frank realized after hearing Deacon Burgess' speech and the way he fumbled around questions, that he was much more a follower than a leader. Although many church deacons found themselves rising up to head a church Frank didn't see this man becoming a savior. There was also the UHCC to consider and the binding contract Larry had signed. Technically they owned the church, the land it sat on, and all church property. Frank wondered if the UHCC would want to appoint someone to take over as Pastor or let the church decide. Everyone had looked to Mrs. Anabelle Gilmore for answers during the funeral, but all she did was weep behind her black veil. She hadn't any answers anyway, that had been Larry's department. She hadn't even informed the UHCC of Larry's death. Mr. Banther hadn't been at the funeral and Frank wondered how long it would take him to find out about it. Frank thought this might be the first time Banther would have to make a ruling on something like this, or perhaps someone above him would tell them all who would head up Motte Lutheran Church.

The UHCC hadn't given much information on how their organization functioned. They only pushed membership, rules, and penalties for breaking those rules. Frank realized this was probably to keep people like him from finding ways to screw the system.

The old reverend didn't discuss the UHCC or his take on the issue. He merely recommended that Deacon Burgess call a meeting with the church elders for a meeting Friday evening at the church. The deacon agreed and Frank excused himself so he could go check on Daniel who in the back of his mind was on stage vomiting all over the good folks of Tall Rock Baptist.

Frank dove into his wife's car and made a bee-line for his home turf. The eulogy he'd promised the widow had been delivered. It was gracious and touching (and mostly bullshit). He'd put all his years of practice into its creation and delivery. He was worried that Daniel's inexperience must be making him do poorly by comparison. He shouldn't have put the young man in that situation yet. Frank knew his first sermon was well written, but he was concerned the execution would be just that. He thought, 'A congregation isn't looking for Shakespeare or any nonsense acting. They want a genuine, honest to goodness, bible thumping guru.'

He arrived as the first cars were leaving. Tony Walter's pickup truck was one of them. For an instant he wanted to ram his truck head-on and beat his ass afterwards, but he decided his marriage was soon to be over anyway. The church was all he had left fighting for. He pulled into his driveway and walked over. He looked at his watch; it was a little earlier than he was used to. The crowd was coming out of the front doors like they usually did.

"Well hello Reverend," said Mrs. Lorraine Hendricks, "Your new man sure did a fine job! He gave us a homework assignment too."

"Oh, did he?" Frank replied.

'Homework assignment?' He couldn't help but realize the irony in that he had just left the side of a weeping widow, and this old widow was all smiles.

He greeted more departing members when he spotted Daniel and Elizabeth talking with Charlie Earp and Leslie Goodson. They all seemed to be smiling as they spoke, which was a relief. At least no major disaster had occurred.

Charlie had seen Frank walk in, "Hello sir, Welcome to Tall Rock Baptist. I'm afraid you missed the service. It starts at seven."

Frank shook his hand and went along with the joke, "Oh is that so? Who's your arch-bishop? I'd like to meet him."

"Actually it's Pope Daniel the nineteenth, but you may call me, Your Eminence," Daniel said.

This drew a laugh from all. Jane Dixon was pretending to text on her phone while actually trying to listen in on the conversation. Everyone raved to Frank about how good Daniel's first sermon had been. Mrs. Dixon finally left but Leah and Beth were lingering by the door. Daniel excused himself to go speak with them. He hadn't seen either of them since they dropped him at Leah's house and were made to go back out for the night. The first thing out of her mouth was, "You need to get a phone, preacher."

"Oh? I do?" He mocked. They were nearly whispering. Beth just stood there grinning.

"Yeah, this whole going to church thing just to talk to you is a pain in the ass," she said.

"Well if I've ever met anyone who needs to go to church it's you two heathens," He replied.

"I'm only gonna come to church if you keep partying with us. You are freaking crazy. Do you know how many times I wanted to text you funny stuff about the other night but I couldn't?"

"I'm sure. I guess I'll just have to keep chaperoning to keep you two out of trouble."

Beth piped up, "Elmo says we have to teach you how to handle your liquor before you go off the deep end again."

Daniel smiled. It sounded like she'd rehearsed that line and delivered it a bit flat.

They both were smiling back at him, all three knowing his drink had been tainted and no one wanted to get into it while standing at the front of the church.

"So…why don't you meet us at Helen's café Friday around dark-thirty?"

He sighed, "Fine, I'm gonna go ahead and start praying now."

Frank stayed in his office the rest of the evening watching the video of the day's service that he'd missed. He downloaded it from the video camera to his computer that sat off to one side of his desk. He leaned back in his swivel chair wishing that he had a small glass of brandy to sip on while he watched. There hadn't been an opportunity to replace the bottle he and Larry had gone through.

He watched the video with a pen and paper in front of him so he could take notes of things Daniel needed to improve on. He never picked up the pen. The old reverend was too mesmerized by what he saw. Daniel was so much better live than when he practiced. It was like watching him play his part as Prince Moreau again only more exciting. Daniel added in a lot of little things that made the sermon better than it was on paper. Little pauses, expressions and hand gestures helped his character become real.

Unlike most churches, Tall Rock Baptist rarely saw a microphone in use. There was one that came with the speaker system, but Frank just didn't like to use it. He felt like his voice sounded good and was loud enough that he didn't need it either. Daniel too had good vocal chords, just not quite as deep. Occasionally he would get louder just to keep the audience intrigued. Then to Frank's amazement he watched him pick up the bible and start to slowly walk as he was preaching. Reverend Catoe stood only behind his pulpit when preaching; he felt like a rock, unmoving and solid. This rock was rolling around the church, even going off camera a couple of times, but he still sounded good.

The sermon ended and Frank sat and thought about it. It was damn near perfect according to his judging system. He grabbed the audience's attention, delivered the message, and left them wanting more. Daniel Montclair had done it right. He'd proved his worth as an actor and a preacher on his first try.

'Damn he's good. Of course he has a different style than me. Maybe I should take some acting classes. He reminds me of John Worthy.'

The last time he'd felt that way after watching a sermon, John Worthy was doing a revival in South Georgia. It was before he'd met Elizabeth, back when he was still learning the trade from Big JW, the best God-damned preacher man alive. It was beginning to look like that title was in contention. He watched the video again.

The next day he woke up smiling and earlier than usual. This so far had been one of the most exciting weeks of his life. He's introduced Daniel to his church on Sunday, met his new UHCC representative, and murdered Larry Gilmore. Monday he'd lied to the police (and everyone else) about it and went to visit the widow (who he thought might be suspicious of him). He'd worried and prepared all day Tuesday. Wednesday was a victory. Both he and his young apprentice had delivered in fine fashion.

Chapter 29: Drafted

It was Thursday morning and Frank sat with his coffee on the front porch making plans. He had to contact Deacon Burgess and make sure he'd informed the right people about the meeting at Motte Lutheran Church Friday at seven o'clock. He would contact Greg Banther himself and inform him of the situation. Frank wanted the UHCC to stay out of the day to day operations but he also realized they were running the show to some degree, or at least thought they were. Like it or not the old reverend had brownie points to earn.

During breakfast he complimented Daniel on the fine job he'd done. Frank could have gone further in praising him but he didn't want the youth to get a big head and cause him to slack off at his work. He told Daniel he was to read the bible until lunch time and work on another sermon in the afternoon.

Daniel waited until they were crossing the lawn to the church to tell Frank about Leah's plans for Friday night, "I wasn't sure if it was her or her mother's idea so I just went along with it."

Frank had all but forgotten about the fiasco Daniel had been put through by the mother-daughter ho' train.

"Go," He paused and thought. "Yeah, go. Don't drink anything, don't eat anything that girl or someone else could have fooled with. In fact be boring, a real stick in the mud. What the old folks like to call church-proper."

Frank hadn't been stern with him like this yet, "Her mother is the one we need to worry about. She's got all the power to sink you and if she is behind this 'date' be a stick in the mud for her as well. Be terrible in bed, no good whatsoever, and she just might lose interest in you too. You see last time you performed so well for each of them that they want an encore. Just suck at it."

"Trust me, I can suck. Last time it was the drugs that made me so wild. If I stay off that shit I will be my normal boring self this time."

"Good," Frank agreed, "I don't think I can take much more excitement for a while."

Frank's day progressed. He made his call to Deacon Burgess who'd left Mrs. Gilmore in charge of contacting members. Pass the buck, what a leader. She was e-mailing the senior church members about the meeting and Frank didn't blame her for not calling. While many folks might not check their e-mail it was so much quicker than calling.

Mr. Banther was on a conference call when Frank called his office, but he returned the call that afternoon.

"Mr. Catoe, what is this I hear about a dilemma at our Motte Affiliate?"

'Is that their new name? Goodbye Lutherans you're all nondenominational now!' Frank thought.

"Pastor Larry Dixon was killed in a car wreck Sunday night," He let that sink in, "I gave the eulogy at his funeral yesterday evening and didn't see you there, figured that no one had informed you."

"No I hadn't been notified," Mr. Banther was very monotone. "Does he have a replacement?" He asked.

"Well the church has called a meeting for tomorrow night at seven to discuss it. You see Larry and his wife ran that church and she can't do it by herself. There is a deacon who has talked about filling the role but isn't so crazy about the idea. Really isn't much of a leader though. He's always been a backup man. I think his real job is in a factory."

"Let me look up the numbers," Banther said. Frank could hear him clicking away at a keyboard.

"Our Motte affiliate had a preliminary attendance of seventy-nine people. That's a larger number than yours Mr. Catoe. Would you care to transfer over to Motte if the Deacon isn't up to the task?"

"No, Tall Rock is my home. I wasn't sure if you were going to let the church decide or appoint someone yourself. And what happens if no one is up to the task?"

The UHCC representative had to think on that, "Well, I guess officially it's my call who heads the church. I can let them nominate someone for a trial basis. If not, the UHCC will have to appoint someone from inside the organization. The problem is we haven't begun training anyone yet. I was on a conference call this morning and was told to look for young Christians, out of school, to be trained for roles in our organization. They are opening the UHCC Academy later this year."

"Who would train them?" Frank asked.

"It would be experts at our headquarters in Cincinnati. It's like a college. The students go for something like six months to a year. They get free room and board while studying in exchange for a work contract."

"That sounds pretty nice. This contract..." Frank paused to reword his question but Banther cut him off.

"Well if we are going to provide room and board for that long they are expected to work for a set rate for a set amount of time or they would be expected to pay for the education they received if not."

"No, I understand why they have contracts. What types of roles they will be filling?" Frank asked.

"Oh, well a variety really. We have many different positions and are creating them quicker than we're able to fill them. Worship leaders, recruiters, musicians, technical specialists for lighting and sound. They're going after the youth hard. Teenagers are the main focus. Some have jobs, which means possible revenue. They all have parents with some source of income. The church knows children are the key to building a future. I'm afraid you, Mr. Catoe, like myself are too much of an authoritative figure to draw in the youth that don't attend church."

"Oh Mr. Banther, I know I'm not a spring chicken anymore. I was thinking of my young protégé. Remember me introducing you to Daniel Montclair the other night?"

"I recall meeting him, yes."

"Well I've recruited him from a performing arts program not too long ago and I've been working with him. I had to attend Pastor Gilmore's funeral Wednesday so I let him conduct the worship service at Tall Rock by himself. HE DID AMAZING! I had the whole thing recorded and he had the crowd on the edge of their seats."

"Well Mr. Catoe, it seems like I'd better make that meeting at our Motte affiliate tomorrow to meet…whoever it is that they nominate as a replacement. I think I'd like to stop by your church beforehand and watch that video and possibly speak with your young man about furthering his career with us."

Frank felt like they were making significant strides to his goal. If he could get Daniel into that UHCC Academy they would have inside information about the organization. Information that could help him expose the corruption and how mandatory umbrella membership was stripping away the freedom of religion to all Americans.

Again he wondered how much he could really do. What difference could he make? And Daniel, could he be trusted? Could he succeed at this new college?

Frank came out of his office and just cracked the hallway door to peer in at his pupil. He was sitting eight rows back in the pews, right where the Worlitz family liked to sit every Sunday morning. He was studying the bible passages intently as if it were a suspense novel at its climax. Frank chose not to disturb him yet. He went back into his office until dinner time and tried researching the academy on the internet with no luck. By dinner time Daniel had written out one complete sermon and was working on another. Frank relayed the info Mr. Banther had just told him about the academy and his coming visit. Daniel was interested.

The next morning Frank gave Elizabeth his bank card with instructions to take Daniel to Motte and buy him another suit and a new pair of shoes. New clothes was the least Frank felt he owed him. His new apprentice had worked hard with no complaints, it was time for a payday.

Of all the things they'd discussed salary hadn't come up. Daniel understood it was coming out of Frank's own pocket and that it wouldn't be much, especially because his food and room were paid for. He really thought about how much he was worth and how much this job demanded of him. It was twenty-four seven. He had originally taken the gig as an out. A way from having to go back home to the family in shame, to hearing his father complain about all the time and money he'd wasted and why he should have been in engineering school instead. When Frank had pitched him the idea he did like it, but in reality he could have asked him to sell cotton candy at the zoo and he would have said yes. Anything to get the hell out of Alabama. That was a week ago, he was already starting to forget his old life. His classes, his apartment, the play…

Frank remembered Daniel's date night was that evening with Leah (and possibly her mother) and wanted to tell him to pick up some condoms while he was out in Motte (or as far away as possible). He couldn't just text his wife something like that. He needed to be able to contact that boy and vice-versa if he got into another bad situation. Frank called his wife and told her to go by Motte Tech Store and add another cell phone to their plan. No internet, only talk and text, he didn't mention the condoms.

Frank's dislike for social media was obvious. Nearly every other church around had a blog or network page. He felt it wasted much more time than it was worth. That was one thing he and his wife argued about on a regular basis. When they returned Daniel and Frank exchanged phone numbers and he set his new device up to charge.

"Don't give your number away to anyone unless they specifically ask you for it, mainly the Dixon's," He commanded. "Leah would bother you constantly and her mother would have you at her beck and call. If they think you are still without a phone, at least they'll have to come to church to harass you."

Only moments later they heard the new phone tweet like a bird. They looked at it. A text from Leah.

'Hey D. this is Leah…you still going tonight?'

Frank silently cursed Elizabeth. It must have been her sharing the boy's number so quickly with Jane and Leah.

"That is my wonderful wife's doing I bet," He said in contempt, "Ignore it for now."

Greg Banther, briefcase in hand, arrived at four-fifty, ten minutes earlier than he said he would. He and Frank went into the office and watched the video of Daniel's first sermon. Many times during the video Frank looked over at Banther but his expression never changed. Frank wondered if a shot of tequila would make his face change any.

"He seems well suited for a role with us. Is he vital to your operation or can he be farmed out?" Banther asked after the video ended.

'Farmed out? That kind of made Daniel sound like a rented mule.' Frank thought.

"Well he hasn't been with us very long but he's already starting to build some strong bonds with us and our members, but if it helps the organization I guess it needs to happen," Frank answered.

They called Daniel in. He and Banther sat in the two office chairs opposite Frank at his desk. Daniel was sitting in the one Larry Dixon had sat in and held a gun on Frank only days before.

Banther explained to Daniel the UHCC's interest in young men like him and their plans to start training at their academy. He handed Frank a copy of an e-mail, it read:

Attention all UHCC District Representatives,

As you may know our organization is always planning for growth and looking toward our future. Our most untapped source of revenue and membership is the teens of this country ages 13-19. They spent 4.7 BILLION DOLLARS last year on consumer goods (i.e. clothes, cell phones). The best way to get these teens to spend money in our donation baskets is to get them into the churches on their own will. They in turn will bring their friends and siblings and our business can continue to grow.

However we need fresh young faces enticing them to participate. We need young men and women ages 18-25 to step into new roles we are creating that are aimed in bringing these teens in the doors. We are now taking applications for our UHCC Academy in Cincinnati, Ohio. The Academy will be held every semester starting this fall. One semester completes the program. Candidates recommended by district representatives must fill out an application. The form is 00179-LH2 available at our website. Those candidates selected from those applications will then take an over the phone interview.

If we then select them for the Academy they must agree to a contract that binds them to work for the UHCC for at least two years at a set salary that varies by job and qualifications. In return they will receive a fully paid tuition, a room (possibly shared), and one meal a day from our cafeteria. Students who fail to finish the semester for any reason are required to repay the prorated amount of their expenses. Failure to repay will cause the debt to be assumed by their sponsoring church. Every student that completes the program will earn a monthly discount in membership fees for their sponsoring church for the length of their contract.

Applicants should be between the ages of 18 and 25, have at least a high school education, and be excited about Christianity. They must have a sponsoring church that is in good standing with the UHCC financially. DO NOT publicly advertise this as space in the academy is limited. WE ONLY WANT THE BEST! You are our talent agent and will receive a bonus for every student that completes the Academy. If you know someone who fits please speak with them about this opportunity.

Blessed, Elijah Norwood

Frank gripped that paper in between his thumb and middle finger ever so tightly as he read it. That inter office memo was exactly the type of hard evidence that wasn't meant to be copied and seen by the public. It would expose the greed of the UHCC and their lack of religious ambition. He set the paper on his desk hoping Banther would forget about it, but he didn't. The old man picked it up and handed it to Daniel who also carefully read it. He handed it back to Banther who slid it back into his brief case.

"Well Mr. Montclair, are you interested in going to this academy?" Banther asked.

Daniel and Frank had already had that discussion, the promotion was key. Frank was too old to climb the corporate ladder and Daniel was his fountain of youth.

He answered as Frank had coached him to. "I would love the opportunity to represent Tall Rock Baptist at the Academy Mr. Banther. I just started preaching the other day and it made me feel so good to share the teachings of the lord with-"

"Wonderful, wonderful," Banther cut him off. He looked to Frank, "And Mr. Catoe, will Tall Rock Affiliate endorse this young man?"

"Of course," Frank nodded. He felt sure Daniel could pass whatever course work the instructors gave him. However he was still learning the bible and he had just dropped out of college over one bad experience. What was the price of tuition if he failed to complete the semester? It would fall back on Tall Rock, his sponsoring church, if he didn't pay it. Still it was a risk that had to be taken.

"And how do you feel about being an interim worship leader at our Motte affiliate until we find a replacement for Mr. Gilmore?" Banther asked.

He and Frank hadn't talked about that possibility. He looked to Frank who himself was debating the idea.

Banther added, "That is if no one in Motte steps up or is qualified. I saw your Wednesday sermon and I feel sure you could handle the services. If you have any questions on paperwork or procedure I'd only be a phone call away."

"This would just be temporary you say?" Frank asked.

Banther nodded, "Until we could prepare a more permanent leader. Maybe a member at Motte who can be trained over time. By the time he goes to the academy it should be handled."

They all agreed that Daniel was ready to give it a try. Banther produced another document from his briefcase and set it on Frank's desk. It was form 00179-LH2 (Academy application).

"Fill this out so I can send it in for you," Banther insisted.

"What?" Frank asked. He'd been daydreaming of ways to kill Mr. Banther without leaving any evidence.

"The form. Go ahead, take care of it," Banther said tapping his finger on the first page.

Frank and Daniel each filled out their parts of the form and handed it back to the professional gentleman sitting before them. Then the meeting was over and it was time to go to another one.

Chapter 30: The Motte Affiliate

Deacon Steve Burgess was wearing a suit and sitting outside the church doors in a folding chair when the Tall Rock guests showed up. Frank, Daniel, and Elizabeth were followed by Banther who drove himself ever so slowly and carefully. Motte Lutheran was larger and newer than Tall Rock Baptist. About five years before Larry had pushed hard to collect the funds necessary to have it remodeled bigger and better than it had been. The outside was brick. Pale grey not bright red like most others. It had the classic cathedral design, meaning it looked like a cross from the sky. Maybe pastor Gilmore wanted to make sure God knew it was a church and not just another brick building people prayed in. The design also looked good in aerial photos.

Frank introduced everyone to Deacon Burgess and they made small talk until the others arrived. Mrs. Gilmore walked over from her house next door as more cars drove in and parked. She was wearing a nice floral print dress and flats. Her eyes weren't red as they had been lately. She had finally run out of tears earlier while talking with her attorney. Five other cars showed up bringing a total of eleven church members. All of them were over fifty and had been with the church for years and years, many since the beginning. The crowd didn't go into the main prayer room. Instead they walked into a room on the east side of the church. It was filled with long rectangle tables and folding chairs set up so they all could look at one another.

Banther didn't say anything right off. He just let them go right ahead with their meeting. Everyone sat down except for Mrs. Gilmore.

"As you all know, Larry and I started this church nineteen years ago. It was mostly Larry, I was just here helping when I could. Now that he's gone I can't do his job, we have to figure out what to do…what becomes of Motte Lutheran Church? Our biggest problem is who could replace him?" She had a seat and let the conversation take off.

An elderly man with a full head of white hair said, "I can help with things. Organizing, setting up music and lights…But I'm not a preacher."

Two other gentleman had a similar notion. They could help behind the scenes but wouldn't have a speaking part near the pulpit.

Frank was watching Banther. Mr. Banther was watching Deacon Burgess who was silently waiting and hoping for someone to save him from having to take the preaching job. Finally all the members had piped up except for him.

"Well help is something anyone who heads a church will need. I can't devote as much time as I'd like because of my job and all, but I could do the sermons and-"

"That won't be necessary," Banther cut in. He stood up and straightened his jacket. "For those of you whom I haven't met, my name is Greg Banther. I'm your regional representative from the United Holy Christened Church. The UHCC reserves the right to appoint delegates to available positions within the church. I am appointing Mr. Daniel Montclair as your new worship leader for the time being."

"Who?" Deacon Burgess asked.

"That would be me sir," Daniel raised his hand as if he was back in school, "I've been training under Reverend Catoe."

The deacon ignored Daniel and continued speaking to Banther. "So you're just going to give the job to a kid we've never even met?" His tone became harsher as he went on. "Without even asking the members what we think?"

"Yes," He replied coolly, "It's obvious that you aren't ready for this kind of commitment right now," He pointed to Daniel. "He is."

The Deacon was turning red, embarrassed that this outsider was telling him how things were to be done.

"That's fine. Whenever you two show up we'll just lock the doors and go on about our business. And how many dues do you think we'll pay you then?" the deacon was fuming.

"This church and property it is on now belongs to the UHCC and if anyone gets locked out it will be you sir," Banther said.

This made the crowd grumble under their breath a little.

He continued, "Now Reverend Catoe here is going to be helping Mr. Montclair from a religious standpoint. I will be helping with policy and compliance. It would be a show of good faith if you all would help him in all other aspects. Services will be held at their normal times. I'm leaving for now. I will return Sunday morning to a normally functioning church or there will be more changes."

He calmly picked up his briefcase and walked out of the room and down the hall.

The room was silent. Everyone was looking at one another. They were all stunned by what he had said and his brisk departure, few knew how to react.

Frank broke the silence, "Mr. Banther is just a businessman. He isn't much of a people person and we don't like him or what he represents…But, we have to do his bidding. Even if we don't like it."

Deacon Burgess was furious and stormed out of the room. There was another round of grumbling amongst the old folks as they complained and slowly made their exit. Mrs. Gilmore stayed to show Daniel and the Catoes around. She gave him a spare key that unlocked most of the doors and another for the office that still had Larry's things in it. They stayed for a while, talking about aspects of the church and the UHCC policy.

Chapter 31: Threads

Daniel Montclair, Prayer Leader of Motte Affiliation of the United Holy Christened Church. It was a title he fell into but one which he was well suited for. Membership was at an all-time high as rumors of his late night escapades lured in rotten youth from all over. He still lived with Frank and Elizabeth, still studied his bible and practiced sermons daily. He filled the old shoes of Larry Gilmore and then some. Mrs. Gilmore and other church members did their part and helped him with the chores of running a church, bill paying and paperwork mostly. A couple nights a week he met with Leah Dixon. It was a weird situation for them because they had a thing for each other. When it was just the two of them alone Leah would pick and flirt, but if they were with her friends she would act like she was to cool to be getting chaperoned by a preacher boy. They hung out with her friends and Daniel did his best to be 'church proper'. He never ate or drank much when he was around her, just in case she tried to roofie him again. They would have a good time together then later in the evening he would fuck her mother. Leah never mentioned it and neither did Daniel, but he knew she was keen to what was going on. Her mood would change the closer it got to the time he had to meet her mother Jane. Her words became colder and the flirting stopped altogether when it was time to say goodbye for the night. She always seemed to forget about it the next time they would meet, that her crush was having sex with her mother. She never acted mad about it, it was her mom's way of conducting business.

Sometimes Leah would drop him off at her house, but sometimes Daniel would get dropped off at the Tall Rock Baptist parking lot and Jane would pick him up so they could go fuck somewhere new. She liked having sex outside, in places where they had a slim chance of getting caught. A random cow pasture, in her car on the side of a dirt road, a dark cemetery. Business was good.

Leah and Beth picked him up on a Tuesday night. It wasn't late yet, the sun still hung on the horizon, but he was tired from a studying his bible and helping Frank cut the grass at the church. He wore the same collared shirt and khakis that were his usual going out attire.

"Not much variety in your wardrobe, huh preacher?" Leah teased.

Daniel thought about it, he hadn't brought much from his apartment at college. Although Frank had gotten him a new suit he felt like he could use a few more shirts and pairs of pants. Frank had supplied him with a wallet full of cash, should he need to purchase anything and this seemed like an opportune time to pick up a few things.

"Is there anywhere still open where I can buy some clothes? You could be my fashion coordinators."

The girls laughed with excitement at the opportunity to spend someone else's money on a shopping trip.

"I know just the place!" Leah said and whipped her car around.

They got to the Mall of Motte with over an hour before they closed for the night. They hit three different stores. The first was a little too trendy for Daniel. He didn't like the idea of buying skinny jeans with tears already in the knees. Leah and Beth browsed around joking that he had to buy them each something for being his fashion experts. Daniel didn't disagree with the idea, he just gave them each a twenty dollar bill. They decided to shop around.

The next stop was a department store. He felt more comfortable with the more conservative fashion. The girls shopped hard picking out several outfits for Daniel to try on. He hit the dressing room and would walked out with the ones he liked to get their approval. They gave mixed signs so it was up to him and the mirror to ultimately decide. Beth disappeared to the women's department with the twenty dollars Daniel promised. Leah stayed behind supplying Daniel with more clothes to try on.

She knocked on the door, "Here, try these."

He cracked open the door to grab them and she barged in. Daniel had been in the middle of changing and was without a shirt, the jeans were pulled up but not zipped or buttoned. She looked at his bare chest and offered him a long sleeve purple shirt that Daniel found quite repulsive.

"That, um. Purple and yellow aren't really my best colors."

She folded her arms still holding a pair of green cargo shorts.

"Sometimes you have to wear clothes that you don't like. Someone else tells you to wear them or else…so you wear them."

Daniel took the shirt off the hanger and realized her meaning. He put it on and fumbled with the first button.

"Here, I'll get it," Leah buttoned the bottom and started with the rest.

"Just because someone makes you wear an ugly shirt doesn't mean you have to like it," Daniel told her as she was taking her time on the third button, "You could like some other shirt and it might fit."

Her fingers never put the last two buttons together, but her hands took a good firm grip on the collar of his shirt. Leah pulled down being a head shorter than Daniel, who was already moving in to meet in the middle for a kiss.

It wasn't the wet tongue in his mouth, like Mary Ann had slipped him. Leah's lips were soft and kissed him so gently he held her in his arms and let it be soft and gentle.

Things were starting off slowly but he was half expecting to get naked with her in that small changing room. His hand moved up her ribs and grabbed her breast but she put the brakes on hard.

"I'm not some slut like my mom," she said looking into his eyes, "I'm a virgin and you need to treat me like one."

Daniel didn't know what to believe, "But weren't you jerking me off that night in the pool? I can't remember very much but that sort of stuck out."

"I have a reputation as a bad girl and I like it. That doesn't mean I don't want a boyfriend or at least someone who cares about me.

She left the dressing room back in that stoic mood like Daniel was about to go fuck her mother. He wondered if she was bipolar the way she changed personalities so fast.

Beth came back and Leah disappeared to go shop. They found her coming out of a lingerie store with a tiny bad in hand. She was back to being the bad-girl, hiding her sweeter personalities for another time.

All the bags got tossed in the back including the lingerie. Daniel couldn't help but wonder what she bought but he never got the nerve to ask.

Chapter 32: Flower Pipe

The drive back was routine until they crossed the Kenia river bridge. A sheriff's deputy was running radar and hit them with the blue lights. Leah pulled over cussing under her breath. In her mirror she saw Deputy Brantley Wainwright get out and approach the vehicle.

"God damn, that's just my luck," She whispered.

"You should stop breaking the law," Daniel teased.

Leah didn't think it was funny. The deputy knocked on the window so Leah lowered it halfway.

"Going a little fast aren't we Miss Leah?" Deputy Wainwright asked in a mocking tone. He bent down and peered in at the other passengers with contempt. Beth was a familiar face but Daniel he didn't recognize.

"Step out of the car Ma'am," He said and opened the door. Leah unbuckled her seatbelt and reluctantly got out.

"Turn around and put your hands on the roof of the vehicle," he demanded.

Once more Leah complied. The deputy began frisking her and spent much longer checking her breasts for contraband than the rest of her body. He fondled them like a horny teenager right through the window for Daniel to see. The Deputy handcuffed her and sat her on the hood of his patrol car. Next Beth got similar treatment and Daniel got cuffed as well, although his search didn't involve any groping.

The trio were all sitting on the patrol car waiting as Deputy Wainwright searched Leah's car. They saw him pick up something out of the center console and examine it.

"Shit, he found my pipe," Leah said.

"What kind of pipe?" Daniel asked.

"Just pot," She answered.

"Well it's legal now, what does that matter?" He asked.

"Still considered drug paraphernalia," Beth said, "they harass anyone that has a bowl by arresting them until they can test for other drugs in the pipe."

"Has there been anything else smoked in that pipe?" He asked looking into Leah's eyes.

She shook her head, "No, just a little bit of homegrown I got from Juan. Can't afford the stuff they sell at the headshop."

"Juan? Was that the guy you stopped to see in the trailer park?"

Leah had almost forgotten she'd taken Daniel there and left him in the car, "That's him. Just don't go rattin anybody out preacher boy."

Daniel thought about the way the girls had been treated by the hot-blooded officer who was back to digging through the car. He opened the trunk and went through every bag of clothes. Daniel got to see the matching bra and panties Leah had bought with his twenty dollars. It was much more conservative than he had imagined, almost regular underwear. He wondered if she had purchased them for a special evening out, one where she might try to lose her virginity.

When the deputy was satisfied there was nothing else to find he approached the three and held up the pipe. "Who's is this?"

"It's mine," Daniel said before Leah could fess up to it.

The officer chuckled and said, "You expect me to believe you smoke your rocks out of a pipe with pink and yellow flowers on it?"

Daniel didn't fall for the setup, "I smoke Marijuana or tobacco out of that pipe sir. Nothing else."

Brantley Wainwright wasn't fooled at all by the act but he still had to perform his job by certain standards. He couldn't take Leah to the county jail to test the pipe if this other guy was claiming ownership. He'd been hoping to intimidate her into giving a blowjob in exchange for letting her off the hook.

He looked at Leah, "You gonna let your boyfriend take the fall for you?"

She didn't answer.

"I said it's my pipe dickhead. Now leave her alone!" Daniel shouted, sounding braver than he actually felt.

Deputy Wainwright glared at him. It wasn't often the gleaming star pinned to his uniform let an insult come his way. Most of the local kids knew better than to fuck with him.

"You don't open your mouth until—"

"I want your name and badge number right now officer! I know my rights and you're not about to piss on them!" Daniel said, borrowing some of the dialog from a play he'd been in.

The deputy grabbed him by the collar and shoved him backwards onto the patrol car. "Deputy Brantley Wainwright. Badge number 3-3-7-9-2-8, and you can say it all night while you're locked up."

He took the cuffs off the girls, "You two are free to go, for now." He was talking to Leah again, "I'll get you some other night."

The trip to the Motte County Detention Center was less than pleasant for Daniel. Deputy Wainwright tightened the cuffs almost to the point of cutting off circulation to his hands. They didn't speak during the ride, neither one realizing they had both been involved in Daniels naked run down the highway. The cruiser was buzzed in through the tall fence with barbed wire on top. It surrounded the cinderblock building that housed the Detention Center, the sheriff's office was on the same property. Deputy Wainwright yanked him out of the back seat and led him inside to the bookings room.

The deputy began emptying Daniel's pockets, placing the contents into a plastic tray. Another officer with a mustache, whose face Daniel recognized, came over.

"Brantley, stop what you're doing and come with me."

The deputy looked annoyed, "What about him?"

"Mr. Montclair, you mind staying put right here for a minute?" The officer asked.

"No problem. Could you loosen these cuffs a little? My hands are numb."

The officer took the cuffs off of him completely. Daniel took notice of his name, T. Weaver, and the Sargent stripes on his sleeve. Sargent Weaver led Deputy Wainwright through the door to the next room. Daniel could see them talking through the large glass observation window. The deputy heroically showed the Sargent the plastic bag holding Leah's pipe. The Sargent didn't seem impressed and took it into his possession. They kept talking, it was obvious that Brantley was mad at something but he was talking to a superior officer. He glared through the window at Daniel as to intimidate him and then left through another door.

Sargent Weaver came back for Daniel and told him to collect his things from the basket.

"You're free to go. The deputy thought you were suspicious because of the pipe, but I assured him that you were no harm to anyone."

"Thanks," Daniel said, "I recognize you from Tall Rock Baptist but I feel bad not knowing you any better. You can call me Daniel."

They shook hands, "Tom Weaver. I've been going to church and listening to Frank preach for almost twenty years now. Would you like me to drive you somewhere?"

Daniel didn't want to be a burden and decided Leah needed to come get him for all the heat he'd taken for her that evening.

"No, I'll have someone come pick me up," Daniel said.

"Well you're welcome to wait in my office until they get here."

"Sure. That way I can explain how Frank's protégé ended up arrested," Daniel said.

"Well, you hadn't been booked yet so nothing is official. But yeah, I'd like to hear your story."

They went to the Sargent's office and Daniel retold most of the story while waiting on Leah to pick him up. He left out the romantic details about the shopping trip. When Leah text that she was in the parking lot he thanked Sargent Weaver and promised to do his best to keep Leah and her friends out of trouble. They both agreed she didn't need the pipe returned to her so it was thrown in the trash.

Leah was standing outside the entrance shivering from the cold. She looked beautiful and Daniel was glad he'd saved her from the Deputy Wainwright experience.

"Are you Jailbird Taxi Service?" He asked.

She laughed, "I guess so. This almost feels like a movie. Me sitting here in the cold, waiting on my man to get out of prison."

"Your man?" He asked, "Well, I sure am glad you waited so long for me to serve my time. It was lonely in prison."

He kissed her for the second time that evening. Only this time he didn't grab her breast, he just held her tightly around the waist. She was a completely different person than her mother, and he was falling for her.

Chapter 33: Moral Obligations

At dinner one Tuesday night Frank unfolded a piece of paper and read it to the 'family'. It was a letter addressed to Mr. Franklin Catoe and Mr. Daniel Montclair. It explained the goals of the UHCC Academy and what to expect, bring with, and prepare for. Daniel had already switched over to the Church's new official Bible and found that it wasn't much different although it did omit some of the more taboo and unjust stories. He kept studying hard. The orientation was just over three weeks away.

Both Daniel and Elizabeth seemed excited but it was all for show. The young clergyman was just getting comfortable at his new job in Motte. People were looking to him for guidance and he was showing them the Lord's way, even though he didn't really believe in it. His social life was great but his sex life had come to an abrupt halt when he refused to screw Mrs. Dixon anymore. He didn't feel it was right for him to have feelings for Leah and still be nailing her mom. However it was a two sided sword. Mrs. Dixon wouldn't let Leah go out at night for ruining her fun. They went to Tall Rock Baptist for church on Sunday's but Daniel was still preaching in Motte as a substitute for the late Pastor Gilmore.

Elizabeth was disappointed the gossip would go away. She was in the loop more than ever with the papal stud living under her roof. Jane had kept her informed of all the juicy details about their romps and those of other people. In fact she was starting to fantasize about the young man herself.

Daniel and Frank went on about their business as usual, but by the end of the week half the people in Motte and Tall Rock knew Daniel would be leaving.

Sunday morning Mr. Banther came to discuss Daniel's replacement. He'd made arrangements for another deacon from Summerville to fill the void for a while instead of Deacon Burgess. Daniel introduced him, Deacon Collins; and then gave another fine sermon. Mr. Banther set up a camera and filmed it. He acted calm and uplifting just like always. Greg Banther took notice of all the young people in church today and how they all wanted to speak with Daniel after it was over. Banther had to wait another thirty minutes before the hang-rounds had finally left. He took survey of the collection plates. Not a bad take for the average age of participants.

Daniel's flight to Cincinnati was breaking personal boundaries for him. Not only had he never flown before, he'd never been north of Manchester, Kentucky where his Great Aunt Ethel lived. He took a cab to the UHCC Academy that wasn't far from the airport. It had previously been a small technical college that had closed because of funding cuts. He wasn't the only one hauling luggage up to the front doors. Several others were also checking in. Some had rolling luggage, others duffel bags, suit carriers, book bags. Daniel had a duffel and was wearing one of his two suits.

He signed in and was told to have a seat in the lobby. Other 'cadets' were waiting and chatting with each other. After a few more arrived a bearded man with a nametag TODD walked in and asked all the young men to follow him. They walked across the campus to a dorm building and he gave them room assignments. Daniel was paired sharing a room with Clayton McBride, eighteen years old and fresh out of high school in Missouri. It reminded Daniel of his first dorm assignment freshmen year of college except the room was already furnished. Two twin beds, two desks, two lamps.

They had a couple of hours to kill before orientation so they explored campus together. Clayton was enthusiastic. He spilled out his boring life story in a few minutes and how he'd always wanted to, "spread God's word to all the children".

Together they wandered the campus; finding the library, computer center, auditorium, dining hall and a couple of other buildings that they assumed were administrative offices or classrooms. Other cadets were wandering about asking questions and meeting one another.

Orientation started in front of the main building and it led them through all the buildings Daniel and Clayton had explored. The tour concluded at the auditorium, or the "Prayer Hall" as they referred to it. They all sat down and waited for the speaker. Daniel looked all around him and did a quick guesstimate that there were upwards of a hundred and eighty there, most of them in their early twenties like him. A man walked from backstage right up to the microphone. He was older than his audience, probably late thirties or early forties, wearing a stylish suit, with his hair and beard dark and well kept.

"Hello cadets!" He said, "I'm Terrance Martin, and I'm proud to be the Learning Coordinator for the UHCC." He spoke in a booming voice that echoed throughout the Prayer Hall.

"I'm glad you're here. I'm so pleased that young people still want to teach others about the Lord and help each person on their path to heaven. Now many of you already possess skills of the many different facets of church operations. We have brought you here to refine those skills and to expand them to new heights. We need you to be the new face of Christianity, to make it uniform, streamlined. In other words perfect. 'Perfect?' You may ask… No it isn't easy, but we have the lord on our side."

'I didn't know he took sides,' Daniel thought.

"All of you will start with church policies. They may be a little different than the former policies of your sponsoring charters which is why you must learn it well. There will be no variance from one affiliate to another. When that is over you will be split up into different majors if you will. Sound and Lighting; Recruiting and Youth Services; Preaching and Guidance; and Church Administration. Of course you will be cross trained in each subject. It makes things run smoother when you have a solid grasp on the big picture."

"Now, do not forget we take learning very seriously here. You will be given ample time for prayer and bible study. Your classes will last for around half of the day depending on your major. The rest of the time you are free to study and practice at your own pace. However I recommend that you use your time wisely. This is not a spring break party getaway. While you are free to socialize do not let it interfere with your progress in your studies. That's all I'm going to lecture you on for now. Church policies 101 will begin here tomorrow morning at eight o'clock sharp. Be prepared to take notes and learn."

The same cadets sat in the same prayer hall the next morning. The instructor was named Mr. Wentman. He went over church policies as a college professor would lecture History. It was obvious some of the kids right out of high school weren't used to it, constantly scribbling down everything that came out of his mouth. Daniel just jotted down the key words and listened.

It was all business, no religion. The structure of the organization reminded him of his first day of ROTC in high school. He had transferred out after his first semester. Wentman covered the Local Chain of command, required meetings, training schedule, requests for time off, and basic operational duties.

Wentman was boring. Daniel knew the type of professor he was. Just there for the paycheck and not much else. He didn't take questions or cite many examples, just straight robot reading and some hand gestures. After two hours of this he announced a twenty minute break. He and Clayton got up and walked outside for some air as did most of the cadets. How many of them would be sent home embarrassed after dropping out? He thought about how their churches would have to pay their tuition. That would stir up some bad blood if they dropped out and then left their tuition to be paid by the church. His own parents were already upset about him dropping out of college. He knew they would be disgusted if he couldn't even pass a Bible College.

The class lasted another two hours, then they were told to study at their leisure the rest of the day. The following day was more of the same. Thursday they took a test. It was ninety questions and covered every major topic they had been lectured on. No multiple choice either, fill in the blanks or 'In a few sentences explain…'

It took Daniel almost an hour. He was one of the first ones finished and he felt as if he'd done well. Some of the others were struggling.

Frank was on the ready, carefully chewing his Tuesday night supper. On his left sat his wife Elizabeth, on his right sat Jane Dixon. Elizabeth had cooked meat loaf and mashed potatoes, Jane had brought green bean casserole. He was very suspicious of the way both of them had been acting. The Cougar slut didn't usually make dinner socials. 'What was her game?' He wondered, but it was Elizabeth who dealt the first blow.

"Frank, I almost forgot to ask you again. I saw Elliott the other day and he was wondering why we were changing financial advisers. I said I hadn't the slightest idea what he was talking about and he said you'd withdrawn a lot of our savings," She took another small bite of potatoes.

He was a bit thrown by this. His wife rarely pried into their financial positions. He wanted to slap her for bringing it up in front of company. He smiled instead and shot off a quick lie.

"I've been keeping an eye on the stock market for a while now and it looks to me like it's ready for another crash," He paused to see if they bought it. "I took the money out and put it into some more secure investments. You know, low risk. Government bonds and cash mostly, I'd just hate to see us lose everything in the market."

"And don't you think you should have discussed that with your wife first? I mean it's her money too," Jane said with conviction. Frank wanted to grab her by the throat and choke-slam her right through the wall.

"Yeah, I have a right to know what happens to our money," Elizabeth agreed with her friend.

"Well it's been a while since you've even asked about our savings so I decided not to bother you about it, Honey."

Dinner continued. Frank understood Jane was helping Elizabeth plan her escape and getting at least half of everything was part of the strategy. The pair of drama lovers weren't satisfied but they let it go for the time being. They made chit-chat about the latest television shows they were following, with the season finale coming on Friday. They finished eating and Elizabeth took the dishes into the kitchen. While she was gone, Jane leaned toward Frank and whispered, "I need to speak with you privately sometime. My house tomorrow for lunch?"

Elizabeth walked back into the dining room. Frank gently nodded in agreement to be there.

'What would she want to talk to me about and keep it hidden from Elizabeth?' He wondered.

The women then went into the living room to watch a different show than they had been discussing previously. Frank went over to his church office to think and do research. 'Shit, it's turning into a soap opera around here. What could she want to talk about now?'

He pondered the question for a long while trying to have a possible battle plan for whatever she was going to hit him with next. Some ideas came to mind. Late that night after Mrs. Dixon had left and Mrs. Catoe had gone to bed, he took his old pickup truck on a late night cruise over to the twenty-four hour drug store in Motte.

<u>Chapter 34:</u> Casual Acquaintances

After the first week nine cadets had been sent home for various reasons, at least that was the rumor going around the students before and after class. Daniel was making friends and getting a feel for possible allies in his plight. Most of the people there were genuinely friendly and looking for friends too. He figured having a little support group might help him advance, maybe even gain an ally on his mission. More often he wondered if he and Frank were the only two doing the secret agent idea, and if the UHCC was looking for it.

Travis and Lacy sat on either side of Daniel during the first day of sound and lighting class. They were all about the same age from what Daniel could tell. Travis was one of the few black guys that had long hair that wasn't an afro or in dreads. It was very neatly combed. He was from a large church outside of Philadelphia, formerly The New Zion Full Gospel Church of God. Now the UHCC – New Zion Gospel Affiliate. Travis was in training to preach the gospel when he'd been nominated by his elders to go to Cincinnati. Daniel wondered if he was overly animated like many of the black Ministers on the internet sermon videos he'd been studying. They had a style all their own.

Lacy was from The Light of Christ United Methodist Church in Tempe, Arizona. Lovingly renamed UHCC - Light of Christ, Tempe Affiliate. She was a pretty girl, almost six feet tall, wavy brown hair up in a ponytail. It seemed to Daniel that she knew more bible verses than Reverend Catoe. Having a verse for any situation was important he realized. Just like anything else it took practice, and that took time.

He already was in class and studying on his own over ten hours a day. The rest was sleep and small social encounters. He knew Frank was paying him good money to succeed in this school and learn, to gain a good enough position to have access to incriminating information. The problem was Daniel didn't really know what he needed to find out. Maybe the financial aspect. He could see if they'd been cooking the books and cheating on taxes. Maybe their gross revenue was so big it would show the public it was big business not big worship. Frank had mentioned the idea of making up a sex scandal, but they both knew it would have to be huge to not get covered up or disproved.

The sound and lighting class was more laid back than the other classes so far. They divided into groups of three. Daniel and his neighbors Lacy and Travis looked at one another and all nodded in agreement. They were a fairly diversified group, all they needed was an Asian or Native American girl and they could have been in a brochure.

The professor explained it was a team building exercise. One person would become familiar with the basics of lighting, another would learn music and the third would learn production coordinating. Then they would be responsible for teaching the other two what they needed to know during and after class. Daniel took the lighting, as he knew a good bit from a theater class back in his college days. Travis volunteered for music which he seemed to know well. That left Lacy coordinating. She seemed to be up for whatever task she was assigned. They each watched instructional videos on their tablets with headphones covering up their ears.

'Lazy-ass professor,' Daniel thought as he watched video after video of how lighting is handled safely and used effectively.

Each student spent the remainder of the class staring at their tablets with headphones over their ears. Class ended for the day at two-thirty. The three teammates met in the auditorium to share what they'd learned in class. Daniel began, aided by a list of key ideas he'd jotted down on a sheet of paper. He elaborated on each point. It was mostly common knowledge and safety. Don't plug too many things into an outlet, if the outlet smokes unplug it, and don't use electrical cords with exposed bare wire. He moved through the info at light-speed compared to the tutorials.

Daniel took a seat and listened as Travis gave his lesson 'The Musical Process.' It also started with safety. Choirs can only stand on risers that are rated for their weight and have nonslip bases. Then he got into other basic areas like what to do if the organ player or band didn't show up…have a CD and player ready. He was almost done when Daniel looked up from note taking and realized that Travis hadn't been reading from a cheat sheet. He was spouting all that from straight memory.

When he finished Daniel asked him, "You memorize everything you read?"

Travis gave a big grin that seemed to show nearly every tooth in his mouth, "Yeah it's not quite photographic but I'm pretty good at it. I can remember just about every bible story, just not word for word." 'That's handy,' Daniel thought.

It was Lacy's turn, who was the opposite of Travis. She had taken detailed notes and went deeper into each subject than either of the two young men had. Again safety was the majority. Fire exits, hand rails, wheel chair ramps… She read and spoke rapidly, as if she was nervous to speak in front of others.

Daniel thought, 'She definitely needs a public speaking class but I bet she was the valedictorian of her school.'

They finished their study session in under an hour. It was Lacy who recommended they go to the cafeteria for some ice cream. The academy was the main thing they talked about, but then they each told a little about their backgrounds. Daniel said he quit college and became more involved with church. He left out the part about vomiting in his crush's mouth and the fact that Frank was paying him to destroy the institution they were currently attending.

Travis was in line to be a fourth generation pastor. Needless to say he wasn't in school from lack of knowledge. His father was going to retire soon rather than deal with the UHCC and their changes. He knew every single person in his church by name (over four-hundred) and they were all his friends or family. The way the New Zion Full Gospel Church of God worshiped was indeed full of gospel.

They got to church around nine o'clock Sunday morning and talked about whatever happened during the week. At ten worship service would begin and last until eleven thirty, during which time they would hear a sermon and sing at least five or six songs. A full day at church by most standards, but then they would go to the dining hall or out to restaurants and eat lunch. Instead of going home and changing they go back to church and worship for a few more hours. Travis was groomed to be next in line at the head of the church. He was the brightest mind his community had to offer, so failure wasn't an option for him.

Lacy's family church was small, about the size of the one Daniel had been presiding over in Motte. It was at the center of her neighborhood. According to her that's how many neighborhoods in Tempe operated. Lots of small churches and more personal. She'd been offered a softball scholarship to Arizona State but decided to stay close to home and make the church a career, but she wanted more than just the little one in her neighborhood. She already had a rough outline of how her career would climb the holy ladder to heaven. 'The Nun CEO,' Daniel thought, 'and a pretty one too.'

That became the habit after class for the next two weeks. Study after class together and then go out for ice cream or some kind of dessert. The trio's friendship blossomed through mutual interest and the fact that their grades were kicking the holy crap out of their peers. Grades were posted outside the auditorium at the end of the second week. It was a number average not letter. Twelve students had a perfect hundred percent, a good many nineties, but the majority were in the seventies and eighties. Around thirty percent were failing with a sub seventy average. Daniel's roommate Clayton was one of those. Daniel noticed he was always on his laptop playing games during free time and after class. Even a couple times during class. He seemed to be enjoying himself until one day. When Daniel got back to the room that evening Clayton was lying on his bed staring at the ceiling, eyes red as if he'd been crying. Daniel started to ask if he was alright, if he needed help studying. But he could read Clayton's mood, he'd already given up. Three days later he was sent home for cutting class.

Chapter 35: Old Demons Never Die

The Dixon home was clean and tidy Wednesday when Frank arrived for lunch. He wore his slacks and brown sport coat that he would give the sermon in that night. Ms. Dixon let him in and acted like this was a normal social call, knowing damn well this was anything but normal. Frank played along with her bullshit. He was a spy undercover as a reverend. After disposing of his last adversary and covering it up, he faced this new, perhaps even more dangerous challenge. But he was excited and ready as they sat down and began spooning salad into their bowls.

Frank said the blessing, "Oh Father, thank you for this food. We pray that we can show our appreciation by doing our best to live our lives in your image. We are your children and this food you provide gives us life to serve you, to help one another and let us fight the devil's sin. Amen."

"Amen," Jane responded. Frank began on his salad, they both drank sweet tea. Pasta salad and chicken and rice were sitting on the table in serving dishes. They both ate, waiting on the other to begin the conversation. Frank had only commented on how he liked the English walnuts that were chopped into the salad. He was nearing the bottom of his bowl when she made the first move.

"So, Reverend. I was hoping to talk to you about a problem I have."

"Of course, how can I help?" He asked with concern.

"Well, Daniel came over to see Leah one night week before last, but she wasn't home... Out with her friends again. Anyway to be polite I invited him in and offered him a glass of wine like I was having," She paused as if it was hard to get the words to come out of her mouth. "I'd had a few glasses already. He took advantage of me…I wouldn't exactly say he raped me, but he seduced me while I was vulnerable."

"Oh my," Frank became solemn. "My Daniel? Daniel Montclair?" He wanted to laugh out loud but controlled himself. She was full of shit, but did she know what he knew?

She nodded, "I haven't told anyone because I didn't want to hurt his reputation at the church, or your reputation…I was just going to let it go but…but now I'm pregnant," Her voice grew more like a cry and she covered her face.

He took a few moments to take it all in. This was one of the possible scenarios he'd imagined it could be. Frank had driven to Motte the night before to think and to prepare. He'd come to her table ready to complete this unholy quest.

"Oh Jane, it hurts my heart to hear what he's done to you. I really thought he was more of a Christian than to do such a thing. Even acts of passion have to be carefully planned and on the-"

She sobbed, "Excuse me," as she rushed off toward her bedroom still hiding her face.

Frank didn't have any time to waste. He reached for his left pocket and felt a small glass container. He felt the cap, wrong one and dug into his right pocket for the right one. This glass container was a dark brown vile with a medicine dropper cap, labeled PENNYROYAL EXTRACT. He'd heard years before that women used pennyroyal to make their uterus shed. It would make them start their period early so it wouldn't happen at an inconvenient time, such as at finals week in college or on vacation at the beach. Frank also knew it could be taken to abort a pregnancy, and that was exactly what he was planning.

He unscrewed the cap and held the dropper over his tea glass. He pressed the bulb gently and counted as eight drops came out. He put on the lid and stuffed it back in his pocket, then stirred the tea with his spoon and switched glasses with Jane. All in less than twenty seconds, but she still had to drink it, at least some of it. He'd been reading on the internet about pennyroyal (and other chemicals he'd purchased) and how much to use. The most common way for women trying to start their period early, was to put four drops into a hot cup of tea, if it didn't happen after two hours repeat the process. He figured that if it didn't work the first time he wouldn't get a second crack at it, so he doubled the recipe with eight drops.

He sat there listening for Jane but heard no sound other than her muffled cry. Her glass was nearly full and much of that was ice.

'The ice is going to melt and dilute it. She might only drink a sip- if any the way she's crying.'

He grabbed for the bottle again, leaned over to her new glass across the table and dropped in four to begin with, then four more just in case. Another quick stir. Again the bottle was put into his right pants pocket.

'Now what?' He thought. 'She's gotta drink it or it won't work.' He waited for minutes that seemed like hours.

When she came back in she was wiping her eyes with a tissue.

"I'm sorry, I'm just worried. I haven't been pregnant since Leah. I didn't even know it could still happen as old as I am," She said as she sat back down. Frank thought it was unlikely for a woman her age to get pregnant but certainly not unheard of. Either way he had to do this just to be sure.

"You need not apologize. It's me that should be apologizing to you for the way my pupil has acted. He's disgraced me…I only hope you won't let it disgrace the name of the good church."

"I just wish it were that simple. People will want to know who the father is. My family and my friends, my adult daughter. It's bad enough having a child out of wedlock. Imagine how hard it would be to keep that a secret forever," She started crying again.

Frank was thinking more about that tea glass sitting in front of her than what she was saying.

"Here, eat some food. " He moved the salad bowl from on top of her dinner plate and began dishing up the rice and pasta salad.

"I can't eat, not now," she said.

"My dear, there is a passage in Psalms. 'I will hasten and not delay to obey your commands. Though the wicked bind me with ropes, I will not forget your law. At midnight I rise to give you thanks'."

She'd stopped crying and was listening. "Now what that means is even in the hardest times we must continue to do what we should. Praying, sleeping, and yes eating so we may stay strong and continue. Do that and we will be rewarded with forgiveness and help."

It worked. She took one hand from her face and took a bite of pasta salad, then another. Frank was on pins and needles when she reached for her glass. She took a sip and set it back down. No facial changes. If she tasted a difference she didn't show it. She ate slowly as did Frank. His plan seemed to be working, he was outfoxing the fox.

"It's not just keeping the secret Frank. I can't afford to have another child to raise. Leah can't support herself yet and having a baby to raise would just bankrupt me," she glanced into his eyes for the first time since she came back from crying.

Frank chewed the large bite in his mouth. He was still playing like he was upset about the situation but he could have done cart wheels in celebration.

"Tall Rock Baptist may not believe in Daniel anymore but we believe in making things right. We may not be rich but we will help you raise that child financially, as well as any other way we can help. AND it will be kept private."

"Thank you Frank," She took another sip of pennyroyal tea.

They ate quietly, each thinking of the agreement they'd concocted. The chicken and rice was dry and salty.

'Good, all the more reason to drink,' he thought.

They both finished eating their food and still sat thinking. Jane's white blouse was moving in and out with her chest as she was still breathing deeply, Frank noticed, but she still looked fine. He was caught looking.

She asked, "What should I say when people ask who the father is? I just can't say nothing. People will talk and spread rumors."

"Well, you could say it was just the last guy you were seeing," Frank insisted.

"I haven't dated much lately, and it's been a long time since I've been with a man…maybe that's why I was so easily seduced. So that wouldn't work," She said it very flirtatiously.

"How long has it been?" Frank asked with a grin, knowing exactly what she was doing.

"Far too long," She drank the rest of her tea and got up took the plates into the kitchen. When she came back to the dining room not one, but two of the buttons on her blouse had been unbuttoned. He could see a little bit of white bra and an eye full of cleavage.

"Some more tea?" she offered.

He let himself get caught looking this time. He smiled and answered, "I'd love some."

He got an even better view when she bent over to pick up his glass. She went back into the kitchen. It almost thirty years since he'd had it thrown at him like this, and even longer since he actually fucked a woman other than his wife. She came back with his glass full of tea and spilled some of it right in his lap when she set it down on the table.

It was ice cold but old Frank was heating up.

"Oh I'm sorry, I'm such a klutz sometimes," she immediately grabbed his napkin off the table and began to dry up his lap. She wasn't really trying to dry him, she just found his cock and stroked it with the napkin several times as it got hard. Her tits were basically in his face and he noticed another button was gone.

"Well you might want to take off those pants and let me throw them in the dryer for a few minutes," she advised.

"Sure thing," Frank said.

He got up and followed her to a bathroom beside the laundry room. He knew she had planned it this way but he didn't care, he was too excited. He told himself he'd stop it before it got too far, he just had to see what was next.

"Go in there and take your pants off and rinse'em off, shirt too. It looks like you have spot right there.

He did as commanded. Took his belt off and emptied his pockets. Keys, wallet, phone and two little vials of liquid. He put it all on the counter.

'Nope, can't let her see that,' he slid his shoes off and hid his magic potions in the left one. Then he undressed and rinsed his clothes. He was only wearing an undershirt and a pair of briefs. He had a huge boner so he wrapped a towel around his waist.

He came out and handed her the clothes. She grinned at the pink towel he had on. She walked just a few feet to the laundry room and put them in the dryer. The washing machine sat beside it with a basket of wrinkled clothes on top. She closed the dryer door and bent over it to the controls and then looked back to see if he was watching her. He was.

"What's the towel for reverend? You know a pregnant girl can't get any more pregnant."

He pulled the towel off and let it fall to his feet. His staff was pointing straight at her through his white briefs.

"Lead me not to temptation… for it's hard to resist."

She pushed the button to start the dryer and it shook to life. Still bent over, she grabbed her skirt and pulled it up revealing her bare ass and pussy, "I know."

The good Reverend Franklin Catoe and Miss Jane Dixon had been fucking on top of the dryer for about five minutes when Jane started cramping. She was screaming in pain so Frank thought he must be doing well, then he noticed a sticky feeling of blood on his cock and looked down at it.

'Damn pennyroyal worked like a charm,' he thought as he kept pounding her. Jane couldn't do anything other than close her eyes and moan. She passed out there on top of the dryer, blood dripping out of her.

"Mother Fucker," Frank whispered as he pulled out. "I might have used too much."

He waited but she didn't move, she just lay there bent over the dryer, skirt pushed up on her waist. He didn't want to call for help and then get caught up in the consequences, no matter what they would be. If she woke up later alright then he didn't want to be around to talk about it. If she died he needed to distance himself as far away as possible and clean up any evidence before he left. He decided to clean himself up first, hurrying back into the bathroom, which had become the emergency dick washing station, to clean off the period blood. There was some on his briefs. That wasn't going to wash out so he took them off and set them on the counter. He had to get his pants and shirt out of the dryer.

He peeked his head out the door. She hadn't moved, the dryer was still vibrating away. He'd have to move her to get in the dryer, so he grabbed her ankles and spun her legs toward the washing machine. The vibrating stopped as he opened the door and grabbed his clothes. He had one leg in his pants when her limp body fell, her head hit the tile floor with a thud that made Frank wince. He just continued to dress himself and think about what he needed to do.

'Who knows I'm here?' He wondered, 'Elizabeth thinks I'm in town. Would she have told anyone? Maybe text someone?'

He needed to check her phone. He went looking for it in the kitchen and didn't see it so he wandered through the house. He found a bedroom with teen posters on the wall, which must have been Leah's. Then a master bedroom. There were clothes on the bed, even more on the floor; but he couldn't find her damned phone anywhere. He was panicking now and looking in the same places two and three times expecting it to show up. Dresser, night stand, bed.

Then he saw the door going into the master bathroom. It was sitting on the counter, plugged into the wall charger, just within reach of the old claw-foot bathtub. He swiped it up and pressed the button to wake it up. Lock screen, the type you have to touch a certain pattern. He didn't even try to guess, he just unplugged it and took it with him. He was going back towards the laundry room when he saw the table with the glass of tea sitting on it.

'That's evidence, my finger prints are all over it. Shit, they're everywhere now.' He tried to think back to all the places he touched since he'd been there. It would be nearly impossible to wipe every print away and then he'd have to wash out the glass…all the dishes, so it would look like she hadn't had any company. How much time did he have before Leah came home?

It was getting riskier by the second and too much to clean up when he remembered an old trick from years before. 'Burn this bitch to the ground and get rid of all the evidence at once.' Only this time he wasn't at Low-tide's Marina and didn't have any gas to start it with. He finished getting dressed and reloaded his belongings into the slightly damp pants pockets. Jane's body was still lying where it had fallen, a pool of blood had formed around her head where she'd hit.

He went into the kitchen hoping for a gas stove. Instead it was electric, still it made heat. Frank opened some cabinets and found what he was looking for, a bottle of vegetable oil. He opened it up and began splashing it on the stove, on the walls and the floor. Then he poured a line of oil as he walked back into the laundry room and poured the rest on top of his former lover. He had to go back into the kitchen and turned on all four burners to start it up. He grabbed a pot out the sink and filled it with water. The vegetable oil ignited after a couple of minutes. He was backed up in the dining room and the flames were starting to spread. He flung the pot of water onto the fire and flames exploded everywhere. The smoke alarm went off as he ran out the front door. He hurried to his truck hoping no one would see him. As he drove away down Mayflower Road he looked back for signs of smoke but it was too early and he wasn't waiting around.

Frank wasn't a mile away from his latest crime scene when his leg vibrated. It was Jane's cell that he'd put in his pocket. He cursed that he hadn't left it to burn up with the rest of the evidence. He took it out and pressed the on button. The lock screen had a message banner that read: Message form Elizabeth Catoe – How's he taking the big news??

'Shit. Elizabeth knew where I was the whole time. Fuck. Now that's a problem I didn't expect.'

Frank was busy contemplating his wife's allegiances. Could he tell her what happened? No, definitely not. Could he make up a story that she'd believe? Maybe, but then he'd have to stick to it and make the investigators believe it too. His arson plan relied on Frank not being tied to the crime at all. Without even a memory of it, he drove past the spot where Larry Gilmore had bit the dust.

He realized he was getting very close to home and didn't have a plan yet to deal with Elizabeth. By the end of the day she was going to be weeping for her lost friend and questioning what happened. Her car was in the driveway. He drove past into the church parking lot and eased his old truck back into the woods near the river where his chopping stump was.

The good ole ax was tucked away behind the bench seat of his truck just like always. Some men do their best thinking in a favorite recliner, others on the toilet or in the shower. Franklin Catoe had his mind at its sharpest when he was splitting firewood. He wasn't fast about doing the work, just steady. The rhythm and exercise was his key to deeper thought. What deep thoughts he'd plunged into. Reliving the crime, the escape, the future string of lies he might have to tell. For what? He'd given up drug dealing and crime years before. Turned straight for over thirty years, living the clean Christian life and earning respect through perseverance and leading prayer. In just a matter of months he was plotting, murdering, and lying all in the best interest of the church. Frank's world was burning fast.

"What could I do? She was asking for it."

The axe came down hard into an oak log.

"Extortion on a church! That bitch deserved it…So did Larry Fucking Gilmore! She wanted to fuck him! She didn't know I do the fucking around here. Fucked her whole god damn afternoon. Probably a stinking ass bar-b-q over there by now, I hope it fucking hurt like hell if she wasn't dead already," he set another piece of wood on the stump.

"I could tell Liz I went by and she wasn't home. What are the odds that someone saw my truck in the driveway and paid attention to it being there?" He swung the axe even harder.

"No, I was there talking with her and she said she was about to start cooking fries on the stove. GODDAMNIT, I SHOULDN'T HAVE FUCKED HER! I could have just left'er there to die on her own. Can't trust the internet for shit. Would have be..."

Elizabeth had seen his truck drive back to his woodpile, so she walked back to accuse him of cheating on her with Jane. His meeting with Jane was a setup they'd planned, giving her a reason to divorce him.

She stayed quiet while Frank shouted at himself, revealing his various sins. Her eyes were wide with disbelief when Frank saw her standing there. He knew right away he'd given up everything.

They stared at each other, both breathing rapidly but for different reasons.

"I poisoned your friend Jane. Then I fucked her and burned her house down," He surprised himself he said it so calmly. Her expression of confusion didn't change, she only breathed harder.

"I did it because she was a no-good lying tramp, just like you. Yeah, I know about you and Tony Walters. Jane was threatening to ruin the church and that's all I've got left. She wanted the church's money and you're not running off with it either!"

She turned and ran toward the house.

He dropped the axe and darted through the trees to cut her off. This was speed he didn't even remember having. She heard him crashing through the brush and changed her course. She was just running, fleeing for her life from her husband who'd never even been rough with her. He was getting mad at her for being silly and running away like a child. She made it to the river bank and splashed out into the slow, black water. She was waist deep when Frank grabbed a handful of hair and yanked backwards. She fell into the water and came up shrieking.

"JUST SHUT UP AND LISTEN TO ME!" he demanded, but she screamed even louder. He grabbed her by the shoulders and dunked her head under water. He held her under for a few seconds and pulled her back up. For those few seconds she was under all he could hear was the river bubbling past. Peaceful like the eye of his hurricane.

She gasped for air and began wailing like a siren again, only this time she was fighting back. She punched and clawed at Frank and he was almost too surprised at this to defend himself. She landed a couple of weak slaps to his face before he dunked her again. She came up fighting again, and again he put her under water. But this time it was for much longer, and the silence was such a relief.

He had now murdered four people and it didn't even bother him anymore. In fact he was enjoying it a little. She would never cheat with Tony Walters again.

Her body floated slowly away down the river.

Chapter 36: Checking Out

There was never much of a line at Tall Rock Citizens Bank. Frank walked in calm and quietly. Susan Willis was at the teller window talking to the two tellers at the counter. Not another customer in sight. He walked past the first open glass office door and ignored a teller saying, "Hello, can I help you?"

The next office door was closed. The sign 'Paul Bowman – Bank Manager' was printed on the glass. Frank stood in front of it and stared in with no kind of emotion on his face. Mr. Bowman was talking on the telephone and had both feet crossed and kicked up on the desk. After a moment he saw Frank looking in at him. Frank folded his arms and kept staring. Mr. Bowman pointed at himself as if to ask, "You need to see me?" The old Reverend nodded slowly. The bank manager cut his phone call short and motioned for him to enter.

"Reverend Catoe, what can I do for you today?"

Frank took a chair and did what he was becoming so good at these days.

"I've got a problem Paul. A man, who I have never laid eyes on, came into my office today and claimed to be with the IRS. Agent Luckamn or Luckman or something. He showed me many, many documents pertaining to my personal finances and those of the church."

Mr. Bowman had a confused look about him but remained silent.

"He showed me my income taxes from the last ten years. He had information on all of my accounts. Savings, my investments, he even knew what the church has in the scholarship fund. Oh, and not to mention having mine and Elizabeth's social security numbers and all of my credit card numbers," Frank was on a roll.

"He then went on to inform me that I owed the IRS over thirty-nine thousand dollars in back taxes due to some kind of calculation errors or some crap."

Mr. Bowman spoke with his hands as much as his mouth. He held his palms up at Frank, "Slow down, we'll get to the bottom of it. Have you contacted your tax associate yet?"

"No I haven't. The only person I've contacted so far is the IRS. You see they don't operate like that. First they send you letters, many, many letters. Then they call you. The last thing they do is send an agent out to Tall Rock to try and collect. Also they don't have anyone by that name. They said it's a scam and I need to call the police to file a report."

"You...why haven't called them yet then?" The banker asked surprised.

"Because that takes time. Time I don't have. I've got a sermon to give in an hour and a police report would take too long. He's probably watching my house anyway looking for that. In the meantime, he's got all my information. Passwords, account numbers, access to every dollar I've ever saved. "

"Oh, Lord," The banker was rattled by Frank's story. "It's going to be fine Reverend Catoe. I'll just put a lock on your accounts and put your credit on Fraud Alert Status. Your money will be safe."

Frank looked him dead in the face, "I know it will, because I'm withdrawing every dime out of each of my accounts until we can get to the bottom of this. And I want it now."

It was his money. It had been his and Elizabeth's but that bitch just hadn't been the loving and faithful wife he'd expected her to be. What the church fund had in it was his too he felt. After all he'd built the damn thing.

He stuffed all of it into the briefcase despite the bank manager's protest. Four hundred twenty-nine thousand two hundred twelve dollars and fifty five cents.

As he was walking out to his truck in the parking lot he felt like a bank robber, but the feeling faded as he cranked the old machine up. His rough plan was to pack up a suitcase and get the hell out of South Carolina. He might be in the clear from his adventure on Mayflower Road, but it was only a matter of time before Elizabeth's body was found or people started wondering where she was.

The good reverend returned home and began packing. Socks, underwear, shirts, suits, ties. No sense in being a poorly dressed fugitive. He retrieved the money in the bedroom safe, his emergency cash. He reached in and set the remainder of the contents on the floor, car titles, and the deed to the house, old photographs and records. He wouldn't be able to use any of it. He pulled the false back out of the safe. His old pistol was still there, wrapped up in an oily cloth to prevent rust. He thought back to the last time he'd fired it… it had killed a man.

He took all his luggage and put it in his truck. For an instant he'd thought about taking Elizabeth's car since she wasn't going to be using it but his old truck had gotten him this far, and he was looking for familiar things to hold on to. He locked the house and walked over to his church office for his bible. Sitting on top of his desk where it liked to lay, the good ole book with the worn leather cover had been a stone for the last thirty years, just like Frank. He grabbed it up gently as if it were a child.

He flipped it open to the bookmark and read. That passages made him think of others and then more ideas followed. He looked at the clock. It was almost a half hour before the first of the congregation would start to arrive for Wednesday service. That was all the time he needed to write his final sermon at Tall Rock Baptist Church.

He had the front doors open and the regulars filed in taking their seats. Normally he and Elizabeth were waiting to greet them as they walked in but Frank was in his office and Elizabeth was still floating down the Kenia River. He came from his office without his suit jacket, only his white shirt with the sleeves rolled up and bible in hand. He took the altar and gazed out into the sea of eyes, all those faces he knew and loved…except for two men. Mr. Banther the UHCC representative, sat with his arms folded. He listened with the usual frown on his face.

Another man sat alone near the aisle on the back row, his long salt and pepper hair and beard fell down over an old flannel shirt. He had a bulge in his left cheek, quite odd for someone to have a dip in their mouth during service. Frank couldn't place him right off but the wrinkled face was familiar.

He didn't take the time to ponder on it long. There was silence today instead of organ music. It was show time.

"There you are. Friends and family. Those who I love. The people who I've seen grow up from children and have some of their own. The people who offer their hard earned money so they can hear this old man talk a couple of times a week. Think back and ask yourself how many years have you been coming to this church. And now think and try to remember how many sermons you've heard me give you from this pulpit. So many, I can't remember them all, some better than others. Maybe you have a favorite, one that stuck out, maybe even made you live a little better because of it. Today you are going to hear a sermon a little different then you're used to. It's going to be the most important thing I ever teach you. If you've been coming in here and sleeping for the last twenty years now is the time to wake up and take this one as the gospel."

Frank unloaded a sermon that held nothing back. He felt like it was his finest moment. The mysterious man with the flannel shirt and chewing tobacco was smiling, exposing his grungy teeth.

Chapter 37: *Wearing the Holy Cloth*

The office in which Daniel and his friends waited was well lit with humming fluorescent lights and no windows. Paintings of Christian icons hung on every wall, and the furniture was nicer than they'd grown accustomed to in their new college lifestyle. Lacy and Travis sat beside him on a fancy leather sofa. Katelyn, another cadet, was in a matching chair.

They had all been summoned just before class ended for the day. This was normally ice cream and study time. Terrance Martin, the learning coordinator, was the one who came and got them from class. He'd left them in this room and instructed them to wait.

Glancing around the room Daniel noticed two LED cameras. That meant recorded surveillance by campus security. The large oak door across from the sofa was opened by a man in a black suit. He was in his fifties, short neat hair and a three day old beard on his face. Pure businessman by the looks of him.

"Hello, I'm Elliott Ricnor, Chief Executive Officer and Grand Bishop of the UHCC. You are here today because of your hard work and immense potential. Your teamwork and skills separate you four from your peers," he paused and smiled, "and that's why you are the first to be offered career opportunities with us. I'd like to begin with you Mrs. Moore. This way please," he motioned for her to join him in the office. He closed the heavy door behind them.

"Cool, we're getting jobs," Travis said without much enthusiasm.

Twelve minutes later the door opened and they came out, "Mr. Montclair, your next."

Inside the office was classically decorated with paintings and sculptures. The walls were a dark polished maple. The desk was large and important looking, with a few papers and a computer screen on the top of it.

"Have a seat," Mr. Ricnor said and Daniel obliged. The businessman parked himself behind the desk in the large executive chair.

"Mr. Montclair, you seem like the glue that binds your study group together. You're a few years older and more educated than most of the cadets here. We've been watching your progress from afar and have also pried into your background. I know why you're here," he said.

Daniel was getting really good at hiding his real emotions. He just smiled back but on the inside he could have shit a brick, "Oh, really?"

"Liberal arts, theater, acting. You are a performer and one of quality. That's a solid foundation for a religious career. Your sermons were quite impressive. I take it you've had some proper training before you came here on how to write and give them. Or are you just a natural?"

Daniel relaxed a little.

"Well thank you sir. The theater and public speaking classes in college really gave me a good start. Reverend Catoe, the head of my church, taught me how to write sermons."

"Most students stick around for their final year of college. Just why didn't you? Did the Lord call you to serve?"

"An arts degree, majoring in theater only helps you do two things. Either be an under paid, underappreciated actor, or be a teacher that wishes they'd done something else. Reverend Catoe came to me looking for an apprentice. The UHCC requires dues and he wanted me to stir up some excitement in his old church, get some young blood and new money coming in on Sundays. It was a real chance, a real show with a real audience. I couldn't say no. I'm a performer, that's what I do and it's what I love," Daniel said and wondered if he'd told too much about his motives.

Ricnor gave a stern look and slammed his hand down on the desk. Daniel jumped a little.

"Finally a student that understands the game. Every student and most of the staff members who've sat in that chair have been so sidetracked with praising the Lord that they forget we are a business. This is the one place you can turn off the praying and the acting, just cut the bull and talk business. That's what I DO, and that's what I live for. I need folks here that are business minded like me, from performers to pencil pushers and everyone in between," He took a sip from his coffee mug.

"You are now the main campus assistant event coordinator. It's a new position, but don't let the 'Assistant' title fool you. It's quite important. You'll finish your training and be meeting with myself and other associates a few hours a week. I'll be giving you and some of your colleagues some advanced business training. Bishop Norwood is the figurehead of the church but I'm the power behind the throne. You and he will be doing the sermon writing. By next month all our churches will be wired for video feed. The plan is to have you stand on stage and give the sermon a few days early…but perform it like its live television. We record it on video file, several times to get it right if necessary and then email it out to each church leader."

Daniel jumped in, "That way everyone gets the same message."

"Exactly. The church leader plays your video. They mix in some local flavor, 'let's say a prayer for our recently deceased, Blah-Blah-blah' or 'We need a homerun in the donation basket this week.'"

Whenever a church leader gets sick, quits, or dies your video sermon fills the void. As long as we have someone there to turn on the lights and press play we don't have to rely on those lazy sheppards.

Daniel held up his hand as if he was asking a question in class. "Just how many churches are in the organization?"

"Well, haha," Ricnor chuckled and glanced over at his computer screen. "Currently there are over three-hundred-thousand in our system. Sixty thousand or so are on probation for not yet complying with our bylaws. Some of those are going to be closed down and some will be re-staffed. Twenty five hundred are what we call Mega-Churches, with attendance over two thousand in a single weekend. Those are our money makers, our golden geese if you will."

"Any idea how many church members are under the umbrella? And employees too?" Daniel asked.

"Pheeeew, well there are about seven thousand employees right now. It's a payroll nightmare but we hired a company that's getting that worked out. As for members, it's hard to get an exact number. Some people only go twice a month, others go three times a week and others go on Easter Sunday only. I'd say about a quarter of all Americans go to one of our churches at least once a week."

The young man's eyes wandered up at the ceiling as he tried to imagine how many people that was. "Wow. That's big. I don't think Broadway can hold a candle to that."

"Don't go getting stage fright on me now before you even begin."

"Oh don't worry, I've got a game-face from hell. What's this gig pay before I accept?"

"Well it's a new position so we're still working on all the benefits packages still. Probably around seventy-five thousand a year, three weeks paid vacation, holiday pay, travel expenses, full insurance."

Daniel remembered a trick his father had taught him on negotiating. "That's not a bad start, but it's a lot of responsibility for only seventy-five a year. I mean writing inspiring sermons is certainly not kids play."

The businessman was pleased, "We will do better than that salary if you meet my satisfaction on your first ninety days after training ends. Plus there are other perks, take my word for it."

Chapter 38: Allies

Those top four cadets spent a busy four weeks finishing their classes. Each had been given security badges that allowed them to enter campus buildings with just one swipe. Daniel looked stoned in the picture on his but no one bothered to look at the I.D. card.

They now included Katelyn in their study group. They were the four horsemen after two o'clock. Study time was run more efficiently, even with another person in their group they covered more ground. Katelyn was sharp. She had been chosen to be Elliott Ricnor's personal assistant. That meant she would have access to the books, all monies and important business. She was certainly the one for the job.

Lacy was in the technical operations center. Her main job was to make sure every church had at least two employees qualified to log onto the UHCC website and open the sermon videos and broadcast them on a projector or computer screen. The company had an army of technical geeks on phones all day long certifying people and testing them via an online test format. She'd go to class, then study, then either go for more advanced training or head to the technical building to look at the daily progress and try to fix problems after hours. She stayed up late most nights reading reports and making task lists for the tech geeks. They all could see the stress was wearing on her.

Travis was the new Youth Leader Assistant. He worked with a team of recruiters/salesmen armed with the task of recruiting new young members. Travis was their go to black guy, as he put it. He helped them target ads in print and online aimed at attracting the young blacks back into church. (Many had shut down or gone underground when the UHCC began charging dues.)

Travis wasn't thrilled about his job, but he didn't dare decline it. All he wanted was to return to his church and help it flourish. One day he would be the fourth generation of King Pastors at his church. Needless to say he wasn't very crazy about the UHCC changing the world. Really not one person that he knew was gung-ho about the company. At the same time, trash talking the church was one of the taboo subjects on campus. Cadets becoming romantically inclined was another. There were a lot of young attractive people studying each other's bodies just as much as their bibles. Lots of masturbation after hours was the only responsible outcome.

Daniel decided he was not the only one there with an ulterior motive. A little help could make all the difference, but he knew it could ruin him at the same time. Tactful caution was important. He knew Travis was the first to speak with. He'd began referring to the UHCC as the Monopoly Church.

Daniel waited on him outside the Dorms late in the evening, "Hey there preacher, got a minute?" Daniel teased.

Travis, not to let a joke die, jumped right into character as a minister.

"YEEEEESSSSSS, my son. I always have time for one of my flock."

"Good because I need some counsel," Daniel nodded for him to follow as they walked back towards main campus.

"I'm glad we're getting some good jobs and all…but I'm just not crazy about the way they run things here. It's all about money. Money and power. They're all about throwing a concert every week to keep the kids entertained. I guess the messages are good but it's not the same as when I was a kid. It's not personal…You know?"

"Oh, do I ever. My grandfather was the first to warn me about it. Even before the Fair Worship Act was passed. He told me that's how the government gets rid of something it doesn't like. It didn't like the churches being tax free. The taxes are how they control us and Uncle Sam gets all put out when he can't control us or at least get our money. Of course the church gets corrupt too. The government is getting paid, but the United Holy is getting rich, stupid rich."

Travis hadn't talked like this to another cadet and suddenly remembered where he was.

Daniel pressed his palms together as a sign of agreement, "Don't worry about me, I'm on your side."

They were walking slowly and talking in low whispers to not be overheard.

Daniel said, "My reverend didn't want to join, but in the end we had no choice, it was either join or be shut down."

"Yeah, same with us," Travis said, "My father wanted to organize a march in Washington but once he saw how all the rallies were being shut down so violently we decided we'd better get on board and wait for a better opportunity. We figure the system will get hit with a scandal sooner or later. Right now it's just too strong….too many on the band wagon."

"But what's going to happen while we wait on the church to hiccup along the way. Think of the poor folks that lose out in the meantime. People who started churches are being pushed aside for better entertainers. The common man will basically have to pay to pray in a house of God, and if they don't, their church will be boarded up and sold."

Travis stopped walking and looked Daniel in the eyes, "My brother, you are preaching to the very head of the choir."

"Well what if we could change things sooner than later? Instead of letting the church make a mistake, what if we ruin them first?" Daniel pressed.

Without a pause Travis came back, "But how? They aren't going to stop taking in money. They aren't gonna let anybody make them look bad. They've got too much power, too much influence on the media. We can cry wolf and they'd catch the words midair and cram them back down our throats. The big dogs have plans in case of a disgruntled employee or two, trust me on that."

It was time for Daniel to take a chance, "I hope this conversation is in confidence."

Travis nodded in agreement.

"I came here to shut this bitch down. It's my only purpose for being here. I don't want a job or respect or to be rich. I just came here to end this bullshit. And I have some ideas but I need a little help....maybe from the good Lord himself."

For maybe the first time since Daniel had met him, Travis wasn't smiling. "You and I are on the very same quest. What we're doing is lying, a trick of the Devil. Brother, don't feel like we are evil or alone. We have Jesus on our team."

That contagious smile came back and Daniel realized he was talking to the only real Christian he knew.

Chapter 39: The Lam

Mr. Banther was less than happy with the sermon. They waited on everyone to else to leave. Frank shut both doors. He was holding his old Bible, considering if he'd ever given a more powerful sermon.

"Reverend Catoe. That was NOT an approved message! I'm afraid your church is going to be fined for several infractions."

Frank smiled, "Oh really?"

"There was no greeter at the door. No music. Not a single song was sung. You didn't even pass around a collection plate!"

"Yeah, it felt good to not have to rob my friends for once," Frank laughed. He turned and walked back towards the altar.

Banther followed behind him, growing louder and angrier.

"I don't think you understand how serious this is Reverend. You're about to lose your church if you don't change things immediately. Starting with that book in your hand."

Frank stopped in the middle of the church and turned to face Banther.

"If you don't use your approved Bibles, I'm going to replace you with someone who will," Banther threatened.

Frank held up his Bible, "You mean this old thing. It must be about worthless then, right?"

Mr. Banther nodded his head in agreement, "It's about time you realized that."

Frank still had on his happy face, even though the fire inside him was blazing.

"Well, just wait a minute. I can still think of one thing it's good for."

Mr. Banther opened his mouth reply but Reverend swung his Bible with both hands and stuck him across the face.

The older man fell on his back, stunned by the blow. He was too stunned to be afraid as Frank stood above him.

"This one is much thicker that your version," the reverend said.

Frank came down with a fury of blows. Each thudded against Banther's skull until he was braindead.

Frank's truck rumbled on like a champ through the night. He almost wanted to take the risk and keep on driving it. Having to leave behind so many lifelong possessions hurt his old sentimental heart. No, the truck had to go before they were searching for it. He'd dropped some mighty hard clues in his last sermon, almost to the point of an encrypted confession. It was the easiest sermon he'd ever given and all off the cuff.

'How many murders does it take to make a serial killer?' he wondered.

He was on the interstate heading west through Georgia. He had a briefcase full of money and a suitcase with everything else. His plan was to leave his truck where it would be found by the police. Then commandeer another vehicle and head north without being followed. He was using cash only. Not just because he cleaned out his accounts, but it was also impossible to trace. And why not? He had just shy of four hundred thirty thousand dollars. Most of the bills were pictures of Benjamin Franklin. The bank was all but wiped out after he left.

He left the old Dodge on the side of I-75 between Macon and Forsyth. It was the first time he'd ever ran it out of gas. In fact the last time he'd abandoned a vehicle he'd set it on fire. This wasn't quite the same, it was bitter sweet. At three A.M. as he walked away with bags in hand. No gunfire of sirens. He told himself the truck had more good years on it. It would go to the police impound and eventually be sold at auction. Maybe it would be some young fella's first truck. He walked on hoping it wouldn't rot as criminal evidence.

He could have easily used his pistol and carjacked a ride, but the cops would be called, and he'd have more heat on him than before. Overpaying for a car with no questions asked was simpler. He had plenty of cash to throw at someone. He walked into the outskirts of Forsyth and found a cheap hotel room that took cash. The next morning he walked to a breakfast-house and ate. He ended up paying eighteen thousand dollars to Jake, the cook that fixed his omelet. He got a nine year old white sport utility vehicle that was worth less than half of that. Jake had agreed not to report it stolen for three weeks.

It rode much smoother than Frank's old truck but the driver's window motor was shit and had to be pushed up by hand. He'd driven to Georgia to throw off investigators who would guess he was heading either to Alabama or Mexico. Going south of the border wasn't a bad idea, but he hadn't given up his reputation and freedom to grow old in a place he knew nothing about. His course changed north to Ohio, Cincinnati in particularly. He and Daniel hadn't spoken since earlier in the week and he didn't want him freaking out when he heard the evening news. They never had talked about their diabolical plan over the phone. Frank didn't trust cell phones or land lines as being secretive enough. Still he had to be able to call Daniel. He stopped at a Dollar Mart and bought a prepaid smart phone. He called Daniel's phone at eight that evening but there was no answer. He tried again an hour later.

"Hello?" Daniel answered expecting a wrong number.

"Daniel, it's me," Frank said, "No matter what don't let anyone know we've spoken. I'm wanted by the police…or I will be soon."

The young man wasn't ready for that. He was in the technology operations center with Lacy. She had been showing him how they could link the video sermon to phones and tablets.

"Ohhh, ok, Sure. I'll just call you back in a few minutes Dad, and we'll talk about it. Ok…... Yeah….I can…..Ok, bye."

'What the hell is that all about? Shit, Frank is wanted? Fuck!!' he thought.

"Everything fine?" Lacy asked.

They were the only ones left in the building. She had an office upstairs above 'the pit', an open sea of computers, tables, and printers. She spent more time in her office than her bed.

"Yeah, Dad's trying to figure out what to get my mom for her birthday. She's kind of hard to shop for."

"Aww, that's sweet of you to help," She said. They'de been flirting with each other all day. He started it by letting her catch him looking at her during class. He'd just smiled after he was busted. At study group she'd been talking about the video sermon app she was working on and Daniel acted interested like he really gave a damn. Of course she invited him to see how it worked at the tech center.

"Mom and Dad have been married for twenty-nine years now. He still can't figure her out," he laughed.

"Well some women are just hard to read," she smiled and looked away from his eyes. They were standing a few feet away from one another.

He stepped closer, "Some aren't," he replied.

Lacy had that look on her face that meant she wanted to be kissed. He leaned in slowly, nose first. Their lips touched and she kissed him back with force. It wasn't a sweet first kiss between teen sweethearts. This was an aggressive make-out session fueled by weeks of sexual frustration and work. Daniel wasn't holding back, he grabbed her breast and squeezed. She groaned with excitement. It wasn't long before her clothes were on the floor and her legs were wrapped around him.

Frank got a hotel room near the Cincinnati Zoo. When Daniel called him back he told him to meet at the zoo entrance. It was almost midnight when Daniel's taxi pulled up. Frank was parked on the street and drove over in his new wheels. Daniel got in and listened to the whole story. Jane being pregnant, the pennyroyal poison, the arson, Elizabeth, Mr. Banther, the bank and his last sermon. Frank certainly wasn't proud telling the tale. Daniel assured him it's what had to be done, even though he wasn't so sure. Frank had admitted to Daniel three murders. It was good to have someone that understood his struggle and accepted his actions as unavoidable. What a relief it was for Frank, who had been pretending to be a saint for so long, could now act however he wished. He realized that sliding back into his old ways was only natural, and there was no going back to being a reverend.

Daniel heard Frank's story and was floored by it. The reverend was risking everything to do what he felt was right for his Christian way of life. It was a crusade against evil and Daniel was in too deep to turn back. He had no regrets about Mr. Banther having meet his end. Elizabeth had always been kind to him but had cheated on Frank. Daniel gave his mentor a pass on that one too. His only regret was Jane Dixon and not because of their sexual romps. He knew Leah's world would be turned on its head. He hadn't heard from her all week and that must have been why. He didn't feel bad for nailing Lacy. After all

Leah wasn't his girlfriend, as much as he would have liked it. She was exciting but so was his new enterprise.

The main Campus Assistant Event Coordinator, Mr. Daniel Montclair, gave his fugitive, ex-reverend the low down on what he'd learned of how the UHCC operates. About how he was working together with Travis and fucking Lacy to gain her trust and possibly another ally.

"I can think of a lot of ways to screw their system. I don't have access to their money or revenue income numbers…but Katelyn probably does. She's a tough cookie. Very career minded, very professional. If we could get her on our side we might have a little ammunition to work with. A bribe might work but it could backfire too."

Frank shook his head, "Having access to their bank account wouldn't do any good. They have checks and balances, security, and the law on their side. Just say you got into their account and could get their millions, just what then? Donate it all to charity? I doubt any one person has the authority to move that much money without alarm bells going off. Besides they would just cry foul and it would be put right back. You'd get tossed in prison, I'd be tossed under the prison and tortured. We need another angle."

Daniel admitted he was right.

"Well what now?" he yawned. It was late and he had to get up early for class.

"Keep doing what you're doing for now. I'm at that motel around the corner from the zoo. Whenever they come asking about me just play dumb. If you need to talk to me come by my room, it's number 319. Say, how long before those video sermons start going out?" Frank asked.

"Uuuhhhh, at least a couple weeks. Still waiting on some new servers to be installed. Lacy says we'll have more viewers than most network television stations. Can you imagine when it goes live in every church? That's got to rival the Super Bowl…every Sunday too."

Daniel tried imagining that many people stuffed into a huge church watching him give a sermon. He still hadn't spoken in front of more than a few hundred people yet.

Heading back to Campus he decided there had been too much chaos to abort his mission. He didn't want all the suffering to be for nothing. In his mind Frank's ethics and sanity weren't in question.

Chapter 40: Lies

It was eleven days after Reverend Catoe's exodus before the FBI came to ask Daniel if he knew anything about Frank and Elizabeth's disappearance. He'd already turned off his cell so he wouldn't get bombarded with questions from people in Tall Rock.

It was early morning and Daniel was getting ready for classes when there was a knock on his door. There was no peep hole to look through but he was mostly dressed, shirt still unbuttoned and missing shoes when he opened the door. It was Elijah Norwood and another man. Daniel knew he was in for an interrogation but had prepared for it.

"Good morning?" Daniel managed to ask and look sleepy eyed at the two men.

"Good morning Mr. Montclair. This is Agent Lewis with the Federal Bureau of Investigation."

"Hello," Daniel gave him a sleepy blink and nod.

The agent started in right away, "Daniel, we've pulled your phone records. When was the last time you spoke to Reverend Franklin Catoe?"

"Oh…it's been a while since I've heard from Reverend Catoe…a couple of weeks at least. Why?"

"What did you talk about? The last time you two spoke, did he seem normal?"

Daniel thought for a second, "Well I told him how school has been. He likes to know how my sermons are coming along."

Agent Lewis was impatient, "Is that all?"

Daniel thought again, "Oh and he told me he was getting over charged on his cell plan and how he planned to change carriers and that I shouldn't use my phone unless it was an emergency," he shrugged, "Frank pays my bills right now so he calls the shots. I just turned my phone off. I didn't really use it much anyway." He pointed to the phone sitting on his dresser, "What's up? Is he alright?"

The agent ignored the question, "So you haven't spoken to anyone in Tall Rock either? Social media maybe? Or called on a land-line?"

"No I stay pretty busy with school and I don't really have time for social media these days," he replied as he buttoned up his shirt.

"We do give our students quite a work load. Mr. Montclair is one of our top students, always studying and working on his sermons," Mr. Norwood interjected.

"Has something happened to Reverend Catoe?" Daniel asked.

"No, I just need you to call me if he contacts you OK? If he mails you a letter or a postcard or sends you a new phone give me a call. If he shows up here don't tell him I was here asking about him. Just talk about normal things and afterwards call me. No one is in trouble. The bureau is just investigating some issues and we need your cooperation on this." Agent Lewis handed him a business card.

"You are willing to cooperate aren't you Daniel?" Mr. Norwood asked.

"Yes sir, of course," Daniel said.

"Good, then don't mention this to anyone else. And remember to call when he contacts you," Mr. Norwood said, "Now have a good day."

They left him standing there still without shoes and walked back down the dorm hallway.

Daniel realized he was becoming the character he was portraying. Many top actors claimed that was the only way to be believable. He was a spy. Fuck the FBI, he had a mission to complete.

That was Tuesday, but by Wednesday Tall Rock was on the National News. Elizabeth Catoe's body had been found miles downstream by a kayaker. She and Frank were already "Missing Persons" on the local news but it took days for the Motte County Sherriff investigators to put together the Jane Dixon death and disappearance of the Catoe's. It wasn't until Mr. Bowman of Tall Rock Citizens Bank came forward that anyone suspected Frank of anything. Mr. Banther's body was found later stuffed in the storage closet in Tall Rock Baptist and an all-out federal investigation was launched.

Chapter 41: Casual Sex

Frank gave himself a makeover and paid Benji, a graphic artist, six hundred dollars for a first class phony driver's license. His new license listed him as Earl McWhite, from Hopkinsville, Kentucky. His new look with no beard, crew cut and glasses was a stark contrast to the 'Reverend on the Run' that everyone was supposed to be on the eye out for. He changed to another crummy hotel that took cash along with a deposit. Benji also introduced him to Keith his pot dealer, who was a little skeptical of Frank who wanted to buy an entire pound of the strongest reefer available. It was far stronger than the legal amount of THC allowed. It was the same strain that had made several people die from Brain Hypoxia. The THC had slowed down their breathing so much that they'd acquired brain damage or had a stroke. Frank didn't care if it was illegal or dangerous, he wanted the best high available. He also begun reading on the internet the latest in surveillance equipment and what to do with it. Frank knew he had to be clever to catch the UHCC with their pants down. They had a state of the art security system on campus and they had an entire office dedicated to cyber security.

Saturday they had a graduation for the students who had managed to pass all the classes. Over three hundred students had begun the school but only one hundred-thirty had passed. Most of those had been assigned a job in the organization, although many were not thrilled to move somewhere new and take over a church that didn't really want them.

It was low key, as far as graduations go. No cap and gowns. No valedictorian speeches. No walking across the stage. A good many parents and preachers packed the auditorium to show support. Elliott Ricnor gave a sermon type commencement speech. Frank snuck in to watch, but also to learn. He took notice of the surveillance cameras, the campus layout, and put a few names to faces. He took notice of one in particular, Mr. Ricnor who usually stayed behind the scenes but on this occasion was sitting on stage as the names were read aloud. Frank dared not approach Daniel on campus, he just blended with the crowd and left without saying a word to anyone. He didn't realize he'd been identified by a smart camera as he was leaving.

By Monday all the classes were over and had been replaced by work and meetings. Most of the recent graduates were packed and headed home but about forty remained for work on campus. They were told to continue living in the dorms for the time being.

There were department meetings on Wednesdays, Fridays and Sundays. Monday and Tuesday was considered their weekend time. Daniel met with the production department every Wednesday. He'd presented two or three sermons to a panel of men that resembled a board room meeting. They listened and took notes. Mary, another former student transcribed each sermon and sent out them in email to the department panel. They met on Fridays and discussed changes they'd come up with. Then after the final draft Daniel would practice the rest of the day. Sometimes the panel would tell him to add a couple of passages or to cut something for time, but usually they liked what he came up with.

He spent Saturday morning dressing up and performing his sermon in front of a live audience of church employees and occasional visitors. It was run like a movie set. There was a full camera crew, director, and rock band with accompanying choir…not to mention a small army of people behind the scenes.

Occasionally Mr. Ehlms, the director, would cut the scene and retake it telling Daniel to speak more slowly or change the lighting. He would deliver part of his sermon, then introduce the band. After a song or two about something pertaining to his sermon, he would give a prayer and go back to preaching. Saturdays were busy. He would have lunch break for two hours so he could eat and change clothes, all the while practicing for his next recorded sermon that same afternoon. He met with Frank on Mondays. Frank, who was slowly reverting back to his younger days on the other side of the law.

Daniel would walk to their new meeting place, Pilot Park, which was the median of a pedestrian street without cars. He would walk into the park, sit down on a bench somewhere near the middle and read his bible. Sometimes he would get there early just because he liked reading outside and jot down some notes to use in a sermon later. Between two in the afternoon and two-thirty, Frank would be across the street watching Daniel, and more importantly to see if anyone else who was watching him. At two-fifteen Daniel would get up and walk to the bus stop on Seventh Street. When Frank was sure they hadn't been followed he'd join him at the bus stop and then they'd head out, usually walking. Once they'd taken the bus but they didn't like having to whisper to avoid being overheard.

They shared any news. It was mostly Daniel telling Frank about the computer systems or how the hierarchy of The UHCC worked. Once he brought a security handbook that was issued to the web nerds in the Technology building. He'd swiped it after going to see Lacy one afternoon.

Frank was thrilled. He'd been learning the ways of a computer hacker, although for a dinosaur like him it was slow learning. His new toy was called a ghost computer, a laptop that was nearly untraceable. He'd paid three thousand to have the top of the line hacking machine. The guy he bought it from was named Cooper and was more paranoid than Frank.

Lacy was another subject. Ever since the first time they'd fucked she was wanting it more often than not. Not quite a nymphomaniac like Jane Dixon but she was building up to it. She liked to talk afterwards, mostly about work but also personal things like her family. Daniel was worried she was wanting a relationship but she must have sensed it and reassured him they were just 'naughty friends'. He eventually went out and bought a new cell just to be able to communicate with her and Travis more easily. He didn't want the FBI to catch Frank so they kept meeting once a week in person to talk. Travis sent him the phone numbers of many other UHCC employees. From members in the band to members on the board of directors, he had connections.

Lacy never bothered him during work hours, though they often saw one another at meetings and on campus, but after hours she let him know when she was horny. They had plenty of late night fuck sessions. She would text him things like:

Lacy Let's go on a mission trip

Daniel Wtf ?

Lacy whoops I meant, let's do missionary ;) hehehe

Lacy Or doggystlye…it's whatever…How about 10:30 here??

Daniel OK

She was also on campus, a cautious three minute walk to get inside her room. It was in the C – building where the females on campus lived. He would peer in the small glass window in the double door. If the auto lights were off he was clear to enter. They would turn on but two seconds later he was in her room that she'd left unlocked for him. She was under the covers, with only her head visible. He knew the only thing she was wearing was a pair of socks. He locked the door and began his goofy stripping ritual, bobbing his head from side to side to the tune of the only techno beat he could remember. He stripped down all except his socks also. And the show began….

Twenty minutes later the huffing and puffing had subsided. Lacy got up to use the toilet and Daniel quietly sprang into action. He'd brought one of Frank's new toys with him. To the average person it looked just like and old flip phone because at one time it had been. Now it was repurposed as a spy tool. It had two functions. The first was to piggy-back the signal from Lacy's phone calls and send it the second signal to Frank's ghost computer and download it to an audio file. Any conversations she had would be picked up by the spy phone as long its battery was charged and she was within a ten meter range. Its second function was similar. It grabbed text message signals as they were sent and received and that gave Frank a lesson in millennial text lingo. Daniel hit the power button and set it behind a shoe box in the top of her closet.

Frank got to read lots more redundant texts from Lacy than he cared for. He didn't know who the messages were to or from, only that they were nearly all pointless. He also had an audio file come through. It was a phone call from Lacy's mother back in Tempe. It was useless information but it gave Frank a chance to learn modern day spy work.

The old reverend had a standing order with the hotel maid service not to clean his room, which he had turned into an office. He had his ghost computer and another laptop at the small dining table where he spent many hours a day reading about new surveillance techniques and of the doings of the UHCC.

He made an anonymous profile on unholychurch.org, a forum that talked a bunch of crap but did little. It was mostly disgruntled pastors and unhappy Christians looking for a community of others to vent their frustrations. They were collecting money to try and lobby in Washington, but Frank knew the UHCC had more money and power than any right wing websites could even imagine. He did find a few individuals who seemed more like revolutionaries, but it's easy to talk tough on a keyboard, but building real alliances proved difficult.

<u>Chapter 42:</u> Other Voices

Daniel Montclair was quickly becoming a celebrity. All UHCC churches were required to show a broadcasted sermon during service on Sunday and Wednesday. They were able to download and view a choice of five sermons, each from a different "Worship Leader". There had been such blowback when Daniel was the only Worship Leader for a church to choose from, Elliott Ricnor decided they needed to culturally diversify, which meant they needed people other than just a white guy. The UHCC hired top religious leaders that were already well known and liked.

They often used the same sermon as Daniel but they made changes to better fit their preaching style. Occasionally one would get permission to stray from the Alpha Sermon and preach something they had written. This created much more work because it had to be approved through the UHCC council. Having five more people at the meetings was five times as chaotic, as they were all used to being a voice that was meant to be heard. Then there were five more tapings of sermons, all with band changes because one musical style doesn't fit all. To put it simply, things had become more than complicated.

Pastor Fredrick "Full Gospel" McKnight was a well-known speaker in the black community. He would read the same sermon as Daniel but it would take twice as long. Of course he added plenty of 'Hallelujahs' and 'Amens'. It was his own style and he did it well.

Manuel "Felipe" Hernandez, the Texan born from Mexican parents, was the heartbeat of Spanish Gospel in the southwest. His sermons were primarily Spanish but he knew to throw in a few English words when the time was right. For being in his early forties he had way of speaking to every generation and making everyone feel equal. His sermons created the most trouble because none on the council spoke any Spanish, therefore they had to hire a translator to verify that his sermon was very close to what Daniel had written before it was approved to be broadcast.

Helen Osborne was there for the white women to have a voice, and a soft soothing voice it was. She was a thirty-six years, old married mother of two. On her first sermon she brought her whole family up and introduced them because she often mentioned them during sermons. After taking her father's job of preaching after he'd had a second heart attack, she'd then built up Southern Omaha Methodist Church. Within three years thay'd merged it with sixteen other Methodist churches in Nebraska, Kansas and Oklahoma. It became, The Lord's Service Methodist Church, and with almost seven thousand members was the largest in the region. Helen Osborne had shown the other church leaders how they could all save and gain members by banding together. Three years later the UHCC had made it all for nothing.

Zeke Agala was a long haired Hawaiian that was Daniel's age. He was young and hip with the kids, exactly what the UHCC was looking for. His style was more like a west coast surfer, which is what he was before he learned that surfing didn't pay the bills. Much like young Franklin Catoe had done, Zeke bounced around to any kind of church or prayer service that would let him pass the plate around. He started giving his sermons through a webcast and found quite a following; though it was less affluent and more of a grass roots crowd. They sent in donations with digital currency and he was becoming quite wealthy even after the UHCC tried to get him shut down. Finally the IRS began investigating him but the UHCC pulled some strings and he became a Worship Leader for them.

Maya Robinson was another young up and coming star in the Christian world. She had a voice that could lead a gospel choir and a personality to match. She had what it took to bring younger people into the pews…black and white. Often she would burst into song during the sermon or grip the altar as if the good Lord was making her faint.

Daniel Montclair. Worship Leader. Sermon writer. He was the least experienced of them all and yet he was the most influential with the UHCC board of directors. His sermons were like gold and adhered exactly to the church guidelines. That was something the other Worship Leaders, accomplished sermon writers themselves, weren't used to. Fredrick McKnight almost quit his first day when he found out he wasn't able to use his own bible. Many of them gave Daniel ideas for sermons, but they all gave him respect. He saw it as an opportunity to meet new allies but also enemies, for he knew the UHCC would be paying those big names lots of money and they might not be keen to the idea of him and Frank trying to kill their golden goose.

Daniel used every chance he could to engage in socializing with his new colleagues. Frank gave him the idea of using food to bring people together. A lunch out, just the Worship Leaders…on the dime of the UHCC. Daniel got it approved and they even turned him loose with the company expense card for the afternoon.

They all met at the House of Steak, an expensive restaurant near campus. None of the colleagues had a problem spending the company dollar for a nice meal and a glass of wine. Mrs. Osbourne ordered a chardonnay first and so did Mr. McKnight once the ice was broken. Daniel decided to partake in the drinking, hoping someone else would loosen up and show their hidden dislike for the UHCC.

These were professionals who knew the bible cover to cover and knew people as well. Daniel was wired with one of Frank's new toys that recorded the sounds. He played the greenhorn and admitted his lack of experience with live performances.

"I'm sure it's gonna happen to me one day, I haven't bombed in front of an audience," he was saying.

"Full Gospel" McKnight spoke up with advice, "It's gonna happen sooner or later," He said after swallowing a bite of ribeye, "The trick is to realize what's happening and turn it around. That's where you have to give them a classic phrase. I like to use something like 'Jesus loves you…show him your love.' It's easy as a simple catch phrase like that…then work back into the sermon."

Daniel took a sip of wine and nodded.

Helen Osbourne chimed in, "Yeah, you need a slogan, a calling card if you will. Something that no one else uses. You write some wonderful sermons but like any artist you should sign them with your own special touch."

The conversation drifted to dress clothes and then food but Daniel listened for disdain toward the UHCC without being the one to get it started. Manuel seemed a little upset for all the rules he had to follow since he was used to doing things his own way, but he dropped the subject when the others fell silent. Full Gospel didn't even mention having to use their new bible. They all were leery of speaking against the church. Daniel wondered if they all were angels of death like he or perhaps they were spies that would get a bonus for turning in a heretic. Who was what? Daniel wished they would all get drunk and throw their caution out the window but the dinner was wrapping up before a second round of wine could be ordered.

When the group dispersed Daniel drifted towards Pilot Park. He had time to kill before meeting Frank, so he stopped in another restaurant, straddled a barstool and ordered another glass of wine. He drank one glass and then another.

What a poker game it was, and how he wished he could see what hands the other players were holding. He felt like he had some allies, but even more enemies. 'I need more allies,' he thought, 'I need the Lord's help on this one…Hey, that's not bad, might use that in a sermon.'

He paid his tab and walked out to rendezvous with Frank, his heretic spiritual leader. He never noticed the man who followed him down the street.

Chapter 43: Kidney Punches

Frank's paranoia was finally justified. He sat inside the Mad Cat Coffee Shop with a window view of the park. On time as always, Daniel strolled up and carefully selected a bench with a good bit of sunlight. As he sat and read his bible, Frank sipped coffee and spied a man behind Daniel that was watching him.

The man's hair was short and grey with a large bald spot on top. He wore jeans and a sport coat. Frank figured he was at least forty years old. He'd been walking on the park trail when Frank spotted him, but he cut across to the sidewalk to put some distance between him and the young man he was tailing. He took a cell out of his pocket and leaned against a building, appearing to be texting. Frequently he glanced up to peer at Daniel.

Frank didn't like the damn Feds watching Daniel. They may or may not catch the 'Reverend on the Run', but they might catch wind of Daniel trying to screw with the church.

Bald spot sat there waiting on Daniel to move and he finally did. As usual, he walked to the bus stop on Seventh Street. Frank sat still, sipping his coffee and watching the man shadow Daniel down the street. Frank waited a couple more minutes and left in the opposite direction back towards his hotel, cursing himself for the sins he'd committed and the justice that would one day follow.

Daniel was oblivious that he was being watched by anyone other than Frank. He waited at the bus stop as the routine normally went, but after five minutes he knew something was wrong. The old man had been like clockwork, until today. That meant shit had gone wrong, either Frank had been caught, or there was a reason he couldn't approach him. He'd read about some larger cities using facial recognition cameras to catch criminals, but he wasn't sure if Cincinnati was using them yet.

His worry turned again to guilt. After all wasn't it his whoring around with Jane Dixon that got Frank into this trouble.

Finally a hand grasped his shoulder, "Whew," he gave a sigh of relief that Frank had just been late, but as he turned to greet his partner it became clear this man with a bald spot wasn't part of their team.

"Get in the car," he growled, just as a black Mercedes flew up to the curb. The man had Daniel by the shoulder still and forced him into the back seat of the sedan. The car sped off from the bus stop. A light skinned black guy was driving. Bald spot pulled a 9mm out of his jacket and aimed it at Daniel's lap.

"Don't say a fuckin word and you won't get shot in the dick," he told Daniel, who decided it was a good idea to comply.

The driver zig-zagged towards the north side of town apparently trying to lose anyone that might follow them. The pace finally slowed and they pulled into a parking garage. The Mercedes climbed the upward spiral floor by floor until they were on the rooftop level. The only other vehicle was a grey SUV and they parked beside it.

"Get out," said bald spot. Once more Daniel complied, not wanting to get shot in the dick. Bald spot was right beside him.

The back window of the SUV rolled down. The man sitting there was an older white guy with sunglasses and two bad scars on his face. They started on the top left forehead and crossed over his nose to the right cheek. "I don't know what kind of shit you're up to kid, but I know you better be careful. Hell, you are an important guy. Big job…a big job that rides on your image and your reputation. You have a lot to lose."

Daniel didn't have the first freaking clue who the old guy was and decided on doing a little acting to look tough.

"I don't give a damn who you are, if you don't-" the old man nodded his head and bald spot hit Daniel in the lower ribs with a sucker punch that doubled him over.

"Aaaaaahhh, god damnit," Daniel cried out.

The man sneered, "A holy man no doubt. Frank Catoe's piss-ant-choir-boy."

Daniel looked up and slowly regained his posture.

"Yeah, I know all about the Reverend on the Run and that he trained you for the job you're at now. And I also know that you meet Ole Frank every so often. He does good staying in the shadows, keeping a low profile. You two are smart enough to fool the Feds, but Leo here could piss in a beer glass and fool the Feds. So don't bullshit me boy," He said with contempt.

Daniel knew this old guy was bad news but he tried to look tough and show he wasn't scared.

"Okay, so what do you want?" Daniel asked.

The old man nodded again ever so slightly and Daniel was rocked even harder, this time square in the gut. He dropped to the concrete on his hands and knees gasping for air.

"You fucking millennials don't know how to shut up do ya?" He asked.

"I've got a video of you, PRINCE MOREAU. Yeah a video of you acting like Bill Shakespeare and then upchucking down a girl's throat. A video like that gets out…linking you and the bigtime church across town to that…You'd have a little explaining to do. Wouldn't ya?"

Daniel was on all fours still but his brain was on alert listening to the old man.

The old man lit a cigarette and took his time. Daniel dared not speak again for his new fear of Leo's right fist.

"What I want is Frank Catoe. THAT SNEAKY FUCK!"

Chapter 44: The Plan

For the two days since he'd been abducted on the street, Daniel's life was a wreck. While still nursing an aching ribcage, he was getting burnt out on the constant pressure to write and perform new cutting edge sermons twice a week. Constant paranoia of FBI agents and whoever wanted to get Frank didn't help his concentration either.

He'd blown off meetings with Travis and Lacy so he could have more time to think and hope Frank would get in touch with him. Lacy reminded him often that he could come to her room and "de-stress" as long as they didn't get caught.

Frank didn't dare approach Daniel until he was sure no one was watching, and even then he came in disguise. It was a security guard uniform from the Happy Time Clothes and Donation Outlet down the street from his hotel. He also started smoking cheap cigars. It made him feel a little like Clint Eastwood in an old western, but more importantly it was a way for him to observe his surroundings while maintaining the image of a working guy on smoke break.

He was casually strolling the sidewalk on campus when Daniel noticed him.

He first took notice of Frank and thought he might be a federal agent tracking him. Then he recognized the facial structure and posture of his accomplice. A wisp of cigar smoke gently rolled out of his mouth and their eyes met briefly. Daniel pulled his phone out and pretended to play a game.

He lazily strolled over to a picnic table at the campus property line beside the wrought iron fence. The fence had brick columns every ten feet and Frank was leaning with his back to the column facing the other direction. They were only ten feet apart but to the casual observer they were unaware of each other.

"I got shanghaied by a couple of jerks the other day, wasn't the Feds," Daniel said.

"I heard the whole thing from your transponder. We had some shit happen over thirty years ago. A drug deal went bad and some people got killed. I thought it had been lost in the past until I heard his voice. His Name is Douggy."

"Ha-ha that's just great…" Daniel snickered, "Drug dealer, why does it not surprise me?"

Frank wasn't his normal calm self and fired back, "I wasn't always a reverend and I never claimed to be a saint."

"NO SHIT FRANKIE!!" Daniel fumed and turned to talk to the brick column Frank was hiding behind, "But I'm not used to being jumped by the redneck godfather and getting the shit kicked out of me. I've never been investigated by the FBI, I didn't sign up for this shit!"

Frank took a long drag and changed his tone, "I know. I know. I never thought in a million years things would get so crazy…You're handling it better than even I cou-"

"Don't kiss my ass and don't give me any more fucking sermons. If I hear one more I'll get a fucking aneurism and fall over dead. That's if I don't get shot and thrown in the river by your old friend or arrested for conspiracy to murder."

The thought had crossed his mind what kind of trouble he could be in for getting caught with a double murdering arsonist.

Frank likewise had cringed at the idea of leading Daniel into even more dangerous waters.

Frank said, "If you want I can pay you off and leave you alone. I can try and go it alone from here and I won't ever bother you again or rat you out. And I wouldn't blame you if you walked away."

He didn't wasn't pushy and gave Daniel time to think.

Daniel set his phone on the picnic table and put his hands on his forehead.

"I'm trying Frank, but I don't see us making any progress. All we have is some phone conversations of people being boring as fuck. We don't have any proof of wrongdoing or anything. I mean it's a great try, but I can't get any dirt doing what I do. I'm just too busy writing these damn sermons."

"Do you know what the tabloids do when there isn't any juicy gossip?" Frank asked, "They make something up. They lie and crop two pictures together and it gets attention. The attention gets people talking, investigating and sometimes…well sometimes the conspiracy theories are true…and that little spark starts a forest fire." His cigar was just a nub and he threw it down.

"I've got an idea, but it'll take you, me and Travis too. If it works my name will be cleared and Douggy goes down with the UHCC… And we're gonna have to lie our asses off to make it happen."

Of course Daniel was going to help. Danger was his vice, and in a strange way Frank was his idol, "Just how in Shakespeare's shithole are we going to do that?"

"We have to get a phone inside Ricnor's office…while he's in there… and neither one of us can be there."

Travis and Daniel met in the campus courtyard at 8:15 pm. They took the sidewalk and got away from the UHCC security cameras, already thinking about evidence in a possible upcoming investigation. Daniel relayed Frank's plan.

"So you need me to get this spy-phone into the boss's office and send a text using his phone number," Travis said.

"Frank says all you'll have to do is get close enough to him–or to his cell to hijack his phone's signal. Ten feet, so anywhere in his office, and then just send a text that's already saved to a number that's already saved as Douggy. It's gonna say something to let Douggy know where he can find Frank."

Travis shook his head, "That's the part I really don't understand. This reverend of yours. Who is wanted for double-" He looked around and lowered his voice, "He's wanted for double murder and you're going to give him up to a drug dealer who wants to drop him off a building. And then you want to lie to the Feds and tell'em it's the church's fault?"

Daniel had been thinking of flaws in the plan all afternoon. "Frank meets with the drug dealers, they beat the shit out of him…But I get the FEDs there in time to save him."

"What if they just shoot Frank as soon as they set eyes on him?" Travis asked.

"I guess we'll have to pray for him," Daniel said. "Then the Feds investigate. Frank tells them he was kidnapped weeks ago by Douggy and that Ricnor paid him to do it. They'll see a text message sent from Ricnor to Douggy and then you and I play stupid."

Travis nodded his head, "Yeah we can play stupid. This is stupid. We're both gonna go to prison for conspiracy to being stupid. Why would they believe the church would do something like that anyway?"

"Because of me. I'm gonna say that I was gonna quit writing sermons and go back to South Carolina to protest the church like

Frank was planning to do, but they nabbed Frank and held him ransom so I'd keep working here like a slave."

Travis shook his head in disbelief, "Ya'll been watching too many movies man…or maybe not enough. They're gonna find out the truth, this isn't a sermon to people who are your congregation. The Feds want facts not some smooth lies and text messages. How do I get into Ricnor's office anyhow? The only time we've been there is when he gave me my job."

They stopped at the corner of a busy intersection and just talked as cars went by.

"He likes to intimidate people, show he's boss. It's the power. I bet he likes firing people too," Daniel exclaimed.

"First you want me to be an accessory to conspiracy, and now you want me to try and lose my job. A job that I had to work my ass off to get. Are you crazy?" Travis asked.

"You could grab Katlin's boobs. You get to play with her melons and it lands you in the principal's office," Daniel argued.

"What makes you think she won't like it? I mean she has been playing hard to get but those are the ones that want it the most. You know what they say, once you go black…"

"What your credit score goes down?" Daniel teased.

"Ha-Haaaa. This man's got jokes. You actually found a black guy in Cincinatti with a job, and now you want me to get fired? Now that's a joke," Travis said.

"It's the best chance we've got to stir up some shit before I get hammered by Douggy again, or Frank gets popped by a cop that recognizes him. We've got to try something and that's the best we've got."

Travis nodded and they began walking back toward campus. They walked silently in thought for a while before he agreed.

"Ok. I'll stick my neck out there and get it done but you have to put your ass on the line too."

"Alright," Daniel was curious, "How's that?"

"Doing what you do best," Travis replied.

Chapter 45: Endgame

Frank had done his research. He'd looked at all the possible scenarios again and again. He figured that their plan had a fifty-fifty shot at best but he liked to think that if there was a God he might make the odds a little better.

He'd wiped his hotel room for fingerprints and vacuumed before he left the door wide open and walked away without dropping off the key card. Most of his money he'd buried in a duffel bag two feet deep in Lockmore Park between two large shrubs. At a little after two in the morning he'd dug the hole with his bare hands and covered it with mulch it as best he could to make it look untouched. He took a mental picture so he could describe it to Daniel later that morning.

Leaving the hotel with only his briefcase in hand he began the walk to the parking garage. He figured it was a good place to meet Douggy, somewhere familiar where he probably did drug deals or whatever he was into these days. Frank had taken a GPS signal with the spy phone that was on Daniel during the rooftop meeting. He'd carefully scoped the place and found there weren't any cameras, something Douggy already knew.

As he walked up to the garage he glanced at his wrist watch, three fifteen, plenty of time. Travis was supposed to start the party around four and let him know. Frank strolled in past the gate where tickets are given. There wasn't anyone working the booth; just a couple of signs that read, $7 per hour weekdays - $9 Weekends, towing enforced.

Then he paced and waited for the text. % meant Travis had done his part, but >> meant it hadn't worked. Frank had given both Daniel and Travis many instructions and he hoped they could remember it all under pressure.

At four o'clock Travis was at the office of ELLIOTT RICNOR, President and CEO of the UHCC, as was printed on his door. Katelyn his assistant was in the outer office like a secretary when he walked inside. Travis had tried to flirt with her to for weeks but she wasn't having it. She looked at him with disapproval as he walked in.

"Hey girl, I need to see Mr. Ricnor."

"You don't have an appointment. I can try and schedule one but it will be sometime next week…maybe Tuesday, let me see…" she began tapping the computer monitor for the calendar.

"I can't wait until Tuesday. This is an emergency, I've got to see him right now," He insisted.

She cut her eyes at him, "Just what is your emergency?" She asked.

"I can't tell you, it's private…but he has to know right now." He leaned over the desk and put both hands down on it flexing his forearms and bulging his eyes. It was an intimidation tactic his father liked to use on occasion. It backfired.

She stood up eye to eye with him and threatened, "Don't you try that with me! I can have security here with the push of a button! Now Mr. Ricnor is in a meeting and you're going to have to wait until it's over before I can even ask if you can pry into his busy schedule but don't think—" She stopped short when the intercom buzzed.

"Send in Mr.-?" Came the voice from the intercom.

"Mr. King." Travis answered.

"Yes, just a moment and I'll let you in," The voice said calmly. Travis realized it wasn't Ricnor.

The lock clicked and the door opened. Travis looked at Katelyn for a moment and walked in.

Mr. Ricnor was sitting behind his desk with his arms folded looking a little surprised to see Travis. Across from him in one of the visitors chairs sat a man close to Ricnor's age that Travis had never seen.

"Take a seat won't you, Mr. King?" He motioned to the last vacant chair. "This is Douglas Goings. Don't mind him, he's just part of our financial department. You can speak freely in his presence."

Mr. Goings nodded and forced out an irritated smile.

"Now what can I do for you?" Ricnor asked.

Travis' mind caught up with the situation. He had work to do, sneaky work. He had to send a text message linked with his boss's phone, but this other guy was watching. They were both watching him.

"My role here is to lure students into going to church by showing them our diversity, our youth, but look around campus it's almost all …" he paused.

"White guys?" Mr. Goings asked.

"Well yeah," Travis agreed.

Ricnor added. "That's true. As a whole the UHCC is sixty two percent white, but here on campus it's closer to eighty-five percent. Your main concern is being more diversified, yes?"

Travis had planned to catch them off guard but they seemed ready to discuss the issue. "Well…eh. I think this campus is the heart of the church and we should bring more people in to see and be involved. Sunday school trips, tours, that kind of thing. But if a tour bus full of black kids comes here to get excited about church and all they see is white guys in suits they aren't gonna be so hyped. It's just not what they're used to. You understand my meaning sir?" He was really just hoping for an interruption on Mr. Ricnor's side. A phone call or him searching his computer for a number.

"Well, most of our on-screen staff is very diverse. From our sermon leaders to the band and the choir too. That's what the masses see, a harmony of all races under one church," Mr. Ricnor advised.

This meeting was becoming too professional. Travis didn't want to pull his phone out while debating but the men left him little choice.

"I saw a video the other day about tours at the Natural History Museum. They had a behind the scenes tour that was more popular than the main tour itself. Let me see if I can find it," He pulled out his spy phone and started to go through the linking process just as Daniel had showed him. He made sure to hold the phone close like a poker hand he didn't want Mr. Goings to see.

SpyPhone: LINKING… …LINKING…LINKING…CONNECTED.

Mr. Goings asked, "Why do we need behind the scenes? The people will be happy with what we give them, not the editing room, not the boardroom, not the cafeteria."

Spy phone: CONNECTED TO E. RICNOR CELL

There were four saved numbers in the phone's contacts:

E. Ricnor - LINKED

DOUGGY -

DANIEL-

FRANK-

He selected DOUGGY – SEND SAVED MESSAGE

…SENDING MESSAGE…MESSAGE SENT.

"Perhaps he has a point," Ricnor interrupted, "MAYBE the people need a destination, a pilgrimage if you will. This is the best thing we have right now. We could charge a small fee to let groups sit in at the filming of every sermon….Maybe they even get on TV. It would have the pull of a gameshow…"

Mr. Goings' phone chimed. He reached in his jacket pocket for it.

"That's what I was getting at," Travis said. "We would have more people interested in the church…let them eat in the cafeteria with us to."

He cut his eyes back to Mr. Goings for a reaction but he was too busy looking at his phone. Travis continued, "I could lead a tour around campus and give a sermon at the end. Answering some questions is the best way to recruit. You see, by getting folks involved with our program they become our free advertisement. They tell everyone how great of a time they had in Cincinnati visiting our campus."

"Sorry to get off topic but I've got an issue we must look into," Mr. Goings said to Mr. Ricnor and he leaned across the desk to show Ricnor the phone. The text message read:

FROM: E.R. Rev Catoe. $80,000 cash. Meet at 5:30 top of parking garage like last time.

"Did you send me that just now?" Goings asked Ricnor, who read the message and was confused as well.

"No I..." He reached for in his desk drawer and pulled out his own cell to look at it.

"No, but that's my number. It's…Wait who would have written that?" They both looked at Travis. He'd already slipped the phone into his right pocket and pulled his real, more modern phone out his left pocket.

Goings told Ricnor, "Send your secretary out on an errand."

He pushed the intercom button on his desk, "Katelyn, go over to Pizza House and get a large pepperoni with mushrooms and olives. Oh, and stop by the grocery store and see if you can find some sweet ice tea."

"Yes Sir," She replied.

Mr. Goings took up the questioning on Travis. "So what's going on kiddo? You and Daniel playing some games with us eh? Frank too?"

Travis tried playing stupid, "What do you mean? I don't play games, I'm serious about these racial inequalities regarding minorities at this institution!"

"Oh, ok," Mr. Goings who was still standing at the desk set his phone down and slapped the hell out of Travis with the back of his hand almost knocking him out of the chair. Travis grabbed his face, both hurt and surprised. Before he had a chance to even look up Mr. Goings had a nine millimeter pistol pointed at his nose.

"Now I'm an old man, and I don't have the patience I used to have, so either you get to talking or I start unloading. Oh and I want your cell phone." Travis handed him the phone he held.

"And now the other one, the one that looks like it's older than you."

Travis didn't move.

He reminded him, "It's in your right pants pocket."

Travis reluctantly pulled the phone out and handed it over as well. Goings handed it over to Ricnor who began inspecting it.

"You aren't going to shoot me. You'd never get away with it. There would be evidence everywhere and people would hear it, Douggy."

Douggy Goings was leaning on the desk with the gun on Travis. He reached into his pocket and pulled out an object that looked like a piece of water-pipe and began threading it onto the end of the pistol barrel.

"I tell the head of campus security what to do." He nodded toward Ricnor, "Shit I tell him what to do sometimes. You see I'm not your typical financial consultant like Elliott here introduces me, you see I kill people when it helps me, but sometimes I let them live. Now which do you want to be?"

Travis was beyond scared, he was on the edge of pissing his pants in terror. "I want to live," he said.

<u>Chapter 46:</u> Shit Gone Wrong

Daniel was in his room, missing a meeting with the other prayer leaders. It was just a brainstorm session for the Christmas season that was months away. Not that he wouldn't skip anything for what was about to happen. Travis was going into the lion's den. And Frank!! He hated to think of what Frank was getting himself into in a few minutes. As soon as Travis gave him the go ahead he was ready to call up Agent Lewis and lie to a federal investigator, which was not a small thing either. He heard the spy phone vibrate.

>>

"AWW SHIT!!" A failure Daniel thought. 'What could have gone wrong?' He knew it wasn't the best plan to begin with. 'Maybe Ricnor wasn't in his office today.' The phone then began to vibrate again.

INCOMING CALL: TRAVIS

He immediately answered, "Hey, what happened?"

Travis sounded odd to him, "Have you called the FBI yet?"

"No, I'm waiting on your signal. What happened? Did it work?" Daniel was almost beside himself.

"You and Frank get the hell out of that garage and get up here to Ricnor's office. I'm alone on his computer. I'll explain when you get here."

CALL ENDED 00:16

He sat there digesting what he'd just heard. The >> had meant the plan failed in some way, and Travis knew he wasn't at the parking garage with Frank. 'He's warning me. It has to be, he wasn't supposed to even call only text from here on out.'

He had to break the rule also and call Frank and let him know something was fucked up.

Frank was smoking a cigar when the phone rang. He picked up the call without saying anything.

"Hey it's me," Daniel said, "Travis just called and somethings not right." He wasn't even sure Frank was on the other line until he whispered, "God Dammit".

Daniel told him word for word what was said.

"Ok, it's time for you to bolt. Get somewhere safe and do what we talked about by this time tomorrow night. Get rid of this phone RIGHT NOW!" Frank shouted, "If someone's onto us this is probably the reason. "

"Yeah, but what if Travis screwed up the signals and he is really on Ricnor's computer waiting for us?"

"Then I'll meet you tomorrow night before you dig it up. You can go back in and say you got sick or some shit like that…you always were good at lying with a straight face. I'm glad you're on my side but I'm also sorry I got you into this mess," Frank admitted.

"Good luck," Daniel said

"You too," Frank replied and ended the call.

Frank started to drop his cigar but thought better of it and puffed it a few more times on his way back down to the ground floor. He took the elevator this time being in a rush to get back to the campus. With no ID card to get him in, he was going to have to walk in the front door or find another way in.

He managed to flag down a taxi after a couple of blocks. He still had a brief case with eighty thousand in cash and his old bible. In his left pocket was a pair of trick handcuffs that looked secure but he could easily slip out of with the right movement. His plan had been to be waiting for Douggy hands cuffed as if Daniel had taken him there by force. The money was to distract Douggy from searching Frank and finding the gun holster riding uncomfortably beside his balls. The gun in the concealed carry holster was his old .38.

'So much for that plan!' he thought. It had been ballsy but it only pinned suspicion on the tail of that evil empire. The new plan he was forming was to go for the head of the serpent.

Back in Elliott Ricnor's office, Douggy was barking orders over the phone to one of the security guards on staff.

"That's right, delete the last hour of footage and turn off all video recording until I say so. What? Yes all the cameras….Good, and keep an eye on the monitors for anything suspicious. Call back this phone if you see anything and I will tell you how to address the situation. You understand? CALL ME FIRST!" Douggy hung up the phone.

"You'll get Catoe and I'll keep Daniel Montclair writing those beautiful sermons that he's so good at, but what becomes of our friend here, Douggy?" Ricnor asked.

"Who? This asshole? We'll let him go home, as long as he knows how to keep his mouth shut. If he doesn't my boys can drop him off somewhere that no one will ever find him. Either way young Preachers are a dime a dozen on this campus."

Ricnor was speaking to silence the hope in Travis' mind, "And what if he goes to the police with a wild story of corruption and scandal in the church?"

"Then the dues at his Daddy's church triple and we have him arrested for sexual harassment, or assault. In fact that's why he broke into the security office and deleted the camera footage. Trust me, I've got guys in the Cincinnati Police. FBI too," Douggy bragged about his corrupt connections.

They heard Katelyn come back into the office. Douggy put his index finger to his lips for Travis to remain silent. Ricnor slipped into the outer office to intercept her from coming in.

"Thank you very much Ms. Womack. We won't be needing the tea, my visitors have both left…that Mr. King stormed out of here very upset. Anyhow it's almost five o'clock so you might as well take off for the evening. I'll eat some pizza and finish up my paperwork."

"Okay, have a good evening," She said and she began to shut down her computer and gather her things.

After she left Ricnor went back into his office with the pizza and gallon jug of tea.

"Looks like we're having a pizza party when our other guests arrive," He laughed and set the food on a shelf behind his desk. "I never would have imagined that Montclair would betray us like this. Unlike all the other Jesus freaks that come in here, I really thought he got the big picture."

Chapter 47: The Last Hoora

Daniel packed a book bag with a change of clothes and things he couldn't easily replace. It was time to split, but he had to play his last card before he left. He hurried over to the technology center not caring if he was being watched. Lacy's office was open.

"Hey your holiness, to what do I owe the pleasure?" She asked as he walked in.

He held up a USB drive, "Mr. Ricnor wants you to send this out ASAP as a supplement to tonight's sermon. It's an introduction to our new format and explains more of how we work here at headquarters."

"Oh, Hi. Good to see you too," She was pissed with him for ignoring her last couple of texts.

"I'm sorry, I've been working on this almost non-stop the last few days trying to get it ready for this release. He gave me a deadline, and I had to rewrite twice and perform it seven times until he was happy," he complained.

"Well a quick response would have been nice. 'Hey I'm busy' or 'Maybe this weekend I'll pound you're pussy when I'm not pounding the pulpit'," She sneered. "Anyway I can't release this until it's approved by the committee and uploaded into the system."

Daniel knew that was the protocol but already had a lie conjured up. "That's what I told him too but he said it's just a supplement and not a sermon so he could push it through with no problem."

She didn't feel like calling to verify and if it was going out tonight she had to get it sent out quickly.

"Okey Dokey, let's see what we've got." She inserted USB stick into the drive, "That's a big un'. Gonna take a while to upload it to the system. Is it going out to everyone, every church?"

"Yeah, can you attach it to play before every sermon?" She nodded. "No matter which sermon they choose?" Daniel asked.

"Uh-huh preacher man. You do realize this is what I do for a living, right?" She clicked on the keys for another minute.

"Ok, it's transferring to every church in the U-S-of-A, so once that finishes I'll see if there were any problems."

"How long you think? For the data transfer to finish," Daniel asked.

"PPPHHHhhhh, at least fifteen or twenty minutes. What's the rush?" She asked irritably.

"Oh no rush…I was just hoping we had enough time to catch up," he said and smiled.

She raised an eyebrow and cast a naughty smile at him, "Where? Here?"

"Well yeah, given we don't have time to go jump into bed. I wouldn't mind bending you over that desk again Miss Moore."

It was ten minutes until five and there were still plenty of other people in their offices on the same floor. The pit down below was busy wrapping up the work day. The room had an outside window and a door with blinds. Daniel grinned at her and slowly closed the door. CLICK. The lock was in place and no one was walking in on them. He didn't have to fool with the blinds as they were already closed.

She hadn't had sex anywhere but her dorm room for a long time and the idea made her super excited. She began to unbutton her blouse, "We have to be really quiet," she whispered.

He didn't even bother with his shirt, just went straight to opening his belt and unbuttoning the pants. She reached under her knee length skirt and slid her pink panties all the way down over her leather pumps. By this time Daniel's pants were around his knees. He left his briefs on so she could 'help' him with that part. She pulled the elastic band back with one hand and reached in for his cock with the other. It was already growing to towards its full potential, so when she stuffed it in her mouth it didn't take long to make him rock hard.

He did as promised and bent her over her own desk. Legs spread wide she grabbed her computer monitor and an empty spot on the desk. He lifted the skirt up to her hair and held onto both with his right hand as he slapped his rod against her sweet spot. When he thrust it in it wasn't any way gentle. More like a revenge fuck he thought. This was his last chance before he hauled ass and he didn't hold anything back. Lacy, who normally didn't typically make much noise, was having little high pitch moans escape from her tight pressed lips. They grew louder as he got going faster and deeper. TAT-TAT-TAT-TAT-TAT, the skin of their bodies slapped like two hands clapping. As he pulled her hair and humped even harder, she let out a "OOOOHHHHH, YES, OOOOOHHH!!" so loud Daniel felt sure plenty of other offices around could have easily heard. He didn't care. He would have fucked her in front of the whole auditorium since he was about to fly the coop.

He only let go of her hair so he could grab her breasts. That was her favorite thing, and he normally fondled them during foreplay but this was rough. He reached around and grabbed one in each hand. She was still wearing a pink bra and unbuttoned blouse but his hands squeezed hard and his cock thrust harder, as he had a better handle on his lover. Lacy had never been fucked so hard or rough before and she couldn't control her moans anymore. She didn't care at that point, it was so good she didn't care if the Pope himself was in the office next door.

"THAT'S IT, OOHHH FUCK ME, OHHHHH YEAH!!!"

Daniel was ever cautious about pulling out but this time he couldn't stop himself from exploding inside her hot tight pussy. That sent her into orgasmic overdrive and every muscle in her body tightened up and she moaned at the top of her lungs, "OOOOHHHHH GOD FUCK MEEEEEE!!"

He was thinking about how much better it was than usual when he heard a soft bang in the distance, like rolling thunder before a Carolina thunderstorm. Bang, bang…bang. And then he knew it was gunfire. The Adrenaline Alarm Bells Band went full orchestra as his pelvic thrusting ground to a stop.

"Don't stop!" She whined, "Keep going, it's so good!"

"Is the video done yet?" He asked.

"What?" She leaned her head backwards to look at the monitor. "Yeah, well all but a couple but that's…" She was still breathing heavy, "That's normal for a couple of programs to have technical glitches." She never turned around but started rocking her hips and sliding on the hard rod still inside her.

"I've never been fucked this good before Daniel," She said, but he wasn't listening. His mind was already elsewhere thinking of the danger his friends were in. He pulled out and began pulling up the pants and underwear from around his ankles.

"We were way too loud. I need to go before we both get into some real shit," he said not realizing how true his excuse actually was.

"I can be quiet, and we could wait for a few minutes since most everyone is leaving soon."

She turned around to give him the slut eyes but he wasn't discussing it any more. Even if it was the best sex of his life he had to get off campus before the place was locked down. He grabbed her behind the neck and kissed her with real passion.

"You're great! I wish I could stay," He grabbed his bag and was out the door. A few heads were leaning out of their office doors and Macy Tisdale was standing in the middle of the hall pretending to be on her phone. They all wanted to know who had turned sweet little Lacy into a moaning slut. As he hit the door for the stairs he could hear a woman giggling, "Well I guess it's hump-day, hahaha!"

<u>Chapter 48:</u> Death Incarnate

Frank had the taxi drop him two blocks from the back of the campus. During the ride he'd taken the spy phone apart and crushed all the memory sticks. He tossed all the parts down a storm drain and headed towards the UHHC campus. There were three entrances other than the main one but they all required an ID badge to scan in. Frank had once gotten ahold of Daniel's spare but he'd gotten rid of all incriminating evidence before he fled the apartment. It was a few minutes until five, and he hoped someone would hit the door a couple minutes early to beat the afternoon rush. Just as good, an old man with salt and pepper hair wearing a janitor uniform was sitting in a folding chair beside the door. He had the top off a can of chewing tobacco.

"Pinch-O-Pete Reverend?" the man offered as Frank walked up.

"No thanks. I-" Frank looked at the man like he was looking at a ghost and remembered that phrase and the lines on his face. "Well actually. Why not? It's been a while," he said. For a moment he hesitated and as the man smiled at him and held the can out for get what he wanted. Then with his thumb and finger grabbed a pinch of the black chew.

The janitor took some also and snapped the lid back on the can. He gave Frank a grin exposing his brown rotting teeth, Frank smiled back. Then he recognized that familiar visitor at his last sermon who sat on the back row. It was a face he hadn't seen in years. He was a janitor that cleaned up messes and the sins of his children.

"The pews are as solid as the day you built them. Thank you Billy, for everything."

The former carpenter turned janitor had a retractable lanyard with an ID card. He stretched it out to the key pad and it flashed green. He opened the door for Frank still wearing that same snaggletooth grin.

"You'd better get going reverend, it's almost five o'clock…all hell's about to break loose."

Their eyes locked as Frank was passing through the door. Every hair on his body was standing up.

Reverend Franklin Catoe had never considered himself a hypocrite. While he'd never believed in God or Jesus he believed in the wholesomeness of church and those who did truly believe. He'd stood at the pulpit countless times spreading advice on how to be good and fair to others. Heaven and hell were just tools to him, tools to keep his congregation afraid of not being good and fair. The name of God had been Frank's strongest tool. Until now. Now God seemed to be the guy holding the door and saying, "Go on Frank. It's your destiny." This was more than a coincidence to Frank, he hadn't seen Billy in over thirty years for goodness sakes.

He made his way through the building and exited to a courtyard. It was still a good walk but at least he was already on campus and wouldn't need an ID to get in anywhere else. He'd already decided he liked the Ole-Pete classic. The pungent flavor slowly spread from his cheek and gum to make his mouth water. He spit on the side walk, careful none got on his favorite suit. He felt invincible.

He looked at his watch, three minutes till. He'd had that watch for most of his life. Elizabeth had bought it for him their first year in Tall Rock while they were still building the church. She'd told him it wouldn't do for the new Reverend in town to be late to his own service. That was back when they'd really loved each other, before she'd became so worried about gossiping and fucking around with scumbags football coaches. That was years before Jane Dixon had moved into town…years before he'd killed them both.

That made him take stock of himself. Along with his watch he was wearing his favorite suit. Nothing flashy, just a plain black suit that fit his body well. His briefcase he'd had for a long time but it wasn't really that sentimental. The eighty thousand inside it represented years of savings he and Elizabeth had put away.

The Bible he'd had from his start with the church, before he'd met his future wife, when he was traveling from town to town preaching with. He'd used it to beat Greg Banther to death, but he needed more firepower for his next adversary.

His oldest possession was by far his pistol. The old .38 revolver that hadn't been fired since the night he'd talked to Douggy on the phone back on Mobile Bay by Lowtide's Bait and Gas. It was strapped inside his leg and Frank decided he needed it where he could get to it faster. He entered the main building and immediately hit the first men's room. It was empty so he had no witnesses or security cameras to see him unzip and pull the gun through his fly and stuff it in his belt behind him where the jacket would cover it.

While Frank had never been to Elliott Ricnor's office he knew about where it was, on the second floor with a secretary in the outer office. Daniel had given him as many details as he could remember. He'd even drawn a couple of maps of the campus for Frank.

Even for his age the old reverend preferred to take the stairs over the elevator. He felt like a little exercise wouldn't hurt, and he'd heard too many horror stories of people being trapped in broken elevators for hours. For all he knew, the building security could shut off the power to the elevators and trap him until the FBI arrives. They would have the upper hand. He knew he was walking into a trap.

He climbed the stairs thinking about Charley Earl, the mayor of Tall Rock, who Frank played in a game of chess occasionally. Charley was a fair enough player by most standards, but he had problems when playing against Frank who had a better vision for the game. Charley's best strength was his use of the 'knight'. He could dance them all over the board, wreaking havoc if they survived until later in the game. Early in one game Charley used an odd tactic, the queen sacrifice, to try and level the playing field between Frank and himself. It worked, and they ended up trading 'fighting men' until Charley's 'knights' could ride all over Frank's remaining men. It was the only time the ole captain ever got the best of Frank, although they had plenty of other good games.

He opened the door to the second floor hallway. This was the executive wing. There were twenty offices, a couple of conference rooms and a lounge. Frank passed a few offices with the names printed on the door. The door for A. Schuler was standing open and he could hear a man on the phone talking about football. A bead of sweat began forming on his brow as he passed the lounge area. The clear glass window left him in plain sight of the four people chatting around the community fridge but none of them took any notice.

ELLIOTT RICNOR- President and C.E.O. of the UHCC, was on the glass of a large imposing office door. Frank walked in expecting to see Katelyn. Instead he saw Leo, the bald man who had followed and abducted Daniel was now sitting behind the desk.

"Come in Reverend Catoe." Frank closed the door behind himself. "And where is Mr. Montclair?" Leo asked annoyed.

"He's on the way. Should be here in a couple minutes," Frank lied, hoping the thug would wait on Daniel and not frisk him.

"What's in the briefcase?" Leo asked.

"A million buck. Are you gonna let me in, or should I turn around and hit the road?" Leo looked as if he was about to get pissed off but the door clicked open as if to answer his question.

Frank smiled and walked in with the briefcase in hand.

Travis was still sitting in the chair. Frank had never seen a black person turn pale but it seemed to be happening to the student. Ricnor was behind the desk still inspecting the spy phone and Travis' personal one also. Douggy was standing beside the desk reading from a file folder.

"Won't you have a seat Reverend?" Douggy said and nodded to the chair he had vacated.

Frank pushed the door closed and tossed the briefcase on top of the desk before he slowly took a seat. Douggy dropped the folder to reveal a gun in his right hand.

"I can't believe you're really here Frank…it's been a really long time."

The silenced gun stayed casually fixed on Frank's chest.

"In fact I had given up finding you years ago. I'd rattled every bush in the underworld knowing eventually you would start selling pot in Mississippi or steal a car in Memphis," he shook his head, "but my boys couldn't find anything. I figured you either overdosed or finally caught the bullet you deserved. I never thought to look in a church."

"How the hell did you end up here? A Bible college of all places?" Frank wanted to know.

"I got tossed in jail after you killed those cops in the Mobile Bay. I learned how to use my influence to make miracles happen. The dope game was getting all the attention from the law, and was less and less profitable. Political corruption. I found that's where the money is. I get paid to twist the arm of a congressman once, and after that he respects my commands. I make scandals disappear and dead hookers too. The UHCC needs an enforcer looking for maniacs…like you, and I beef up their security. I make their problems go away. Then the FBI shows up looking for you of all people. Hell, I barely remembered your name when they called you Reverend Franklin Catoe. You learned to dress nice and preach, but you're still wanted ARSON and TRIPLE

HOMICIDE! The security cameras caught you sneaking around a few weeks ago at graduation. I saw your face on camera and it brought back years of hate for you and Steve. I knew you'd be around somewhere, trying to start a fire. Me and my boys have been waiting to piss it out."

"Good to see you too Douggy. I brought you a little peace offering," He said and tapped on the briefcase.

"Is it my reefer you ran off with?" Douggy mocked.

Frank thought for a second. "Not exactly, but I know a guy on Lincoln Avenue that can hook you up with some." He leaned up and popped open the latches opening the case. The money was there along with his bible. The cash wasn't stacked as neatly as in the movies but it did bring a small smile to Douggy's face.

"You think that little pile of money is gonna save your ass now? SHIT!! They offered me ten times that to find you and get rid of you. I might burn it just to let you watch your life savings go up in smoke."

"That money is so you forget about Travis here," he said glancing at Ricnor. "I've got another two hundred grand in my car so you'll let Daniel go free," Frank said coolly.

"Oh no, I don't think so," Ricnor said sternly. "That boy is going to keep doing exactly what he does now. You should be proud though, he's the future of this church. He's going to be writing sermon's for us until the day he dies, whether that be from natural causes or a bullet. But I guess for the cash we'll keep him alive for now."

"Are you done?" Douggy looked at Ricnor. "I decide when—"

Frank leaned up and went for the revolver tucked in his belt. Douggy saw it coming and fired first. The bullet hit Frank in the gut. The shot wasn't silent but it was nothing compared to the deafening thunder and fire Frank's .38 let out. His hollow point hit Douggy center mast and a mist of blood shot out of the exit wound onto the bookshelf and wall behind him.

Frank managed to hear the door click despite the ringing in his ears. Still sitting in the chair he turned to see the bald man rush into the room pistol in hand. This time Frank got the first shot off and thunder boomed again. The bullet caught him about three inches below the navel, but he too returned fire. His bullet unsilenced caught Frank in his right armpit. The bald man, in shock from having his bladder shot out of his ass collapsed on Travis and then onto the floor moaning, grabbing at his wound.

Frank changed hands with his weapon having his right arm crippled from the bullet in his shoulder. He cocked the gun and fired awkwardly with his left hand. This bullet punched through the side of his head and splattered on Travis.

'Daniel would thank me for that,' Frank thought.

Ricnor sat there, mouth agape in disbelief of what had happened. Travis had closed his eyes when he saw Frank aim for the finishing strike on the collapsed man. Frank looked down at his own belly; the red circle on his shirt was slowly expanding. He knew that unlike his shoulder this was a fatal shot, only it would take a couple minutes for him to bleed out.

"I'll be damned," was all he could think to say. He lifted himself up out of the chair slowly hoping the burning pain would ease off if he took it easy. It didn't. He re-cocked the hammer and pointed it at Ricnor who pissed his pants and said, "No, please, please, don't. "

Frank stood beside the cowering man and pointed the gun at his temple. "You took my church, I want it back," he demanded.

"Okay, Okay It's yours. Please don't--."

Frank pulled the trigger and blew his brains across the room. He looked at Travis who still had his eyes closed. "You need to come up with some really good bullshit or get the hell out of here. Or both."

Travis just sat there horrified from what he'd seen. He wanted to run but he just shook his head as if to say, "I can't move."

Frank took a tissue out of a holder on the counter and grabbed the barrel with it. Then another tissue to wipe his finger prints off of it. He then put it in Ricnor's limp hand and pressed his fingers on it. He then let it drop to the floor beside Ricnor's chair.

"I brought them this money as a payoff. You don't need to know why. Then he," pointing at Douggy, "handcuffed me." Frank pulled out his cuffs and clicked them on himself. "They started arguing about who would get the money and then they started shooting. That's when you crouched on the floor and kept your head down until the shooting was over."

Frank slowly walked back and sat in the chair again. He was hurting worse with every breath. He pressed the tissues over his stomach wound, he was still bleeding to death quickly but the pressure helped.

The old reverend rolled his head back and looked up. "Try not to mention Daniel…or any dealings with him or me…" he took a deep breath, "and remember why we had to do this. Now go."

Travis got up and grabbed his cell phone off the desk. He stepped over the puddle of blood still leaking from the dead man at his feet. He took one last look at Frank who looked like he was staring up at heaven. Then he ran out the door and into the hallway. Reverend Catoe began his last prayer.

Chapter 49: Blood Money

Daniel followed the mob of employees hurrying to leave campus. Some from just getting off work, others scared it was another active shooter trying to set the new high score. He heard sirens approaching and walked towards the bus stop. He needed to get away, hide until he could watch the news that evening to find out what happened. He waited at a bus stop but it was crowded and he didn't want to be around anyone. He took off walking again and found himself going towards the park Frank had told him about.

It was a big park with plenty of people. He noticed many of them glued to their phones more than usual, probably due to the breaking news in their city. Daniel didn't have a phone on him and for once was glad.

There were three picnic shelters on the park map and he had to go to all three of them until he found the one with the flower bed but no playground. The flower bed had a variety of flowers and bushes. In between the Dogwood tree and the Holly bush is what Daniel was concerned with. The wood chips looked freshly moved. 'That's it. That's the loot.'

Frank was as always accurate with directions he remembered, while trying not to stare at the spot too hard. He wondered how Frank had dug the hole and what he'd done with the extra dirt. He decided Frank would have used a shovel but now that the dirt was loose he could use his hands if need be. Not in the daylight though, not until he knew what happened to Frank. He wondered what had become of his friend. The more he worried about Frank, the more he realized just how crazy their plan had been. Not just the last twenty-four hours, but the entire scheme to expose a church organization that had legally done nothing wrong.

He couldn't see any cameras watching the park. A sign at the entrance listed the operational hours as sunrise to sunset. That was a rule he planned on breaking soon, just like Frank had.

'Franklin Catoe, that's a good role model in life,' he told himself again.

He imagined getting arrested with hundreds of thousands of dollars. It would be the scandal of the decade, if the UHCC didn't cover it up.

Chapter 50: The Sermon of all Time

Daniel Montclair stood at his podium looking into the camera.

"Hello friends. I'm here today to give you a different kind of message than you are used to hearing. In fact, it's the opposite of what I've been told to say. I'm doing this because it's the right thing. Regardless of the consequences, it is what's right." He held up his bible.

"This is a bible, my bible. Inside is truth and guidance to help us go through life…CLOSER to the image of God. There is nothing wrong with this book, as there is nothing wrong with your bibles. Not your UHCC bibles, I mean the ones you've been using for years. YOUR bibles, not the politically correct garbage they shove down our throats...And that includes me," he said raising his hand.

"I'm on the payroll. They pay us well, better than many of you watching take home per week. And it's YOUR money! Why should some corporation get to have your money? You earned it, you built the churches you're sitting in. Who are they to take it away and tell you what bible to read from?" He slammed his raised hand down on the pulpit.

"I'm glad if I was able to help any of you. I always felt like the messages were good and true but I am ashamed of the way I presented them. Church is about being there with each other, listening to a person you know. A leader in your community whom you chose! Not some jerk on a screen, reading from a script. This is my last sermon for the UN-UNITED UN-HOLY UN-CHRISTIAN CHURCH! I'm not proud of having worked for them…but if anything good came out of it, it's this one message: NO MORE!"

"Don't pay any more dues, not one cent! See how long they can operate without YOUR hard earned money. Elections are coming up next year. Vote out the pigs that that supported the Religious Freedom Act. They are corrupt as this corporation that calls itself a church. They'll revoke the bill if their jobs are on the line."

"Freedom of religion is a right we have to take back!"

"Our freedom to assemble we must take back!"

"If we all stand together we are more powerful than any corrupt congressman and any so called church representative. Take back your true name! You aren't a UHCC affiliate if you don't want to be! Is there a guy there now enforcing church code? Throw the bum out the door! IT'S YOUR CHURCH!!!"

He paused for time. While the room he was in was silent he could imagine all those crowded churches erupting with applause. Travis was behind the camera smiling.

"Don't expect me to lead you anymore. If I'm sure of anything it's that I'll be silenced. But you already have a leader. Whether man or woman, whether you call them pastor or priest or reverend or whatever, they are once more the voice of your church. We can't lose this fight. This is your right, your eternal soul is more important than some rules written by man. Jesus didn't always play by the rules…He did what was right…and so should you!" Again he waited knowing this would cause a stir.

"So get talking, start planning. Think about how you want to worship and make it happen. Talk to other churches and come together to push back. Let heaven and earth know you mean business. Turn off this video and worship the way you used to. My name is Daniel Montclair, and I believe in GOD."

Daniel slung his bag at the bottom of a barstool he straddled at a bar and grill on Magnolia Street. He ordered a beer and cheeseburger. A basketball game was on one TV, but the other had -BREAKING NEWS- covering the shooting that took place at the UHCC headquarters.

Reporters Ashley Meyers was interviewing Susan Lekowski, a woman Daniel recognized as working in the finance department. She had been crying and was telling about the gunshots in her building and how she hid underneath her desk until the police found her. "Now back to Jamie and Rob in the studio."

The neatly groomed Rob Austern began by saying, "We now have confirmation that four people are dead. We are not yet sure of their identities, or if it is Daniel Montclair, worship leader who earlier today denounced his own church in a sermon and called for total rebellion from the UHCC."

Four people dead. 'That means Frank and Travis and hopefully some bad guys.' He still had no understanding of what had gone wrong and now he assumed his cover was blown somehow.

Daniel's sermon began playing, with the words –WORSHIP LEADER CALLS OUT CHURCH- in red letters at the bottom of the screen.

He drank a beer and watched himself punch the church in the mouth. It may have worked. The video had caused an uproar and politicians were already being interviewed concerning possible support for change in the Religious Freedom Act. Many called for a complete abolishment.

"…and police are looking for Daniel Montclair for questioning about the shooting that took place today as it may be related to the viral video that has the nation buzzing," the news anchor said.

Daniel cautiously peered around looking for anyone who might recognize him. He needed a disguise like Frank had done. He could grow a beard but that would take some weeks. He decided he would shave his head, buy some blue jeans and a pair of glasses to throw people off. He got his burger and fries and ate but only halfheartedly.

Rob's co-anchor Julie Westgate took her turn to deliver some dirt she referred to as an interesting fact.

"Prior to his time at the UHCC, Daniel Montclair was a student at Birmingham Arts and Tech. He was an actor in the drama department and had a lead role until things went sour. I have to warn you the footage you are about to see is very graphic. Please look away if you are easily sickened."

A video showed his one and only performance as Prince Moreau during his big love scene with Mary Ann.

Daniel: "He may be skilled but I am the son of King Tinious, The slayer of the Gauls, death runs in my line."

Mary Ann: "Oh I am such a silly girl that one I love must die to satisfy me and it would only make me undone."

Daniel: "I would not think of you a silly girl even if I lay dying by the sword of your father."

Mary Ann: "Then how would you…"

Then the kiss. Daniel thought it started out so good, so real, but then the vomit started spewing and the audience began to shriek in horror.

'Mother Fuckers. I just gave the sermon of the century and they want to play that shit.'

He was really more upset about Frank and Travis. 'I should have been in that office too, sacrificing like my friends,' he thought.

He'd only taken a couple bites of his burger and a few fries but he downed his beer and paid in cash.

The next night he wore jeans and a sweat shirt. His new buzz cut wasn't perfect as he had done it himself in a cheap motel room. The new pair of sneakers completed the makeover, and he liked the way they felt as he cruised quietly through the park. It had been confirmed that Reverend Franklin Catoe, fugitive from the law, was one of the four killed in the UHCC headquarters.

That gave Daniel even more reason to get the hell out of town, but not without the money. He dared not wait too long either. The idea of a park landscaper finding the money didn't really appeal to Daniel much. He felt like he'd earned at least part of the cash for putting his ass on the line for Frank and ruining his own career...possibly his entire life.

Daniel was mentally exhausted as he entered Lockmore Park. He dug in the flowerbed, looking for the duffel-bag full of cash. Frank had wrapped it in plastic so no groundwater would seep in. Damp money and large bills both get cashiers suspicious. He couldn't do anything about the large bills but spend them cautiously. He tore the plastic off the duffel and put it in a trash bin as he left the park. He'd never carried around so much cash it was a burden. The stacks of hundred dollar bills were making him sweat in the cool night as he left the park. He headed towards the highway. He couldn't rent a car or even buy a ticket out of town without taking a chance of the FBI finding out, so he decided hitchhiking and walking was the best way to go.

Chapter 51: Exodus

In the seven weeks following the shooting at UHCC headquarters, the entire United States was in an uproar and some claimed on the brink of revolution. Countless rallies and demonstrations were held at every state capital and in small towns too. Washington was in gridlock for three weeks straight.

Daniel's last sermon had been huge, and some say the key event needed to mobilize God's soldiers. Churches were in an uproar, some were tossing the UHCC representatives out the door, and others were waiting to see what happened next. When Daniel couldn't be found there was a void in the young revolution, it needed a new leader.

Pastor Fredrick "Full Gospel" McKnight stepped up and called for, "Every person who calls themselves a Christian, to march on the capital and protest in a violent peace."

Over fifteen million made the pilgrimage to camp on every street and park in the city. After two days the police gave up trying to arrest them all. Those jailed for nonviolent protest were turned free and tossed right back into the madness. The harassment of Congress and the President was round the clock as protesters chanted, "Free the Churches" or "Let-me-Pray-my-way-OK". The Religious Freedom act would have been revoked sooner but most politicians wouldn't leave their homes without extra security. Even the ones that had voted against it originally still feared the mob that occupied the streets.

When Congress finally came together to vote it was 72 votes to repeal and zero against. The congressmen who didn't vote were all replaced the next election. Daniel Montclair had set in motion the largest mass protest and political change the world had ever seen, and yet his whereabouts remained unknown.

Most assumed he was silenced or killed by the UHCC or the ties that had been revealed to organized crime via Douggy Goings. He had drifted through truck stops and country roads heading west.

Sometimes he hitchhiked, sometimes he took a bus, but he managed to see most of the national parks west of the Mississippi river. When he met people along the way he called himself Carl Smith, a common name that was easy to forget. He made up a character with a back story but most of the time he acted like his normal self.

At first normal had felt strange to him, for most of a year he'd been in character saving souls and plotting with Frank. Afterwards he was living like a man on vacation. It was fun but he had so much time to think. That's what he needed, to think of his next move. Where would he go? Would he ever see Leah again?

He regretted not having been able to go to Frank's burial service. The town of Tall Rock demanded the body be returned and buried as soon as the official investigation was done with him. They buried him behind Tall Rock Baptist Church in the cemetery next to his wife Elizabeth. The casket was opened and they had placed another bible in his hand because his was federal evidence. All the national news teams were there looking for a story and they got plenty…All about Reverend Catoe being a kind and innocent man. That's how Daniel got to see it.

The FBI never came up with enough evidence to make any charges, being that most of the witnesses were dead, and Frank had done a good job covering his tracks. Tall Rock's mayor and Frank's good friend, Charley Earp, gave a beautiful eulogy and threw out a theory of his own.

"Reverend Catoe was the victim of the corrupt church and the underworld. After the Reverend showed signs of resistance to the UHCC he mysteriously vanished... and after he helped Daniel Montclair write his last sermon he was unjustly martyred."

His headstone was simple, just as Frank would have liked it.

Franklin D. Catoe

A Loving Husband, Friend and Man of God

He will be missed

For more info visit www.pasantoslit.com

www.ingramcontent.com/pod-product-compliance
Lightning Source LLC
Chambersburg PA
CBHW070639310726
48982CB00001B/334

9781733250900